of the Great War

Rebekah A. Morris

Bible quotations taken from the King James Bible

Copyright March 2011

Copyright © 2012 Rebekah A. Morris

All rights reserved.

ISBN: 1469972883
ISBN-13: 978-1469972886

Photos by Heather Johnson Ueland

All rights reserved

DEDICATION

To all the families of our armed forces and to those who have fought in every war, I dedicate this book with a grateful heart. Thank you all for your sacrifices.

CONTENTS

	Acknowledgments	i
1	Chapter One	1
2	Chapter Two	15
3	Chapter Three	30
4	Chapter Four	38
5	Chapter Five	49
6	Chapter Six	63
7	Chapter Seven	81
8	Chapter Eight	94
9	Chapter Nine	109
10	Chapter Ten	121
11	Chapter Eleven	139
12	Chapter Twelve	157
13	Chapter Thirteen	175
14	Chapter Fourteen	185
15	Chapter Fifteen	197
16	Chapter Sixteen	211
17	Chapter Seventeen	219
18	Chapter Eighteen	231

19	Chapter Nineteen	241
20	Chapter Twenty	253
21	Chapter Twenty-One	269
22	Chapter Twenty-Two	279
23	Chapter Twenty-Three	293
24	Chapter Twenty-Four	305
25	Chapter Twenty-Five	319
26	Chapter Twenty-Six	326
27	Chapter Twenty-Seven	343
28	Chapter Twenty-Eight	361
29	Chapter Twenty-Nine	377
30	Chapter Thirty	385
31	Chapter Thirty-One	395
32	Chapter Thirty-Two	409
33	Chapter Thirty-Three	427
34	Chapter Thirty-Four	435
35	Chapter Thirty-Five	449
36	Chapter Thirty-Six	461
37	Chapter Thirty-Seven	475

ACKNOWLEDGMENTS

I wish to express my gratefulness to my mother for suggesting I write this book to begin with and for the hours she spent proofing and correcting each page. I couldn't have done it without you, Mom. To my sister, Sarah, for listening to the "audio" version of each of my stories as they were being written - or even the ones that didn't get written - as well as coming up with names when I needed them. To Lydia Hansen for naming Lydia Ruth and her doll. Special thanks goes to my special friends and heart sisters, Anna Christensen and Hannah Cass who helped pray me through the process of writing this book. I truly don't know what I would have done without you girls. Thanks! Also to Mrs. Sylvia Long for her encouragement and support. It is with many thanks that I think of all the readers of "Country Woman" who took the time to share their memories of growing up during the early 1900s with me. I received many ideas, and though I couldn't use them all in this book, I know they won't be wasted. Thank you to my test readers who willingly read this book and gave me their honest opinions: Anna Christensen, Hannah Cass, Hannah Covington, Emily Swager, Lydia Hansen, Jerusha Hardin, Jana Courville, Joanna Ueland, Hannah Christensen, Susanna Thornton, Mrs. Sylvia Long, the Noran Family and the Steffes Family. I may not have taken each suggestion, but I hope you enjoy the finished book. This book wouldn't have been the same without Heather Johnson Ueland's wonderful photography. Thank you, Heather! Thank you, Dory Athey for starting the final proofing process. Cousins are great! And finally, a special thank you to Mrs. Kathy Hansen, Heidi Hansen, Mrs. Ann Bollinger and Mrs. Sylvia Long for being willing to jump in at the last minute to finish the final proofing. If it hadn't been for you, I still wouldn't have gotten it done.

1941

Mr. Mitchell
Mrs. Mitchell (Emma)
Edmund - 21 (Ria's oldest brother, usually called Ed)
Jimmy & Johnny - 19 (Ria's twin brothers who like to tease her but greatly enjoy their younger sister)
Chris - 15 (the youngest of the Mitchell boys and the closest to Ria in age)
Maria (called Ria) - 13 (A very lively, energetic and only girl. Slightly spoiled by the twenty older brothers and boy cousins in "the gang" but still sweet.)

Mrs. Smith (Lydia's Mom)
Lydia Smith - 13 (Ria's friend from school)

Corporal (Ria's next door neighbor who loves to have her visit)

1915

<u>Kansas, United States</u>
Lawrence Foster (Father)
Helen Wallace Foster (Mother)
David - 15
Emma - 13 (called Lucy by Edmund)
Edmund - 13
Carrie - 9
Vincent - 7
Georgie - 4
Rosalie - 2

<u>Nova Scotia, Canada</u>
Dr. Frederick Foster (Father)
Amelia Dawson Foster (Mother)
Edith - 18
Maria - 13
Mark - 8
Lydia Ruth - 3

CHAPTER ONE

"Maria and Lydia, you will be partners. Lucas and Andrew . . ."

Ria Mitchell didn't listen to the rest of the partner list. After all, she knew who she was with. Glancing across the school room, she caught her friend's eye and smiled. Lydia returned the smile. They were to do this project, whatever it was, together. It would be such fun! Much more interesting than alone.

"All right, class," Miss Bryant's voice broke into Ria's thoughts. " It is now time for your assignment. Together with your partner, I want you to prepare a report on some hero or heroine of the Great War. We have studied the war quite a bit, and you should have no trouble. I want a five hundred word written report as well as an oral report to be given on April 17, the day we remember the entry of the U.S. into the war. That is the day the entire school will be giving their presentations on the Great War. That gives you all two weeks in which to get this done. Are there any questions? Yes, Max."

"What if we choose someone that someone else chose?"

Miss Bryant smiled. "Then we should know a lot about that person when you are done. Yes, Hannah."

"Can we do it on a group of people, like the lost

battalion or the Choctaw code talkers?"

"Well, I suppose that would be all right, but it must be a very special group of heroes or heroines without a prominent figure. Are there any more questions?" Miss Bryant glanced around the room. "Amber?"

"Can one person write and one person do the oral report?"

"Only if you both worked on both parts."

A few more questions were asked and then class was dismissed.

"Oh, Lydia!" Ria exclaimed, grabbing her friend's hand and almost dragging her out into the bright sunshine. "Just think! We get to do this together! Now, who shall we choose?"

Lydia tossed her blonde braids back over her shoulders and squinted around at all the other groups that had formed around the yard. "I don't know."

"Well, I don't want to do anyone really famous like General Pershing, Eddie Rickenbacker or Alvin York. Some others are bound to do them. I'd rather do someone that no one else would think of doing. Some forgotten hero." Ria's dark eyes sparkled, and she gave a little skip of excitement which caused her dark hair to bounce as well. Her eagerness was contagious, and Lydia, usually quiet and more reserved, squeezed her friend's hand and sighed,

"Wouldn't that be grand! But who could we do?"

The two friends fell silent, and their steps slowed as they pondered. They still hadn't said a word more when some five minutes later they turned up a shady walk to Lydia's house.

"Why don't we ask your mother?" Ria suggested. "Perhaps she knows someone we could write about."

Lydia looked a little doubtful, but it wouldn't hurt

to ask. Mrs. Smith shook her head when the question was put to her.

"Girls," Mrs. Smith spoke slowly and with a strong French accent, "I was just nine years old when the war ended. I don't know of anyone except General Pershing or one of those well known figures. Maria, perhaps your mother would be of more help."

Ria caught at the suggestion eagerly. "Mrs. Smith, may Lydia come home with me? Perhaps Mom does know someone, and then we could get started. I'm sure one of my brothers would come with me to see her safely home later." She looked hopefully at Mrs. Smith.

"Oh, please, Mama," Lydia begged.

"If you are sure your mama wouldn't mind," Mrs. Smith said, hesitating a little. She knew Maria Mitchell quite well as she nearly always stopped by for Lydia before school and walked home with her afterwards. And Mr. and Mrs. Mitchell weren't complete strangers to her, yet she didn't know them really well. She didn't want her daughter to be a bother.

"Oh, Mom won't mind at all!" Ria exclaimed, sure now that Lydia could go. "She loves having us bring our friends over. And my cousins are always stopping by, but they are all boys, and sometimes Mom and I wish for at least one other girl."

Mrs. Smith smiled. "All right. Lydia, just make sure you are home by 5:00."

"Yes, ma'am."

It was two very excited but out-of-breath girls that arrived panting at the Mitchell home several minutes later. Ria's home was set back a little ways from the tree-lined street in the small town of Plainville, Kansas. The house was in a quiet neighborhood where everyone knew and watched out for each other. The Mitchell home, with its wide front porch and large windows, was the usual gathering place for all Ria's brothers and cousins, but the only one home when the girls reached the house was Mrs. Mitchell.

"Come on, Lydia," Ria urged, opening the screen door. "Mom, where are you?"

"Right here," a cheery voice sounded from the kitchen.

Ria rushed in, followed a little more slowly by Lydia. "Oh, ginger cookies!" Ria dumped her books on the table and quickly sat down and reached for a fresh, hot cookie that was filling the air with its spicy aroma.

Mrs. Mitchell laughed, "Make sure you save a few for the gang. Hello Lydia. Come, sit down and have a few cookies. How was school today?" she asked, sitting down herself after pouring two glasses of milk for the girls.

Ria nodded, her mouth too full of cookie to talk for the moment. As soon as she was able, she began. "Mom, we need your help. We are supposed to do a report on a hero or heroine of the Great War, and we don't know who to write it on. We don't want it to be about any of the usual famous people. We were hoping you knew of someone."

"Do you each have to do a report?"

"No, we're doing it together. We're partners. Can you think of anyone, Mom?"

Mrs. Mitchell became thoughtful. Ria finished her last swallow of milk and waited in silent anticipation for her mother's answer.

"Well," Mrs. Mitchell began slowly. "I can't think of anyone, but," she added as she saw the look of disappointment pass between the two friends, "I do have some old letters that I wrote to my cousin Maria during the war. Perhaps we could find someone in those, but don't get your hopes up too high."

"Oh," Lydia sighed. "Mama says that there are mysteries in some old letters. She has one from someone she has never met. It is really old and only signed with a first name. We can't read the name, though I think it looks like it could be Mary or some such thing. She doesn't know where it came from, but it is addressed to her. She said one of her sisters found it somewhere and sent it to her. She wrote to ask where it came from, but no one has answered yet."

"Where did your Mom come from?" Ria questioned.

"Well, from Florida, but she said when she was really little she lived in Quebec. And she knew lots of girls named Mary, but she is sure none of them wrote the letter, so I suppose it will have to remain a mystery." Lydia looked as though she didn't like that thought.

"Maybe we will find a mystery about a long forgotten hero or heroine that we can report on from your letters, Mom!" Ria was all eagerness.

Mrs. Mitchell laughed. "I don't think you'll find any mysteries, and I'm not sure about heroes in any of my old letters, girls." She stood up and untied her apron. "But if you are ready to go help me look, we'll see if we can find them."

The attic, large and dusty, with its strange assortment of boxes, trunks, old furniture and what not, was lit by a single bulb hanging from the rafters. Mrs. Mitchell, Ria and Lydia gathered around an old chest and carefully sorted through it, pulling out anything that might be a letter.

"Mom, don't you have any that you wrote? All I can find are ones addressed to you from Maria."

"Yes, my Aunt Amelia sent me all the others after my cousin died. I think they might be in the desk downstairs."

At last, when not a scrap of paper that might possibly be a letter had been left in the trunk, the three searchers departed the warm attic for the cooler region below. In the desk, as Mrs. Mitchell had thought, a stack of old letters all tied neatly together was found. Ria could scarcely contain her enthusiasm.

"I just know we'll find someone to write about!" She seized Lydia and whirled around the room.

"Hey, what's going on?" a voice exclaimed from the doorway.

"Yes, what is all this excitement?" The speakers were two tall, identical looking lads about eighteen years of age.

Ria stopped breathless in the middle of the room. "A school project! Lydia and I have to do it together," she panted, but her eyes sparkled with enthusiasm as she looked at her twin brothers. "It is just the most wonderfullest project I've ever had to do at school before!"

Lydia had quietly moved over to Mrs. Mitchell and had begun to try to help her sort all the papers gathered from the trunk. She didn't know these two brothers of Ria's very well. Oh, she knew their names, though not which one was Johnny and which Jimmy. At times she envied Ria who had four older brothers and who was herself the youngest of the family. Lydia was an only child. Her family had moved to Plainville only last year, and it had taken Lydia some time to make friends with most of the girls at school. Ria was an exception. She had at once befriended the quiet, shy girl who spoke French as well as English. Lydia listened to the friendly teasing going on between the twins and Ria joined soon after by Ed and Chris, the eldest and youngest of Ria's brothers.

"Ria," Mrs. Mitchell finally called, "I thought this project was for both of you. Come over and help sort."

With a few more merry words to her brothers, Ria skipped over to the table and began to help. Many of the letters were folded together, but some had become separated after so many years and it was with difficulty that at last nearly one full year of letters lay neatly together.

"I'm afraid I wasn't very careful with my cousin's letters," Mrs. Mitchell remarked somewhat ruefully. "I didn't even keep them in the same place. If we find some letters missing, we might have to go look at Grandma's house. I don't know if we'll find any, but there might be a few here and there in the attic or somewhere. Do you girls want to read these yourselves or would you rather I read them out loud?"

"Out loud!" exclaimed both girls in one breath, Ria adding, "It'll be much more interesting that way."

Mrs. Mitchell smiled. "All right. What time do you have to be home today, Lydia?"

"By 5:00."

"Then," glancing at the clock on the wall, "we won't start these today seeing it is so late. If your Mom is willing, come tomorrow, and we'll begin reading them. That will give me a little more time to sort some more of these."

Lydia nodded. "I think she will be willing if I'm not a bother."

"Of course you're not a bother! Be sure you tell your mother I'd be more than happy if she could come someday too. Sometimes we need a few more females around here, don't we, Ria?" Mrs. Mitchell laughed. "Ria, why don't you go find out if one of your brothers can go with you to walk Lydia home."

Ria departed to return a moment later with Ed. The trio departed, Ria chattering eagerly with Lydia while Ed walked quietly behind them, smiling at his sister's ambition of finding some lost hero. Mrs. Mitchell watched them until they were out of sight, then turning back to the pile of letters, she fell to work again.

By the time the girls arrived at the Mitchell home the next day, all the letters that had been found were sorted and ready for reading. Eagerly they settled themselves on the porch swing with their cookies and milk to listen.

Mrs. Mitchell opened the first letter. "I think you girls should know that I and my twin brother were thirteen when this first letter was written. That would make my cousin thirteen as well, for she was only three days younger than we were. We lived out on the farm where Grandma and Grandpa still live near Codell here in Kansas while my cousin lived in Nova Scotia, Canada in a small fishing village." Then she began to read.

Saturday
February 27, 1915
Codell, Kansas
USA

Dear Cousin Maria,

How are things in Princeville with Uncle Frederick gone? Have you heard from him yet? I can't imagine what it would be like to have Daddy gone to war. At least Uncle is a doctor, not a soldier. Is Mark being a good man of the house? Do you still have snow? We have a lot. In fact, we have so much snow that we aren't going to school now. Probably the children in town can get to school, but all the folks out of town are kind of snowed in. Or should I say, snowed out?

It snowed on the 23rd. Huge flakes came down rapidly. So rapidly that they didn't have time to melt like much of our snow does. At times it was almost a white out! It was quite exciting. Vincent and Georgie ran from window to window to see how deep the snow was on things. One of our little pine trees got so loaded down with snow that it bent completely over, making a little arch. Daddy and David had to tie a rope from the house to the barn, so they wouldn't get lost. It snowed all day Tuesday and a little bit on Wednesday, just enough to look pretty when the flakes came down. Yesterday we had such fun that I will tell you all about it.

It was a great day for playing in the snow. It was cloudy and cold, but there wasn't any bitter wind blowing. The snow was perfect for packing. After breakfast, we all, even Mama and Rosalie, bundled up and headed out. Edmund and I were the first ones out the door. When Daddy and David came out, we pelted them with snowballs. That started the fun. Soon everyone was throwing snowballs! That is except Rosalie. She just played with the snow on the porch and watched us. After a while, Edmund suddenly whispered to me, "Follow me!" I did, and we slipped away around the house. Once we were safely out of sight, Edmund said quietly, "Now quickly, up on the porch roof." I looked somewhat doubtfully at the snow-covered roof. You remember it isn't steep or very high, but I wasn't too sure about all that snow on top. Before I could protest, Edmund had climbed the tree and was on the roof. "Hurry!" he urged me. I scrambled up the tree, and Edmund grabbed my hand and helped me step across onto the roof. Once I was up, it wasn't too bad. Quietly we made our way to the corner of the house and began to make snowballs.

"Now," Edmund whispered, and we began to fire snowballs as fast as we could. Edmund is a good shot, and one of his snowballs hit David on the side of the head.

Carrie saw us first and started shouting, "On the roof!" Everyone turned to look. That is when the snow really began to fly! Everyone turned on us. Soon we were out of snow.

"Come on," Edmund whispered. "Let's crawl back where we can get more snow." I nodded and began to slowly inch my way backwards. David caught on to what we were doing and running around the house began to bombard us from behind. I decided to go forward and let Edmund go back. The roof hadn't been too slippery with all the snow on it, but now that the roof was scraped bare it was beginning to get slick. I was afraid I would slide off.

"Edmund," I said as I ducked snowballs. "Let's surrender."

"Surrender?" Edmund exclaimed. Just then a large snowball hit him right in the face! A shout of laughter sounded from the ground. When he could talk, Edmund shouted, "We surrender!" The snowballs stopped. Now we just had to get down. That wasn't easy.

Edmund asked where the nearest pillar on the porch was. Some said left and some right. Finally Daddy said he was right in between them. Edmund crawled backwards until he was right above one. Slowly and carefully he lowered himself then disappeared off the roof. A moment later I saw him on the ground. "Come on, Lucy!" he called encouragingly. "Your turn now."

"Go forward," Daddy said. "You're closer to that pillar." I crawled quite slowly until I was told to stop. For some reason, as soon as Edmund was not on the roof anymore, I felt very unsafe. I was told to crawl backwards towards the edge of the roof! I started slipping a little as I crawled.

"Stop!" Edmund shouted. I froze. "You're right above the pillar, so reach back and grab the gutter; it will hold you. Then wrap your legs around the pillar and slide down!" It sounded simple enough, but I wasn't so sure it was going to be that easy. I took a deep breath, and with one hand grabbed the gutter. There were shouts of excitement from the ground as I grabbed the gutter with the other hand. Slowly I slid until I was off the roof. "Wrap your legs around the pillar," Edmund directed. I tried, but I couldn't move. My legs were twisted up in my skirt, and my skirt was caught on something.

"I can't!" I called down. "My skirt is stuck!"

"Can you fix it?" Daddy asked.

"No!" I answered.

"Boys," Daddy ordered "go free your sister!"

"Hurry!" I wailed. "My hands are starting to slip!" David and Edmund each rushed for a pillar and climbed up. Hand over hand on the gutter they came to my rescue. David managed to unhook my dress from a large nail, and I slid down the pillar to safety. Maria, don't ever climb on a snow-covered roof even if Mark coaxes and coaxes! Finally, with all safely on the ground, we went inside to drink hot cocoa.

Georgie's birthday was the day before we got the big snow. It is hard to believe he is five years old now! He is just as funny as ever. The morning of his birthday he wouldn't comb his hair. But that isn't anything unusual. When he came down to breakfast, he was a sight. His hair stuck up in some places while in others it lay flat against his head the wrong way. He had his shirt buttoned all wrong, and his shoes were on the wrong feet. Edmund said he wouldn't let anyone help him dress. Daddy took one look at him and nudged Mama who was at the stove. When she turned around, she started laughing.

"Georgie," she said with a chuckle, "you wore that shirt on Saturday and got a stain on it, and I haven't washed it yet. Vincent, run and get him a clean shirt, please."

Vincent ran off and soon returned with a clean shirt. Daddy helped Georgie put on and button the clean shirt before he asked if his feet didn't hurt. Georgie nodded.

"Well," Daddy said, "your shoes are on the wrong feet." Georgie's eyes opened wide and he looked at his feet.

"But Daddy," Georgie said, clearly confused, "these are the only feet I've got!" Daddy smiled broadly and showed him what he meant. Once his shoes were on correctly and before Georgie could slip away, Daddy pulled a comb out of his pocket and began to comb Georgie's unruly hair.

"No! My hair!" Georgie wailed, trying to back away from the comb.

Mama smiled and remarked, "No combed hair, no breakfast." That has been the rule in our house for as long as I can remember, but Georgie never seems to believe it. Since we were having pancakes, fried eggs, and sausage, Georgie decided to submit this once to having his hair combed.

Oh, we got a letter from Uncle Philip Vincent Bartholomew Wallace III last week! As I told you before, he was visiting friends in France, and when the Germans went to war, Uncle Philip joined the French army. He is with the "Chasseurs." I think that is how to spell it though I have no idea how to say it. Uncle Philip's handwriting is very hard to read. Mama said it has always been that way. Uncle Philip is Mama's "baby brother" as she calls him still, and she used to try to make him write nicer. It never worked. Before Uncle Philip left for France, he thought he might become a news reporter because he loves to tell stories and write. The only problem is that no one except Mama and himself can read his writing! Sometimes even Mama can't figure it out. Uncle Philip said he was in the Vosges Mountains and having a "bully good time." Daddy said that he thought the Vosges Mountains were a part of the Alps. I will let you know when I hear anything else of interest from Uncle Philip.

A couple weeks ago, Edmund and I walked through the woods to Mrs. Conway's house. (Everyone calls her Grandma.) We were taking her some things Daddy had picked up in town for her. While we were there eating cookies and drinking milk, she told us about something that people used to do on February 14. She said they called it St. Valentine's Day. People would make or buy beautiful lace and cute (Edmund thought they were ugly) cards for their sweethearts or ones they wanted to be their sweethearts and give them to them. Sometimes the ladies would give the young men locks of their hair. Grandma showed us a few that she had saved. One said:

> You're as charming as the violet,
> As lovely as the rose.
> In two more days you will be mine.
> With all my love, your Valentine.

Wasn't that just elegant? Grandma said that she thinks St. Valentine's Day used to be a pagan celebration, but she wasn't sure. She didn't know who St. Valentine was either. When we went to school the next day, we asked. I'll tell you what we found out.

Most people think that St. Valentine lived during the reign of the Roman Emperor, Claudius II. As Edmund so bluntly puts it, Claudius II was rather stupid. He decided that married men didn't make good soldiers, so he made a law that said no young man could get married. St. Valentine didn't think that was very nice or wise, so he secretly performed marriage ceremonies for couples. I also heard that St. Valentine helped the Christians who Claudius II was persecuting. Claudius didn't like that, and he had St. Valentine killed.

I thought that was quite interesting. I don't know how much of it is actually true, but I thought you might enjoy it.

I am out of things of interest to write about now. Though that doesn't always stop me from writing as you should know by now. You always were a good listener, so I am assuming you are just as good a reader. Do you still read as much as you used to? I don't read much. Though I read more in the winter than in the summer. Maybe sometime I will read more. I used to, but now . . . I think I just read too many books and got tired of reading. Anyway, I am going to end this letter before it gets too uninteresting.

    Edmund is leaning over my shoulder reading this as I write. He says it's not uninteresting, it's just almost boring. Now he says I wasn't supposed to write that. Sorry, too late now. Edmund said that he didn't have anything to tell you other than what I have told you already.

    Good-bye, my dear cousin. God bless and keep you! Please let us know anything you hear from Uncle Frederick. We are praying for him and your family!

With all my love,
Emma

    Ria and Lydia exchanged eager, excited glances as Mrs. Mitchell ended the first letter and picked up the second one. Neither one spoke, however, and after a slightly amused glance at the waiting friends, she started reading again.

CHAPTER TWO

Thursday
March 25, 1915
Princeville, Nova Scotia
Canada

Dearest Emma,

Greetings from the cold northlands of Nova Scotia, and to be more precise, from bonnie Princeville. We have snow still, or I should say, again. I don't expect this to last too much longer as it appears to be snowing again, and more than likely it will turn to rain before it stops. Such is the way of the weather. We are all well here. Mama isn't quite herself, but let me tell you why. Another baby is on the way! Mama said we should expect it sometime in late May or early June. Oh, I wish Papa were home! I don't know what we will do without him when the baby comes. Pray for us, Emma dear. I'm trying not to worry, but some days it is hard to cast my cares on my Savior and leave them there. The younger two don't know about the baby yet and probably won't until it comes.

We received a letter from Papa yesterday. Actually we received three wonderful long ones! These are the first we have received since he left for Europe, other than a short one saying that they had all arrived safely. Papa said that they arrived at Plymouth (Now this is the British Plymouth not the U.S. Plymouth though how I wish it were the U.S.), on October 14, but now they are in France. They arrived on the 11th of February. He didn't say where they had landed in

France. Maybe that is censored information. Papa hasn't done much doctoring yet though he had his hands full of seasick men when they crossed the English Channel. He says the men are all hoping to be sent to the front soon. Papa is not sure just where he will be, whether up in the front with the army or in the rear at the hospitals. Either way he says,

"I will do my best for Christ, as a Soldier of the King, as I strive to help my fellow men with their physical and spiritual wounds."

Doesn't that sound just like Papa? He also thinks that the war will be over soon, now that the Canadians have come to help. I pray that it will. Surely the Germans won't keep fighting for very long. Please keep praying, Emma, as I know you will.

Emmaline Louise! How could you climb on a snow-covered roof just to play snowballs! Sometimes I think you are impossible. Though on second thought, it's not you, it's Edmund that is impossible. Tell him that I thought he had more sense than to actually encourage you in something like that! I'm very glad to hear that you made it safely to the ground. Have no fear for me, Mark could plead until he was blue in the face, and I still wouldn't get on our roof. When I read your letter to the family, Mark declared that he could do that if we had any trees close enough. Edith raised her eyebrows and said, "You would most likely slide right off the roof and down the cliffs. And then where would you be?"

"In the water," Mark answered with a grin.

Edith continued, "And by the time you were rescued from the water, you would be so cold and frozen that it would take Mama and Maria two days at least to thaw you out."

Mark shivered at the very thought and observed, "Well, it would probably take longer than that because I wouldn't be able to get more wood for the fire." We all laughed. I don't believe Mark has any intention of climbing on the roof. At least I certainly hope not!

Please be sure to give Georgie a birthday hug from us

all. Lydia Ruth says to give him a kiss for her and one from Ab'gail. (That is her favorite dolly.) She has just told me she wants to send Georgie a letter from her, so I will do my best to write it down.

Georgie, I like my hair combed. When you write de newspapers, will you please write 'bout me an' Ab'gail? Can you come play with me sometime? Don't bring any doggies. They frightfull me 'cause once a doggie tooked Ab'gail and runned off. Papa bringed her home. Love, Lydia Ruth

Speaking of Lydia Ruth, let me tell you what she did the other day. She was supposed to be taking a nap, but instead she rolled around until she was all tangled up in her blanket. Since she couldn't get untangled by herself, and I suspect she wanted to know what was going on downstairs, she struggled out of bed, staggered to the stairs and tried to go down. Being all tangled up in her blanket as she was, she couldn't see the steps and ended up tumbling all the way down the stairs until she reach the closed door at the bottom. She didn't cry. I think she was so well padded with the blanket that she didn't feel a thing. Edith and I were sitting in the front room knitting socks while Mark read a book to us. Mama was lying down resting in her room. Suddenly Mark stopped reading and said, "Listen." We heard bump, bump, bump, a dull thud, and then silence. We looked at one another, puzzled at the noise. Edith stood up, remarking, "I'm going to go see what that was." Mark and I followed her to the stairs. When the door was opened, out rolled a bundle, and we heard Lydia Ruth say in muffled tones, "I went bump, bump, bump all de way down de stairs."

"Lydia Ruth!" Edith exclaimed. "Are you all right?"

"Uh, huh," Lydia Ruth replied from the depth of her blanket. We quickly untangled her, and Edith led her back to bed still saying, "I went bump, bump, bump. . ." Mark and I went back to the front room where we looked at each other, and Mark said softly, "Bump, bump, bump." Then we both laughed.

It has begun to rain, as I thought it would. The weather rock is quite accurate. Have I ever told you about our weather rocks? If the rocks are wet, it is raining. If they are warm and dry, the sun is shining. If they are white, it means snow, and if you can't see them, it is foggy. What do you think of them? Perhaps Edmund can find a weather rock for you. Just remember, they have to be a certain kind of rock, or they might not work. They are truly accurate as long as they are kept outside. Mark wanted to go outside and play last week, but it was raining, so what did he do but go and bring the weather rock inside and put it by the fire. In a little while the rock was warm and dry. Mark then went to Mama and asked if he could go outside. She shook her head saying it was raining.

"Mama," Mark said, " the weather rock says it is sunny and dry." With a grin, he then produced his rock to prove his point. Mama and Edith laughed heartily. So did I when Edith told me the story that night as we were getting into bed.

That was fascinating about St. Valentine. I didn't know any of that. I find I am inclined to agree with Edmund in regard to Claudius II. I would have loved to see those valentines. They sound quite charming. Do you think we should try sending some valentines next year? Who would we send them to anyway?

I do read still. Not as much as I used to because I have read all the books in the village. Well, I haven't read Mr. Campton's law books yet. I did look at them the other day, but I couldn't make head nor tail out of any of it. So please just keep writing long interesting letters, and I won't have to resort to law books for something new to read. I have continued somewhat with my drawing though I haven't done much lately. I am hoping to pick it back up with the warmer weather.

I really must go now. I am sorry this is so short. Tell

Edmund to keep off the roof. Give my love to everyone. Everyone else here sends their love as well. God bless each of you!

Your loving cousin,
Maria

P.S. If your uncle is with the Chasseurs, then you pronounce it "Shaaa-Sur." You are supposed to make the "r's" do something, but I can't write it on paper. Don't you know anyone who knows French? I mean besides me and your uncle.

"Mom, you sure could have used Lydia then as she can speak French."

Mrs. Mitchell smiled. "I once tried to get my uncle to teach me French, but it did no good. I still can't pronounce anything correctly. He said I slaughtered every word, so I gave it up. Now, should I read more or are you tired of them?"

Both heads nodded eagerly as the girls pleaded for the next one.

Tuesday
April 20, 1915
Codell, Kansas
USA

My Dear Maria,

It was a delight, as usual, to get your letter. Things seem rather quiet up there. There was a little excitement here three weeks ago, but now things are almost back to normal. Spring is definitely here. The trees are all budding, the daffodils are in full bloom along with tulips and irises. There are still some crocuses blooming, but most of them have finished. The redbuds and dogwoods look so delightful as do the apple and cherry trees in the orchard. A robin has her nest right outside the boys' window, and a cardinal nest is outside ours. A house wren built a nest on the porch roof near the kitchen. They are noisy little things but so cute and friendly that no one minds the noise.

Let me tell you about the excitement we had on Saturday the third. The morning was beautiful! Deep blue sky with piles of white fluffy clouds and wonderful, bright sunshine. A pleasant warm breeze was blowing from the South, and Mama and I thought it would be a perfect day to wash clothes. Carrie helped, and by midmorning the clothesline was full of clean clothes snapping gaily in the wind. Just after dinner Mr. Jones came riding up to ask if Mama would please go stay with his wife who was about to give birth. He was going for the doctor. Daddy headed at once to the barn to hitch Royal up to the buggy while Mama got ready to go. Since Royal was being unruly, Daddy said he would go with Mama as he knew that we could handle things here. Mama hurried out to the buggy while giving last minutes instructions to us all. She didn't know if she would be able to be home in time to start supper, but if not, I was to make soup. Rosalie began to cry as Mama and Daddy drove away, but David picked her up and comforted her.

"Come," I said briskly when the buggy was lost to sight around the bend. "Let's all work really hard and see if we can get the house clean before Mama comes back, as a surprise for her."

"But I worked all morning, and I want to play now," Vincent grumbled.

"Yeah, me too," Georgie echoed.

David looked at the little boys with a "don't start complaining" look as he admonished, "Well, grumbling won't let you play any sooner, so you might as well smile."

"Besides," Edmund added, "we are done in the barn until evening chores, so we will all help."

With all the help, it didn't take long to clean the house. When we finished, I noticed that it was beginning to look like it could rain. Quickly I checked to make sure the windows were shut before hurrying out to bring in the clothes. Carrie came out with Rosalie and, leaving her on the porch, came to help me. The little boys were running around enjoying their freedom. Suddenly the wind began to blow harder, and I looked up to see a large dark funnel heading in our direction! "Carrie!" I yelled. "Get Rosalie, and get to the cellar! Vincent! Georgie! To the cellar!" I hugged the basket of clothes closer in my arms as I ran after the children. The wind was whipping my dress and hair and almost taking my breath away. I reached the cellar as Carrie tried to open the heavy doors with Rosalie in one arm. Quickly I grabbed the handle with my free hand, but even with both of us pulling, we couldn't get the door open more than a few inches because of the wind. Suddenly Edmund was there, and with a strong pull he jerked the door open.

"Inside, quickly!" he ordered.

Carrie and I hurried down the dark steps, quickly followed by the boys and dogs. The rain began to fall just as the wind slammed the door shut behind Edmund, leaving us in total darkness.

Rosalie was crying, and Georgie begged, "This is too scary. Open the door."

Edmund struck a light, and by the dim flame he found a lantern left here for just such times and lit it.

"We might as well sit down and wait," I observed cheerfully, and taking Rosalie I sat down. The others followed my example in silence. The noise outside was dreadful. It sounded like someone was dropping hundreds of marbles on the doors. I looked at Edmund who sat with one arm around Georgie.

"Hail," was his brief answer to my questioning look. All of a sudden I noticed that someone was missing!

"David!" I gasped.

Hurriedly I put Rosalie on Carrie's lap and was standing up when Edmund caught my arm and commanded firmly, "Sit down, Emma. No one is going anywhere right now!"

"But, Edmund, David . . ."

"Lucy," Edmund interrupted and gave me a look which made me sit down again, take Rosalie back on my lap and hide my face in her hair. I felt Edmund gently squeeze my arm, and I knew what he meant. There was no way we would be able to open the cellar door in this wind, and even if we could, how would we find David and get back to the cellar?

"Let's pray for him," Edmund said. So, in the quiet of the cellar with the rain pounding on the doors as if seeking entrance, and the wind howling and whistling outside, Edmund led us in prayer, not only for David's safety, but for Mama and Daddy's and anyone else who was in the path of the twister. A peaceful feeling came over me as he prayed.

After what seemed like hours, but were really only minutes, the storm passed. The rain stopped, and the wind was quiet. Edmund stood up, ascended the stairs and pushed the door open. The air that came in was quite cool, and for a moment Edmund stood in the doorway looking around. Then he turned to us and beckoned, saying as he did so, "You can come on out. Vincent, blow the lantern out. Carrie, can you bring the basket of clothes to me? I'll carry it to the house."

Soon we were all outside. There didn't seem to be much damage done. A few branches were down, and a small part of the fence was broken. Together we walked to the house. It seemed undisturbed, and Georgie opened the door for us. We had no sooner gotten inside when Georgie asked, "Where's David?" I think that was on all our minds, for everyone looked at Edmund.

"You all stay in the house or on the porch. Emma and I will go look for him," he said. Quickly we headed out. "He could be in the barn," Edmund suggested.

"Could be," I consented, "but don't you think he would have come out by now?" Edmund didn't reply. We decided to each go a different way around the barn. As I rounded the corner, I looked out toward the pasture. Suddenly I began to run, as I shouted, "David!" When I reached him, I saw at once that he was injured. He was lying unconscious on his left arm and a gash was across his head. In a moment Edmund was there too, and pulling a clean handkerchief from his pocket, he pressed it against David's head while I chafed his hands and wrists and called his name. Soon he opened his eyes and looked at us in a confused way.

"What happened?" he murmured.

"There was a tornado," I replied.

Edmund added, "It looks like you got hit by something." David gave a weak smile and some of his humor came out.

"I always did want to see the eye of a tornado. If whatever hit me hadn't knocked me quite as hard, I might have gotten to see one." I smiled a little and hoped he never would see one. "I don't know why I'm just lying here," David continued as he started to sit up. It was then that he noticed that his arm was hurt, and he leaned back against Edmund with a stifled groan.

"Here," I pulled my apron off and began to make a sling for his arm. "maybe this will help until we get you to the house." Slowly and carefully we helped him stand up. Then we headed for the house with David leaning on Edmund's shoulder and me supporting his arm.

All the children were gathered around the porch as we came up. Their comments sounded just like them.

Carrie exclaimed, " David, you are completely soaked!"

Vincent shook his head, observing, "You won't be doing chores tonight."

"I'll write you for my newspaper! I'm sure you'll sell a lot!" Georgie added eagerly. That last comment made us all smile. Edmund helped David upstairs to their room while I tried to calm the children and start supper. Before long the older boys were back down, and David had dry clothes on, much to Carrie's relief. She was afraid he would catch pneumonia. David sank onto a chair holding his left arm and looking worn out.

Edmund came over to me and said in a low voice, "I think he needs a doctor."

"I wish Maria were here," I sighed. "She'd know what to do."

Edmund grinned and pulled a piece of my hair that had fallen down as he teased, "Should I go telegraph her to come on the next train?" I made a face at him then glanced at David.

"Don't be silly. Go ask David what we should do. After all he's the oldest." When the question was put to him, he said he could wait until Daddy came home.

Just then we heard Daddy saying cheerfully, "Well, Rosalie, where is everyone else? Did they blow away in the storm?" The younger boys rushed out and practically dragged Daddy into the kitchen, both of them talking at once. Daddy looked a little bewildered until he saw David. After hushing the boys' chatter, Daddy went over to him and asked with a smile, "What's your story?"

"I tried to ride the twister, but it threw me off." There was a general laugh before David told how he had not seen the twister and had gone to check on the animals in the pasture. When it began hailing, he turned to run to the barn, but something hit him on the head, and he knew nothing until Edmund and I found him. While David talked, Daddy was quietly examining his face, which now that he was in the light, one could see was covered with small bruises and scrapes. Daddy started moving his hand over David's arm, but David started and caught his breath in so sharply because of the pain that Daddy let it alone.

"Well," Daddy responded when David's story was finished. "Let's see if we can take care of your face, and when the doctor comes, he can see to your arm. Emma, can you put some water on to boil?"

"Daddy, when is the doctor coming? When, Daddy, when?" Georgie was jumping up and down with excitement. The prospect of the doctor seemed to fill him with delight though I don't know why.

"When he brings your Mama home," Daddy replied patiently.

Soon the water boiled, and Daddy, Edmund, and I went to work. Suddenly Edmund sniffed the air and questioned, "Do I smell something burning?" I sprang to my feet with a cry of dismay, nearly knocking Edmund over in my haste to get to the stove.

"My soup!" I wailed as I pulled the lid off the pot and let it fall with a clatter to the floor. "I scorched it!" Everyone started laughing though I couldn't see anything funny.

"Oh, Lucy," Edmund chuckled. "You can't do two things at once."

"Then why don't you make supper?" I demanded.

"He can't do two things at once either, Emma," Daddy consoled though he still smiled.

"What am I going to do, Daddy?" I questioned looking at the pot of soup in front of me. It was Carrie that came to the rescue by suggesting that we pour the soup that wasn't scorched into another pot and make more. Edmund offered to scrub the scorched pot for me. Hardly had we gotten things fixed and cleaned up when Mama and Doctor Pierson came in. The doctor said that David's shoulder was out of socket, and he had sprained it severely. After taking care of David, Doctor Pierson stayed for supper at Daddy's request.

The soup really wasn't too bad, though Edmund couldn't resist muttering under his breath just loud enough for me to hear, "I just ate a scorched potato." I kicked him under the table, and we both grinned. By the time I got to bed that night, I was exhausted.

Oh, Maria! I can't believe I have written this much already and only told you about one day! If I continue to write this much about each day, it will take you a week to read it! I really didn't mean to write that much, but there didn't seem to be anything I could leave out. Edmund laughed when I told him that and said he could tell the story in one sentence. So could I, but it wouldn't be nearly as much fun.

Now let's see, what else has happened? Carrie turned ten last Monday. She hasn't changed much since you saw her last. Only grown taller, and she doesn't have her little girl look anymore. Carrie found Callie's kittens on her birthday. There were six of them. Don't ask me what their names are because I can't remember. I don't seem to remember ordinary things like that very well.

How is Aunt Amelia? Mama was so excited to hear the news. A new cousin, I can hardly wait! Please let us know when you hear from Uncle Frederick again. We are praying for him. No news from Uncle Philip. Thanks for telling me how to pronounce Chasseurs. I know a family who speaks Swedish, and one other person who speaks a little bit of French but doesn't read it at all. We really haven't heard much news on the war. It all seems so far away. Almost as though it isn't happening. I know it doesn't seem that way to you with Uncle gone.

I did hear an interesting story that happened aboard the USS San Diego. I heard the story, well, read it, from my cousin Margaret (Mama's younger brother John's only daughter), who had heard it from her friend, Mary who lives in California and whose father is a fireman on board the USS San Diego. What a long sentence! I am going to copy the story from Margaret's letter, which she copied from Mary's letter, which she copied from her father's letter, and I suppose you will copy it from my letter and send it to someone else. Another long sentence, but here is the story:

I was busy in fire room number 2 on January 21, when Ensign Cary came in to take the half hour readings of the steam pressure from the boilers. Everything seemed normal, and Ensign Cary had just stepped through the electric watertight door into number 1 fire room when the boilers in my room exploded! Second Class Trinidad of the Philippines and Second Class Daly and I were half blinded by the steam of the ruptured boilers. I for one didn't know just what to do or where to go. Suddenly Ensign Cary's thundering voice came through the steam yelling for us to get out of the room. Trinidad and I followed his voice to the door where we found him holding open the door which was being closed electrically from the bridge. I was coughing and choking and couldn't see very well, but Trinidad noticed that Daly wasn't with us and rushed back into the room. He soon returned with an injured Daly across his shoulders. Ensign Cary had held the door open for an entire minute with the steam all around him so that Trinidad could rescue Daly. Just as Trinidad was entering fire room number 4 with Daly, the boilers in number 3 fire room also exploded. Trinidad had no thought for himself, but passing Daly on to me, he returned into fire room 3 and assisted in rescuing another injured man from there. He was burned about the face by the blast of the second explosion. We were all given medical treatment and are all doing well now, thank God! The ship is all right and the boilers now fixed. Ensign Cary was awarded the Congressional Medal of Honor as was Second Class Fireman Trinidad.

Lydia Ruth sounds darling. I loved her little letter. Georgie said he would come play with her in fifty years, and then he would comb his hair. I don't think Rosalie will ever tumble down the stairs wrapped in her blanket. She isn't a wiggle worm when she goes to bed.

I asked Edmund if he would find me a weather rock. He thought a moment before agreeing. He found one, and it works. Most of the time. Sometimes Vincent takes it into the barn, and then it doesn't work.

What a long letter. This ought to keep you from resorting to law books for something new to read. At least for a little while. I didn't mean to write this much, but then I never mean to write a lot, and yet I usually do. Please give Edith a birthday hug from me. Also one from Mama, Daddy, and Carrie. The boys send birthday greetings. Edmund said to tell you that he was on the roof of the house and the porch roof. He and Daddy were fixing the roof where it was leaking in the attic when it rained. David would have been up there with them except that his sprained arm wasn't all the way well.

I must end this and go help with supper. I don't want to have scorched anything this time, or I would never hear the end of it. At least Mama is here. May God bless you, my dear cousin! I am praying for you.

Your affectionate cousin,
Emma

"Well, girls, I think that is going to have to be all for today," Mrs. Mitchell remarked, folding up the letter she had just finished and slipping it back into its envelope.

"Oh, just one more, please!"

"Do we really have to stop?"

Mrs. Mitchell laughed. "If I don't stop and start on supper, you'll have to explain to your dad and brothers why there is no supper."

Ria made a face at the thought but brightened instantly. "You don't have to go home yet, Lydia, so we can talk about them at least." She perched herself on the railing, her feet dangling above the porch.

There was a moment of silence between the two friends as each was lost in thought.

"I didn't notice any heroes yet."

Lydia shook her head. "Me either. Unless we did it on your mom's uncle."

"Uncle Philip Vincent Bartholomew Wallace III?"

"Uh, huh."

Ria frowned. "I don't think he was a hero because he didn't do anything except get wounded. If the U.S. had been in the war, we could do it on the guys on the USS San Diego. Perhaps we should wait until Mom has read more letters.

Lydia agreed, and soon the girls were busy with something else.

CHAPTER THREE

"Oh, look at that rain! Lydia we'll be soaked." Ria and Lydia stood at the school door and looked out at the sheets of rain. "I don't think even an umbrella will do much good."

"Ria!"

Ria turned and saw her brother Chris hurrying down the hall. "Al is here with their truck and ROTC is having a quick meeting, so he could take you both home now if you want."

"We do want, don't we Lydia? You can go home with me again, right?"

Lydia nodded. She had no idea who Al was, but she thought it must be okay. When Chris rushed away, she asked.

"Oh, he is one of my cousins." Ria replied. "The best of them all in my opinion. He always sides with me in anything. The others are nice, but Al is even nicer. When the gang meets at our house, he is the peacemaker."

"The gang?"

"Yah, there are twenty of them, and they are all older than I am. Only five are not my brothers or cousins. They do all kinds of things. But come on, there he is."

A quick dash through the rain and then the girls were scrambling into the truck.

"It's just a little wet out there today," Al remarked pulling out into the street.

Ria tossed her wet hair. "Al, this is my friend Lydia. We are working on a school project together, so you can take us both to my house."

"Pleased to meet you, Lydia. Only stop -- Aunt Emma's. Johnny mentioned your project. How is it coming?"

"Well, we still haven't decided who to do it on yet, but we have heard some really ridiculous stories, and we know who we aren't doing it on." Al nodded but neither he nor Lydia could say anything, for Ria kept up an incessant stream of chatter the entire way home. "Thanks for the ride!" she called from the front porch as her cousin climbed back in the truck.

Soon the girls were settled in the cozy kitchen with their cookies and milk and listening as Mrs. Mitchell began to read.

Wednesday
May 26, 1915
Princeville, Nova Scotia
Canada

My Darling Cousin Emma,

I'm sure you have heard the news about the "Lusitania." We were shocked that even Germany would do such a thing! I can't imagine how many people died! Do you know the number? I haven't heard it yet. It sounds much like the Titanic, only this time someone sunk it on purpose, and it was near the Ireland coast instead of Newfoundland and Nova Scotia. I know the "Lusitania" was a British ship, but it was only a passenger ship. I haven't heard a whole lot about it. If you know more, please let me know. I heard that the German embassy in Washington sent a warning to the newspapers. What did it say? I wonder if anyone heeded the warning. I am still in shock. The whole ship sank completely in twenty minutes!

We are waiting anxiously for letters from Papa, having heard of the second battle of Ypres. (You pronounce it 'Ee'-pr'.) Ypres is in Belgium not too far from the French border. The Germans used poison gas on April 22. I don't know where Papa was. This is the hard part, hearing about battles from the newspapers and yet not hearing from Papa. You wonder how accurate the news is. We are constantly praying for Papa. I know you are too, and that is a comfort.

From hearing about your tornado, I am thankful that we don't have any here. I am glad you didn't follow Edmund's advice and tell that story in just one sentence, or you would have had to answer a host of questions. You can write such long, interesting story letters. I don't see how you do it. I try, but I can't make them as interesting as yours are. Your letters are so interesting, to tell you truly, that I have saved them all, and we read them like story books. Everyone loves them. Why just yesterday I was outside with all twenty-one of the village children, and I read them the story you wrote last year about Georgie taking a piglet to bed with him. The children think they're great fun. Florence Stanly, who is eleven, told me your stories were as good as <u>Anne of Green Gables</u>! So don't ever stop writing like you have been.

Edmund sounds like he still likes to tease. At least he didn't let you go out into the tornado! I do wish I could have been there to take care of David. That would have been such fun. I haven't had anyone to nurse, except Mama a little, since Papa left. I wish someone would be sick or get hurt, so I could nurse them. I don't mean I want them hurt or sick just to please me. It's just that I do so enjoy helping them, relieving their pain and helping them get well. Of course I know that only the Lord can heal, but He allows us help, and I'm so glad. I only wish that Papa were here, so I could go with him out of the village to where folks are in need of help.

    Friday, May 28,

I wrote all the above two days ago before I got

interrupted. I was writing on our porch overlooking the water and enjoying the beautiful day. All the children were outside playing. Lydia Ruth and Ida were playing on the porch nearby with their dolls. Suddenly I became aware of a commotion down where the other children were playing. I looked up and saw twelve-year-old William Campton running towards me waving his arms wildly. I called the little girls, and we went to meet him. He told me breathlessly that eight-year-old James Lawson was hurt. It turns out that he was climbing the cliffs to see some Kittiwakes (I'll tell you about them later.) when he slipped and fell. I rushed over with William and the little girls trailing after. On reaching the spot, I pushed my way through the crowd of children to find James lying with his leg bent strangely, gasping for breath and blinking rapidly as though still a little dizzy. He told me he was all right though I knew at a glance that his leg was broken. After I felt him over carefully to make sure nothing else was broken, I let him sit up and lean on Mark who was kneeling anxiously by his friend's side. The children all continued to stand in a tight group around us and stare until I told them to move back so that James could breathe. They all took two steps back in silence but continued to stare.

Jennie, James's little sister asked quite tearfully, "Are you dead?" James assured her that he was not dead, only a little shaken up. After looking at his leg a moment, James told me that he didn't think he could walk home. I agreed with a smile and looked to see who could help carry him. I had almost decided on William and Charles, though Charles is only nine and rather small, when I noticed Edward Campton, William's sixteen-year-old cousin coming. He had come to find William and tell him his mother wanted him. When he saw James, he offered to carry him to the house. So with Edward carrying James, and me supporting his leg, we headed for the village with a long line of now talkative children following closely behind us.

On reaching the Lawson home, James was carried inside and laid gently on the sofa while the children scattered across the village to find Mrs. Lawson. She came sooner than I anticipated having been only at the Morris's house. She hurried in with a white face and threw her arms around James with a half stifled sob. Mrs. Lawson is a widow, and James and Jennie are her only children. (Do you remember me writing you about the night Captain Lawson perished at sea?) James reassured her that he would be fine. I was wishing that Papa was here to set his leg. Someone, I don't remember who, suggested that I set it, but I shook my head. This wasn't just a simple fracture that needed a splint put on to keep it still; this looked to me like something more serious. I told them that a real doctor needed to see it. As the grown-ups were discussing what was best to do, I fixed a cup of tea for James and tried to make him comfortable. Soon it was decided that Mrs. Lawson, Mr. and Mrs. Stanly, and I would take James to Pictou to see Doctor McNeel. I asked Mama why I was going. She said I was needed to remember all the doctor's orders and to keep James company. Edith was going to take care of Jennie and Lydia Ruth. Mark was to stay and help, though we didn't know where he was. Some of the village boys told us that they would find him. Mama was going home to rest.

Before long we were on our way. I could tell that James was in much pain though he never once complained, and I only heard a few quiet groans when the carriage went over a rough part in the road.

Doctor McNeel was glad to see me though he looked grave when he first saw James. Several times I had gone with Papa and a patient to Pictou to see Dr. McNeel. It made me miss Papa even more. The doctor soon was taking care of James's leg while he asked questions about Papa. He told us that he had tried to sign up to go to the front but was told that he was too old. He laughed when he told us that and added, "I told them I wasn't too old. After all, I'm only sixty-three years old plus six." Before we left, Dr. McNeel told me that if I ever run out of things to do then just to come to him as he always has plenty of patients. James's leg is going to be fine though he has to stay off of it for six weeks! That is hard on him. He is so active and was such a help to his mother. When we arrived back home, and Mr. Stanly had carried James in and helped him to bed, Mrs. Stanly brought Jennie home. After promising Mrs. Lawson that Mark would be over to bring in firewood and run errands for her the next day, I headed home.

It was growing chilly since the sun was going down. It was so quiet; I could hear the waves lapping against the boats down at the dock and the rustle of the pine trees in the gentle breeze.

Upon arriving home, I found Edith and Lydia Ruth setting the table for a late supper. Mark was no where to be seen, and Mama was resting on the sofa. I found Mark out on the porch. He was greatly relieved to hear that James would be all right and gladly promised to bring wood and run errands for Mrs. Lawson.

James is doing quite well now. Mark is utterly devoted to him, as are a few of the others. Mrs. Lawson has let me have almost complete charge of him, much to my great delight. James is a very easy patient though at times he pretends to be difficult. I think it will be harder to keep him still in a few weeks. Please pray for him. Dr. McNeel said he would come up next week and check on him. He promised to check on Mama too. There is no baby yet.

This story didn't take as long as yours. I am sure that if you had written it, it would have been much longer. I love your long detailed letters. I haven't had to read law books yet. The story about the USS San Diego has now become a favorite among the boys. They have enjoyed acting it out though you never told the name of the man writing the story. If I was writing to anyone else besides you and Papa, I would send the story along. As it is, I just read it to the children. James and Mark have heard it so many times that they can almost quote it.

Oh, you never told me about the Jones' baby. Was it a boy or girl? What is its name? Did the doctor arrive before it came? You see what happens when you don't give enough information.

Now let me tell you about the Kittiwakes. They are some of the cutest birds here. A Kittiwake is a kind of gull or tern. We don't see them much except during mating and nesting season because they spend their winters out over the open ocean. They are about 16 - 18 inches long. The adults are white with light gray back and wings. Their legs are black as though they had walked through a pan of black ink and then dipped the tip of their wings in it. They build their nests on the top of a cliff or ledge. We surprisingly have about 5 or 6 pairs nesting on the cliffs by our house. The young are not scared of people at all. Of course if they left their little moss and seaweed cup nests, they would fall. The young ones are darling with their little grayish white furry bodies and black eyes looking up at you as though wondering what kind of bird you are. They have black bills when they are younger, but as they grow older, they change to yellow. The children all want to see a baby bird so badly that Edward told them when the eggs hatch he would see if he could borrow one for a little while. If you lie down at the top of the cliffs and look over the side, you can see the nests. Only the older children are allowed to do that. I saw the eggs just once when the mama Kittiwake moved for a minute. There were two pinkish-buff spotted eggs. You should hear the parent birds when they call each other. They have a harsh cry as though they were upset with someone, then it will change into something a little sweeter that sounds a lot like "Kittiwake! Kittiwake!" The first one of the village who hears them when they arrive in the spring runs through the village shouting, "Kittiwake!" Then everyone begins to watch and listen.

I believe I will end this now as the wind is starting to pick up, and I don't want this letter to blow out to sea. God bless and keep you, dear.

With love and prayers,
Maria

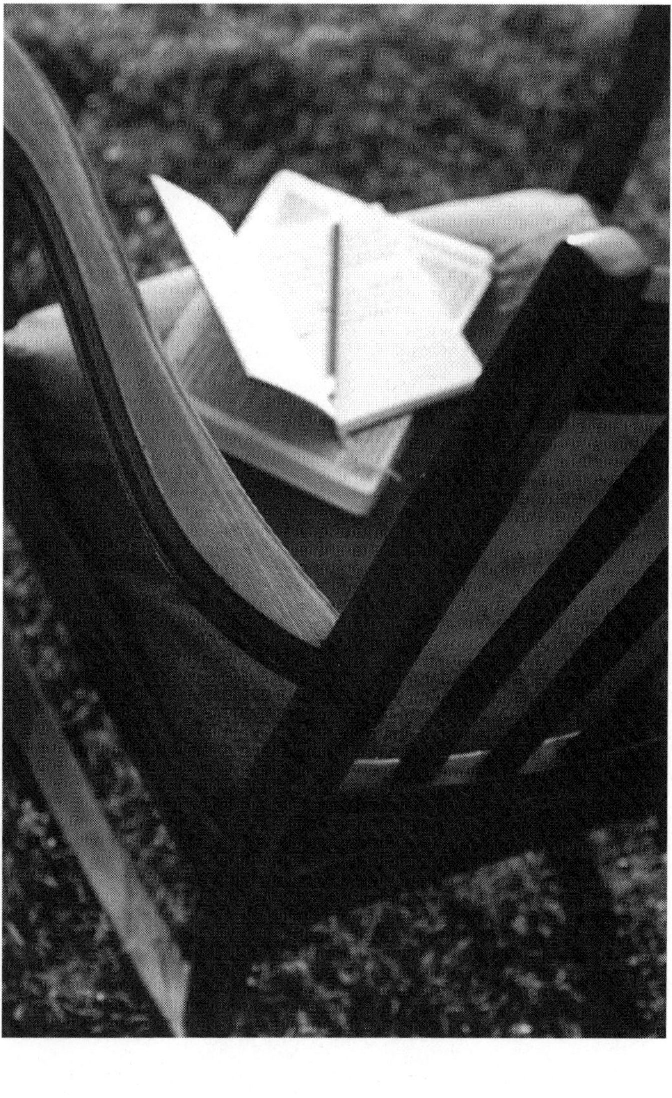

CHAPTER FOUR

Sunday
June 27, 1915
Codell, Kansas
USA

Dearest Maria,

How could you read my letters like story books? Do you honestly read them to the village children? You might want to be careful, they could get some ideas you don't want them to have. I have saved your letters also, only I don't read them over and over to the children. Maybe that is because we are too busy. My letters aren't even close to <u>Anne of Green Gables</u>. I suppose Edmund could be Gilbert if he really wanted to. My hair is too dark to be Anne, and I don't want to be Diana. Personally, I like <u>Pollyanna</u> much better. Have you ever read it? If you haven't, you should. It was written by Eleanor H. Porter in 1913. It is about a little girl who goes to live with her aunt after her parents die, and of her efforts to be glad about everything. It is such fun to read. I hope Eleanor Porter writes another book about Pollyanna.

So, you have heard about the *Lusitania* too? News about that seems to have traveled quickly to every corner of the world. There were 1,924 persons on board. The newspapers said that 1,198 persons are reported missing! Out of that, 128 were Americans! The German Embassy did print a notice in the papers. Here is what it said:

NOTICE! Travelers intending to embark on the

Atlantic voyage are reminded that a state of war exists between Germany and her allies and Great Britain and her allies: that the zone of war includes the waters adjacent to the British Isles: that in accordance with formal notice given by the Imperial German Government, vessels flying the flag of Great Britain, or of any of her allies, are liable to destruction in those waters and that travelers sailing in the war zone on ships of Great Britain or her allies do so at their own risk. IMPERIAL GERMAN EMBASSY Washington D. C. April 22, 1915.

I don't know if anyone heeded the warning or not. I think I would have. I wonder how many even saw the notice. Edmund and I were talking, and he said that if he were already planning to depart on the "Lusitania," he would probably already know when it was leaving and so not even look at the paper the day before the ship left. At least the Germans did put a warning in the paper though I would have thought that they should have put it in a few day earlier. Still, it was a passenger ship! I suppose even a ship flying the flag of Canada would be in danger now since you have gone to help Great Britain. I don't mean you personally you understand, but the nation. I wonder if any more Great Britain passenger ships will be sunk. Daddy said that the American government was highly displeased with Germany and protested the sinking of passenger ships. Germany has ordered their submarines not to attack neutral or passenger ships now. I wonder how long that will last.

I did hear of the second battle of Ypres. Thank you for telling me how to say it. It sure looks like a strange name. We are praying for Uncle Frederick. We heard that the Canadians held the line when the French fled because of the poison gas. I want to hear where Uncle was too. I know you will write us when you get letters again. How are they going to get mail across the ocean with the U-boats? I hope they make it. Other than the sinking of the "Lusitania" and a little news in some of the papers, the war appears quite distant.

What would it be like to be living in Belgium or France right now? Daddy said that Belgium was supposed to be a neutral country. I asked him why the Germans invaded it then, and he said he wasn't sure. He thought that the Germans thought it would be an easier route to Paris if they went through Belgium. Maybe the mountains were in the way if they had gone around Belgium. All this makes me wonder where Uncle Philip is.

Oh Maria, you will never guess what scrape we got into a little over a week ago. Yes, I did say we. Edmund and I, even David. In fact all of us children, except Carrie and Rosalie who were with Mama and Daddy, were involved. It was rather fun while it lasted. But let me tell you about it. It was the 18th, which was a Friday. Daddy had picked up some red paint earlier in the week to paint the barn with. That morning during breakfast Daddy said, "Children, I want you to paint the barn today while your Mama and I are in town."

"Isn't Carrie going with you?" I asked as it was her turn.

Daddy looked at Mama who smiled. "All right, we'll count Carrie out. Also, since you will all be painting, no one will be able to look after Rosalie, so we'll take her too," Daddy agreed. "Do you think the rest of you can handle it?" Daddy looked at each of us as he spoke.

We nodded. It sounded like fun to me. Carrie was excited about going shopping in town. She was getting new shoes. So we managed to clean the kitchen up and wash the dishes in record time.

"Make sure you children put on old clothes before you start to paint," Mama instructed. "You're liable to get paint on you." Little did she realize how true that last statement would turn out to be. Hardly had the wagon started to town when the five of us children raced to our rooms to change into old clothes. Believe it or not, I was the first one ready. I dashed outside, eager to start. The sky was a beautiful deep blue. The sun was quite warm already though the grass still felt cool underneath my bare feet. Soon the boys came trooping out of the house, Georgie's hair standing on end, as usual. David and Edmund soon had three ladders up and ready. Edmund was going to start at the very top of the barn, David and I were below him on either side, while the little boys were to paint from the foundation up as high as they could reach.

We had painted steadily for over an hour before we stopped for a short drink break.

"Lucy," Edmund grinned, "I think you should try to keep a little more clean."

I glanced down. The only paint I had on me was a little on my hands. I looked at Edmund who was quite covered with paint and retorted, "Maybe you can get a little more paint on you so we'll match."

"That might help, but let me brush that spider off your face first," he teased as he reached out a hand covered with wet paint.

I screamed and backed behind David exclaiming, "Don't touch me! David is there really a spider on me?"

"Not even anything close," David reassured me shaking his head.

I looked back at Edmund with an idea in my mind though I didn't think he would fall for it. "Edmund!" I exclaimed in pretended horror. "What it that?" I pointed to his face.

"What is what?" Edmund asked.

"That thing on your face!" I gasped. Edmund instinctively put his hand to his face. "Not on that side. It's on the other side, by your nose." As Edmund brushed his face with his hand again, I said, "Oh, it's only paint."

David exploded with laughter and gasped, "She got you that time Ed!"

Edmund looked a little sheepish at being caught by his twin with his own idea but laughed anyway.

"Say, Emma," David began just before we started working again, "don't you think we could have a sort of picnic out here for dinner? We're all so paint decorated," and here he glanced at Edmund slyly, "that we'd be sure to mess up Mama's clean kitchen."

"Yeah, let's! Please!" Vincent and Georgie chimed in. I couldn't see any reason not to, so I went to prepare it while the boys continued to paint. When I had finished, I brought out the basket, set it in the shade of a tree, and hurried back to help. Edmund and David were having a lively discussion about automobiles to which I listened but didn't join in. It wasn't quite noon when I glanced down to see how the little boys were doing. They were nowhere to be seen.

"David, where are the little boys?" I asked. Before any answer could be given, two little "Indians" came around the corner of the barn with feathers in their brown hair, tomahawks in their belts, and bows and arrows in their hands. You should have seen them, Maria. They had taken off their shirts and painted themselves red! Barn red. I must say they looked rather cute for they had forgotten to paint their feet. The biggest "Indian" raised his bow and shot at Edmund. The arrow didn't even come close, but my twin was a good actor anyway; he dropped his paint brush with a groan and slid down the ladder to fall moaning onto the ground clutching his chest. I hurried down my ladder crying, "Oh, they have killed him!" The paintbrush that Edmund dropped hit David right on the side of his head, leaving a bright red splotch and paint dripping down his face. David is as good an actor as Edmund for he climbed down his ladder and staggered a few steps before collapsing to the ground. The "Indians" looked astonished that one shot had brought such happenings.

Vincent looked concernedly at his brothers and stammered, "Are . . . are they really hurt?"

"Not a bit," Edmund declared sitting up and grinning.

"Only a little paint spattered," David added cheerfully.

Suddenly I had an idea. "I know what we can do," I cried. "Vincent and Georgie, you be the good Indians now, and come and help us."

"That is too many white men for them," Edmund declared. "Besides, I was killed, so I'll be an Indian too."

"Emma, you be the Indian squaw, and I'll be the only white survivor," David suggested.

"But I didn't get killed," I protested.

"But alas, when you saw that I, your faithful lover was dead, you died right then and there of a broken heart." Edmund's voice was a little too tragical for me, and when he clutched his heart and fell back on the grass as he uttered the last words, I tickled his nose with a fox tail making him sneeze. The other boys laughed.

"I'll be your squaw if you aren't foolish," I said.

So it was agreed that the four of us would be Indians, and David would be the injured white man. Edmund and I didn't paint ourselves as much as the little boys had, but we were rather red when we finished. We found enough feathers to make Edmund a chief and even a few for me.

I'll give you the short version of what we played; otherwise I'll be here all day writing. Chief Edmund sent Vincent and Georgie out to hunt. They returned with an injured white man and a basket of food from the wagon train that had been attacked. I prepared the food for the Indians and David. Though David was "injured," he still managed to eat a lot. Finally, through the care of the Indians, the white man became well and joined us in hunts, fights, moves, and many adventures. We were just in the midst of hunting in the woods when we were interrupted and startled by a shrill whistle.

Suddenly I turned around to the boys exclaiming, "The barn!"

David gasped, "I forgot all about it!"

"Me too," Edmund groaned.

We really had forgotten all about it, Maria. The little boys were farther in the woods looking for nuts. "Vincent, Georgie!" David called.

"We had better get moving," Edmund said, "or we'll be in even worse trouble."

"You two go on, and I'll come with the little boys as quickly as I can," David ordered.

Edmund and I turned and began to run toward the barn. Before we reached it, we heard another whistle. We tried to go faster, but I was gasping for breath as it was. Finally we reached the barn, and rounding it we saw Mama, Carrie, Rosalie, and Daddy standing by the fence.

"Where have you been?" Daddy asked rather sternly. For a minute neither of us could answer for lack of breath. Then Edmund gasped out, "In the woods."

"Where are the others?"

"They're coming," I panted. Just then the other three came around the corner of the barn. Mama took one look at the five of us all standing before them and burst into a gale of laughter. Carrie and Rosalie just stared.

I saw the corners of Daddy's mouth twitch a little, though he only said gravely, "Need I ask what you all have been doing?"

"Playing Indians, Daddy," Georgie piped up.

"How long has this been going on? David?" Daddy questioned.

David drew a deep breath and answered, "Since just before dinner, sir."

Daddy looked at us in silence a moment before he asked, "Whose idea was it?"

Vincent walked up to Daddy and said, "It was all mine. I thought of it first and shot and killed Edmund, and Emma died of a broken heart, and David almost got killed but . . . ."

"The good Indians comed, and we taked him to the chief and his squawk." Georgie interrupted, longing to tell at least part of the adventures.

How Daddy managed to keep a straight face over that last word of Georgie's is a puzzle to me. Somehow he managed to, though Mama was shaking with laughter. Daddy turned and walked over to Mama then together they walked a little way apart. I knew they were discussing what our punishment would be. I glanced at Edmund. He was staring at the ground, and I could tell he was trying not to laugh. Carrie came over with Rosalie clinging to her hand.

"You all look funny," she said eying us with astonishment. "I'm glad I didn't stay. I would hate to look like you. Emma!" she exclaimed, "You even have paint in your hair!" Rosalie began to giggle.

Daddy and Mama came back, and Daddy said, "You are to finish painting this side of the barn now before you can eat your supper. Then tomorrow you are to finish painting it. I was going to help you tomorrow, but since you all seem to like paint so much, you can do it by yourselves. I hope this will be a lesson to you to keep your mind on what you are supposed to be doing and not on what you want to do."

"But Daddy, I'm hungry!" Georgie cried.

"Me too!" Vincent echoed.

"Then you had better get busy painting," Daddy advised smiling. Mama was still laughing as she, Daddy, Carrie and Rosalie went up to the house.

When they were gone, we looked at each other and sighed. Then I burst out laughing and raced for my ladder. "What's so funny?" Edmund demanded climbing his own ladder.

"We are!" I chuckled. "Can't you just picture someone's face if they were to come by and see us? We look ridiculous with bright red paint all over us!"

David and Edmund laughed too, and we all fell to work. Everyone worked diligently for about thirty minutes before Georgie began to complain that he was hungry. Knowing that he would probably continue to complain and not work, David sent him to go find the lunch basket and take it back to the house. This he did eagerly only to return from the house with a sad face and begin to paint again. Carrie came out and, perching herself on the rail fence, watched us and told us about their trip. It was almost dark when we finally finished and put things away.

"I don't know about you all, but I want to clean up before I eat," Edmund declared.

"I do too," I agreed while David nodded.

"But I'm hungry!" Georgie wailed.

"You're always hungry, Georgie," I laughed.

"Me too," Vincent said rubbing his stomach.

"You two can go eat," David told them. They ran to the house joyfully. It took quite a bit of scrubbing to get all the paint off of our faces and arms. I didn't even try to get it out of my hair as I figured I would get more in it the next day. You have no idea how good supper tasted that night.

When I told Daddy good night, he smiled and said, "Good night Indian squawk."

The next day we spent painting again. I don't think any of us were quite as eager to start as we had been the day before. The barn was finished before supper time, and we were glad! I think we did learn our lesson though. At least David, Edmund and I did.

I am glad you finally have someone to nurse. How is James doing? We are praying for him. I expect there is a baby now. Boy or girl? Oh, the Joneses had a boy. A dark haired, dark eyed baby named Paul Raymond Jones. I am sorry I forgot to tell you in my last letter. Dr. Pierson did arrive before the baby came, but Paul came about the same time as the tornado. Thankfully the tornado went east of them. Daddy said he stood on their porch and watched it. Mrs. Jones was sick for about a week after the baby came, but she is doing fine now. Carrie, Edmund and I went over there last week for a little while to take care of the children while Mr. and Mrs. Jones were in town. They took Paul with them, much to Carrie's disappointment. However, she had fun with two-year-old Catherine Jones.

I wish I could see a Kittiwake. They sound so fascinating. How can they winter over the ocean? Don't they have to land somewhere? Do they swim like ducks? That seems strange. Can't you draw me a sketch of some Kittiwakes with their young? The children want to see one.

So do I. Georgie said he will put it in his newspaper. Edmund asked him what his newspaper was called.

Georgie thought a moment and then with a frown declared, "I just forgot to name it!" He still hasn't named it. He loves to tell stories. Edmund teases me that I have been telling him too many, and he is picking up the habit.

Guess what! Daddy said that Carrie and I get to have a horse of our own if we can train it! He said he would help us. Daddy told us that he would bring her home some time this week he hoped. We haven't decided on a name yet. We think we will wait to see what she looks like. David and Edmund keep teasing us. I believe they don't think we can train a horse. I think we can if Daddy helps us. Don't you? Mama said she was sure we could. We have all the rest of summer to work with her. I can hardly wait.

I don't believe there was anything else I was going to tell you. Oh, yes there was. The reason I didn't tell you the name of the man who wrote the story about the *USS San Diego* is because I don't know it. Since I don't know it, I guess Mark and James will have to give him a name.

Well, Edmund is calling me to go with him somewhere, so I had better end this. Please tell Mark happy birthday from us all. It is hard to believe he is going to be nine years old! Time seems to be going much faster than it used to. Doesn't it seem that way to you? May God's blessings be with you. We will keep praying.

With all my love,
Emma

Hardly had Mrs. Mitchell finished reading the letter before Ria burst into a merry fit of laughter. "Oh, Mom," she gasped, "I didn't know you could be so silly. I can't believe you painted yourself barn red!"

Mrs. Mitchell chuckled too at the remembrance of painting the barn and playing Indians. "I'm sure we were a sight to behold with red barn paint all over us." She shook her head. "I don't see how my mother lived through us all. Shall we continue?"

"Yes, please. I want to see what Maria says about it," and Ria giggled again.

CHAPTER FIVE

Saturday
July 24, 1915
Princeville, Nova Scotia
Canada

My Dearest Emma,

Yes, there is a baby. A darling boy whose name is Andrew Frederick. You see, we reversed Papa's name for him. He arrived four days after I wrote my last letter, on June 1, which means that he is almost two months old. I was intending to write you sooner, but it never happened. Several times I sat down to start, but each time I was called away to do something else. Then I was expecting your letter any day, so I waited. Your letter must have gotten lost for it took over a week longer than it usually does to reach me. Do excuse me, I see I haven't told you a thing about Andrew, and that just won't do. He has almost black hair, and his eyes are hazel. Mama can't figure out where he got his dark hair or his hazel eyes for that matter. Andrew is a very wide awake little laddie, and oh, Emma, he has one dimple just like Papa! Lydia Ruth has two dimples while the rest of us have none. It is even on his left cheek just like Papa! The first two weeks of his life he cried if he wasn't eating or sleeping. That wore us all out. Edith and I took turns walking him when he cried. Lydia Ruth was so miserable because she wasn't getting enough sleep, and she hated to hear Andrew cry. Mrs. Stanly offered to let her stay at their house. That was a tremendous help. Mark spent most of his waking time doing chores here or spending time with James since I was so busy. All the village women and girls have helped so much. It is a great blessing to have help. On the morning of the sixteenth, when I was holding Andrew and trying to stay awake so I wouldn't drop him, he opened his eyes and looked at me. I fairly held my breath fearing he would begin to cry. Not a sound did he make but looked around as though suddenly interested in what was going on. He hardly ever cries now. Lydia Ruth is back to sleeping at home, and I am free to do other things. Mama is doing quite well. I still try not to let her do much, at which she smiles and tells me I'm acting like Papa. I don't mind. I'd rather be like Papa than anyone else except Mama.

You wanted a picture of a Kittiwake. Well, I did try once to draw a picture of one for you, but I couldn't. It happened this way. It was a delightfully warm day. The sun was shining brightly and a warm breeze was blowing off the ocean. I had an hour or two with nothing I had to do, so I thought I would try to draw your picture for you. I gathered my paper and pencil and headed out to a special place on the cliffs where I sometimes go. It is a charming little place even if it is a little scary getting down there. Once there however, I can see all the nests of the Kittiwakes or look out over the ocean toward Pictou harbor and see the fishing vessels. If it is the right time of day, I can see a small speck that is the ferry going to Prince Edward Island or returning from there. The place itself is a large ledge which juts out from the cliff. It has a moss-covered seat where I can sit and lean against the cliff while enjoying God's creation. I reached the place in safety and was getting settled when I dropped my pencil. That would have been all right if when I reached for it I hadn't accidentally knocked it off the ledge. It fell to the ground below, and I must say, I sighed. It would take about thirty minutes to work my way back up to the top of the cliff, walk around and then down the cliffs to the path that leads to the bottom of the cliff, retrieve my pencil and then retrace my steps. I decided to go quickly and not waste my time wishing it hadn't happened. Leaving my paper behind, I began my ascent. I hadn't gone more than a foot or two when a large rock came loose above me. I clung to the side of the cliff and prayed! Upon looking up, I saw the rock had stopped only a few inches from my hands. It was firmly lodged right in the middle of the path! There was no way I could climb over it and only a very small creature could go under it. There was nothing to do but go back to my ledge and wait.

I was rather shaken up from the experience, and when I had safely reached the ledge again, the first thing I did was to thank God for His protection. Then, having nothing to do but sit, I dreamed of you and wondered what you were doing and what the farm must be like now that summer has reached you. Then my thoughts turned to Papa. How I long to see him again! I thought of the soldiers: the French, the British, the Canadians, the Belgians. I even thought of your Uncle Philip in the Vosges Mountains. At last I began to try to think of a way to get to the top or bottom of the cliffs. Now I can just hear Edmund saying, "Jump." I didn't intend to. I was sure that by now Edith would be expecting me back to help with supper. I didn't know if she would send Mark to find me or not. Then I remembered that he was at the Lawsons with James. Upon carefully looking around, I noticed a small ledge running along the side of the cliff toward the sea. It sloped gradually upward, and I thought it might continue to the top of the cliffs around the bend. I decided to try it. First I dropped my paper over the cliff after my pencil. I hoped someone would find them both, or else I would just get them in the morning. Carefully clinging to the rocks above and beside me, I worked my way over the ledge and around the bend where it suddenly ended. I must try to paint a word picture of where I was. I was standing on a ledge less than six inches wide while I clung with clammy hands to some rocks. There were another two feet or so of rocky cliffs above me before the top could be reached. Below me the cliffs dropped some twenty feet before they reached the ocean. From where I was, I could hear the waves crashing against the rocks. Scattered with light pink clouds, the sky was turning purple and the sun began to sink in the west. You may think it strange, Emma, but I wasn't terribly frightened. I was more worried that Mama might try to find me and wear herself out and become ill. I prayed, and hardly had I finished when I heard a deep voice calling my name from somewhere up above me. I shouted back though I wasn't sure of my voice being heard above the waves. It must have carried though because the voice got closer and closer. Suddenly a face appeared over the cliff. It was Mr. McLean!

"Lassie!" he exclaimed when he saw me. "Didnae ye ken we've been a lookin' fer ye? Here, lad, lend a hand will ye?"

This last was over his shoulder, and in another moment Alan's face was also to be seen above me. Reaching down, they grabbed my wrists and pulled me up. I managed to thank them for their help before flying to the house to make sure Mama was all right. She was. She said she hadn't even left the house. Supper was ready soon after I arrived. After I had a good cry on Mama's shoulder (though I don't know what I was crying for), I slept quite soundly. Oh, someone did find my paper and pencil and brought them home. I haven't been back to try drawing the Kittiwakes again. So now you know why there is no picture. Maybe next year.

I wish you could have been here on Dominion Day, Emma. And you too, Edmund. I know you would have enjoyed it. Dominion Day is much like Independence Day in the US except that Dominion Day is not a celebration of a declaration of independence but rather a celebration of the uniting of all the provinces into one government called The Dominion of Canada in the year 1868. That seems like such a long time ago. The celebration was so much fun. All the villagers attended. Even those who don't really live "in" Princeville came. One of the highlights of the day was the "barrel race." We weren't able to have it the last two years because the sea was too rough. This time it was perfect. There were a dozen contestants, all men or older boys. Each was to get on an empty barrel and paddle 100 yards out to sea and then back. Oh, it was quite a sight! I had forgotten how comical this was to watch. Several barrels turned over right at the first, dumping whoever was on them into the water. Most men straddled their barrel like horses. Mr. McLean was one of the first to be rolled into the water by his barrel, so instead of trying to sit on it again, he laid across it, feet in the water on one side and hands in on the other. I don't remember who won, but those of us who were on the shore watching laughed until our sides ached.

The other highlight began at dusk. All the children, and most of the adults, hurried to their houses to change clothes. When we heard the skirtle of the bagpipes begin to play, we all rushed out. The older ones were given torches, and we formed a procession and marched all over the village. Almost everyone was dressed up. Mr. McLean and his oldest son Alan were in full Scottish dress with kilts and tartans. They both played the bagpipes. James and Mark, along with a few other lads, were dressed as soldiers. Since James was not allowed to put weight on his leg yet, he was carried on a stretcher. I was a red cross nurse. There were Indians and statesmen, well-to-do ladies, and a schoolteacher. Each was dressed to represent Canada's past or present. When the procession was nearing its end, the bagpipes began playing "It's a Long, Long Way to Tipperary." We all sang it as we walked. The second verse is so ridiculous. It goes like this:

"Paddy wrote a letter to his Irish Molly O,'
Saying, 'Should you not receive it, write and let me know!
If I make mistakes in "spelling," Molly dear,' said he,
'Remember it's the pen that's bad, don't lay the blame on me.'"

Even if the song is Irish and not Scottish, it is still fun

to sing.

When I read to Mark, Edith and Mama about you painting the barn, they laughed until they cried. Edith said she could just picture you all covered with bright red paint and with chicken feathers in your hair. Mama added that she could see why Aunt Helen couldn't keep from laughing. Carrie must still not like getting very dirty, or was it just the paint she didn't like? I'm not sure I would have joined you in painting myself red, though I do wish I could have seen the little boys looking like Indians.

I would love to hear one of Georgie's stories. They must be interesting. Couldn't you try to write one down for me? Perhaps I should ask Edmund to. He doesn't seem so busy.

How is your horse training coming along? Have the boys stopped teasing yet? Maybe they were just jealous that they weren't getting a horse. What color is your horse? What is her name? It is a girl, isn't it? There are hardly any horses in Princeville because we walk everywhere or use a boat. Horses do get used to go to Pictou though.

No, I have never read Pollyanna. I hadn't even heard of it before I got your letter. It does sound interesting. Hasn't Eleanor Porter written something else? Mama thinks she recognized the name.

We are still waiting and praying for letters from Papa. Not much war news has reached the village recently. I don't know what that means. Are no battles going on? Is the war almost over? Sometimes I get so lonesome for Papa that I want to get in a boat and go find him in France. I am glad Andrew is here. He is a distraction. As James is back on his feet, I am out of patients to nurse. I have thought of taking up Dr. McNeel's offer, but if I did I wouldn't be able to live in Princeville. And I suppose I am rather young to be on my own. Not that I really want to be. I will try to stay busy anyway. Maybe I should begin to study the law books. On second thought, perhaps I should just end this letter, so you can write another one of your exceptionally long letters to me. If I don't write you before your birthday, be sure I will be thinking of you both and most likely be wishing I could be there with you. Please give everyone there my love. Kiss Rosalie for me. I have already kissed Andrew for each of his cousins and his uncle and aunt. Oh, you should see him when I kiss him! He smiles and gets all excited, and his one darling dimple shows! I will end this now. May God be with you, my dear cousin.

Much love,
Maria

Tuesday
August 31, 1915
Codell, Kansas
USA

Dear Maria,

I don't know if this will be a long interesting letter or not. I think it will be interesting, but whether it is long or not, will depend on how fast I can write and how long Edmund will let me. You see, I have injured my back, and this is only the first day I've been allowed to sit up. I like to think that if you were here I'd have been sitting up earlier. I declare Maria, I've never known Edmund to be so fussy! Why, sometimes I scarcely dare breathe without asking him. He will rarely let anyone do anything for me because he wants to do it all. He is very gentle and patient with me even when I get cross. It is just so hard to have to lie here day after day. I thought that I would have been up within a week after it happened, but everyone said, "No!" so emphatically that I didn't dare to try. Do you want to hear all about it? What a question; of course you do. It will help you stay away from those law books.

To begin with, Daddy did bring Carrie and me a horse on June 30. She is a beautiful, chestnut-brown two-and-a-half year old. We have named her Jessie. Jessie had been somewhat trained before we got her, and with Daddy's help,

Carrie and I didn't have much trouble. The boys continued to tease us some, but we didn't mind. By the end of July, Jessie would stand quietly while we saddled her. But, though she would let us mount and ride her for a time, she would only go a little while before either bucking or stalling to get the rider off. Daddy had us ride in the pasture, so someone could watch us. David and Edmund weren't allowed to mount Jessie until she was all the way trained. Around the middle of August, Carrie and I could ride Jessie for a long time around the pasture without her acting up. The boys hadn't seen us though. At dinner on Wednesday the 18th, I asked Daddy if I could take Jessie for a ride around some of our land.

"Where would you ride her?" Daddy questioned before he took a bite of Mama's bread.

"Down to the creek," I replied, ignoring Edmund's grunt.

Daddy looked at Mama, but before he could answer, the teasing began.

"How many days will you be gone?" Edmund inquired.

"Do you plan on arriving there before dark?"

"You won't make it to the creek. At least not in one day!"

"Bring me some cattails, will you?"

I only laughed and looked across the table at Carrie who sighed.

"All right, boys," Daddy checked the teasing, "I wouldn't be too sure of anything. You might be eating your words before the day is out." He then turned to me and said I could go. Carrie and I grinned.

A little while later, after the kitchen was cleaned up, we headed out to the barn yard. It was quite a crowd; Daddy, David, Edmund, Vincent, Carrie, Georgie and me.

"Will you please bring me a cattail all my own, Emma," Georgie begged.

I kissed him and said, "I'll bring four of them. One

for each of you boys who don't believe I can do it."

Vincent declared that he thought I could do it. I smiled, mounted Jessie, and with a wave of my hand started off toward the creek in high spirits. Oh, Maria, the ride was simply glorious! Jessie behaved beautifully. It wasn't more than fifteen minutes before we reached the creek. I dismounted, tied Jessie to a tree limb, and stepping lightly on half-submerged rocks, crossed the creek to get the cattails. After I had four, I started back across the creek, pausing a moment in the middle to watch a dragonfly. Back across, I untied Jessie. I probably could have just left her untied.

September 1,

Well, Maria, Edmund wouldn't let me write anymore yesterday, so I will try to finish today.

When I mounted, I decided to go home another way than I had come. I thought it might take a little longer, but I really wanted to ride Jessie down the big hill to the barn. Everything was going beautifully until suddenly, right in front of us, a pheasant flew up with a loud noise! Poor Jessie, she was so frightened that she reared up. Before I was able to get a grip on anything, I was thrown off, and I remember thinking, *don't let go of the cattails*. Everything went black then until something kept nudging me. I opened my eyes to find myself lying on my back while Jessie nudged me as though trying to tell me to get up. It took me a few minutes to remember where I was and what had happened. When I tried to sit up, pain seemed to shoot through my every limb. I lay back catching my breath and collecting my thoughts. How was I to get home? Should I try to send Jessie back? I prayed, I assure you. As I lay there, I noticed that the cattails were still clutched in my left hand.

"Jessie," I muttered determinedly, "I am going to ride you home. We'll just have to go slowly." I began moving my arms and legs carefully just to make sure nothing was broken. They seemed to be fine. Slowly, very slowly, I stood up. The pain in my back was quite intense. I felt rather lightheaded as I leaned against Jessie's side. She stood still, only turning her head to look at me as though urging me to mount. Shifting all my weight to my right foot so I could put my left foot in the stirrup, I let out a cry of pain as my ankle gave way, and only by clinging to the saddle was I saved from falling. There was no doubt that I had hurt my ankle. It was with great difficulty that I managed at last to pull myself into the saddle. Everything seemed to be spinning, and I thought I was going to fall again. I leaned down against Jessie's neck while I hung on to her mane and the reins with my right hand.

"Home, Jess," I whispered, closing my eyes to shut out the whirling ground and praying she would go the right direction. Jessie set off at a steady pace. Finding that my back hurt less leaning on her neck with my feet out of the stirrups, I rode all the way to the barn that way. The barn and yard were deserted when we rode up.

"I suppose they weren't expecting us back so soon," I murmured to Jessie as we entered the barn and stopped by her stall. Now I had to dismount. Oh how I wished someone would just pick me up, carry me to the house, and let me lie down and not move until I didn't feel so lightheaded. I slowly slid off only to find that my legs didn't want to hold me, and I sank onto an upturned bucket. Just then I heard voices.

"Are you sure you saw her come home by herself, Ed?" David sounded rather doubtful

"Look, there she is. Emma wouldn't leave her just standing there if she were here."

The boys had by this time come up on the other side of Jessie.

"Oh, I wouldn't, would I?" I challenged, trying to keep my voice sounding natural.

"Emma!" both boys exclaimed hurrying around the horse. I was glad the barn was quite dim or they would have noticed right away that something was wrong.

"Your cattails, sirs," I offered, holding them out with a shaky hand only to withdraw them quickly as I added, "But

I think I will wait until we get to the house."

The boys laughed a little sheepishly at that and began to unsaddle Jessie.

"How did she do?" David inquired, removing her saddle.

"Beautifully!" I bit my lip to keep back a groan. I was in a lot of pain, but I wasn't about to admit it yet. Soon Jessie was unsaddled and taken care of.

"Come, Lucy, let us escort you back to the house as the heroine of the day," Edmund proposed, offering me his arm. I took it and stood up. I think the weight with which I leaned against him made him wonder, for he looked at me and questioned, "Are you okay? Lucy, what's the matter?"

"I think I hurt my ankle," I moaned.

The boys made chair with their arms and carried me out of the barn. "Lucy!" Edmund exclaimed. I looked at him in time to see all the color fade from his face leaving it a chalky white. I wanted to ask him what was the matter, but my back was hurting and everything was getting so blurry that it took almost all of my concentration to keep from fainting. "Mama!" Edmund shouted before we even reached the house. "Mama!"

Mama came out on the porch. "Shh, boys! You'll wake . . . Emma! What has happened?" Mama's tone quickly changed as she saw me. No sooner had the boys set me down in a chair in the kitchen than Mama grabbed a dishcloth as she ordered, "David, go . . ." She didn't have to finish as David was already outside. Only when Mama pressed the clean cloth tightly to the back of my neck did I realize that I must have cut it on a rock when I fell, and that is why I was so lightheaded. The little boys rushed into the kitchen, eagerly asking if I had brought them cattails. I held them up though my hand shook. Each began clamoring for his own. To my surprise, I couldn't open my hand. I had gripped them so tightly that it just wouldn't open. Edmund had to pry my fingers apart.

Daddy, David, and Carrie hurried into the kitchen

then, and Carrie exclaimed, "Oh, Emma! We can't ride her?"

"Sure we can. She behaves beautifully!" I declared.

"Then what has happened to you?" questioned Daddy.

I explained in a few words adding, "Really, I will be all right. Please just let me go to bed." I was in such pain and was so exhausted that I feared I would faint.

"Bed is probably the best place for you, young lady," Daddy admitted taking me in his arms. Maria, that bed felt so wonderful! I closed my eyes as the room was still spinning. I heard Edmund say something about my ankle then I felt Daddy's strong but gentle hands remove my shoes. He began moving my foot, and as he did so a keen pain shot through me. I started up quickly only to fall back with a sharp cry of pain.

"Emma!" I opened my eyes to see Edmund leaning over me with a face full of concern. "What is it?"

"My back!" I gasped.

He held my hand, and I squeezed it, hard. Everything seemed to be slipping farther away as though into a fog. Daddy was talking to David about going somewhere, but I was too tired, and it was too much of an effort to think about what he said. All I cared about was that Edmund was beside me, and Mama and Daddy were near.

September 2

Day three of writing. Edmund just won't let me write long enough to finish this letter. I thought I would finish it yesterday, but no, Edmund took the paper and pencil right out of my hands! I think I will have to insist that I finish it today, for it is already long past time for this to be sent. But back to the story.

I must have fainted or fallen asleep then because I don't remember anything until sometime later when Edmund kept calling my name. It was with difficulty that I opened my eyes. I saw Edmund and could feel his hand still in mine. When he saw that I was awake, he turned to someone in the doorway. Then I saw Dr. Pierson. He smiled at me and said something. I couldn't understand him. I don't really remember the rest of the day or for a few days after for that matter except that I was in pain, and Edmund never seemed to leave me. Mama told me later that he never left my side for more than five minutes at a time. The only way they could get him to eat was for Daddy to bring a tray with his food on it to my room and then order him to eat while he watched. The doctor said the pain, shock and loss of blood caused me to be very ill for several days.

Everyone tries to amuse me and help in any way they can. Edmund doesn't allow much help. He seems jealous if he is not the one getting things for me or doing something for me. Georgie has told some of the cutest stories. I couldn't write them down though. Vincent once came in to stand on his head for me. He did very well, but when Georgie, his faithful shadow, tried, he knocked over the vase of flowers, spilling the water and breaking the vase. He had also forgotten the snake he had in his pocket. It slid out and disappeared in the room and no one knew it for several hours. I had slept for an hour before Carrie came in with a cup of tea for me. When she was beside the bed, she suddenly screamed as only Carrie can scream, dropped the cup and scrambled up onto the nearest chair where she stood and continued to scream. Of course the tea spilled all over the bed and me. I glanced down and let out a shriek too. There coming out from under the sheet was a snake! Edmund was the first to rush into the room. He only noticed the mess the tea had made, for the snake had slid back under the sheet.

"Carrie," he began with a sigh, but I cut him short.

"Edmund, get the snake out of my bed!"

"The what?" Edmund jerked back the sheets and found the snake. It was only a garter snake, but I don't like them in bed with me! Carrie and I were a little nervous until we found out that Georgie only had one snake.

I am enclosing a copy of "Pollyanna" for you. Aunt

Ester who lives in New York found a new book called "Pollyanna Grows Up." She didn't know if I had "Pollyanna" or not, so she sent me both. I am so glad Eleanor Porter wrote another "Pollyanna" book. (Now I am starting to sound like Pollyanna.) I haven't gotten to read it yet.

We were all so excited about our new cousin. Andrew Frederick is a charming name. How I wish I could see him! Babies grow up so quickly. The last time we saw Lydia Ruth she was only a baby. I wish we could come visit you.

That is all right about the Kittiwakes. I am so thankful you didn't get hurt! Did Edward ever

Maria,

I have told Emma she can't write any more. She has already been sitting up more today than the doctor said she could. I know you will agree with me. She said to tell you happy birthday! I send my greetings too. Now, since Emma insists that this letter must go out today, I will end it so that Emma can get some rest before tomorrow. Don't tell her, but the doctor said she might be moved downstairs tomorrow, so she needs to rest now.

Edmund

CHAPTER SIX

Tuesday
October 5, 1915
Princeville, Nova Scotia
Canada

My Darling Emma,

How are you doing? Please do be careful when you ride Jessie. I should hate to hear of anything else happening to you. I now know why I felt such a burden to pray for you in August. I certainly do wish I could have been there, though I might not have been as lenient as Edmund. Please tell him that I agree with him about you. He'll know what I mean. You certainly have a wonderful twin, Emma. It almost makes me jealous. Never mind, I have Edith, and you don't have a big sister. How has Carrie fared on Jessie? Are the boys allowed to ride her now?

I had a wonderful birthday. The only thing that could have improved it would have been Papa here in person. As you know, on our birthdays we girls have a tea party using Great-grandmother Dawson's tea set. It is genuine silver from England. Mama asked me who I wanted to come to tea. I told her I wanted you, Edmund, and Papa, but as I couldn't have any of you, I decided to ask Widow Campbell to come since no one is close to my age here. David McLean is the closest to my age, being sixteen, of those that are older than me, and William Campton at twelve is the closest to me of the younger ones. Mrs. Campbell was delighted! She is eighty-seven years old and has been widowed for twenty-six years. All the children call her Grandmother. I wish you could hear her talk. She is Scottish in the way she dresses and most of her speech. Sometimes she starts to speak Gaelic, but the only ones who understand that are the McLeans and a few others. If you look really puzzled she usually realizes who she is speaking to, laughs, and tells you what she said. I tried to learn Gaelic once, but I got it so mixed up with French that when I tried to say something, everything was so mixed up that even Alan, who speaks five languages, couldn't understand me. After that I didn't try to learn it any more.

When Grandmother arrived at our house in her lovely Scottish dress and cap, all in the Campbell plaid, I greeted her at the door with Andrew in my arms.

"Ah, Lassie," she said, " I didnae ken the wee bairn was so birkie."

I smiled as Andrew wiggled excitedly in my arms. Grandmother is such a delight. We had a wonderful time. Edith had even made Sally Lunns for tea. She had used Mrs. McLean's recipe. Grandmother told us stories of her "hame toon on the brae beside a runnel near Loch Loman." I had such a lovely day. That night as I pulled back my covers, I found a letter on my pillow. It was from Papa! Mama said it had arrived the day before, so she saved it. Wasn't God good to give me a letter from my dear Papa on my birthday? It is the first birthday I have ever had without him.

I have just come back from taking Lydia Ruth to play with Ida and Anne at the Camptons. That reminded me of what happened on the 21st. It was quite humorous once it was over, and yet it was such a mess! The Stanly girls had come to play that day. Florence, Edie (her real name is Edith but she is called Edie to distinguish her from our Edith), and I sat on the porch and talked. Mark was off somewhere with James, and oh, Jennie was here too. Edith and Mama were somewhere else, I don't remember where. I had just put Andrew down for his nap and had rejoined the girls on the porch. Lydia Ruth and Ida had been playing just around the corner of the house with their dolls and Lydia Ruth's almost full-grown kitten. Lovey is a dark gray kitten, and Lydia Ruth loves her. I think that is where her name came from. We four were talking about <u>Pollyanna</u>. Thank you so very much for sending it. I am quite fond of it! So are all the girls. Is the second book as good as the first one? Mama said that the next time we go to Pictou we will look in the bookstore for it. Now, back to what I was saying. We must have been there talking for at least three quarters of an hour before I thought that the little girls were being remarkably quiet. I rose to check on them, only to find that they weren't there anymore. I called to Florence asking her if she had seen the little girls. She replied negatively but offered to go look inside for me. I remained where I was, my eyes searching the nearby trees and hills for signs of the girls until I heard Florence calling me to "come quickly." Catching my skirt up with my hand, I ran up on the porch and paused in front of the open kitchen door. There I stopped in blank dismay staring at the scene before me. There stood two little girls, one with dark brown hair and the other with blonde. Both had white paste smeared all over their hands, faces, dresses, shoes, and even in their hair! The floor was covered with the sticky mess of white footprints while the empty paste-plastered water bucket and dumped flour sack explained what the mess was. Why it was there I could not begin to guess.

"Girls," I sighed, "what were you doing?" I was completely unprepared for the answer I received. Do you think they were trying to bake a cake or a scone? No!

"Wanted a white titty like Anne have, so we maked one," was Lydia Ruth's innocent answer.

"Where is the kitty?" I gulped, not quite sure I really wanted to know.

"She runned away, she did." Lydia Ruth declared.

Ida then informed us that, "De kitty not white, but she not black no more."

I looked at the other girls. Edie and Jennie had their hands over their mouths and were giggling. Florence just shook her head, looking aghast.

"We go find Lovey," Lydia Ruth offered, but I shook my head and told them to help clean up. Following Lovey wasn't as hard as I thought it might be, seeing she had left a trail of flour behind her. After following for a few minutes, I saw the tracks led to Mama's room where the door was partially opened. I quickly stepped into the room, glancing around for the cat. Suddenly I scolded, "Get out of there! Shoo! Scat!" Lovey was in the cradle with Andrew! She sprang up right on his face and leapt for the dresser. "No!" I wailed, "Not there!" I rushed forward but not in time to catch the vase that fell with a loud crash to the floor. Andrew was awakened by the commotion and began to cry loudly. I grabbed Lovey by the scruff of the neck, and turning towards the door I beheld all five girls standing in the doorway. Ida reached for the cat, but I thought Florence might be able to hold her longer, so I gave Lovey to her. Quickly I hurried to pick up Andrew and calm his fears.

"Mia," Lydia Ruth began, but when I saw her standing on Mama's bed getting flour and paste all over it, well, I picked her up and carried her in one arm and Andrew in the other back to the kitchen. Emma, it certainly is amazing what a mess flour and water can make! When I reached the kitchen, there in the doorway stood Alan and David McLean! I could tell they were trying not to laugh.

"Ah, lassies," David grinned, "hae ye been a tryin' to make bannocks?"

I knew he was only teasing but right then I felt like sitting down for a good cry. It was hard to have all this mess when I had just cleaned the whole house yesterday. Alan must have understood my look for he chided, "Och, let-a-be David. Let-a-be. Here Lass," he then added to me reaching out his arms, "let me take the bairn. We hae come lookin' fer the lads."

I told him I didn't know where they were as I gladly handed Andrew to him. Alan has a way with the children. He said David would look around "a wee bit fer them." Soon I had the two little girls outside at the pump with Jennie and Edie trying to get them clean, while Florence and I cleaned the house. Oh, we let Lovey outside, and when she came back, she was her usual color. Edith came back before the house was clean, and she helped. Alan was kind enough to keep Andrew until he fell asleep. You have no idea how hard it is to clean up paste unless you have tried it. If you use water, it makes more of a mess, and yet it is not dry enough to sweep up. By the time Mama returned, the house was clean, and I could laugh about the whole thing. I surmise that between Mama, Edith and me, we have convinced Lydia Ruth that her kitten is just the color God made it, and she can't change it. Also that you don't use water to clean up flour.

Does Georgie really carry snakes around in his pockets? How perfectly dreadful! Aren't you afraid he will pick up a poisonous one? I shudder at the very thought of a snake in my bed!

Oh, I haven't told you about the second battle of Ypres yet. Papa wrote us all about it. I will copy part of his letter as it will sound more interesting than if I try to rewrite it.

We (that is the medical corps) were well behind the front lines on 22 April. I am sorry, but I can't give you the exact place. The battle had been rather stagnant with neither side moving. A little after five o'clock we saw a large yellowish cloud which appeared to be moving in the direction of our troops. Back where we were, there was great speculation at first what it was. All too soon we found out. The Germans had released deadly amounts of gas into the French and Algerian trenches. The result was panic. The troops fled choking and gasping toward the rear of the army. Many died before they reached safety. Very quickly, the entire medical corps was busy. We worked into the night with many staying up the entire night. The gas was determined to be chlorine and the other troops were told to hold a cloth soaked in water over their mouths and noses if it were to happen again, as chlorine is a water-soluble gas.

The next day didn't bring more gas casualties; this time it was the machine-guns that did the damage. Before dawn on 24 April, another cloud of chlorine gas invaded the trenches where our brave Canadian troops were. Although some collapsed from the gas, our lads held the line, though the Germans managed to take Saint-Julien.

Two thousand casualties were inflicted on the British troops by the German artillery on the 26. This war is terrible. Almost the entire medical corps were working around the clock. I myself have done 32 operations in one day. Though I miss your help, Maria, I am thanking God that you are not here to witness this horrific slaughter. I am beginning to think this will be a long war. After several gas attacks the countryside has changed. No longer are the trees and grass green, but everything is yellow. It is a sickly yellow at that. The smell in the air is not that of fresh growing things, of spring and flowers, but it is a sour, penetrating smell. The second battle of Ypres dragged on and on. Finally on 25 May, things seemed to have stopped for the most part. I don't know the casualties for sure, but I know they are high. Oh, the families at home! How my heart bleeds for them. One lad, a French boy of about nineteen, grasped my hand just before he died and pleaded with me to write to his mother and five sisters. He said he had no one to take his place. His father was already dead, one of the first casualties of the chlorine gas. On being assured that I would try to write his family, he smiled and asked if I would pray with him. He was not afraid to go, and he passed on to his reward with a smile on his face.

Oh, Emma, I can't write any more about that now. It is too heartrending. Papa did add that he was being assigned to a stationary hospital someplace else. The exact location is unknown. He also said to tell you all that he feels your prayers and to keep on praying. I know you will.

I'm sure that by the time you receive this, autumn with all its beauty will be there. It has already arrived here. There are only a few trees which change colors here as most of our trees are pines. It is usually a cold wind that blows off the ocean now days. We could get snow any day now. Mark is longing for it. We are back in school. Mr. Stewart is teaching this year.

I must end now and prepare breakfast. I awakened early this morning and decided to write you before the distractions of the day began. God bless and keep you and all your loved ones, my dear!

                    Your affectionate cousin,
                          Maria

"Mom," Ria began as her mother folded away the letter with care, "did you understand all those strange words? Why did they talk that way anyhow?"

"Well, we didn't understand them very well at first, though we did later. The little village they lived in--"

"Princeville?" Lydia asked.

Mrs. Mitchell nodded. "Was settled mostly by families who had come over from Scotland, and that is why they talked that way. The younger ones spoke English better than the adults did, but listening to them all talk could be quite a challenge at times."

"Why didn't Maria write it in English?"

"Would it have been as fun to listen to if she had?"

Ria shook her head. "I suppose not, but it does sound funny. Can you read the next one?"

Friday
November 19, 1915
Codell, Kansas
USA

My Dear Cousin Maria,

You were certainly right about autumn being here. The trees, what we have, are simply gorgeous! Daddy calls them "Georgeous!" We have flaming red maples, yellow redbuds, elms, and pecans, brown oaks, and silver birch. We have finished picking the last of the apples from our trees. Yes, I helped. My back is much better. It still bothers me some, but not much. Usually if I sit too much or try to carry something too heavy it will begin to hurt.

School has started as I'm sure you know. There has been some talk of starting another school closer than Codell. You see, it is hard on all the younger ones to have to walk all the way to and from school every day. Most of the little ones can't come if the weather is bad. Besides, when it snows, half the time none of us who live in the country can get through. Only two families who have automobiles drive their children to school. Oh, David has quit school and is now helping Daddy all day on the farm. It is different going to school without him. Georgie can't wait until he is old enough to go. He still wants to be a newspaper man.

Let me think of what has happened since I last wrote you. Edmund won't tell me what he told you about me. I hope it wasn't anything bad. Now let's see. In the first place, I am no longer thirteen. Of course, neither is Edmund, nor are you. Doesn't it seem strange to actually be fourteen? Do you recall us wondering when we were nine years old what we would be doing in five years? On our birthday, before I was taken downstairs, Edmund and I had a delightful long talk about those long ago days. So much has happened. What do the next five years hold for us? Will we all still be here, or will God have called some of us home? Will He add more to our families? I read a verse this morning in Psalms 90 which said, "So teach us to number our days that we may apply our hearts to understanding." How true that is. We don't know when our call will come. I think all these thoughts came from reading Uncle Frederick's letter about the nineteen year old boy and the fact that Mrs. Grandma Conway died two weeks ago. She was ninety-six years old, and she lived all by herself. I will miss her. She wanted to go home so much. The last time I was over to see her, she told me that she was the only one left of her family. Her parents, brothers, sisters, husband and even children had gone on before her. She was ready to join them, and she so wanted to see her Savior.

I must write something more cheery and glad, as Pollyanna would say, or I'm afraid I will start crying. I am so "glad" you like "Pollyanna." Yes, the second one is just as good. It starts off when Pollyanna is around thirteen and then it skips until she is twenty. She is still just like herself. There is a mystery in this book just like in the first one, and at the end of the book. . . Well, I won't tell you because it would spoil it if you haven't read it yet. Speaking of reading books, almost every evening Daddy reads some of <u>Freckles</u>. It was written by Gene Stratton Porter. We all like it ever so much. Daddy is such a good reader! He seems to make the stories just come alive. It is such fun in the chilly evenings to sit around a warm fire all together and listen to a story.

I must tell you about Vincent and Georgie! You know that most of my stories begin with how beautiful the day was? Well, this day wasn't beautiful. It was cold and rainy. Not a steady rain that sounds soothing against the windows and on the roof; this was a miserable drizzle. The little boys wanted to play outside, but Mama said no. They were told to find something inside to do. Daddy had the older boys helping him in the barn, and Carrie, Mama, and I were baking in the kitchen. Rosalie kept getting in our way. She would stand right behind or beside us. We tripped over her several times.

"Vincent," Mama finally called, "come get Rosalie, and play with her please."

Vincent appeared and led Rosalie away. Presently we heard laughter, and in another minute Vincent and Georgie came in the kitchen pulling Rosalie on a blanket. She was holding on and giggling. Every time the boys would stop, she would bounce up and down and urge, "Go! Go!" We all laughed and then shooed them out of the kitchen. How long that lasted I don't know for sure, but we were suddenly startled by many bumps, squeals, a crash and then much laughter. Before any of us could go find out what this new pastime of the little boys was, Daddy and the older boys came in. Maybe I should start calling David and Edmund the men instead of the older boys.

"Brr! It's cold out there!" Edmund shivered as he pulled his gloves off and put his cold fingers on my neck.

"Edmund!" I gasped ducking away from him. Crash! We all jumped and quickly rushed into the hall.

"Boys!" Mama exclaimed, "Are you all right?

"What were you doing?" Daddy questioned. Georgie lay sprawled on one side of the hallway half on a pillow. He looked like he wasn't sure whatever-it-was had been such a good idea. Beyond him lay Vincent laughing and hanging onto a little wagon Daddy had made them.

"Oh, Daddy! It worked!" Vincent cheered getting to his feet. "Watch! You'll all have to move down there so you can see and not get hurt. C'mon, Georgie! It's great fun!"

Vincent continued to chatter as he ran up the stairs pulling the wagon after him. Georgie followed a little more slowly. I don't think he really was very eager to do whatever-it-was again. None of us watching were quite sure of what was happening or going to happen. My thought was that they had slid down the stairs on their "stair sled" and crashed into the wagon. (If I have forgotten to tell you what a "stair sled" is, it is a smooth board with a rope on the front to hang onto. Daddy made it so the boys could sled even in summer. Remember that at the end of both our stairs is a long hall, and the stairs make great hills.)

From where we were standing, we could see the lower

stairs, most of the upstairs hall and part of the attic stairs. We watched and soon saw Vincent and Georgie sliding down the attic stairs on their sled. A slight crash was heard along with Vincent's cheers. Then we beheld a sight that made Mama give a little scream and hide her face. Carrie backed behind David and wouldn't look, while I stared in a fascinated horror and held my breath! The boys were coming down the upstairs hallway on their wagon. Vincent was lying on it, and Georgie was hanging onto Vincent's legs while his own dragged on the floor. Then they reached the stairs! Vincent was hanging onto the wagon and grinning with delight as they began their treacherous descent. Georgie, gripping Vincent's legs with all his might, kept his eyes tightly closed. His legs which were dragging behind the wagon, bumped loudly as though trying to match the wagon's own ruckus. The fact that much of Georgie was dragging was probably the only thing that kept them from tipping over. That and God's mercy. Crash! Bump, bump, rattle. The noise was almost deafening. Finally Georgie was dragged down the last step, and both boys tumbled off in a heap.

When Mama saw that they were all right, she shuddered, looked at Daddy and begged, "Lawrence, please!" Then she hurried back to the kitchen. There was no mistaking her look and words. It meant "don't let them do it again!" Carrie hurried after her. I lingered in the hall with Edmund and David to see what would happen. Daddy sat down on the stairs and called the little boys over. Vincent began to look like maybe it hadn't been such a good idea. Daddy gave them a gentle lecture on the danger of what they had just done. He informed them that the sled was fine to use on the stairs but not the wagon. I entered the kitchen with Edmund to finish getting the food on the table. Mama sent Edmund to go find Rosalie as it was almost time to eat. Before long everyone was called to the table. We were missing Edmund and Rosalie, but before I could go look for them, they came in. Rosalie was lying on Edmund's shoulder still looking half asleep.

"You want to guess where I found her?" Edmund inquired with a grin, setting Rosalie in her chair.

"On the sofa."

"In the middle of the floor."

"Under a bed."

To each guess Edmund shook his head, his smile growing bigger and bigger.

"We give up. Tell us quickly, so we can eat," Daddy pleaded acting half starved.

"She was in my closet!" There was a laugh, and then Daddy asked the blessing on the food.

I can't imagine what a mess you had to clean up after Lydia Ruth and Ida got through with their "white cat!" I certainly hope that never happens in our house! At least we don't have any house cats. We don't now anyway. Mark probably thought it was all very funny, didn't he?

You probably have never heard of Margaret Sanger have you? I can't believe that woman! Uncle John, Mama's brother and Aunt Ester's husband, the one who lives in New York, wrote a letter to Mama the other day and told us about her. She was arrested for sending information through the mail about limiting the number of children in your family! Can you imagine? Why would anyone even consider it? It would seem as though you knew more than God. The Bible says children are a blessing. Now who in their right mind would want to not be blessed? Anyway, Uncle John was at the trial of Mrs. Sanger, and the court ruled that, "Family limitation is contrary not only to the law of the state, but to the law of God." I am thankful that our nation believes such things.

Booker T. Washington died on the 14th of this month. I'm sure you remember me telling you about him. He was fifty-nine years old. Well, no one knows for sure just when he was born, so they can only guess at how old he was. Did I ever tell you that Daddy once visited Tuskegee? He said it was fascinating.

Yesterday was so pleasant that we played outside once we got home from school. Even Daddy joined us. I had to leave and help with supper, but I could still watch them out the windows. Once Daddy hurried in and whispered something to Mama. She laughed a little, dusted her hands off and hurried out. I watched as he lay down in a pile of leaves, and Mama covered him completely up. The pile didn't even look like he was there. Then Mama came in really quickly, and together we watched out the window. All the children (wouldn't Edmund just hate it if he knew I was calling him and David children) came around the house looking all around. They all moved rather slowly. Rosalie was on David's back. Oh, I forgot to add that before Daddy hid, he pulled his boots off and mostly buried them in another pile of leaves. Carrie soon spied the boots, and they all cautiously gathered around. Then Georgie pushed the boot a little. Nothing happened. Vincent reached out, and just as he grasped the boot, a loud "Kerchew!" came from behind them, and they all jumped and turned around. Nothing could be seen. Then they suddenly noticed that Vincent had the boot in his hand.

"Vincent, did you pull his boot off?" David questioned.

"I don't think so." Vincent got no farther for another loud "Kerchew!" startled them. This time Daddy sat up covered with leaves much to everyone's astonishment. Mama and I laughed and laughed. We had tears in our eyes we laughed so hard. It was the funniest thing to watch.

You are probably wondering what everyone looks like now aren't you, since I really haven't told you much. I will start with Rosalie as she has changed the most. She has gotten taller, and her hair is now a few inches past her shoulders. It is still just as dark and curly. Rosalie talks now. Of course not as much as I did at her age. Mama said I was talking in complete sentences before I was fourteen months old. I wish you could see her. Rosalie, I mean. Her smile is so sweet you can't help smiling yourself when you see it. She is not shy and makes friends so quickly even if she doesn't say a word. Rosalie has gotten thinner and has lost a little bit of her round baby face. I miss it.

Georgie has grown like a weed! He is now almost the exact size as Vincent only Vincent is thinner. Most of the time they act like twins, except that Georgie still won't comb his hair, and Vincent will. Vincent is also very neat about all that he does while Georgie couldn't care less if things are messy. Oh, David has taught Georgie how to write all the letters of the alphabet, and now he can write his name. That is the only real word he can spell, but he loves to write many letters together for his "newspaper." I wonder if he will ever want to be anything else. As I am sure you can tell by this letter, Vincent still gets into mischief at least once a week. He just has such interesting ideas, and he tries them out. A few weeks ago, he put on all of his clothes at once and was going to go to school in them.

Carrie hasn't grown much this past year. She is still fairly quiet unless she has something she really wants to say. She loves riding Jessie and hasn't had any trouble with her. Sometimes the two of us will ride double, and then Carrie will talk. The other day she told me that she wished there was someone in our family who had blonde hair. She is praying for it to happen. I told her that Edmund and I would look really absurd with blonde hair. She said she didn't mean us.

Maria, you should see Edmund! He has started to grow. He is now only one quarter of an inch shorter than me. He told me my days are numbered. I asked him for what, and he said for being taller than him. He may be getting taller, but he hasn't stopped teasing. Just last week we were playing outside when suddenly I noticed that my hair was all falling down. Edmund had pulled my hair pins out without me noticing it! When I finally cornered him, I threatened to put hair pins in his shoes. Of course I didn't do it.

David is taller too. He has finally gotten taller than

Daddy. His shoulders are also getting broader, and his shirts don't fit him right now. We are making him more. Other than that, David is the same. Still rather quiet, but he does like to laugh.

Now my dear cousin, I do hope you will answer some questions for us. We are trying to figure out what these Scottish words mean. We know some of them, and we think we know others, but what does "birkie" mean? Is a "hame toon" a home town? It was as though you had made us a puzzle in your letter. Everyone is trying to think of meanings for the words we don't know. I loved reading the Scottish though I didn't understand it all. Is a "bray" a rock or the lake shore? And what is a "runnel?" The only things we can think of are a tunnel, which doesn't seem to fit the sentence, or a . . . but I forgot the other thing we had thought of. Please satisfy our curiosity, Maria.

What five languages does Alan speak? Doesn't he know French? But I suppose if he did, he would have known what you were saying. Sometimes I wish I could learn another language. I don't know what I would learn though.

Your tea sounded like so much fun! I do wish I could have been there. Edmund said he wouldn't have known what to do and would rather have gone fishing. I think I have heard of Sally Lunns before. Weren't they named for the English woman who first made them?

It is raining today. A good, steady rain. It didn't start until we were on our way home from school. We were glad we had brought our raincoats, for we hid our books under our coats and ran for home. I must say we were quite wet when we arrived. Mama made us change right away, and then we sat in the warm kitchen and drank hot cocoa. We are having soup for supper. Doesn't that sound delicious? The boys were all envious that you probably have snow.

A week from yesterday is Thanksgiving! I can hardly wait. I just love helping fix all that food. It always smells so good! Mama said I can cook the turkey this year! That means I have to get up early. I don't mind. Here is what I know we are having: turkey, rolls, stuffing, cranberry sauce, mashed potatoes, gravy, applesauce, corn, green beans, bread pudding, pumpkin pie, apple pie, rhubarb pie, and I think that might be all. I can almost smell it now. Edmund said that what I'm smelling is supper and it is time to eat. God bless you! We will be praying even harder for Uncle Frederick.

With much love,
Emma

"Now I know why Grandma's hair is so white," Ria remarked. "Having to live with two boys like Vincent and Georgie must have never been dull."

Her mother laughed. "It certainly wasn't. I remember quite a few things that happened as I'm sure you'll hear about in the rest of the letters. Right now we must stop." Mrs. Mitchell gathered the letters and arose.

"You can come over tomorrow, can't you Lydia?" inquired Ria, her voice showing her eagerness.

"Only after all my chores are done, so it won't be until after lunch."

"Ria has chores to do too." And Mrs. Mitchell glanced at her daughter. "So I think after lunch would be the best time after all. And Lydia, do tell your mother that she is welcome to come join us anytime."

"Thank you, ma'am. I'll tell her. She doesn't go out much, but maybe she will come here."

"Mom," Ria began but paused as her brother stepped through the doorway. "Ed, can't you take us to Lydia's house so we don't have to walk in the rain?"

"Sure. I have to pick up Chris anyway. We can take Lydia home first."

"Where is Chris?"

"With Dave. I am supposed to meet them at Uncle Edmund's. They were getting a ride over there somehow."

Mrs. Mitchell nodded and smiled. "I'll see you when you get back. See you tomorrow, Lydia," she called as the trio departed the warm pleasant kitchen for the drizzly rain outdoors.

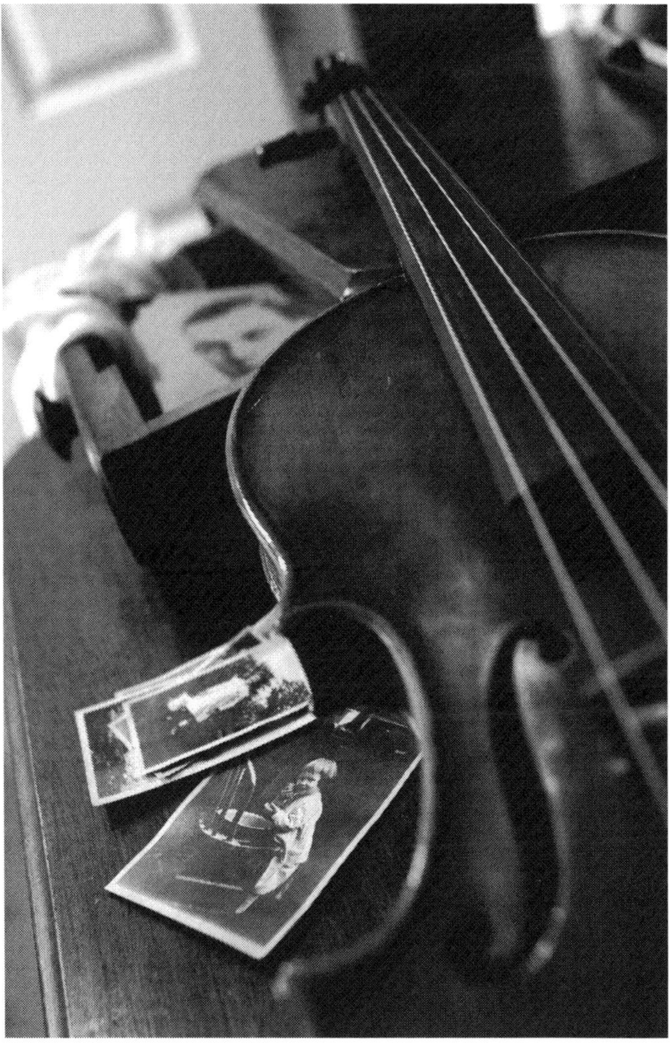

CHAPTER SEVEN

Saturday came and with it glorious sunshine and a warm spring breeze. Ria flew through her chores with such speed and vigor that her brothers began to tease.

"What is the hurry, Sis?" Ed questioned. "Is the Governor coming to visit?"

"No, Lydia is coming this afternoon so we can work on our school assignment!" and Ria dashed out of the room with her arms full of rugs to shake.

When she came back in, Johnny put his hand on her forehead. "Do you feel okay, Ria? Does your head hurt?" His voice was full of brotherly concern, yet the merry twinkle of his eyes betrayed him.

Before Ria could reply Jimmy interjected, "Perhaps we ought to call a doctor. Ria must be sick if she is this excited about a school assignment."

"Don't you wish you had such delightful school assignments?" Ria's merry laughter rang out and covered the groan the twins made at the mere thought.

The hard work paid off and by noon every chore was finished. Then came the hardest part. Waiting for Lydia to come. Ria never was fond of waiting. As she stood on the porch to watch for her friend, she noticed their neighbor, and a good friend of hers, weeding his flower bed. "Good afternoon,

Corporal!"

The older man looked up. "Good afternoon to you, Miss Ria. What is the big excitement at your house today?"

Ria laughed. "Nothing really," she began. "Only my friend Lydia is coming, and we are going to work on our school project together." She jumped off the porch and skipped across the yard. "You see we have to write a report about a hero or heroine of the Great War together."

"That is quite an assignment. Just who is this hero or heroine that is going to be honored by your report?"

"Oh, Mom has some old letters that she and her cousin wrote during the war that she is reading out loud to us. We are hoping to find some forgotten person to write about." Excitement gleamed in her eyes.

"There were many forgotten heroes. There always are in a war." Corporal's voice grew soft, and his eyes took on a faraway look. "Most are never remembered save by a few. They go unthanked and unnoticed. Sometimes they simply disappear before anyone can thank them. Either that or no one even thinks of them as heroes."

A sudden look of wonder passed over Ria's face. "Corporal, you weren't --"

He shook his head. "No, Ria, I was no hero. But there is a group of them that I would like to see honored."

"Who?" Ria was all attention.

Corporal pulled a few more weeds up before replying. "Oh, I think you might come across them in those letters if you pay attention. So, what have you found out from your mom's letters?"

Ria launched forth with an account of some of

the stories told so far, ending abruptly when Lydia hurried down the sidewalk. "I'm sure Mom would let you come listen too, if you want to."

"That is very kind of you; I just might do that one of these days." The older man waved as Ria hurried back to her own front porch.

Situated in the old rocker on the porch, Mrs. Mitchell pulled out the next letter and began to read as the two girls listened with eager interest.

Wednesday
December 29, 1915
Princeville, Nova Scotia
Canada

Dearest Emma,

A merry Christmas and a happy New Year to you and your family! I hope you had a wonderful Christmas. Have you had much snow yet? I am sitting here in the window seat of the front room watching the snow fall gently outside. I just love watching it come down over the ocean. It is so peaceful; the delicate white flakes meeting the dark gray water as though in an attempt to cover it as they have the land. Inside, the fire in the fireplace crackles merrily. The Yule log is still burning. It has two more days left to burn. Mama is seated in her rocking chair with Andrew in her arms. Edith is over on the sofa with Lydia Ruth, trying to teach her to knit. Mark, stretched out on the rug beside the fire, is reading. Everything is so cozy and comfortable here. It is at times like this that my thoughts wander to far off Europe in search of a tall, light brown-haired doctor in a hospital somewhere. A doctor with one dimple. Oh, Papa, where are you tonight? I want to send him a telegram with my love, but Emma, I don't know where he is. Today was the fifth day of Christmas. If Papa were home, he would be sitting in his chair near the fire telling us stories of long ago that Grandpa Foster told him. I'm sure you have heard the same stories. Or he might have been reading a Christmas story. Have I ever told you about Christmas up here in Nova Scotia? I don't believe I have.

Did you know that the people of Scotland aren't allowed to celebrate Christmas? Mr. Stanly told us in school that it was because John Knox believed it to be a Catholic holiday, Christ's Mass. The Scottish who live here celebrate it though. We have a variety of traditions here in Princeville. We celebrate all twelve days of Christmas as they do in England. We have the Scottish Yule log and celebrate Hogmanay. That is the Scottish name for New Years. We eat French desserts on Christmas night, and I'm sure we'll have some belsnicklers come to our house this year too. I have forgotten if they are Scottish or English, but I'll tell you about those later. Here I am rambling on about things I'm sure you haven't heard of, so let me start by telling you about our decorations.

There is much evergreen and holly in our house. Mostly holly though as it is ever so much prettier than just evergreen. Each window in the house is trimmed with green while there is at least one white candle which is lit each night on every window sill. The candle is supposedly to guide the Christ Child through the dark streets. Papa always told us that the candles should remind us that Christ is the light of the world and that we should let Him shine through us as the candles shine through the windows. The mantle over the fireplace is trimmed with evergreen and holly. Papa's picture stands on one side while the wooden crèche that was given him a few years ago stands on the other side. Holly is outlining a few of the main doorways downstairs. Over to the left of the fireplace stands our Christmas tree. It is beautiful! We have put little flags all over it; flags of Britain, America, Scotland, and France. We strung popped corn around the branches and hung cookies on it. We decided not to put candles on it this year for fear they would catch the flags on fire.

On Christmas night we had a feast to celebrate the start of the Twelve Days of Christmas. Since we have a large dining room, we were able to invite the Lawsons, Grandmother Campbell, the McLeans and the Burns. Have I mentioned the Burns to you before? Well, Mr. Burn and the three oldest boys are all with the CEF (Canadian Expeditionary Forces). Mrs. Burn is here at home with their two youngest daughters and youngest son. They aren't very young though. Their oldest daughter is married.

But, back to Christmas night. The table was covered with a snowy white table cloth. Tall white candles in polished silver candle holders lined the middle of the table with each encircled by a small wreath of holly. Edith and I had polished the silver until it shone. Everyone looked so festive in their holiday attire. The Burns, McLeans, and Grandmother all wore their holiday plaids. Since we and the Lawsons aren't Scottish, we were just going to wear our best clothes, but Amelia, Mable and Mrs. Burn made us all plaids. Oh, Emma, I never knew it was such fun to be Scottish! We could not persuade James and Mark to put on their kilts. Mark said he was <u>not</u> going to wear a skirt! It took Alan, David and Mr. McLean fifteen minutes to convince them that it really was all right. Once finally dressed properly, the two boys looked quite dashing. All they were missing, Mr. McLean said, was a claymore. The main dish that night was venison stew made by Mama. There was much talking, all with a Scottish accent mind you. Oh, while I'm on the subject of Scottish words, let me tell you the meaning of the words you asked about. "Birkie" means: lively young fellow. You guessed correctly on "hame toon." Actually a "bray" is a hill and "runnel" is a stream. A stream can also be called a "burn."

Before we ate dessert on Christmas night, I was beginning to get lonely. You see, Mr. McLean, Alan, David, and Theodore Burn (by the way, he's nineteen), were all off in a corner near one side of the fireplace discussing the war. On the other side of the room near the Christmas tree, Mrs.

Lawson, Grandmother, Mrs. Burn and Mama sat. I believe they were talking about Myrtle and the baby who are coming for a visit soon. The three older girls, Edith, Amelia and Mabel, sat together on the sofa knitting socks while they chatted gaily together. Jenny and Lydia Ruth played with Andrew on a blanket in front of the fire, and I don't know where Mark and James were. I stood in the doorway a few minutes feeling sorry for myself because I was left out. I could have joined the knitters because I know how to knit socks, and they would have welcomed me. Sometimes, though, I long for another girl closer to my age to talk to. I don't feel that way very often, so I don't want you to get the idea that I am terribly lonely.

As I stood there, a sudden thought struck me, and I quickly slipped into the hall, quietly closing the door behind me. I hurried across the hall and into the dining room. It was just as we had left it; the chairs were crooked and pushed back, napkins lay some on the floor and some on the table, and none of the water glasses were full. I flew upstairs to my room where I hastily donned my largest pinafore to keep my new clothes clean. Back in the dining room, with the door shut, I fell to work replacing the napkins with clean ones, straightening up the chairs and filling the water glasses before hurrying to the kitchen. Once there I bustled around heating the wassail and getting the thirteen desserts out. Yes, I did say thirteen, Edmund. Are you envious? It's a tradition in our family every year to have thirteen desserts on Christmas night. It came from Grandma Dawson who was French you know. She grew up in Province, France, where the tradition had been going on for hundreds of years. When Grandma married Grandpa and went to England with him, she kept the tradition alive though it has changed somewhat with what we eat. I will tell you all thirteen desserts now. We had: almonds, raisins, taffy, black nougat with cocoa, oranges, fudge, cookies, walnuts, apples, white nougat, dates, candied fruit, and bannocks. Is your mouth watering yet? By the way, you pronounce nougat, "noo - GA." That is if you are French. By the time I got every dessert arranged on the table, the wassail was hot. Now I can just hear Vincent and Georgie asking what wassail is. It is the juice of apples and some water, with spices and pieces of apples all heated up together. It used to have, and some still make it with, ale or liquor, but we don't. It is a delightfully spicy drink.

At last it was all ready. I carefully relit the candles and then began to sing "The Twelve Days of Christmas" as I opened the dining room door. That is how we always call the others in for dessert at Christmas time. This time though no one seemed to notice, so I paused in my singing and got out my violin. I don't know why, but I am shy about playing my violin when others watch. I always seem to mess up. Back in the hall, I went to the stairs, closed the door and sat down in the dark and began to play. I was concentrating so much on the music that I didn't hear the others until the stair door was suddenly flung open revealing everyone crowded in the hall listening. For a second I froze, then springing to my feet, I flew up to my room, shut the door, sat down on my bed, and burst into a a fit of laughter. I had caught sight of myself in the mirror. The pinafore that I had put on was my painting pinafore and was covered with paint spatters. My hair which Edith had so carefully done earlier was a mess. Oh, you should have seen me! Then again, on the other hand, I'm glad you didn't.

Someone knocked at the door, and Edith asked if she could come in. I said yes, and she entered saying, "Maria, are you. . ." then she too began laughing. It only took a few moments to be presentable again, and still giggling, we went down stairs. I was a little apprehensive of going down since they had all seen me, but Edith assured me that I had been in the dark, and no one noticed my attire. At that we both laughed and entered the dining room arm in arm.

The rest of the evening was charming. After everyone had eaten all they could, we had music. I must add here that everyone at the table on Christmas night must have a little of each of the thirteen desserts. Does that suit your fancy,

Edmund? The music was delightful. Mr. McLean and Alan had brought their bagpipes. I, at last, let them all persuade me to play the violin. I think it was really Mrs. McLean who changed my mind. She said she used to have a sister who played the violin, but she died when she was seventeen, and Mrs. McLean had only heard one a few times since. With violin in hand, near the fireplace and Christmas tree, I asked what I should play. No one seemed to care, so I began with "God Rest Ye Merry Gentlemen." They begged for another one, and not wanting to continue to be the center of attention, I turned to Alan who was seated near by and whispered, "Will you sing?"

He nodded with a smile. I played a few notes, and then his rich tenor voice filled the room with "Adeste Fideles." I can't describe that song sung by such a beautiful voice, I can only say it was simply glorious! Song followed song. Some singing, some bagpipes, a few violin, and some a mixture of all until the clock struck one o'clock. Andrew had been in bed for some time while Lydia Ruth and Jenny slept cuddled on either side of Edith.

"Let's have one last song," Grandmother requested.

I was told it was my turn to pick, and so with a smile at Grandmother and then at Mama, I began to play. Mr. McLean's bagpipe joined in, and Alan's splendid voice led us all in "Auld Lang Syne." The final notes seemed to linger as everyone said good-bye and prepared to leave. Theodore carried Jenny, who refused to wake up, home for Mrs. Lawson. The McLeans escorted Grandmother home.

The days that have followed since then have been filled with caroling, visiting, feasting and having a wonderful time. If only Papa were here. Mama, Edith, and I have made figgy pudding every day. That is because when people come caroling to our house they always sing "We wish you a Merry Christmas" and ask for figgy pudding. Perhaps it is because no one else knows how to make it except Mama, yet everyone loves it. It is rather complicated to make at first, but we have made it so many times that I don't need a recipe anymore. Mama said to send you the recipe because Uncle Lawrence always enjoyed it, and she didn't think you had it. So here it is:

<u>Figgy Pudding</u>
1 cup suet
1 cup sugar
3 large egg yolks
1 cup milk
2 tablespoons of flavoring
1 apple, peeled, cored and finely chopped
1 pound dried figs, finely chopped
Grated peel of 1 lemon and 1 orange
1 cup chopped nuts
1/2 teaspoon cinnamon
1/4 teaspoon ground cloves
1/4 teaspoon ground ginger
1 1/2 cups dried bread crumbs
2 teaspoons baking powder
3 large egg whites, stiffly beaten

Mix together suet, sugar, egg yolks, milk, flavoring, apple, figs, lemon and orange peel until all creamy. Add the next six ingredients, mixing well. Fold egg whites into mixture. Pour into generously greased 2-quart bowl or mold and place into large shallow pan and place in hot oven. Fill the shallow pan half full with boiling water and slowly steam pudding for four hours, replacing water as needed.

<u>Sauce:</u>
2 cups milk
1 large egg
1/4 cup sugar
1 tablespoon water
1 teaspoon vanilla
1 tablespoon flour
1 tablespoon butter

Scald milk and allow to cool. Mix together all other ingredients except butter. Add to cooled milk. Cook over low heat until thickened. Take off heat and stir in butter.

Pour sauce over pudding and serve. It tastes best warm, but it is also good cold.

Speaking of figgy pudding, let me tell you about the Drinkwalter brothers. They are three bachelor brothers who are probably as old or maybe a little older than Papa. They aren't in the village much as they spend most of their time fishing. We can count on them every Christmas time to show up for their figgy pudding. Yesterday, late afternoon there was a knock on the door followed by men's voices singing off tune and sounding as if each had chosen his own key in a futile attempt at harmony. There was a general rush for the door which, when opened, revealed the Drinkwalter brothers. Mama stopped them after the second verse by telling them that there wasn't a bit of figgy pudding left in the house, but if they came early tomorrow, we would have some. They looked a little disappointed at first but promised to be here early this morning. Early was right. It wasn't quite 5:30, and Edith and I were just putting the pudding in the oven to start it's four hour baking when, "We wish you a merry Christmas. . ." was heard. We hurried to the door hoping they hadn't awakened the children. The singing stopped as the door opened.

"Are we early enough, ma'am?" the oldest one, Steve, questioned Edith.

"Early?" Edith laughed. "We just put it in the oven."

"Will it be done in ten minutes?" Sam, the youngest of the brothers asked.

"Ten minutes! Goodness! It has to cook for four hours!" Edith couldn't help laughing again. She then told them to come back at 9:30, and it would be hot out of the oven.

At 9:20 exactly, Mark began shouting that they were coming. In another minute the song began. This time we didn't open the door until the whole song was finished. Mama invited them to come in, saying that it would take a few more minutes until the pudding was ready, so they would have to sing for it.

"Us! Sing?" all three gasped in unison.

"Certainly, if you want any pudding."

They looked a little sheepish, then Seth, he's the middle one and has the best voice, began "Christmas is coming." That song was so short that they had to sing something else. They were having a hard time thinking of songs to sing, so they ended up singing "Scotland the Brave." Finally the pudding was done, and the Drinkwalter brothers were made happy.

I see I haven't mentioned the Yule log or the belsnicklers. A Yule log is not from a Yule tree as you might imagine. It is just a log, preferably a green one as they burn longer, that is lit on Christmas Eve or Christmas morning and is supposed to burn until the New Year has begun. You ought to try it sometime. It is such fun to see if it really will burn that long.

Belsnicklers come around on Hogmanay. They are just people dressed up who go to houses singing and making noise. They try to dress so you won't recognize them. If you can guess who they are, they take off their mask and quiet down for cookies. If you can't guess, you have to join them on their rounds. Some favorite costumes are their Papa's nightclothes, big rubber fishing boots, and rain hats. They also like to try to change their voices. It is quite amusing to watch. I am usually good at telling who is who. Perhaps it is because I spend so much time with the children. Sometimes the adults will join them.

I just realized I have forgotten to tell you about Lydia Ruth's fourth birthday! It happened before Christmas on the 21st! Please don't tell Lydia Ruth I almost forgot as she gave me instructions to "be sure to tell Tarrie, and Emma, and Auntie Helen, and Rosalie 'bout de tea clothes on my day. And Ab'gail" A "tea clothes" is a tea party where you get dressed up, or as Lydia Ruth says, "dessed up like a Tween!" Ida Stanly, Edana McIntyre, and Anne Campton all came over for tea. Each one was dressed up in her mother's old clothes. They were simply adorable! Their skirts were all looped up with ribbon so they could walk. Each one had on a hat. I think Anne's hat was the cutest on her. It was rather small for Mrs. Campton, yet it was a little big on Anne. The hat had pink roses all around the crown with pink and white ribbons hanging off the back. Lydia Ruth wore her favorite outfit of Mama's; a white blouse with leg of mutton sleeves, a dark green skirt looped up with white ribbon, a wide purple sash tied into a very large bow in back and a great big hat with feathers. Now Mama never wore all this together, it is just what Lydia Ruth picked out once, and it has become her favorite dress up. The tea party itself was so cute! All four girls had hats on which kept sliding down on their noses and they each had gloves on which didn't fit a particle. They were so sweet trying to sound like grown-up ladies. A whole range of subjects were discussed from dressmaking, to baby dolls (each having brought her favorite doll to take tea with Ab'gail), and from "Autobills" to "Lomacotives." Those are automobiles and locomotives. It took me a little while to figure out that last one, which none of them has ever seen, by the way. They ended their conversation by telling how to make a cake. I do wish you could have heard and seen them!

This letter is growing quite long, and I haven't answered all your questions. Alan speaks English, Gaelic, Scandinavian, Latin, and I think Dutch. I had never heard of Margaret Sanger before. I was as shocked as you were. I hope she doesn't try to do that in Canada.

Your Thanksgiving dinner sounded delicious! I hope it was as good as it sounded. How did the turkey turn out?

I was reading your last letter out loud to the rest of the family, and when I got to Vincent and Georgie's ride down the stairs, I forgot to read out loud until they got my attention again. Edith said, "Just think, if they had done it here, they could have gone down one flight of stairs, down the hall, out the front door, down the porch steps and then on down through the village."

Mama told Mark not to get any ideas. He said he was

too big for such things. He is tall, Emma. Just tell Edmund that Mark is as tall as I am, and he is only nine! I am glad you told me what everyone was like again. You haven't done that for some time. I would do it in this letter, only it is already very long, and I must end it now as Mama says it is time to be heading to bed. Andrew and Lydia Ruth have been in bed for some time now. I am glad I don't have to get up at 4 o'clock to make figgy pudding again. I only have to get up at 5 o'clock.

With all my love,
Maria

P.S. Mrs. McGuire gave birth to twin boys in November. Their names are William Wallace and Rob Roy. Dr. McNeel let me come and actually be there! He said that one of these days he might not be able to come in time, and someone in the village should be able to deliver a baby, at least until Papa comes home.

"Wow! That was some Christmas celebration, wasn't it, Lydia?"

"It sure was," Lydia sighed. "That would be such fun to do all of that."

Ria caught at the suggestion eagerly. "Do you think we could do it this Christmas, Mom? I've never had Figgy Pudding, and we have never had a Yule log, or had twelve days of Christmas, or . . ." She paused out of breath.

Mrs. Mitchell chuckled. "Perhaps we should wait until it is closer to Christmas before deciding. You might not want to do all that extra work."

"I wouldn't mind," breathed Lydia dreamily.

"Me either," Ria chimed in, adding as an afterthought, "at least I don't think I would."

Her mother laughed again and picked up the next letter.

CHAPTER EIGHT

Monday
January 24, 1916
Codell, Kansas
USA

My Dearest Maria,

Here I am, sitting in my room at my desk by the window. It is mid afternoon, and right now the window is being bombarded with snowballs. I think Edmund is rather annoyed, or at least he pretends to be, because I deserted him to come and write to you. We were in school today in spite of the snow. It really wasn't snowing much this morning. All of us who live "out of town" (doesn't that sound funny) were dismissed a little early. When we arrived home, Carrie and I left Edmund and Vincent to play in the snow with Georgie while we came in and changed into warm dry clothes. It was quite something to have to wade through the snow on the way home. I enjoyed it though. The snowballs have stopped now, and I think I hear Edmund coming upstairs. He is probably going to change and then go help Daddy and David wherever they are. Mama told me to write to you now or else I would be downstairs mending with her.

I was delighted to get your last letter and learn about your Christmas and New Years. I had hardly finished reading your letter aloud to the family when Daddy said, "Come on, Emma and Carrie. Let's go make Figgy pudding!"

Mama began laughing and caught Daddy's sleeve as he

was passing her. "Lawrence, that pudding has to cook for four hours. It'll be midnight before it is done."

"All the more reason to make it now; I'll be the only one up to eat it."

There was a clamor of voices declaring that they wanted some too, and Daddy relented saying that we would wait and make it in the morning. We did, and it was absolutely delicious! Thank you for sending the recipe. Edmund loved the idea of thirteen desserts until he heard what they were and that each person was required to have some of each. For some reason he has a great aversion to almonds. He will not eat them. We all think he is rather silly as the rest of us like or at least tolerate them. That is one thing that I can tease him about.

Be sure you tell Lydia Ruth happy birthday from us all, and that we all thought her tea party sounded wonderful. Georgie has written it up for his newspaper. He has a box where he keeps all his news "for when he gets big."

Maria, you never told me you played the violin! How long have you been playing? When did you start? I don't play any instrument, except the dinner bell. Does that count for one? I do sing. The whole family sings actually. How I wish I could have heard Alan sing. That all sounded like such fun. We all went to bed early on Christmas night. We did stay up until the New Year though. I am still trying to get used to writing 1916. I imagine we have heard many of the same stories. Daddy told us one the other night about when the four of them decided to be pirates. Have you heard that story? We could hardly believe Daddy, Uncle Theodore, Uncle Frederick and Uncle James would do such things! Why, some of the stories of what they did . . .! But you know what I'm talking about, don't you? Yet we wonder where Vincent gets his ideas.

I must copy Uncle Philip Vincent Bartholomew Wallace III's letter for you. Well, I will at least try to. Edmund isn't needed out in the barn yet, so he is going to read it to me as I write it down. At least he will try to read it.

The handwriting is so hard to read! I am glad the letter isn't very long. I want to warn you though that you will probably need a dictionary. Uncle Philip uses very large words at times. He wrote this to Mama, and she said I could copy it for you. Now as Edmund is ready, stretched out across my bed with dictionary beside him and the letter in his hand, I will begin.

Lief Sister,

Warmest greetings from -------------, France. (We, none of us, can read what the town or place is in France. Perhaps that is why it wasn't blacked out by the censor.) I am no longer with my comrades in the Vosges Mountains, though I fain would be there still. Instead of being in the fight, I must now be alimented as I indolently lay here on my cot. Such a life. But, my narrative is still waiting to be told, so gather around, settle down, and I will begin. I am beginning to sound like a poet.

It was some time ago when I first received my injury. How long ago exactly, I cannot recall at this time. It was in the opacity of night. I and a dozen or so comrades were moving clandestinely through the mountains to sever the communication lines of the enemy. An explosion of some sort I remember hearing before my memory fails me for a time. When next I recall, it was to find myself benignly borne in the arms of my comrades. Eftsoons I was borne into our camp and placed on my bed which in actuality was no more than a pallet on the ground and which is juxtaposited to the outside door. When I essayed to arise, a keen pain in my right leg caused me to slump back while beads of perspiration came out on my forehead and trickled down my face. My chapeau and roquelaur were taken off, and my comrades essayed to make me comfortable.

I must have fallen into a doze, for I was awakened later by Jean, who because of his knowledge of medicine, had been called in to try to alleviate my pain. He inquired how I felt. I told him I felt qualmish and any movement, even a pandiculation caused much pain. I began to soliloquize then and wish you, lief sister, were at my side as you were when I had the measles. I must have continued in and out of consciousness for some time. At one point, methought I heard the captain satirize my companions for their perfunctoriness that had caused my injuries.

"Ah, me," thought I, "were I not so languid, fain would I essay to join my comrades once more though it were but to join in their satirizing."

My wound increased in pain and a quotidian came over me. Jean now appeared quite concerned when he came to aliment me. One day, as I lay on my pallet, an egregious advent occurred. Obstreperous sounds were drawing towards my hut, the door of which was soon flung open, Jean entered with two, no three other men. One was the captain. The other men I had had no earlier acquaintance with. Both were quite urbane though I perceived the keenness of their eyes. Rife in both of them, methought, was an extraordinary clandestine and a seeming indefatigable spirit. After one of the men examined me, he began issuing orders.

"Jean, bring two other men. Pierre, graith the dogs and the sled. We must hasten to use the darkness to the best advantage."

"Is it wise to move him now?" the captain asked. I believe he really is fond of me.

"It is a risk we must take. If we tarry, he may lose his leg," was the blunt answer.

Now, so as not to cause this to be verbose, I will skip any further conversation.

I was solicitously borne out to the sled, covered with blankets and with many farewells mingled with "Mush," the sled began to move. My two new companions, though they were Chasseurs as well, drove the dogs like Scotty Allan himself. At least methought 'twas so, as I have only heard of Allan and never beheld him at work. Francois and Pierre with their dogs seemed to possess spirits of inamissibleness, for never once did we falter or seem to lose the way. Many a time one or the other would run behind the sled foining it up the hills. When we would stop for a rest, all the dogs would collapse in the snow panting, yet they were always keen to continue when Pierre gave the word. Pierre, I perceived, was the one who always took care of and ordered the dogs. They seemed to be one-man dogs, and Francois let them alone. Nothing Francois did to alleviate the pain in my leg seemed to help much, but I would not be dolesome. On the second day, I asked Franois and Pierre about the dogs, so as to keep my mind off my sufferings. Pierre told how he had traveled to Britain with fifty other chasseurs and was trained by Scotty Allan. I recall reading in the papers about him, don't you, Helen?

As we traveled on, Francois and Pierre didn't talk much, to conserve their energy I think. With nothing to do, I often fell to soliloquizing, that is, when I was conscious at all. At last we arrived at --------------. Those five dogs had been extraordinarily indefatigable. Never once had they been obstreperous. They never had to be catachresticaled but were always impatient to move on.

Now I have been in this makeshift hospital for a few days methinks. The rife thought now in my mind is, when will I see the doctor. I have seen plenty of nurses and one or perhaps two doctors, but I have been told <u>the</u> doctor will see me soon. Ah me, to be languishing here in this sombrous place instead of foining my way surreptitiously through the opacity with incognizable messages. But, I will not remonstrate with my lot seeing that Providence has placed me here.

I have been informed that <u>the</u> doctor is on his way to see me now, and I must stop writing. I am giving the nurse your address, Helen, so that this letter might be certain to arrive. I must bid you adieu now as I see the doctor coming. There is something that seems strangely familiar about him

though I don't know why. Perhaps I met him earlier in France.
>
> In haste,
> Philip Vincent Bartholomew Wallace III

There, I believe I have spelled all those words right. I certainly hope you enjoyed it after I spent all that time writing it. It was longer than I thought it was. At least it took longer to write it than I had thought. Perhaps it was because Edmund had to look up so many words. I just wish I knew where he is. Uncle Philip I mean; Edmund is going to the barn.

Oh, I didn't tell you President Wilson got married on the 18th of December! There were all kinds of articles about it in the papers. He married a widow named Mrs. Galt. Mrs. (Galt) Wilson's former husband had been a jeweler in Washington. It sure seems strange to think of the President of the United States getting married. I know he is a normal person like everyone else, I guess I just never had thought much of such a thing happening.

Tuesday 25,

No school today, so I think I can finish this letter. Let me tell you why I didn't finish it yesterday. Edmund had gone out to the barn, and I was writing the last part about President Wilson when snowballs began to hit my window again. I ignored them at first thinking it was Edmund again, but when I listened, I heard my name called. I quickly stood up and, opening my window, stuck my head out to be narrowly missed by yet another snowball.

"What do you want?" I called down to the little boys.

"Come help us get Rosalie out of the house."

"If she doesn't want to go out, then let her stay in where it is warmer," I said, preparing to pull in my head as the wind was rather cold.

"But, Emma, she's stuck!" Vincent called.

"And she's too fat to come out the door," Georgie

added woefully.

Just then Carrie came around the corner and called, "Emma, you really have to come help us."

In agreement and still wondering, I hurriedly donned my warm clothes and went outside. Mama told me on the way out that Carrie and the little boys had taken Rosalie outside with them. Hurrying around the corner of the house, I suddenly beheld what looked like a little fort. The walls were quite high, as high as the children were able to make them. I saw a small opening in one side which I was informed was the door. Inside this enclosure was Rosalie. She was sitting on Vincent's little wagon and giggling.

"We want to put a roof of snow on this, and we thought maybe Rosalie should be out in case, well, just in case," Vincent explained.

"Come on out now, Rosalie," I called.

With another giggle, Rosalie tumbled off the wagon and stuck her head out the door. "Me tuck!" she exclaimed, delightedly smiling at us all.

I could tell she really would be stuck if she tried to get any more of her out of that doorway. She had been bundled up so much that now she looked quite plump and could hardly move. She didn't seem to mind though.

"Can you get back on the wagon?" I asked her, thinking I would lift her over the sides.

In popped her little head, and I watched her try to get back on the wagon. Since the wagon was frozen in the snow and didn't move, she finally made it onto the top of it. The only problem was that she was lying down. She managed to roll onto her back, but it was impossible for her to sit up without help.

"Oh, dear!" Georgie sighed, "She's never coming out."

"Yes, she is," I laughed at his pitiful face. "I'll just lift her out."

So saying, I reached into the roofless house and tried to lift Rosalie. It didn't work. I could barely reach her hands, and she weighed so much more than usual that I didn't have the strength to pull her up. I was also afraid that if I leaned too hard on the wall, it would collapse.

"I tuck!" Rosalie chuckled smiling. "I tuck. I tuck, I tuck." She seemed greatly pleased with herself.

"Well," I said slowly, "I guess we'll have to get Daddy or one of the boys to get her out."

As the boys ran off after more help, I asked Carrie how Rosalie had gotten in there in the first place.

"We just built it around her," she admitted.

At last Edmund and David came. Edmund reached down, grasped Rosalie's hands and pulled her to a sitting position. He then tried to lift her out, but the angle with which he was trying from made this impossible to do.

"Whew! What have you been feeding her?" he exclaimed in pretended amazement. "I know she didn't weigh this much this morning!"

Carrie laughed. David meanwhile put one foot in the doorway and braced his other foot in the snow behind him, then he caught Rosalie and swung her up and out of the enclosure. When she was safely on the ground, she begged to do it again, but no one would put her back in. As I stood watching the older boys run back to the barn, I heard, "No, Rosalie!" Turning, I saw Rosalie trying to crawl through the doorway to get back in.

Edmund has finally reached his goal. He is taller than I am now by one inch. The way he acts sometimes you would think he was at least six inches taller. I tease him some and tell him that he is still so short that I don't have to look up to him yet.

Maria, please do give me word sketches of everyone. You are so good at doing them. Now I don't mean everyone in the village. Though I would love to hear about the new twins. Did you know that I don't know any other twins?

Any news from Uncle Frederick? Have you heard anything from Grandmother and Grandfather Foster in London? I wrote to Mary Jane in Dover some months ago, but I haven't heard anything. Maybe I will hear from her soon. If I do, I will let you know what she says.

I must end now as Edmund is waiting for me to go for a walk with him. We are going to go through the snow to the creek. I think it will be such fun! God bless you!

With love,
Emma

Sunday
February 20, 1916
Princeville, Nova Scotia
Canada

My Dear Emma,

It is a gloomy Sunday afternoon here in Princeville. We had snow yesterday, but today it has changed to rain, and all the village snowmen are turning to slush. Mama and Andrew are resting as is Lydia Ruth. Edith is visiting Grandmother Campbell who didn't make it to church this morning. I believe Mark is busy with something in his room.

I did so enjoy your letter. Reading about the snow house the children built reminds me of what happened at school. Let me tell you about it.

A few days ago during school, it was decided to have a good snowball fight at recess. William Campton and Arthur Morris were chosen as team captains. I declined to join the fun, partly because I am fourteen now and partly because I am the oldest in the school, and well, I'm sure you understand what I am trying to say. Did I ever mention the fact that there are only five boys in school and nine of us girls? Mr. Stewart decided that he wanted to play also, but that made the teams a little uneven, so he sent Evelyn over to their house next door to see if Finlay would come play too. He came and joined Arthur's team, to the delight of James and Mark. As each side was making their snowballs, Duncan McIntyre came strolling by, stopped, and asked if he could join in the fun. His eight-year-old sister Elspeth was excited to have Duncan on her team. She adores her big brother! When each team had a pile of snowballs in their forts (the forts had been made the day before), Mr. Stewart told the rules. The object of the game was to get the opposing team's flag off their fort and place it on your fort. If you got hit ten times by snowballs, you had to sit down at the Red Cross Station (that was me) until you had counted to 200. I was also the one to fix the girls' scarves and hats.

Part way through the game, Elizabeth Campton, who is six, got hit in the face with a snowball. I left my post of observation by the school house and rushed into the fray. Quickly I brushed the snow from her face, retied her scarf, and after a kiss she was ready to play again. She told me she was going to go throw a snowball at Finlay. Surprisingly she hit him, and he had to come over and count to 200. Elizabeth giggled.

The snowballs flew thick and fast as each team sought to capture their opponents' flag while yet defending their own. Time after time a team would rush from their fort to assault the "enemy." Although several times each flag was taken from its fort, the bearers couldn't get it safely to their own fort. Finally Arthur's team came up with a brilliant plan. I watched as Arthur, James, Mark, Evelyn and Edie left their fort and charged, leaving only Finlay, Jenny and Jean to guard the flag. As the attacking team reached the fort, Edie suddenly dropped to the ground directly in front of the fort and lay still. No one seemed to notice her. Arthur grabbed the flag only to have it jerked out of his hand while he was pushed back into the snow by Duncan. Arthur, James, Mark and Evelyn moved on either side of the fort as a decoy, I saw, for Edie. She was watching Finlay, and when she saw him nod, she quickly reach up, pulled the flag out and lay back down on the flag. Finlay came running over, turned suddenly and shouted, "Victory is ours!"

Then he began to run towards his fort. In an instant the entire opposing team was after him. Finlay is fast, but Duncan is faster, and the gap between them was closing quickly. Finlay noticed and veered off to the left, calling on his team for help. It was then that I noticed Evelyn and Edie racing hand in hand for their fort with the flag safely clutched in Edie's hand. Jean and Jenny were jumping up and down shouting, "Hurry!" Just as the girls reached their fort, Duncan knocked Finlay into the snow and discovered that he didn't have the flag. You should have heard those girls scream with laughter as they joyfully waved both flags. Soon everyone came crowding around the porch steps where I was, all talking at once. Mr. Stewart called for order, and when silence prevailed, he asked Arthur how they had managed to get the flag. With much laughter and many interruptions, he told of their plan and how it had worked. Mr. Stewart asked Finlay if it was his idea.

"No sir," Finlay replied with a twinkle in his eye.

"Whose was it then?"

"Evelyn's!" was the shout that caused Mr. Stewart to gaze at his daughter in disbelief.

Let me share part of a letter with you from my Aunts Marie and Elizabeth who live in Wednesbury, England. They've had much excitement there in the middle of Britain. The letter is dated February 3. I won't give you the whole thing as it wouldn't all be of interest to you.

We were bombed on the night of January 31 and February 1 by two Zeppelins! Why they bombed our little town, we aren't sure, but we have heard rumors that the commanders of each airship thought it was Liverpool! Imagine, our small town as Liverpool! The first bombs at 9:00 fell on King Street destroying, the Smith home and killing all the Smith family except Mrs. Smith who wasn't at home when it happened. Little seven-year-old Ina Smith used to be in Belinda's Sunday School class and was one of Eileen's close friends. Fitzhugh, Belinda and Helen were out for a walk when the bombing started. They saw the silvery Zeppelin in the dark sky above the burning Crown Tube Works at the end of Union Street. On heading up towards the church with the throng of others, a householder opened the heavy doors to his cellar urging people to go down there for safety. Fitzhugh urged his cousins to go down, but the girls refused unless he went with them. No one ended up going down. The three of them didn't arrive home until about 10:30. They were all unharmed, much to our relief. We all went to bed with thankful hearts that we had all been kept safe. At 12:15 another Zeppelin bombed us again. Not much damage was done this time and there were no casualties.

I can't imagine why anyone would think Wednesbury was Liverpool, can you, Emma? Speaking of letters, we received a short letter from Papa yesterday, and surprise, surprise . . . I'll let Papa's letter tell.

"I have kept plenty busy at my new post here. Sorry, but the town name is censored. The other day I was called to a nearby house, which is being used as another hospital, to see a young man who had recently been brought in. I stood by his bed and gazed at him in uncertainty as a nurse told me his name. The young man gazed earnestly at me, evidently trying to remember where he had met me before. Would you believe it, it was none other than Philip Vincent Bartholomew Wallace III! We were both speechless for a moment. Be sure you tell Helen that it is my hope that his leg, though badly injured, can be saved, thanks to the speed in which he was brought in and the care he has received."

Now, though neither of us knows exactly where your Uncle Philip is nor Papa, we do know that they are together. Oh, thank you for copying his letter for me! It was such fun to try to read it. Mark has now added a few words to his everyday vocabulary. Does your Uncle really talk that way, or is that just the way he writes?

You wanted word pictures of us, didn't you? Let me see, I believe I will start with Edith as she has just come in from Grandmother's. Not much has changed with her. She is the same wonderful sister. She hasn't grown taller, and I don't expect she ever will. Edith is usually busy. She, Mabel and Amelia Burn and Sheena McIntyre go into Pictou twice a week to volunteer at the Red Cross. The rest of the time she spends knitting and sewing for the soldiers and helping Mama around the house.

Mark is tall, as I think I mentioned in the last letter. He is getting stronger too with all the wood he has been cutting. If he is not busy with school (which he doesn't particularly enjoy), running errands for Mama, chopping wood, or half a dozen other things, he is off with James. Those two are almost inseparable. They seem to be always helping each other with whatever task is at hand. Mark is a wonderful "man of the house." He is thoughtful of his sisters and of Mother though he sometimes forgets to think about his own safety when we aren't around. I am constantly awaiting some accident to happen to him.

Lydia Ruth is a blessed little chatterbox. Her hair has darkened considerably the last month or two. She still takes Abigail everywhere with her and talks to her or anyone who will listen. She tries to help with the housework. At times though, her help is more of a hindrance. Such as the time she was dusting the book shelves. She took all the books off the shelves, piled them in front of the door and then went off and forgot them. When Mark came in with his arms full of wood, he tripped, and books and wood went flying. Lydia Ruth knows all her letters, and Edith is teaching her to read. It is so sweet. After she has learned something, she will go find Anne, Ida, and Edana and teach them all she just learned. So, in a way, Edith is teaching four little girls how to read.

Little Andrew is getting bigger everyday it seems. He is already eight months old! He will sit by himself for a while if someone sits him up. He has one little tooth which looks so like a little pearl. Andrew's hair is still dark, and his eyes haven't changed color at all. He almost never cries, but when he does, only a few people in the village besides Mama,

Edith and me can calm him down. Those are Mrs. Lawson, Grandmother, Robert Morris, Sheena, Mrs. McLean and Alan. Andrew and the McGuire twins are the delight of the village. I haven't told you about the twins yet. They are identical "wee laddies" with blonde hair and bonnie blue eyes. They are the roundest babies I have ever seen! They are sweet, but not quite as sweet as my little Andrew.

I don't know what to tell about myself. I am almost as tall as Mama now, and Mark is as tall as me. But Mama isn't very tall. I still love reading. Myrtle Belisle (she was a Burn before she got married) is here with her baby daughter, Elsie, and she is helping me with my drawing. Maybe you will get your picture of a kittywake this year. Oh, I am so sorry that I didn't tell you I had started playing the violin. I began last February, and I must have just never remembered to mention it. The violin has been a delight. You can make it say almost anything you want. It can be the wind in the trees, the birds singing, even the waves crashing against the rocks. My favorite time to play is when all is quiet except nature. That seems to happen more in the winter as the children are indoors. I still feel like the Pied Piper when I go out. But I don't mind. I love having them all around me.

I don't remember hearing about when Papa, Uncle Theodore, Uncle James and Uncle Lawrence played pirates. What happened? I remember Papa saying that when the four of them were young, people called them Ted, Fred, Larry and Jim and used to wonder "what those Foster boys would do next!" You should be glad there aren't four boys like Vincent and Georgie in your house.

No, I haven't heard anything from London or Dover. Only Wednesbury. If you hear anything, please send it my way. I wonder if any cousins are in the war now. No news about any battles, but I suppose it is still winter. When will this war be over?

You're right, it does seem peculiar to think of a President of the United States getting married! Please be sure to tell Georgie happy birthday. Six years old! He'll be going to school in the fall. Then he can really start writing his newspapers. Has he named it yet? I do want to hear one of his stories.

    I must be going. Edith just told me that Mark needs a nurse. God bless you!
> Love,
> Maria

    "All that talk of snow makes me almost wish for it."

    "Not me," Lydia put in. "I love spring better. Do read on, please."

Obligingly, Mrs. Mitchell pulled the next letter out of the envelope.

CHAPTER NINE

Thursday
March 30, 1916
Codell, Kansas
USA

Dear Maria,

Spring is coming! I saw a robin this morning on the way to school. Oh, I just love spring, don't you? Everything is changing from drab brown, to beautiful growing green. Some of the trees have the beginnings of little buds on them. The crocuses are up showing their faces as if to say, "We haven't forgotten. The other flowers will be here soon, but we were just impatient to see the sun again." It's still chilly, and we have to wear jackets and sweaters when we are outdoors, but it is getting warmer. Right now Vincent is outside watching the clouds floating in the blue sky. Georgie was with him, but not being able to sit still that long, he is now up in a tree. David and Carrie have gone for a ride. Carrie is, of course, riding Jessie. They should be back before too long. I am down here in the kitchen where I can keep an eye on supper while Mama and Rosalie are out in the barn with Daddy. I believe they are looking at the kittens. Edmund is, well, I'm not sure where he is right now. He is probably outside somewhere.

You haven't heard the story of Ted, Fred, Larry and Jim becoming pirates? When I mentioned how surprised I was, Daddy said maybe that is because Uncle Frederick was the one who suggested it to begin with. Here is how the story goes. The place: a small country village in England near the Thames River. The ages of the boys are as follows: Ted is nine years old, Fred eight, Larry six and a half, and Jim five years old. (Aunt Margaret was a newborn baby.)

"Oh, dear, what should we do? Mama is busy with the baby and . . ." Larry's voice trailed off with a sigh as he sat with his brothers on the old rail fence one fine summer day.

"I duh know." Ted frowned.

Jim's voice broke the silence that followed. "And that girl baby can't even climb trees!" To Jim that was the worst thing that could be inflicted on someone. Not to know how to climb trees!

"I say," began Fred, "let's all go down to the river. I'm sure we'll find something there to do."

"Okay, but we can't go swimming. You know, Papa said we couldn't without him 'cause Mama might fear we would drown." Ted finished this remarkable sentence not caring whether it was grammatically correct or not since it was just his brothers. And so, "Those four Foster boys," as folks called them, ran down to the river to see what they could find with which to fill the time until 5:30 when Papa would be home and could play with them.

Down at the river the four boys discovered a rowboat tied to a small tree.

"Wouldn't it be a fine thing if we could row out to the island and play pirates!" Fred exclaimed.

"It's been ever and ever so long since I've been for a row," Larry remarked with a sigh, forgetting in his eagerness that Mr. Smith had given him a row not more than three days ago.

"Well, we could pretend anyway," Ted said, looking around before jumping in the boat. The others followed his example with such enthusiasm that the rope, which was not fastened very securely to the tree, came loose. "Pull fer all ye got boys!" Ted ordered. "Else we'll be a-grounded." The boys pulled with a right good will and were soon out in the middle of the river.

"Captain! I see another ship a comin'. We've got to get that treasure and get out of here 'fore they sink us all!" Fred shouted, entering into his part as a pirate with great energy.

"It won't be sinking they'll be doing to ye lads if they catch us. We'll all be strung up to the yardarms and then used fer bait," Captain Ted growled. Jim took a quick glance behind them just to reassure himself that his brothers were only playing.

"Land Ho!" sang out Larry as the boat neared the little island. Bump, scrape, the boat grated on a small gravel bed. Out sprang the boys, eager to begin their search for hidden treasure. Before long Ted declared that they "just had to have a prisoner."

"I can't be one 'cause I'm too fat," Larry piped up. Fred declared that he couldn't be a prisoner because he was too big.

"Jim, you'll have to be the one," Ted said pulling out a length of rope from his pocket. Jim knew it was useless to argue and soon found himself tied hand and foot and lying on the ground.

"Now, what're we going to do with the prisoner, Captain?"

"Oh, we'll put him in the hold of the ship and fasten him with irons," Captain Ted said carelessly. So the deed was done, though having no irons they had to omit that part.

"We won't gag him, will we Ted?" Larry asked hopefully.

"Naw, as long as he doesn't call for help. Now, grab those oars, they can be our shovels," Ted commanded. Soon the three boys were in among the trees looking for "treasure" while little Jim lay in the boat and wished they would hurry. After what seemed like a very long time to him, Jim began to squirm around and try to get his arms and legs untied. Suddenly he felt a slight movement and then a feeling of floating. Unable to sit up, Jim could only lie there and wonder what had happened.

Ten minutes passed. Then twenty . . . thirty. Finally Larry said hopefully, for he was rather tired, "I guess Papa is home now." Ted and Fred looked up at the sky.

"I guess he is," Fred agreed.

"At least we can go see," Ted put in, adding, "Why, I wonder Jim hasn't made a noise. Sleeping, I guess."

As the boys came to the place where they had left the boat, Larry looked, rubbed his eyes, and then looked again before saying, "The boat's not here, Ted."

"It's got to be. Fred, you go that away, and I'll go this. Larry, you stay here. We'll find where it's hiding."

So saying, the two older boys each went a different way around the island looking for the missing boat and brother while Larry sat down on a rock to wait. As the island wasn't very big, it didn't take the boys long to walk all around it, and soon they were back.

"Oh! Jim's taken the boat and gone back home! And he left us here!" Fred stamped his foot in vexation.

"He must have," Ted agreed gloomily. All the boys were forgetting that Jim had been tied hand and foot and that there were no oars in the boat. Even had there been, and could Jim have used them, he would have had to row upstream which even Ted couldn't do by himself.

"Well, Papa can come soon then," Larry tried to cheer up his brothers but only succeeded in making them realize that they might have done something wrong.

While the three boys wait with growing impatience and hunger, I will tell you about poor Jim. He had, in his efforts to get untied, rocked the boat off the little gravel bed, and it began to float downstream. For several minutes Jim lay in the bottom of the boat wondering what was happening. "Larry?" Jim's voice wasn't more than a whisper. He tried again and this time his voice was louder, but still there was no answer as Larry was by this time beyond the sound of his voice. "Ted, I don't want to play pirates! Please don't make me!" Jim wailed. "Ted!" Hearing nothing but the water, he burst into a flood of tears, and exhausted and very frightened, he cried himself to sleep.

Deep voices talking above him roused him some time later, and he felt himself lifted up and carried somewhere. There his ropes were undone, and he looked up to see the faces of several sailors.

"Well, sonny, how'd ye get tied up and left in the boat by yer self to float downstream?"

For answer Jim threw himself into the arms of the kind sailor exclaiming piteously, "Please don't make me play pirates! I don't want to do it! I didn't get in the water 'cause Papa said I mustn't, but please don't make me be a pirate or string me to bait!"

It took some time for the sailor to reassure Jim that he would not be made to be a pirate or be strung up for bait. Once Jim calmed down enough to realize that he was with friends, he begged to go home whereat he was asked where his home was.

"With Mama and Papa."

There was a general laugh at that.

"What's yer name lad?" the kind sailor asked.

"Jim, but Mama calls me James, and Papa sometimes calls me Jimmie."

"What's yer last name?" the man persisted.

"Foster. Everyone knows that." Jim was convinced that all of England knew he was a Foster and knew his father.

"What village do ye live in, Jimmie?"

"The one with my house. Please can't I go home? I'm awfully hungry and tired." The sailors, seeing that they wouldn't be getting much more information out of Jim, took him to shore and got him some food. It was there that Mr. Smith saw Jim and hurried over.

"Why, Jim! Your Papa and Mama are mighty worried. Practically the whole village is out looking for the four of you! Where'd you find the boy?" This last was to the sailors who told their story of seeing the boat come downstream and finding Jim tied up in it.

During this talk, little Jim had fallen asleep with his head on the table. He only partially roused with Mr. Smith's gentle shaking. Only enough to murmur, "The boat. It's not mine. Have to take it back."

To Jim, who slept the whole way, the trip home seemed short, and then he was at last in his father's arms.

"Jimmie," his father asked after the first excitement was over, "where are your brothers?"

Jim looked around for them before saying, "I guess they's still being pirates. Unless. . ." a new thought struck terror into his little heart, "Unless the other boat catched 'em and stringed 'em up for bait to arm yards! Oh Papa! Don't let 'em do that! Don't Papa, don't!"

It seemed for several minutes as though Jim would never calm down, but at last he did. Enough for Mr. Foster to find out where the boys had been playing. When he heard, he put Jim down and turning to his wife said, "Margaret, put him to bed; I'll go get the others."

Back on the little island, three very sober boys sat among the trees in the gathering dusk.

"I want to go home," Larry whimpered.

"I wish Papa would come," Fred sighed. "I'm awfully hungry."

The wind was chilly now that the sun had set, and the boys moved back into the woods for some shelter. Keeping close together they sat down. The moon shone brightly and a thousand stars twinkled in the dark sky, but no one on the island noticed, for one by one the boys fell asleep.

"Theodore! Frederick! Lawrence!" The shouts startled the boys from slumber.

"Papa!" they called. The next moment they were in their father's arms while two other villagers stood by holding lanterns. "Thank God you are safe!" Mr. Foster exclaimed softly. Those were the only words he spoke that night about what they had done. After arriving home and eating supper, the three boys were sent to bed where they found Jim already sound asleep. The next morning all four boys followed their father out to the woodshed. A little later, four very sober lads promised their mother that never would they go on or in the water again without permission.

There's the story. I had no idea when I started that it would take up this much room. I guess I won't be telling many "Ted, Fred, Larry & Jim" stories unless I don't have much else to write about. Georgie said he would "newspaper it." Edmund told him he meant "publish it."

"But I don't want to publish it, I want to newspaper it. And that's what I'm gonna do."

I am certainly glad we don't have four boys like Vincent and Georgie! I can't imagine what that would be like. I'm afraid our house would be burned down. On the 15th, Vincent and Georgie were playing Indians (no, they did not have red paint on) in the front room, and they almost started a real fire! I wonder how Grandmother Foster ever survived!

Mary Jane wrote a letter to me, and I received it a few weeks ago. I am enclosing it as it is too long to copy here. You can read all about Kent and Orville's Christmas at the front. They and the rest of the BEF and the French played football with the Germans on Christmas Eve until some officers made them stop and reminded them that they were supposed to be fighting a war. In answer to your question that you didn't ask only wondered about, yes, we do have cousins in the war now. I didn't know it until I got the letter. But I will let you read it for yourself.

I would love to have a picture of a kittywake if you can manage to do it without getting hurt or stuck on a ledge again. What a delightful snowball fight! I'm afraid I wouldn't have been able to stay out of it. I am growing up, but I still love a good snowball fight.

You probably won't believe this, but two weeks ago

Edmund got in a fight at school. It was all over me. Because of it he doesn't call me Lucy except around home now. It all happened this way. Everyone at school, and in town for that matter, knows Edmund's special name for me is Lucy and that I won't answer to it if anyone else calls me that. Well, a new family had just recently moved to Codell, and they have a boy, Lewis, who is about thirteen or fourteen. I don't know which as I never asked. Lewis had heard Edmund calling me Lucy several times, and he also knew that no one else was allowed to call me that. This day he decided to pick on me. First he made sure Edmund wasn't around. I was standing by the side of the schoolhouse watching some of the little girls play hopscotch. Suddenly someone pulled my hair and said in a squeaky voice, "Oh, Lucy dear, what are you doing?"

I turned around. "Lewis," I said patiently, "please don't call me that."

"Why not, Lucy girl?"

"Because I don't like it."

"Oh, but darling. . ." he began, acting like he wanted to kiss me. I felt like slapping him, but restrained myself and just walked away. "Come, Lucy, let's you and me be friends. Lucy and Lewis sound well together." Here he tried to put his arm around me, but I drew away. Just then to my relief I saw Edmund come towards us.

"Leave her alone, Lewis," he commanded.

"I ain't hurt'n her," was the sneering reply as he stepped closer towards me.

"I said," Edmund's eyes were flashing, "leave her alone. Hear me?" Each word was crisp and had a determined tone to it. Exactly what happened next is still somewhat puzzling to me. Lewis leaned over to kiss me, I stepped back as Edmund grabbed Lewis, and somehow I tripped and fell. Before I could get up, Edmund and Lewis were in a fight. Suddenly the principal and one of the teachers were there and pulled the boys apart. The three of us soon followed the principal to his office where we each told our stories. I was dismissed then and sent to class. Some time later Edmund came in looking none the worse. He assured me on the way home that he didn't think Lewis would bother me anymore. The principal told Lewis that maybe there weren't any gentlemen where he came from, but out here there were. And you don't pick on ladies unless you want to find yourself in a heap of trouble. I haven't heard the name "Lucy" off the farm since then.

Oh, I wish I could see Andrew! I miss having a baby in the house. Rosalie is growing up. She is rather quiet still, but very busy. Oh, Georgie has named his newspaper. It is "The Farmhouse Garret." I know it is an unusual name, but Georgie insists on it. You see, he never could remember "Gazette," and as all his things are up in the attic, which the boys call the garret, he insisted that that was the perfect name for the newspaper. Hopefully I can send you a story soon that he has written or at least told.

Everyone here is keeping busy. We sold our sheep last week. Daddy never liked them much and said they ruined the grass because they bite it too close to the roots. I don't mind that they are gone. That means less work for us.

Mama was delighted that you heard from Uncle Frederick and that Uncle Philip is where he is. She is also very thankful that Uncle Philip can keep his leg. Now we know why he thought the doctor looked familiar. After having lived with us for so long, you would think that he would recognize Uncle Frederick. I suppose it has been several years since he last saw him. Yes, Uncle Philip does talk the same way he writes.

You are probably wondering if supper is burning by now. No, we have finished supper and cleaned up, and now it is bedtime for the younger ones. As I am tired and still have a little homework to do before school tomorrow, I think I will say good night and end this.

All my love,
Emma

"There, Ria, now you have gotten to hear a 'Ted, Fred, Larry and Jim' story." Then turning to Lydia, Mrs. Mitchell explained. "She has heard so much about her grandfather and his brothers that we were looking for one of these stories but couldn't find any. I am glad this one is in the letter. Perhaps there are others in them as well."

"Grandpa is Larry," Ria added. "That would be Emma's father in the letters, and Maria's father would be Fred. Right, Mom?" After her mother nodded, Ria said, "But it sure is hard to picture Grandpa as that young, and getting into so much mischief. Mom, do you have the other letter you said you had enclosed?"

Mrs. Mitchell shook her head. "I don't remember seeing it when I sorted the letters. Perhaps my aunt sent it back to my cousin in England."

Home Fires of the Great War

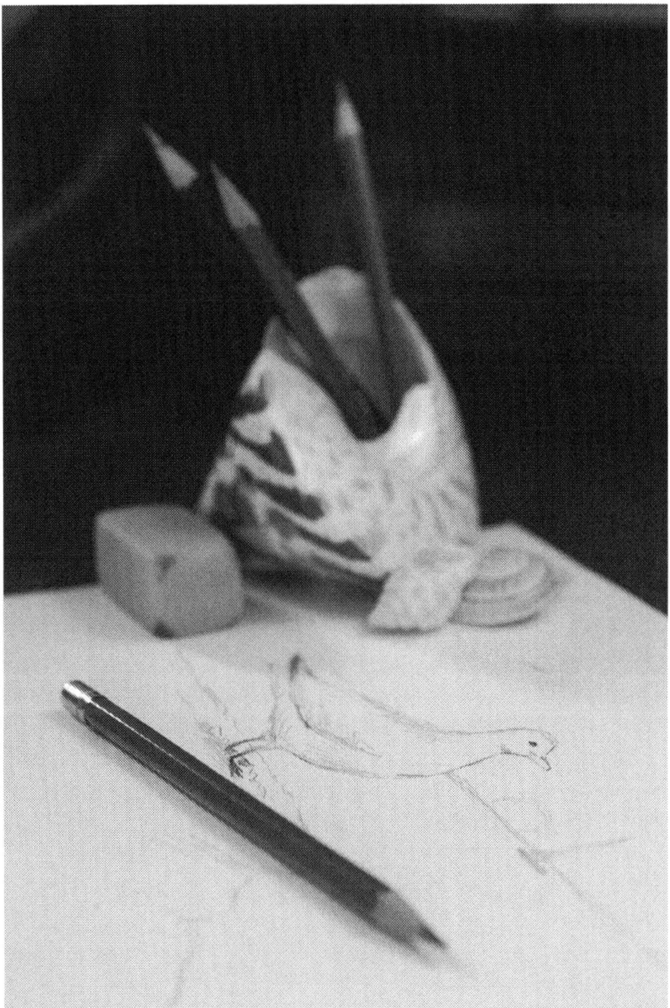

CHAPTER TEN

Friday
April 28, 1916
Princeville, Nova Scotia
Canada

Dearest Emma,

    I am right now in the McGuire dining room seated at the table with Jean, who is working on her school assignment. William Wallace, Rob Roy and Andrew are napping in the next room while Lydia Ruth and Stephen play on the porch where I can see them through the window. Mr. McGuire is fishing, and Mrs. McGuire and Mama, having left the children with me, are helping Mrs. McLean and Mrs. Stewart get Alan and Finlay's things ready. They are both going to war. That is why we aren't in school now. Both will head to the front lines and hopefully meet with Finlay's brother, Malcolm. Now that you know where I am, you will understand if this letter is rather mixed up and random. I have just told Lydia Ruth and Stephen that they must stay on the porch where I can see them. They really want to go for a walk as it is so beautiful out. Yet you know I can't leave the babies sleeping, and Jean must finish her assignment.

    You are right about spring being here. The kittywakes have come, and I have a drawing of one for you. It isn't very good, but it is the best I could do. Myrtle Belisle helped me with it. The ocean is no longer gray but is a deep blue that stretches on until it seems to fade into the azure sky. Flowers are blooming. It's good fishing weather. Almost all the menfolk are out fishing. James and Mark went out today with Robert and Arthur Morris. Mr. Morris is out too, but he's in a smaller boat by himself. The children aren't allowed to go barefoot yet as the sudden showers cool the warm rocks and ground quickly.

I received your letter two weeks ago but not before I had begun reading the law books of Mr. Campton. I don't understand anything that I have read, so Edmund needn't be afraid that I would try to be a lawyer. It happened this way: On April 11, I believe, Charles Campton came running up to our house saying that Edward was "sick, hurt, or something, and Mama wants you to come, please." Mama said I could go. She presumed she could watch the little ones and make dinner. Charles had no idea what was the matter with his cousin, all he knew was that he was supposed to see if I would come. I soon found out that he had slipped on a mossy rock down by the shore and had fallen. He had managed to walk home, and Mrs. Campton had gotten him to bed. There wasn't much I could do. Edward said it was just his back and that he would be fine after a little rest. Not needed then, I went back home only to be called back before dark. Dr. McNeel had come to see Mrs. McIntyre and had been called over to the Camptons. He wanted me to hear all the instructions. Edward was told he couldn't get out of bed or sit up for three weeks at least. He didn't seem to fully comprehend those orders until the next day when he tried to sit up so he could study, and his uncle ordered him in no uncertain terms to lie down and stay down.

The next day, Wednesday, as Mark and I went out for a walk with the little ones and many of the village children, Mrs. Campton came out to ask me if I thought it would hurt Edward to read lying down. I told her I did, and she sighed.

"He is so restless, I don't know what to do."

"Could someone read to him?" I asked quickly, as the children were pulling on my dress and urging me to "please come." She had never thought of that and hurried inside to try it. Later that day she came to me and asked if I would be willing to read to Edward. The law books were too much for William and Charles, and she couldn't read them well at all. I told her I had once tried to read the law books to myself and couldn't understand a thing. She laughed and said she knew just what I meant. I did end up going down with her and found Anne spelling out each word to her cousin while he, poor fellow, tried to make words out of all those letters. You see, Anne didn't put any spaces between the words. Edward told me he couldn't remember a thing that had been read to him and asked if I would mind starting the chapter over. I read for an hour before stopping. The whole time Edward said not a word.

When I stopped he asked abruptly, "Did you understand it?" I shook my head. " You read like you do," was all he said then, and I shut the book and stood up. As I was leaving the room Edward said, "Thanks."

Now I spend at least one hour almost every day reading law books to Edward Campton. He won't let anyone else read them unless it is his uncle because he can't understand what they are reading.

I don't know how much writing I can do now as Rob Roy, who was restless, is now in my left arm sleeping. If I were holding Andrew, I wouldn't be able to write at all as he would most likely decide that he ought to write himself. I just sent Jean to make sure Lydia Ruth and Stephen are still on the porch, as I can't see them. Jean said they were lying on the porch dropping pine needles down a hole.

We all laughed at "Ted, Fred, Larry and Jim playing pirates." James and Jenny came over after I had read it, and Mark insisted that I read it all again. Mama said she doesn't remember ever hearing that story. Mark said he would write and tell Papa about it. I was wondering, does Uncle Lawrence really tell stories like you wrote this one? Papa never did. I can't tell or write like you can, so please forgive these uninteresting letters.

Many thanks for sending Mary Jane's letter to me. I must write her soon. I wonder what would have happened if the officers hadn't stopped that football game. Would the war have ended? Sometimes it feels like Papa has been gone for many years. Oh, how I wish he were home!

Edith got a special letter from Papa yesterday. She will be eighteen on Sunday. Mama thought of having her tea tomorrow, but decided not to since that is when Alan and Finlay leave. It will be so different without them. They will both be greatly missed. Edith will be at the Red Cross in Pictou on Monday, so her tea might have to wait until Tuesday. I hope Carrie had a very happy birthday.

Tell Edmund I was very surprised to hear he got into a fight at school. Though, Emma, I was thankful someone was there to protect you. Edmund, Mark was wondering why you ever started calling Emma, "Lucy." None of us could answer that question. Why did you?

Mama received a letter from her sister, Lynae, who lives on a large ranch in Montana. She is the next to the oldest in Mama's family; Aunt Nicole is the oldest. Aunt Lynae and Uncle Christopher have three children; Chris is twenty, Ginger is fifteen, and Travis is ten. I only remember seeing Chris and Ginger once or twice, and I have never seen Travis. Aunt Lynae said they have fifty-two new head already and expect at least a few dozen more. When Mama read that to us, Mark said, "Where'd they get all the heads? From France?" He has been studying the French Revolution in school. He does really know what Aunt Lynae means by "heads." Aunt Lynae talked about how much time Ginger spends out riding among the cattle with Uncle Christopher and Chris. That would be such a different life. I can't even imagine it. She said their nearest neighbor is about thirty miles away!

It sounds like William Wallace is awake, and I expect Andrew to awaken soon, so I will finish this letter later.

It is evening now, and I am seated on a rock above the village, alone for once, watching the sunset. The sky is a beautiful blue and purple with rosy pink clouds billowing in piles along the western horizon. The sun is a large flaming ball of gold that tinges the edges of the clouds with light. The sun sinks lower. No longer are the clouds rosy pink, they are turning a deep rose red. The golden light seems to be more intense while the sky deepens to blue and purple. An eagle hangs motionless, a dark silhouette against the sun's last golden rays. I can think of nothing but the verse, "The heavens declare the glory of God; and the firmament showeth His handiwork. Day unto day uttereth speech, and night unto night showeth knowledge. There is no speech nor language where their voice is not heard. Their line is gone out through all the earth, and their voice to the end of the world."

A sudden sound has caused me to turn. There on a rock near the edge of the cliff is Alan in full Scottish attire playing his bagpipe. He too seems to be lost in watching the sunset, for only soft notes come from his instrument. Now the notes have become a song, "Amazing grace, how sweet the sound, that saved a wretch like me." Oh, Emma, I can't describe the music. It is different somehow from Alan's usual playing. The notes are full and rich yet have a tender yearning or longing in them as they float out over the water and the village. When I look behind me, I can see the doors of the village houses opening and quietly the people gather to listen and watch. I can see Mama, Edith and Mark on our porch, but not a sound can be heard except the bagpipe and the waves breaking against the rocks. Alan has ended "Amazing Grace" and has begun "Auld Lang Syne." Emma, I know now what he is doing; he is saying good-bye. Good-bye to all the people and places he loves, for tomorrow morning he and Finlay leave for war. Will he come back? Will either of them come back? Oh, I pray the Lord would keep them safe, and Papa. Emma, I . . . The notes are breaking! Don't break now, Alan, keep it strong. There is a step behind me. Mr. McLean has come up to join his son. Nothing is missing from his attire as a Scotsman - kilt, bray, sporran, claymore at his side and bagpipe over his shoulder. With firm even steps he approaches Alan. Shoulder to shoulder they stand. There is no break now in the music. The song ends and is carried away on the evening breeze.

"Aye lad," Mr. McLean's voice comes to me in the stillness. "We'll ne'er be forgettin' ye, donnae ye ken that?"

"Aye," Alan's voice is steady now.

"Then donnae break ye're mither's hert wi' sic dreeful songs. Her een are upon ye frae oor hame, an' it's sair her hert will be if ye are gang far to war wi' out singin' oor favorite hymn. Be ye able to sing?"

There is silence. Alan is gazing out over the water. His shoulders straighten, and he replies, "Aye, wi' David I am." He now turns his gaze to the village while a lively march comes from his bagpipe. David and Mrs. McLean are coming out of the village. The others linger and now are turning back to their houses, no doubt thinking that this farewell has become too personal to watch. I had best be going too; the light is fading though it will be a little while before it is completely gone. Alan just called down to the villagers asking them to please stay. Mr. McLean has begun a melody. Alan's rich tenor and David's perfect harmony blend in "My Ain Countrie."

"I am far frae my hame, an' I'm weary aften whiles,
For the langed-for hame-bringin', an' my Faither's welcome smiles."

Oh, Emma, I couldn't write the song while they sang it. And I couldn't describe it either. I could only sit motionless as the music swelled and dipped around me. Thoughts floated through my mind, "Would we ever hear that rich and beautiful voice again? Would Alan ever come back to this "hame" or would he be "gangin' noo, unto his Saviour's breast." I know we will somewhere meet again. If not on earth "flecked wi' flowers, mony tinted, fresh an' gay" then in "oor ain countrie."

I must end. The tears are close to spilling again, and I don't want to mess up your letter. I am sorry this is short; perhaps my next one will be longer as we are planning on going to Prince Edward Island with the Lawsons in June.

Give my love to your family. May our Savior bless you and yours, my dearest cousin.

                Yours always,
                    Maria

                          Sunday
                      May 28, 1916
                    Codell, Kansas
                            USA

Dear Maria,

You'll never, never guess what has happened! I'm still trying to get used to it, even though they came on the 18th of April. I have forgotten, you don't know who or what "they" are yet, do you? I'm going to start at the beginning and just hope I don't get interrupted, or I may jump to the end or the middle and mix you all up. If my handwriting is hard to read, it is because I'm trying to hurry though I know Mama would say that is no excuse.

It all started Tuesday morning. Well, no, really it started on Monday morning when Daddy went in to Codell to get a part he needed for something. I can't remember what. Codell didn't have that particular part, but Mr. Hoskins told Daddy that he had just been to Plainville the week before, and he saw the part that Daddy needed. So, as I was saying, Tuesday morning Daddy and Mama went to Plainville. It's rather a long trip all the way there and then all the way back. Plus all the shopping took some time. You needn't think that they were just going to get that part, oh no, there were other things to get too. We weren't expecting them home until nearly supper time at least.

The day passed quickly as we stayed busy with different things. I had just put supper in the oven when I heard Georgie shout, "They're home!" Everyone gathered on the front porch to welcome them. We watched the wagon come up the lane, and I suddenly turned to Edmund.

"Who is with them?"

"I don't know," Edmund shrugged. We all stared. One, no, two persons were on the seat behind Mama and Daddy. They both had blonde hair. As the wagon drew nearer, I could see that one was a boy about twelve or fourteen. The other was a girl who looked perhaps five years of age. Daddy brought the wagon to a halt in front of us and climbed out. He looked at us a moment and chuckled before helping Mama down. "What's the matter? Did Emma burn the supper? You look like a group of statues." Here he turned to the children in the wagon. "Welcome home, Karl and Kirsten. I'll introduce all the children to you at supper. It might make it easier to remember their names." Then glancing at us he called, "Boys, come help unload. Then David and Vincent can take care of the horses."

Before long we were all in the kitchen gathering around the table. Daddy gave thanks, and we all sat down. I was seated across from the newcomers. Karl was rather thin with blonde hair and sharp blue eyes. He ate as though he hadn't eaten for a week. Kirsten sat as close to Karl on the bench as she could, only now and then lifting a pair of frightened blue eyes from her plate. Her hair was a little lighter than Karl's and hung down her back in a long braid. It was easy to see that they were brother and sister. Though Karl was gruff and suspicious with all of us, his tender care and protection of Kirsten made us sure that he did have a heart under all his toughness.

Supper was rather a quiet meal. When it was over, Georgie brought Daddy the Bible. Instead of reading where we left off in Acts, Daddy read Isaiah 45. It almost seemed as though Daddy put special emphasis on certain verses. I don't know for sure if he did, but I do remember these;

". . . More are the children of the desolate. . . Enlarge the place of thy tent. . . Fear not; for thou shalt not be ashamed . . . thou shalt forget the shame of thy youth. . . In righteousness shalt thou be established . . . and their righteousness is of me."

When bedtime came, Mama made a pallet on the floor in the boy's room for Georgie and gave his bed to Karl. In our room, Kirsten was to have Rosalie's bed, and Rosalie would sleep with me. Everything was fine until I was going to take Kirsten up to bed with Rosalie. Kirsten drew back in fright, and Karl stepped up beside her.

"Ain't no one goin' to touch my sister unless she wants it. If she's got to go to bed, I'll take her," he snapped.

"Now, Karl," Daddy spoke gently, laying a hand on his shoulder, "Emma isn't going to hurt your sister. If you want to take her to her room, that would be fine. I think it's time all of us headed to bed."

We were all in bed, and just before I fell asleep, I heard a little whimper. My heart went out to the poor little motherless girl, but before I could do anything, Rosalie sat up in bed. "Why, she wants a baby," she said in a sleepy little voice. Then slipping out of bed she took one of her dollies from the chair and carried her over to Kirsten's bed. "Dis baby for you," was all Rosalie said before scampering back to bed. That little touch of kindness seemed to be all Kirsten needed, for she quieted almost instantly.

Before I tell you about the next day, let me tell you how Mama and Daddy came to bring them home. Mama told me about it as I helped her get breakfast the next morning.

It was late afternoon, and Mama and Daddy were almost ready to head home. They were walking near the train station when they noticed quite a crowd by the platform. Curious about what could be happening, they joined the crowd to see a line of children, all different sizes and ages; both boys and girls. It didn't take Daddy long to find out that this was an orphan train from New York. All these children were either orphans or from homes with only one parent who couldn't take care of them. Mama said it almost broke her heart to see the children standing there wondering who would pick them. She said she kept watching two children especially. A man stopped in front of them and looked at the boy.

"You look strong enough. C'mon." He jerked his head towards a wagon.

The boy refused to stir a step. "Youse ain't taken her, ain't takin' me."

The man tried to drag him over, but the boy shoved a fist in the man's face, and the man left in a huff. Before he came back, a couple stopped by and looked at the girl.

"I like her. I think she will do," the woman said to her husband.

"Very well," the man replied. "Let's take her. Come along little girl, you're going to live with us." The man spoke kindly enough, but the girl shrank back in terror behind the older boy.

"Youse guys can't take her without me," he said.

"Now look here," the man began, but before he got any further, the first man was back with a woman who seemed to be in charge and very busy.

"What's the problem?" she asked briskly.

"I want that boy," the first man said.

"And we want the little girl," the lady put in.

"Well, what's the problem?" the matron again questioned somewhat impatiently.

It was the boy who answered, "We ain't seperatin'."

"Of course you must, Karl," the matron frowned. "If they don't want you both, then you must separate."

"Well, we ain't seperatin' and youse guys can't make us. I'll knock down anyone who tries it." The boy spoke defiantly as he planted his feet firmly, squared his shoulders and cocked his fists. His little sister had crept behind him and was clinging to his jacket.

"Karl! Stop that nonsense this instance," the matron ordered sternly.

"Now just hold on a minute." It was Daddy who came over now. He had been watching and listening to the whole thing with Mama. "They are brother and sister, are they not?" The matron nodded. "Well then, I don't blame either one for not wanting to be separated. You won't take the girl?" This to the first man who adamantly refused and then stalked off in disgust. "Are you sure you don't want both?" to the couple who shook their heads and moved off.

The matron was quite upset with Daddy but took it all out on Karl, telling him that no one would ever take two orphans, and if he ever dared to make such a fuss again, he would be sent back to New York without his sister.

Daddy looked at Mama questioningly. She nodded, and he turned to Karl, interrupting the matron. "Karl, how would you and your sister like to come home and live with us?" The matron was speechless.

Karl looked at Mama and Daddy then at the matron. "Don't care," was all he said, but Mama said she saw a slight look of relief come over his face.

Papers were signed, and soon all four were headed home in the wagon. It was a quiet trip. Daddy tried to talk with Karl but only received monosyllables or grunts for answers. Kirsten said not a word. Mama had been told by another matron that they thought Kirsten was mute. They had never had a doctor look at her, but neither had they ever heard her talk at all to anyone, even to Karl, though he talked to her. Mama and Daddy were told nothing about Karl and Kirsten except that they came from New York and Karl was thirteen and Kirsten was six. She doesn't look six at all. She is very small and thin. They were both thin, but they have gained some weight since coming here. We still don't know what their life in New York was like or how they came to be on the orphan train. Perhaps someday we will find out.

All the rest of the week, Kirsten went about with a scared face and clung to Karl almost constantly if she was with him. Karl was quiet, sullen and seemed apprehensive. They both seemed so frightened though Karl tried to hide his fear with toughness. We hardly dared to so much as touch Kirsten when Karl was around because he was so protective of her. By the end of the second week, Rosalie had won Kirsten's heart by her sweet little ways and smiles.

They now share a bed. Kirsten loved the doll Rosalie gave her that first night, and after we explained that it was hers to keep, she carried it around all day.

It was the middle of the third week before Karl and Kirsten seemed to lose their anxious, terrified looks. Kirsten would start to smile at Mama and us girls, and even Daddy and the boys received a few shy smiles from our new sister. Karl didn't smile at anyone unless it was Kirsten when we weren't looking. Of all of us children, Edmund seemed to have the hardest time welcoming Karl into our family. Perhaps it was because they are so close in age. I talked to him once about it. To Edmund, not Karl, you understand. He said he was just being careful, for who knew what he had been doing in New York. I scolded him and told him he should be more friendly. How was Karl supposed to trust us if we wouldn't trust him? Things finally came to a head on Saturday the sixth of May.

It was a beautiful, warm, sunny day. Carrie had taken all the younger children, Kirsten included, out to the orchard to play until dinner time. I entered the barn to find Edmund and Karl engaged in a fight!

"Boys!" I exclaimed, "Stop!" Neither of them even noticed me. "Edmund," I tried to grab his shirt but he pulled away, and I slipped on the wet floor and stumbled back against Jessie's stall. "Quit it, boys!" I begged, almost in tears. "Karl, please," I laid my hand on his shoulder, but he shook me off with such force that I fell to the floor. I was startled for his shirt was wet! Then before I could do anything else, David suddenly appeared, strode over, grabbed both boys by their shirt collars, pulled them apart and held them at arm's length. It was only a few seconds before they calmed down somewhat.

The silence was intense until David said, "You all right, Emma?"

Edmund looked up quickly, a startled expression on his face. Until that moment he hadn't realized I was there. I nodded and stood up, brushing the hay from my skirt. David looked from one to another of us in silence then said, "Dad's in the house with Mama. No one else is in there yet." With that he turned and walked away.

"We might as well get it over with," Edmund sighed looking at the floor. Karl didn't say anything but turned towards the door. I followed, and together the three of us walked in complete silence to the house.

Mama looked up as we entered. She raised her eyebrows somewhat questioningly though she said nothing except to call Daddy. He came in a moment later and sent all three of us to the parlor. Before he followed us, I heard him tell Mama to go ahead and call the children and start dinner. After he had shut the door and sat down, he told us to sit down. There was a long pause before he told me to tell what happened since I was the only female present.

"I don't really know what happened, Daddy," I began, and told him what I have already related to you.

"Well," Daddy said when I had finished, "I don't think you need to stay here any longer. Go eat your dinner." He dismissed me with a smile.

Later that evening as we were out for a walk, I heard from Edmund about what started the fight. Edmund had come into the barn and found Karl smoking on a pile of hay! Without thinking, he did the first thing that came to mind. Grabbing a pail of water that was standing near by, he threw it over him. It doused the cigar and Karl. Karl sprang to his feet in anger. There were some hot words between the two of them which, as you know, ended in a fight. The fight wasn't good, but it seems to have broken the ice between them. I would have thought that things would have gotten worse, but they haven't.

Carrie wants to know where your cousins in Montana go to school. If the closest neighbors are thirty miles away, it would seem that school would be impossible. I can't imagine living that far away from other people. Even though we do live on a farm out here, we do have neighbors, and we see others at church on Sundays and at school.

Mark, Edmund doesn't remember where or why he began to call me Lucy. I don't know either.

Edmund just came in and asked if I had told you about the cyclone yet. As I haven't, I should do that now. There was a cyclone on the east of Codell last Saturday, May 20. It didn't come near us, but it did a lot of damage. And actually it was a tornado not a cyclone. I looked it up in Webster's dictionary. I don't remember what the difference is now, and I don't really want to go get the dictionary to find out again. If you are really interested in the difference, you can look them up.

As I was saying, the tornado did much damage. It started about seven o'clock in the evening, some three miles south of Codell and traveled northeast, the newspaper said, about fifteen miles! At Mr. John Hoskins' place, where it did the most damage, it appeared to be nearly one quarter of a mile wide! I can't tell you all the damage mentioned in the paper, or I'd be here a dreadfully long time. I'll just tell you some of it. At Mr. and Mrs. Hoskins', the cement roof of the smoke house was lifted off and about 400 pounds of meat which was attached to the ridge pole was scattered about the yard, but a bucket of eggs underneath was unmolested. His auto was, and still is I might add, stuck in the side of a tree!

At the time of the storm, Guy Hockett, Blaine Hoskins and the Smith's middle son, Joseph, were passing the Hoskins place. Joseph got out of the buggy and started to get behind a large cottonwood tree, but the others pulled him back in the buggy and made him stay there. Just as they reached the top of the hill, the storm passed only a few rods behind them. The tree that Joseph had wanted to hide behind was knocked across the road! If he had gotten behind it, he would have been killed. The Lord graciously spared his life.

After the storm passed Mr. Overholser's, a board was found with a nail in it and a chicken's heart on the nail. I don't know what happened to the rest of the chicken. Also Mr. Overholser and his family were in their cave and the twister dumped their washing machine and other debris in with them. No one was hurt. The tornado also took a calf that was tied to a tree, carried it about half a mile and dropped it unhurt in a wheat field.

Mr. Jones told Daddy this morning at church that his fields for several hundred yards wide were covered with debris. He's not sure how to get rid of it. He can't safely use horses because of all the boards with nails that are scattered all over. He did say that he found Mr. Hoskin's car's radiator cap. Daddy told him that he could spare two of the older boys if he needed them. I don't know if they will go over there or not.

The last few days our weather has been rain, then hail, then sunshine, then wind. This morning while in church, it hailed quite a bit. It was rather loud, and it frightened Kirsten. We don't think she has ever heard or seen hail before.

Maria, your last letter made me cry. How can you put such feeling into your letters? I have tried, but I can't seem to get it down on paper. I can talk about my feelings most of the time with Edmund or Mama or even Daddy, but writing them is another thing. At least writing them so others can feel the same things. My emotions just won't be put on paper. Perhaps some time I can write like you. Be sure you tell us when you hear of Alan and Finlay.

How I wish I could go with you to Prince Edward Island! You will have to tell me all about it. Why are you going with the Lawsons? Do they have relatives there? Where on Prince Edward Island will you be? I suppose I will find out when I get your next letter.

I love the kittywake picture. It is so well done. It looks like a very sweet bird. Maybe when this war is over, Edmund and I can come visit you and see a kittywake for ourselves. Georgie asked if Mark couldn't catch one and send it to us. Vincent and Georgie then had an interesting discussion about if one would survive such a trip.

Oh, Daddy doesn't quite tell stories like I write them.

Though he did read that story and say it was just like it happened. He said they really did think that "Jim" had rowed upstream and were quite upset with him. I had a great deal of pleasure writing it.

I took Kirsten for a short ride on Jessie last week. She seemed to enjoy it though she said nothing. She still has not said a single word since she came. Karl has been asked if she can speak, but he refuses to talk about it. Daddy says that maybe he is afraid to say she can for fear we'll abuse her to make her talk, or we'll send her away if she can't. So we are just waiting. She might not ever talk, but we love her anyway. Carrie has gotten her wish of someone in the family with blonde hair. Now she has two someones.

I really must be going now, for I don't have much more room on this paper. Besides, Daddy is calling us all. Give everyone my love. Kiss Andrew and Lydia Ruth for me. We are praying for Uncle Frederick. God bless you all!

With love,
Emma

"I didn't know that Uncle Karl and Aunt Kirsten came from New York. Why didn't anyone tell me?" Ria demanded.

"You probably never asked."

"That is why they are so different in looks than the rest of you. I never would have guessed how they came to live with you."

"From an orphan train. I have heard of them, but never truly knew anyone who took any of them in. Was it hard to have new children suddenly join your family?" Lydia queried, turning to Mrs. Mitchell.

Mrs. Mitchell looked thoughtful. "I suppose it was a little at first. They were so different and it certainly took some getting used to. I don't think I ever had as much trouble adjusting as my twin did. I suppose if it had been a girl near my age, that would have made things more difficult. There might have been a few times that I recalled life before they came with fondness, but after a few months, you couldn't have paid us to part with them. They were such a part of our family that they seem to always have been there. I don't even know if the younger ones, like Georgie and Rosalie, even remember that Karl and Kirsten were adopted."

Ria wriggled impatiently in her seat. "Do read the next letter now, Mom. Please!"

CHAPTER ELEVEN

Tuesday
June 20, 1916
Tracadie, P.E.I.
Canada

Dear Cousin Emma,

As you can tell by the place of this letter, we are still on Prince Edward Island and having a glorious time. It is so beautiful here that I don't know if I can adequately describe it, but I will try. Right now I am sitting on the sand near the ocean. Tall, thick grass is growing behind me in the sand, and the ocean waves are gently washing up on the beach. The air has a different smell than I am used to as there are no fishermen near here. They do conduct a lot of fishing here on P.E.I., but there are many farms also, so it just isn't the same. Here I can draw in deep breaths of salty air without the smell of fish. Having wandered off by myself for a little peace and quiet, I am the only one on this part of the beach.

Mrs. Lawson's only sister, Louise Michaels, lives here on the Island and has often wanted Mrs. Lawson to come visit, but it had never been managed until now. It still wouldn't be, I am afraid, if Mama hadn't said we would go with her. Mrs. Lawson has never traveled alone and so was afraid to. There are ten children in the Michaels family. That, plus James and Jenny Lawson and our three younger ones make quite a commotion at the house. Thankfully there are large fields where they can play, and on rainy days they use the barn. Oh, it is all so different here than in our small village of Princeville. Here you cannot see the ocean from any of the houses, but there are ponds and streams where one can swim, row, or fish. Everything is so green and beautiful. Not at all like our rocky, sandy village. I never dreamed that even the trees would be so different! Almost the only trees we have back home are pines, while here there are apple, beech, cherry, and maple, not to mention birch and evergreen. Now please don't misunderstand me. I love my home village, and I think it is just beautiful, but there is a different sort of beauty in a small fishing village than there is on the farms and in the orchards of P.E.I. I am certain that you will agree that there is also another kind of beauty on the farms in Kansas.

Speaking of Kansas, we were all so surprised to hear of the newest members of your family. Are you going to adopt them? Has Kirsten begun to talk? Are Edmund and Karl getting along better? I do want to hear more about my new cousins. So do the others. Are they enjoying life on a farm? It must be quite a change for them to come from New York City to a wheat farm in Kansas. Has life been very different there with Karl and Kirsten? Their names sound Swedish. Do you think their parents were from Sweden?

We have all been having such a delightful time and have been so busy that I don't know if I have time to tell you everything. The Michaels have two sets of twins. The oldest are ten-year-old boys and the youngest are ten-month-old girls. There are six other children, boys and girls, sandwiched in between the twins. I won't give you the names and ages of all of them or you will get confused. The children look alike except in height and length of hair. They all have light brown hair and brown eyes. Add James and Jenny to the list, for they look just like their cousins. Even Mark could almost pass for a relative. I usually don't have much trouble with children's names, but with everyone looking so much alike, I am still mixed up. I know all their names, but putting the right name with the right child is something else. Their mother even mixes them up sometimes, so I don't feel too badly. They all seem used to being called by other names.

Where shall I begin in telling of what has happened? Perhaps I should start with yesterday. Mrs. Michaels, Mrs. Lawson, Edith and Mama took all the girls except me, to a Red Cross sewing meeting at the church. I had volunteered to stay home and make supper. I wasn't really by myself as Mr. Michaels was working nearby in the fields. The boys were all gone on an outing to a nearby pond to row, fish, and enjoy themselves. Mama had asked Mark not to go swimming as the breeze was quite chilly. She said she wasn't at all afraid of his swimming ability as he is used to swimming in the ocean, but she didn't want him catching cold. He promised her he wouldn't. Before long I was the only one at the house. It was quite pleasant to have a little quiet. I gathered my writing things and went out on the porch to write a letter to Papa. I was hoping to write to you as well, or at least start to, but as you know, I didn't get to. Sometime in the afternoon, I saw a group of eager, excited boys hurrying towards the house. I was a little surprised for I hadn't expected them back until later. Putting my writing things away, I waited on the porch, but on hearing my name called, I walked out to meet them. Almost everyone was talking at once, and in the middle of the crowd was Mark, dripping wet. James was beside him and almost as wet.

"Boys!" I exclaimed. "What has happened? Mark, you weren't swimming!"

He made some reply, but with all the clamor of tongues surrounding us, I couldn't hear him. By then we had reached the house.

"Quiet," I ordered, "there will be time for explanations later. Right now, you two boys go get changed and get into bed while I make you some tea."

Mark looked quite tired out. The whole parcel of boys trouped after Mark and James as I headed to the kitchen. A few minutes later, as I carried the tea tray upstairs, I heard the babble of voices. Upon my entrance however, the many tongues fell silent. Mark lay with closed eyes and almost a frown on his pale face. James was half sitting up and looking excited. After giving the boys their tea, I sat on the bed beside Mark and looked around.

"All right," I said, "what happened?"

That was all that was needed. Such a torrent of words filled the room that I was completely bewildered. Who ever said that boys don't talk as much as girls? Every lad in the room, except for Mark, was talking at once, and the volume rose higher and higher as each raised his voice to be heard above the others.

"Hush! All of you be quiet!" I said putting my hands over my ears. "I can't understand a thing if you all talk at once. Now, one of you, begin at the beginning and tell me what happened."

They tried, but you know, I'm sure, how impossible it seems for half a dozen boys to sit by quietly and let one of them tell what exciting thing has just happened. After quite a while I finally understood. Here is the shortened version of what happened.

It seems that while the boys were all on shore by the pond, some of them began to boast about how far they could swim. Somehow word was spread that Mark could swim the length of the pond. None of the boys except James and one or two cousins believed it. When asked, Mark, after looking momentarily at the pond, said that he thought he could. There was much laughter and teasing and urging him to do it. But Mark, remembering his promise to Mama, refused. One of the boys dared him to prove it. Now Papa has taught us all that to accept a dare is foolish no matter what the dare is. He has always said,

"You show more strength of character by refusing a dare kindly but firmly than in giving in. In the end those daring you will have more respect for you because you refused than they would have if you had done what they dared you to do."

Mark remembered his words and had the courage to

refuse. He was teased and taunted. Called chicken and coward, but he just shrugged it off. In the midst of it all, no one had noticed that one of the little boys had gotten into the only boat and was now near the middle of the pond. A sudden scream followed instantly by a splash caused all talk to cease and every eye to turn towards the water. The boat had tipped, spilling its passenger into the waters. A general panic ensued as the boys rushed hither and thither. "He can't swim!" was the only exclamation that Mark heard before knowing what he had to do. He tore off his jacket, kicked off his shoes and dove in. Swimming out to the boy was easy for him as the water was fairly calm, and he was used to the ocean. On reaching the boy, however, he had a harder time, for the lad was so scared that he fought with all the strength he had. (Why is it that drowning people act that way?) By the time Mark neared the shore he was exhausted, and James waded out to help. The little boy was taken home by his older brother while the rest of the boys brought Mark and James home. That is the whole story. Well, almost all of it. After I sent the other boys out of the room and was getting the boys comfortable, Mark asked me if I thought Mama would trust him again since he had broken his promise. I assured him that since he had stood strong through the dares and only swam to save a life, I was sure Mama would consider that he had kept his word. Thus relieved, the boys fell asleep quickly.

Both boys are quite recovered and in fine spirits today. The other little boy is doing very well, and Mama was proud of Mark and didn't consider that his word had been broken.

That all happened yesterday. On Sunday, which was the day before, the Reverend Ardagh preached on Colossians 3:15: "And let the peace of God rule in your hearts." It was just what I needed to hear. I have had such a difficult time letting God's peace fill my heart when I think of Papa. Especially since we haven't heard from him in several months except for Edith's birthday letter which was written in February. The Reverend said, "When you are full of God's peace, it will overflow into everything. Let His peace be your master. Don't let worry or fear have control, for if you do, your life will become bitter and hard. Let your heart be filled with His peace, and you can do anything, go anywhere and let His will be done in your life and in the lives of your loved ones, knowing that your Heavenly Father knows what is best." There was much more in the sermon, but I don't remember all the rest. That was enough for me.

On Saturday, we sent the boys to go pick strawberries to go with the ice cream we planned to make. They were gone for some time, and when they returned, I was outside with the three babies. Andrew was toddling everywhere, (It seems hard to believe that a whole year has passed since his birth. And Papa hasn't seen him! But I must not digress from what I was saying.) while I carried the twins. They are identical and I cannot tell them apart. I saw the boys, and we went to meet them.

"How many strawberries did you get?" I asked, coming up to them.

"We each filled our basket," James said.

I looked quizzically at them. "Then where did you put the berries?"

The boys looked down at their baskets. Only the bottom of a few of them held any strawberries. Most were completely empty. "Why," Mark exclaimed in bewilderment, "where are they? I know I didn't eat that many!"

Mr. Michaels came up then and after much talk, the boys came to realize that they had indeed eaten all the strawberries. They hadn't meant to. They were only going to eat one or two on the way home. It was too late then to send them after more, so they did without any strawberries with their ice cream. Their faces were so astonished when they saw how many "only one or two" berries turned out to be.

Friday was spent in the house or barn, for it rained most of the day. In the evening the sun came out for just a little while, and a beautiful double rainbow shone in the eastern sky. One bow seemed so far away that someone suggested that perhaps it was over Europe. When I wrote to Papa yesterday, I asked him if he saw a rainbow on Friday the 16 of June.

We all went and picked strawberries on Thursday. Well, all of us children did. Have you ever picked strawberries before? At first it was enjoyable, but before we were finished, my back was beginning to ache, and by the time we were done, I felt as though I would never be able to stand straight again. That didn't last long though.

After arriving on Monday, our first three days were spent getting settled and roaming the countryside. Edith and I rode bicycles around the "town" and to the lighthouse. It was all so new and charming. I wish you and Edmund could be here with us. I can just picture the wonderful time the three of us would have exploring the different fields, hills and valleys. Walking along the cliffs by the ocean or along the sandy beaches. The sun shines so brightly though it never seems to be hot. Someday, when the war is over and you both come to visit me, we'll have to come to P.E.I. together.

Oh, I haven't yet told you where we are. We are in Tracadie, which is about nine miles slightly northeast of Charlottetown, which is the capital city and really the only city on the Island. The Michaels' home is about one and a half miles from the ocean.

There has been no news from either Alan or Finlay. Some news has reached us here of the battle of the Great Fleet and the High Seas Fleet. Have you heard anything from your Uncle Philip? We are hoping that letters from Papa will be waiting for us when we return home.

Oh, Lydia Ruth has begged me to ask you to please write another "Ted, Fred, Larry and Jim" story. She had me read the first one to her so many times that she was able to tell it to the Michaels family. Mr. Michaels laughed so hard over it that tears were rolling down his cheeks. Then he told stories of when he was a boy. I didn't get to hear them all for I was busy in the kitchen. Mama said she remembers that Papa once told about him and his brothers being chimney sweeps. Have you heard that story? Mama can't remember it.

How thankful I am that the tornado did no damage at your house. Do you have many tornados? I haven't had a chance to look up tornados and cyclones in Webster's yet. Mark is longing to see what a tornado looks like. I am not, neither is Edith.

The others are coming in search of me now, for I hear them though they do not see me. If I end this now I can drop it off at the post office on the way home, so the postmark will be from P.E.I. We are not planning to depart until Thursday, but I greatly doubt that I will have more time to write. May the Lord bless and keep you, Emma dear!

All my love,
Maria

Tuesday
July 18, 1916
Codell, Kansas
USA

Dearest Maria,

Oh, how delightful your time on Prince Edward Island sounded! Edmund and I wish we could have been with you. I think it is a wonderful idea to visit you when this dreadful war is finally over. Speaking of war, Mama received a letter from her brother Ian yesterday. He is eight years younger than her and is in the Army. Uncle Ian and Aunt Miriam live in New Mexico with their five children. The reason I am telling you all this is because Uncle Ian wrote about being sent to Mexico a few months ago with Brigadier General John J. Pershing. I am going to copy parts of the letter for you.

We entered Mexico on the 15 of March. This was after Villa (by the way, Maria, the Mexican bandit's name is pronounced "Vee-uh") and his men had shot the eighteen Americans on the train and then had raided Columbus, New Mexico. They had attacked the U. S. Cavalry garrison, burned the town and killed nineteen American citizens . . . We are on the march with ten thousand men under command of Brigadier General J. Pershing. Of all the cavalry groups here, it is easy to tell that the 10th Negro unit is Pershing's personal favorite . . . We've been riding over the mountains and deserts of Chihuahua now for some time seeking Villa, but no success. I heard General Pershing say this was like finding a needle in a haystack . . . The 17th of June brought the 10th their first defeat ever. I understand though that is was more the fault of Captain Boyd . . . There were 400 Carranzistas and only ninety American troops. I was one of the 11th Cavalry units sent out by General Pershing to bring the wounded and wandering survivors back to Namiquipa (Pershing's headquarters) . . . I don't know how long we'll remain in Mexico . . . We have a new nickname, Helen. As we ride in the hot, dry land the dust that comes up from our horses hooves settles on us until we are covered from head to boot with fine adobe dirt. Thus our new name is "Adobes" or "Adoughboys" and is sometimes shortened to "Doughboys," for we appear much like the adobe houses sitting on this vast desert . . .

That was about Mexico. We also had another letter from Uncle Philip. I can't decide whether to copy his letter for you again or not. Perhaps I will wait until I write the rest of this letter before deciding. On second thought, I'll just tell you briefly what he said because I don't want to try to read his handwriting! It is worse than usual. He writes that his leg is healing well but slowly. He has made friends with all the nurses and doctors as well as with most of the other injured. He speaks with high praise of Uncle Frederick's skill as a doctor and surgeon. That was about all he said, only he wrote it all in dictionary language. That is all the war news I've heard.

Right now I am sitting out in the orchard under an apple tree writing. We have just finished dinner. The boys are back out in the fields or somewhere working. Kirsten and Carrie are nearby in the field. Carrie is making daisy dolls for Kirsten. Rosalie is napping, and Mama is resting too. The heat seems to be bothering her. The house is quite warm. We have been burning corncobs to bake with as they don't last as long as wood or coal does.

We had a delightful Independence Day! I only wish you could have shared it with us. Maria, we appear to wish often that the other of us was with us. Everyone was up early as we were going to Codell for the day. Chores were done, dinner was packed, and around midmorning we were all on our way to town. Karl and Kirsten watched all the excitement with wonder. Karl finally asked why we were all going to town during the week. Usually we all only go on Sunday to church.

"It's Independence Day!" Vincent told him eagerly starting to stand up in the wagon in his excitement, but David pulled him down.

"What's that?" Karl demanded.

Georgie's eyes opened about as wide as I have ever seen them as he said in an awestricken voice, "You don't know what Independence Day is?"

Karl grew insolent at this exposure of his ignorance and asked roughly, "Do you?"

"Yes."

"Then tell us what it is, Georgie," Daddy directed calmly.

"Well," Georgie began slowly, "it's, . . . it's, . . ." he paused with a wrinkled forehead a moment while collecting his thoughts. Then inspired suddenly he burst forth, "It was when Daddy was a boy, and they shot lots of guns and fell over dead, and George Washington crossed the Del'wear and became Father President 'cause he chopped down his

Daddy's cherry tree."

During this remarkable version on what Independence Day is, David and Edmund both were overtaken with sudden coughing fits, and even Daddy had to clear his throat several times. Perhaps it was the dust of the road. Mama was shaking as though with cold. Somehow I managed to keep a straight face. Karl glanced from one to another and must have realized that Georgie didn't quite have the facts straight for he looked rather incredulous.

"Georgie!" Vincent exclaimed, "That's not how it goes!"

"All right," Daddy broke in, "why don't you all straighten Georgie up on his American history."

Accordingly we spent the rest of the way to Codell giving a history lesson in which, I think, we all benefited.

The day was one full day of pleasure. There were races, contests, speeches and much noise. Why is it, I wonder, that Independence Day is the noisiest day of the year? Speaking of speeches, there were some political speeches. Just some local men speaking for those running for offices. One man spoke for President Wilson. He is running for reelection this year on the Democratic ticket. Another spoke for Charles Evans Hughes. Mr. Hughes was a Supreme Court judge, but Daddy said he resigned in June to run for President. We hear that Teddy Roosevelt is going to run again, but other people say he isn't. Anyway, I asked Daddy who he and Mama would vote for, and he said he didn't know yet. Of course if we were living in most any other state, Mama wouldn't get to vote. Can Aunt Amelia vote?

There was much talk on the ride home. The boys all loved the noise and excitement. Kirsten seemed to be the only one who didn't enjoy the whole day. She clung to Karl or Mama the whole time and cringed when the firecrackers when off. Mama finally took her back to the wagon where it wasn't so noisy.

I must tell you about what Vincent and Georgie did

on the first of this month. It was morning. Mama and I were already busy in the kitchen when Edmund came in from the barn and ran upstairs to waken the little boys. He came back down sooner than we expected and asked, "Have you seen the little boys?"

I shook my head, and Mama replied, "They haven't come downstairs since I have been up. Aren't they in their room?"

Edmund shook his head and muttered to himself, "I wonder where they could be."

"Are you sure they aren't there and that you are not just asleep?" I teased.

Mama laughed, "We have some water here if you need it."

Edmund colored and then laughed good-naturedly. "I'm sure I'm awake this time." He grinned. "And I don't know where the boys are."

Now, before I tell you about the little boys, I should first tell you about Edmund and why we were teasing him.

Only a few days before this, the three older boys and Daddy had spent a long, hard day working and had gone to bed late. In the morning Daddy woke the boys up for chores before heading himself to the barn. Mama and I were in the kitchen when Daddy later came in and asked if we had seen the boys. No, we hadn't, and Daddy went upstairs again. Several minutes later he came back down. "They were all asleep again," he smiled, "but this time I made sure they were up and out of bed."

"My dear, you must have worked them too hard," Mama teased, and amid some laughter Daddy went back to the barn. A short time later, Edmund came into the kitchen buttoning his shirt. I greeted him but only received a grunt in reply. Picking up the basket of eggs Carrie had just brought in, he muttered something about feeding the goats.

"Edmund," I protested, "we don't have any goats." I took hold of the basket, and with a shrug Edmund let me have it. Turning toward the door, he then picked up the

Home Fires of the Great War

broom, shouldered it, and strode outside.

"What is he doing with the broom?" I wondered.

"I think he is still asleep!" Mama chuckled as she looked out the window.

"Mama!" I exclaimed upon joining her, "He's trying to chop wood with the broom!"

"Who is?" David questioned as he and Karl walked in the kitchen.

"Edmund is!" I laughed, still looking out the window at my twin. "He must be still asleep."

Both boys hurried outside to see for themselves. We watched them take the broom from Edmund and there seemed to be some argument between David and Edmund. Karl just stood there smiling. Finally Daddy came out of the barn. It took Daddy dunking his head under the pump for Edmund to fully wake up. He still gets teased about it.

But anyway, back to Vincent and Georgie. No one knew where they were, but when we rang the bell for breakfast they came from the direction of the orchard. When they walked into the kitchen everyone turned to look at them, and a gasp of astonishment came from most of us. Both boys were filthy! And I don't mean just dirty either. They had rolled the pant legs of their overalls up to their knees, and their legs and feet were completely caked with mud! Faces, necks and arms were streaked with dirt while their hands were brown. They were both very hot, but looked quite pleased with themselves.

"Where have you boys been?" Daddy inquired sternly. "Your chores are waiting for you."

"Oh, we'll take care of our chores, Daddy. Won't we, Georgie?" Vincent assured.

As the boys came to the table they were quickly stopped by Mama. "You boys are covered with dirt," she said. "No breakfast until you wash up."

"But, Mama, . . ." Georgie and Vincent began.

"Boys, do as your mother said," Daddy ordered firmly. "And make your feet clean so you don't track mud across her clean floor." Though the boys looked longingly at the food I was dishing up from the stove, they knew better than to argue when Daddy was listening and therefore went with reluctant steps out to the pump. We were half way through eating before the little boys came in. They looked decidedly better even if they did appear as though they had on white shoes. Once they had been served, Daddy questioned them as to where they had been.

"Oh, we had the most wonderful idea! Didn't we, Georgie?" Vincent began, with his mouth full of food. Mama cleared her throat significantly, and Vincent closed his mouth quickly. One thing Mama does not allow at the table is talking with food in your mouth. Vincent was in such a hurry to be able to talk before Georgie that he choked. It was a full minute before he could get his breath back to say anything. He needn't have worried because Georgie seemed to have no interest in anything at that moment except his food. "We will be very busy today." Vincent began again. We all looked at him, and he paused to get a drink of milk. "You may not see us for several days in fact. Isn't that right, Georgie?"

Georgie merely grunted.

"What are you doing?" Carrie asked

"We are digging a hole to China!" Vincent announced triumphantly.

There was a moment of stunned silence before Daddy asked slowly, "Don't you think it will take you a while?"

"Well, it may, but I think we'll be done by dark," replied Vincent easily. "And Georgie is going to write it up for 'The Farmhouse Garret.'."

"No, I'm not going to write it up, I'm going to write it down," Georgie protested.

I could hardly keep a straight face and dared not look at Edmund.

"You know, boys," Daddy cautioned, stroking his chin, "China is a long way away."

"We know, don't we, Georgie? But we can do it.

Come on, Georgie, let's get back to work!" Vincent stood up as he spoke.

"Wait a minute. We haven't had family prayers yet, and then you two need to do your chores first." Daddy pushed his plate back as he spoke, and Vincent slowly sat back down. "Kirsten, would you like to get the Bible?"

Much to our surprise, the boys actually worked most of the day on their hole, and by supper time Vincent could stand up to his knees in it. I mean that is how deep it was. They haven't worked on it since that first day.

I just came back from helping Carrie with one of her flower dolls and found Edmund taking a break reading this letter. He knows I don't mind if he reads them, but this time he said I shouldn't have told you about him trying to chop wood with the broom. I told him it was too late. He really doesn't mind, he just pretends to. Besides, I told him it was news you would enjoy.

Those strawberries you mentioned sounded so delicious! I imagine if any of my brothers had been with Mark and the other boys on their picking expedition, they would have done the same thing.

Daddy said to tell Mark that his father will be proud of him for standing up against the dares. Daddy is proud of him too. He has told us the same thing that Uncle Frederick told you. Daddy said Grandfather taught all four boys the same thing.

Oh, yes, Lydia Ruth wanted another "Ted, Fred, Larry and Jim story" didn't she? I would tell you one now, but I think it would make this letter too long. I will try to put one in my next letter. Which story does she want, Chimney Sweeps or Robin Hood? Instead of that, let me tell you one of Georgie's stories that he wrote for his newspaper. On second thought, I think I will go inside and copy it just as he wrote it, spelling and all.

mi dog Jak

Wun da mi dog Jak an me went to or woodz to hunt a fokz. we ran an ran an srcht an srcht. At lasd we fownd a big wun. He ran uwa. Jak ran uwa to. Jak folod thu fokz for nin milz. thn thu fokz ran in u hl. Jak wuz to big for thu hl. he borkt. "Cum owt n ply." thu fokz sed "no." Jak sed "thn i will dig u owt." "i wil kum owt." sed thu fokz but i can not ply bekuz u wunt to kil me." "i wil not kil u." sed Jak "letz bee frendz." "ok" sed the fokz. An hee kam owt. Jak an thu fokz plad ol da. At supr tim Jak cam hom varee hugree. Jak had a bon fr hiz supr. I sed "gud nit Jak" thu ind.

Don't you think he did a remarkable job for one so young?

I see I haven't told you much about Karl or Kirsten. Kirsten still hasn't said a word. She seems to be enjoying being with us, but any time we go somewhere, she gets a frantic, apprehensive look on her face and clings to Karl. If a stranger speaks to her at all, she winces and hides behind whichever one of us older ones is closer. If a stranger should happen to touch her, she cringes and flinches as though she was struck. Poor little dear! She must have had a very hard life in New York. With Karl it is harder to tell what he thinks of farm life. He seldom talks and only rarely smiles. He and Edmund get along better now. Daddy has kept all the boys working hard here on the farm. Karl is surprisingly beginning to darken somewhat from being out in the sun. Both he and Kirsten have gained weight and begin to look like healthy farm children instead of starving street urchins.

Did you know that on the second of this month, the world's richest woman died? Her name was Mrs. Hetty Green, and she was the wife of the American Consul in Manila. She is believed to have had "in the neighborhood of one-hundred-million dollars!" Can you imagine that much money! I don't know why I told you this except that I thought it was interesting.

Edmund is strumming his fingers impatiently against

the wall on which he is leaning. I asked him if he had anything he wanted to tell you, and he said this letter is long enough and would I please hurry up. He wants to go for a ride before it grows dark, and the horses are waiting. So farewell, Maria, for a time.

       Love and prayers,
       Emma

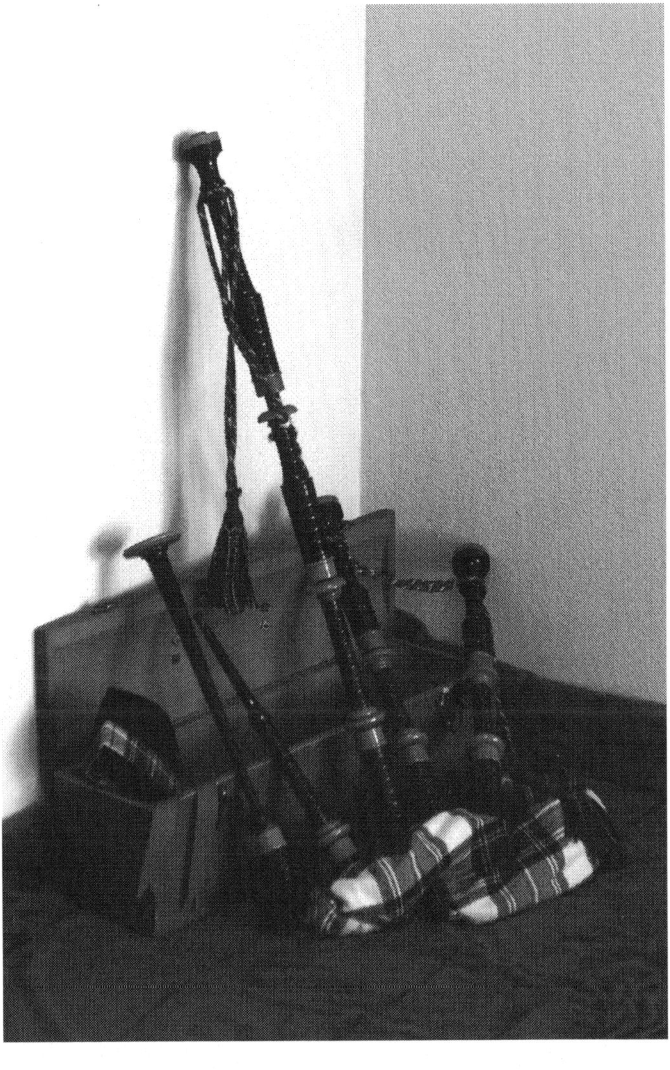

CHAPTER TWELVE

Saturday
August 12, 1916
Princeville, Nova Scotia
Canada

Dear Emma,

News from Papa, Alan and Finlay! I don't know who I should begin with. Papa's would take the longest but would be of the most interest to you. Perhaps though, I should tell about the others first so that I can take my time with Papa's letter. Finlay and Alan both wrote letters to the entire village, which have been passed from house to house. As I have both letters here, I shall copy them for you. Neither one is very long, Finlay's being the shortest.

I am sitting here at [blacked out] station with the rest of my division waiting for the train which will take us to somewhere and then on to France! We are all eager to go. I don't know if I shall ever see Princeville again. The reality of the war has just struck me. Perhaps eternal glory awaits me in France, not earthly but heavenly. I am prepared. I hear the train whistle, and Alan is playing the bagpipes, so can't write more.

Onward to France and freedom! - Finlay

Alan's letter is different. It is longer and of course it is rather Scottish for he writes as he speaks. I have thought of copying it for you in English, but you might enjoy it more as it is, so I will leave it.

Hoo's a' wi' ya a'? I expect to be gangin' morn's morn wi' my division for the front lines. The news here is a' aboot the war. Ye hear o' naething else a' day lang. The battle at Flanders is gabbed aboot muckle. Och! This place isna at a' like bonnie Princeville. The Captain didnae tell us whaur we are to gae, but it doesnae matter. We fight a' the ilk. I's warrant it wi' be nae easy time. The callants are a' brow maun. I feel proud to serve wi' sic a' leal company. I am the piper for the regiment and right glad am I to nae leave my bagpipes at hame! Finlay marches near me an' keeps me company mony a nicht wi' talk o' hame. Ne'er hae I seen sich rain as noo! The runnel has become a linn over the brae. I shall nae be sair to leave England. I maun noo sound lights out. I think o' ye a' aften. Pray for us. - Alan

Now for Papa's letter. It has something about your uncle in it.

Dear loved ones at home,
How I miss you all! I have just received some letters from you, and they help somewhat to ease the ache I feel for each of you. I have almost no leisure hours. As a doctor, there is never a time I don't have new wounded coming in. I have once again been transferred. Not too far away it is true, but still any move means more work; new nurses, new fellow doctors, new buildings or tents and always new patients. I have not yet had to attend any acquaintances other than Philip Vincent Bartholomew Wallace III. I left him in good spirits for the most part, about to leave for somewhere. I don't know where he is being sent. It could be England or some other part of France. I feel that he will never go back to his comrades, the chasseurs, for his leg, though healing nicely, will not, I fear, allow for long tramps through the mountains. At least not for a long time to come. When I told him that, he just shrugged and said he would fly an

airplane, for one doesn't need legs to do that.

Pray for me, dear hearts. I am weary of all this bloodshed. How others get through without the Heavenly Father's strength, I know not. He is my strength. Often have I felt His aid when humanly speaking I could not go on. Days without rest, nights with only an hour's sleep at a time, especially after a battle, is enough to sap the strength of even the strongest man. This was the only time I have had leisure to write . . .

Then he writes to each of us. Papa said he was proud of Mark for not taking the dare, just as Uncle Lawrence said he would be. Oh, it is so wonderful to have a new letter from Papa!

We thought Georgie's story was adorable. Mama said to be sure to save them. Mark said that we would subscribe to the "Farmhouse Garret" whenever Georgie goes to press. I am sure it will be quite the newspaper.

I wish you could have seen Lydia Ruth's eyes when she heard about Vincent and Georgie digging a hole to China. She has spread the word around the village that her cousins made a hole almost to China. That caused quite a discussion among the younger children as to whether or not they should attempt it also. Arthur Morris and William Campton finally convinced them that it really wouldn't work.

Edmund, I am most heartily glad that Emma told us all about your sleep walking. Everyone has found it amusing. Quite often now, when someone has a broom in their hands, the question, "Are you going out to chop wood?" is put to them. No one in the village, as far as I know, has gotten up in their sleep.

I must tell you now, Emma, of what we did last week. The 1st of August was Grandmother's 88th birthday. For a week or so prior to that, Mrs. McLean, Mama and I had been working with all the children on several Scottish songs. Elispeth McIntyre even memorized a poem in Gaelic.

The 1st was a beautiful day. The sun rose in a golden

ball amidst a rosy bank of clouds fringed with lavender which were spread across the horizon. The sky changed from dark ebony to a vibrant azure as the sun climbed higher. All were up and hard at work quite early to prepare. Grandmother knew nothing of the plans which were afoot until the crowd of children, all in Scottish attire, gathered on her porch and began to sing "The Campbell's are Coming." Grandmother was delighted, but before consenting to join them, she first had to make herself ready. When she at last appeared in the center of the village, surrounded by the merry children, she was the very picture of delight. Nowhere in all the world, could you find a sweeter, cheerier, more beautiful Scottish Grandmother! Her white hair was in a bun beneath her tam, and her crisply starched white blouse was half hidden by her stol and vest, while her long kilt reached to the top of her black shoes. Her tam, stol and kilt were all the Campbell plaid: green and blue with a little bit of white woven here and there. Everyone greeted her with pleasure, for truly she has been "Grandmother" to us all. To many she is the only grandmother they know. When she found out that this was all in honor of her birthday, she exclaimed,

"Whisht! Ye donnae mean this is a' fer this auld guidwife?"

"Aye, that we do," answered Mr. McLean, and Grandmother was led to the seat of honor. It was all a festive time and when, after the songs and poem, Mr. McLean and Mr. McGuire, (who had been persuaded to bring out his bagpipe to take Alan's place) began such lively songs on the bagpipes that the children's feet just couldn't keep still, Grandmother said to me,

"What a bonnie sight these canty littlins are wha are capering aboot so gude. Ah, lassie, a bonnie sight indeed fer these auld een o' mine. Gin I were a lass, I might join them."

Just at that moment Duncan stepped before her and very politely asked if she would like to dance.

"I donnae ken but I would," was the laughing reply.

So while Mr. McLean and Mr. McGuire played several

Scottish gigs and dances, Grandmother and the young men danced, for each must have a turn with her. The rest of us stood or sat in a circle around them clapping and stamping our feet in time to the swirl of the music, while the sun shone brightly down and the few clouds danced by on the breeze as though they, too, had come to dance. At last the music stopped, and Grandmother sat down, quite out of breath, but smiling with delight.

"Ah, it hae been mony a lang time sin I hae danced those tunes. Thank ye lads!"

Before long the younger ones were begging Grandmother for a story. She complied readily for there is almost nothing she loves better than to tell stories of her life in Scotland. The day was one long delight, ending with everyone singing "Auld Lang Syne" before the children escorted Grandmother home.

It is late now. The others are all in bed, but I couldn't sleep and wanted to finish your letter. Here on the window seat of our room I can look out over the sea. The light from Pictou harbor is casting its bright beam ever over the sea. I can hear the rumble of thunder and see the jagged streaks of lightning to the north. A summer storm is on the way.

Mrs. Hatty Green? I remember now, she was mentioned in the newspapers here too. Isn't she the lady who wouldn't hire a cab to go to a party in bad weather? Instead she would put a pair of old socks over her shoes and walk! What a strange woman. And with all that money too.

The storm is closer. The waves are growing higher; I can hear them crash on the cliffs. The moon is still shining and the stars sparkle overhead, but the dark clouds are approaching. Even as I write, many twinkling stars seem to have been extinguished.

My heart goes out to little Kirsten. I can only imagine what her life must have been like for her not to talk now if she can. Do you think she can? Do you know anything about their early life? Does Karl know how to read and write? Has he ever been to school? What about Kirsten? We still chuckle over Georgie's version of Independence Day. Neither Mark nor Lydia Ruth have ever been as quaint as Vincent and Georgie.

The storm just broke over us. I must go check the windows.

Now I must finish this and get to bed. Only Mark's window was open, but he was so sound asleep he didn't even stir when a loud crash of thunder shook the house before I left his room. Edith was awakened, but thankfully not Lydia Ruth. I don't hear anything from downstairs, so perhaps Andrew has slept through it as well. Edith is here at the window watching the lightning play across the clouds. I must end as the candle is just about out.

Much love,
Maria

P.S. Lydia Ruth said the "Robin Hood" story please. And thank you "muckle." (The Scottish word for much. Lydia Ruth sounds darling trying to speak Scottish.)

"Scottish. Well, I did understand all that more than I have before. I guess you just have to listen to it enough to get to know what they are talking about." Ria's face showed her satisfaction at being able to understand at least most of the "strange talk" as she expressed it to her brothers.

Lydia agreed, and even Mrs. Mitchell mentioned that it was easier to read it aloud the more she had to read it. "I just don't have the Scottish accent to make it sound authentic. Now Edmund on the other hand can speak with an accent to make even those in Princeville think he is from the Old Country. You should ask him to do it for you the next time you see him."

Ria promised that she would and hoped that Lydia would be with her.

Thursday
September 7, 1916
Codell, Kansas
USA

Happy Birthday Maria,

I picked an apple for you yesterday and ate it to celebrate your fifteenth birthday. How fast the time is going! Didn't I say something like that last year? And the year before that? Are you wondering what we did for our birthday? We had a picnic! The day was the absolutely most beautifulest day of the year; okay, month anyway. I know also that, "Beautifulest" is really not a word, but how else can I explain it? You could find a way I'm sure. Why, I could almost feel the breeze and the warm sunshine on my face as I read your last letter. I was outside in the sunshine when I read it, but what does that matter? You want to hear about the picnic.

Since our birthday fell on Sunday this year, we had the picnic on Saturday. We gathered baskets, blankets and the like and set off over the hills for dinner. Georgie kept us all quite merry with his quaint remarks.

"Does you suppose that if I was to stand on my head every day," Georgie asked as we had all paused at the top of the hill to enjoy the view, "that my legs would grow?"

"Why do you think that, son?" Daddy asked.

"'Cause Emma said that things grow up toward the sun, and I don't want my legs to be short when I get big." He explained. Who else but Georgie would have thought of that?

Then when we were eating, he suddenly threw down his drumstick and fairly shouted, "I have decided!"

We all started in surprise at the sudden and dumbfounding interruption. Kirsten shrank against Karl, her eyes wide and questioning. The rest of us stared at Georgie in bewilderment. After a pause, Mama chided,

"Georgie, you shouldn't shout like that when we are all right here."

"But I did." Georgie didn't look at all abashed.

"I know you did," Mama began, "but you shouldn't shout."

"No, I decided."

Daddy spoke up then. "What is this that you have decided?"

Georgie gave a sigh and picked up his drumstick again. "I decided, but I guess I won't." And he took a bite. No one moved and every eye was fastened on Georgie.

"What did you decide?" Carrie asked at last.

"Oh, I decided to catch some mouses for pets, but then I guessed I won't 'cause Tippet and Teatem might eat 'em." (Tippet and Teatem are the cats. Two of Callie's kittens from last year. Don't ask me why they have those names. Vincent and Georgie named them.)

Can you imagine having pet mice? Ugh! Mama shuddered at the very thought.

Carrie gasped, "Oh, Georgie! How could you even think of such a thing?" Then turning to Kirsten, she added, "Wouldn't that be awful?"

Kirsten eyed her with almost a look of amusement on her face and shook her head.

Most of us looked in surprise at Kirsten. Did she really like mice?

"We used to have a pet rat in New York," Karl volunteered. That was the first time he had ever even mentioned their former life. We all sat in silence. I wondered if he would tell us more. Would we find out if Kirsten could talk? She had shown no signs so far of ever talking. Karl spoke again.

"In that dark, hot, smelly room, the rat was the only thing Kirsten had that wasn't taken from her. No one except me knew about it. It lived in the wall behind the door. Kirsten would feed it crumbs of whatever she had to eat. Though," and he looked fondly down at his now rosy cheeked sister, "she should have eaten it all herself."

Kirsten's blond head was shaken in disagreement, and

we laughed.

Karl lifted his head suddenly and seemed to only then become aware of the rest of us. I saw the look of fear, defiance and pride which had all but disappeared leap back into his eyes. He pressed his lips together and scowled. There was an uncomfortable silence.

Daddy broke into a lively song just as the silence was becoming unbearable. Song after song followed. Many of us took turns picking and starting them. It was such a merry time that no one wanted to end and go back home. Of course we did or you wouldn't be reading this letter.

School started on Monday. It felt so different not to get my books and tramp off to school with Carrie, Vincent and Georgie. Georgie was nearly wild with delight to be able at long last to attend school with Vincent. Kirsten is staying home. Mama and Daddy decided that since Kirsten wasn't speaking, and she was still terrified of strangers, especially men, that she was better off here. Karl isn't going either. Daddy gave him a choice, and he would rather study at home. I think it is partly because Kirsten is home and partly because he is so far behind in things. I can't say that I blame him. David, Karl, Edmund and I all study here at home. Mostly on rainy days and in the evenings. The new school that has been talked about for so long has become a reality. It is just a small one room cabin with a wood stove. But it's only a mile from our house if you cross the fields. By road it's a little longer. Yes, Karl can read. He said he went to school for six weeks one winter and that is all. But can he add and subtract! I have never seen anyone as quick with numbers as he is! David and Edmund are like beginners beside Karl in addition. Daddy is going to teach him multiplication and division.

I wish you could see Rosalie and Kirsten play together. They are entirely silent. Since Kirsten doesn't speak, Rosalie doesn't. It is all motioning, nodding heads and smiles. Without the little boys the house is strangely quiet.

Let me tell you about something that happened that

was not so quiet. It was just a week ago that it happened. I had gone out to gather the eggs as Carrie was busy elsewhere. I had gathered almost a dozen. Reaching into the next nest I felt something move! I let out a scream and almost dropped my basket. I stared at the nest in horror. What had I just touched? I didn't dare put my hand in again. On seeing a slight movement in the nest, I screamed again just as Edmund, David, Karl and Daddy arrived.

"What happened?" they demanded.

"Something moved in that nest," I shuddered, pointing with a trembling hand. David reached in and pulled out a large black snake! Stifling another scream that rose to my lips, I looked away. How the boys laughed!

"Lucy," Edmund laughed, "it was just a nice little black snake."

"I don't care, he scared me. I don't think I dare gather more eggs."

After a little more teasing, Edmund stayed to help. He put his hand in the next nest and exclaimed, "Oh!" in a startled voice.

I gave a little scream.

"Oh, it was only an egg," he said with a teasing grin.

"You!" I exclaimed and gave him a push.

When he had only three nests left, he tried coaxing me to get the eggs again. I shivered and shook my head.

"Look," he reasoned, "there aren't any more snakes." There were only two more nests. "Come on, Lucy," he urged. "I'll get these, and you get the last ones."

Slowly, with reluctance, I reached into the last nest. Then I screamed! There was another snake! Edmund doubled over with laughter, but I shrieked again as the snake poked his head out. Edmund was of no help for he was laughing too hard to notice anything. As the snake began to come out of the nest, I screamed one more time then turned to run to the house. As I turned, I bumped into Karl.

"Karl!" I implored clutching him, "Do something!"

For a moment, he looked at me, the snake and

Edmund. Striding over, he caught the snake, which really wasn't very big, and dropped it down Edmund's shirt! Oh, Maria! You should have seen Edmund's face. His laughter stopped suddenly as he felt that awful snake wriggling. He looked at Karl then burst into laughter once more as he untucked his shirt and let the snake fall to the ground. Karl had joined in the laughter, so I left the two of them to their merriment and their snakes and went inside. See if I ever gather eggs again! I haven't done it yet. I'm not sure I'll ever have the courage to.

Now, before I write more, I should put in "Ted, Fred, Larry and Jim Play Robin Hood," so that there is enough room. I hope Lydia Ruth enjoys it.

This story comes after the "Pirate" one, but only about seven months later as Maggie was beginning to toddle. Ted was almost nine, Fred almost eight, Larry almost six and a half and Jim just turned five.

It was a delightful spring day. The kind of day that no child wants to remain indoors. The four Foster boys were all out in the field behind their house discussing what they would do. "Let's play Robin Hood," Ted suggested.

"Who will I be?" Larry burst forth as the others nodded to confirm Ted's suggestion.

Ted pursed his lips and tilted his head thoughtfully. "You'll have to be Friar Tuck, 'cause you're the fattest."

"But I want to be Little John!"

"Ted is Little John," Fred told him.

"No, I'm not. I'm going to be Robin Hood."

"I am going to be Robin Hood, and you have to be Little John." Fred ordered. "Because Little John is taller than Robin Hood, and you are the tallest."

After a few moments of silence Ted gave in grudgingly. It was his idea, but Fred was right.

"What about me?" piped up Jim.

"Who do you want to be?" Ted asked him.

Jim's eyes sparkled. He got to pick! Usually, he had to

be whatever Ted or Fred decided. Without a moments hesitation he declared "Will."

"Which one? began Larry, but Fred interrupted.

"Let's let him be all three: Scarlet, Scathelock and Stutley. That way we'll have all three of them."

Ted nodded. He really wished Jim could be the sheriff or one of his men, but after what Papa said and did the last time when Jim was the spy and they were in the act of hanging him, . . .

"Come on," Fred was urging. "Let's go to the forest." And so away trooped Robin Hood and his band of merry men to the other end of the village where the "forest" was. Larry found a stick along the way to use as his "quarterstaff."

"But I can't be Friar Tuck," he burst forth suddenly, "'cause I don't got a robe!"

Ted looked around. "There's the church. Got some robes. Come on." So saying, he led the way into the small church nearby.

Before long they found the required robe and, slipping out the side door, they ran across the fields to the forest. Once safely in the shelter of the trees, Larry donned his new garb only to find that were he twice as big, the robe would scarcely fit. Ted pulled a piece of rope from his pocket and using that, the robe was tied around Larry's middle.

"That makes the top fit him better," Fred observed. "But it is still too long."

"Have to cut it," Ted said pulling out his pocket knife. Fred nodded in agreement. The knife didn't cut very well or very straight for it was quite dull. Finally it was cut to the proper length.

"Now," Jim declared, "you just need your hair cut and no one would ever know you're not a friar."

At that, Ted and Fred looked at each other, eyes sparkling with sudden thoughts which both seemed to be thinking for Fred said, "I know where we can get scissors."

"You do?"

"Sure." And without another word he was off. Only a

moment had elapsed before he was back with a pair of scissors. "Borrowed from Mrs. Bernham," he panted.

Ted gave the orders now. "Larry, sit on the rock. Fred give the scissors."

Larry, looking rather doubtful, sat down as he was bidden. He thought surely his brothers were only pretending, but if they weren't . . .

"Don't move, Friar Tuck," Robin Hood said in a deep voice. "Now, Little John, you be mighty careful. Now I must go find Will."

Larry sat on the rock without moving while the scissors went snip, snip, snip. Occasionally he could feel the cold metal on his head, and he cringed. Finally he inquired in a small voice, "You aren't cutting all my hair, are you?"

"Of course not," Ted reassured him. "Even friars have some, just not up here."

"Oh," was the only response Larry gave, though he wondered what his hair did look like. At last the hair cut was done, and Larry forgot all about it in the exciting adventures that befell Robin Hood and his merry men.

Ding, ding, ding. The sound of a supper bell caused all four boys to stop their play. "Supper!" Fred, Larry and Jim shouted.

"Let's go!" Ted added with a whoop, and the boys began a mad dash for home. Out of the woods, over the stream, under the fence, through the field, past the church, down the road, across the yard and into the back door they scampered all out of breath.

Mama turned as they entered and gave a startled exclamation while the platter slipped from her hands and crashed to the floor. She said not a word only looked at them with a mixture of horror, shock, despair, and utter helplessness. Papa, having heard the crash, stepped into the room with Little Maggie on his shoulder. On seeing the boys still with their "swords, quarterstaffs and bows" in their hands, he ordered firmly, "Take the sticks all outside where they belong."

The boys turned to obey, and as they did so they heard Mama cry, "Oh, Theodore! His hair!"

When they were all outside, Ted, Fred, Larry and Jim looked at each other. The realization of wrong doing was beginning to dawn on them. "Maybe we should go away until Larry's hair grows back," Jim suggested.

"We'd miss supper, and I'm hungry," Fred groaned.

"And Papa would find us, and we'd be in even worse trouble." Ted frowned. Why hadn't they thought about what they were doing?

Larry was the only hopeful one. "I don't think it looks too bad." He reached up and gingerly felt his hair. Well, maybe it did look bad, but surely it couldn't be that bad, could it?

"Boys!" Papa's voice came from the doorway. Slowly the four boys reentered the kitchen. Mama was finishing picking up the pieces of the broken platter, and when she was done, she and Little Maggie left the room. All was silent. The boys began to squirm under the stern gaze of their father. "Well," Papa said presently, "what happened to Larry's hair, and where did you all get the black robe he's wearing?"

"We got the robe from the church, and we just . . . well, we . . . we . . . we just forgot to put it back I guess." Larry said slowly.

Papa's eyebrows went up. "What happened to it?" he asked as he untied the rope around Larry's middle.

"It was just too long, Papa," Jim replied.

"I guess we cut it." Fred spoke with reluctance seeing that Papa was still waiting an answer.

Papa looked at Fred. "You guess? Don't you know what happened?" Fred hung his head miserably with a slight nod. There was a short silence as Papa held the robe Larry had taken off and looked at it. "Where is the rest of it?"

"In the woods, but I'll go get it," Ted offered eagerly turning as though to go. He would much rather be anywhere else at that moment than in the kitchen with Papa's questioning.

"Not yet, Ted," Papa spoke firmly. "I'm not finished. What happened to Larry's hair?"

"Papa, it just had to be cut!" Jim exclaimed. "How else could he be Friar Tuck?"

Papa didn't answer or even seem to hear. He was looking at Ted and Fred. "Boys," he said waiting.

At last Ted raised his eyes and confessed in a small voice, "I cut it."

"Where did the scissors come from?"

Larry spoke up then. "Fred borrowed them, Papa."

"Who did you borrow them from, Fred?" Papa wanted to know who it was that would lend one of "those Foster boys" such a thing as scissors!

"Mrs. Bernham," mumbled Fred with his head still down.

Papa looked at him keenly for a moment then asked quietly. "What did you tell her you needed them for?"

"I didn't." The reply was scarcely audible.

With a firm but gentle hand, Papa raised Fred's chin to look directly into his eyes. "Does she know you borrowed them?"

"Oh, she pro'bly does now," Jim broke in. "'Cause we left 'em in the forest."

"Jim, be quiet," Papa said sternly. "Fred?"

Fred's lip began to tremble. "No, sir." His voice began to break. "She wasn't home, but her mending was outside, and I . . . I . . . I stole them!" He could restrain himself no longer but flung himself into his father's arms with a burst of sobbing. For a few minutes Papa let him cry, then slowly but with firm insistence he drew the entire story from his sons.

"Papa," Fred asked at last. "May I please go get the scissors and take them back to Mrs. Bernham and 'poligize?"

"Yes, that would be the right thing to do. In fact," he added looking at the four sober boys before him, "I want you all to go get the scissors, and the rest of this robe.

Return the scissors, and all of you apologize."

"But I didn't take them," Ted interposed.

"You used them, didn't you?" Papa pointed out.

"And we helped forget them," Larry sighed.

Papa continued, "After you have been to Mrs. Bernham's, I want you to come straight home. Is that clear?"

Four heads nodded, but Ted wondered, "Can't we take the robe back, too?"

"With it looking like this and the minister not home?"

Ted squirmed. Papa looked at him, then addressed all the boys. "When you get back home, you can eat and then we'll talk about this all some more."

The boys learned a lesson that day that they never forgot. Not only did they each make a trip to the woodshed with Papa, but they had to work and earn enough money to buy the minister a new robe. Mrs. Bernham was very forgiving, but she no doubt wondered as did many villagers, "Will those four Foster boys ever live to grow up?" Larry had the hardest time of all for his hair did look dreadful, and it took many weeks for it to grow back.

The moral of the story is: always think of the possible consequences of your actions before you do them.

This is now a very long letter, and I still haven't finished! Mama said to thank you for sending the part from Uncle Frederick's letter about Uncle Philip. We had gotten a post card a month or so ago from him. You'd be surprised to see how much he could fit on one of those. Here it is in its entirety.

Leif Sister,

Oh I am faining to be up and about! As soon as Dr. Foster sanctions me to get up, I will enlist with the "Escadrille Americaine." I don't have any flying experience, but I could learn quickly I know. Perhaps you haven't heard, but they now have planes worthy of the German Fokkers. I fairly long to fly one! Those darling Nieuports. Helen, can't you convince Dr. Foster that I no longer require his service, nor will I consent to be sent to England! I will stay in France until this is over! Out of room. Au Revoir. - P.V.B.W. III

Now I have to end, for as you can see, there is no more room on this paper.
>Love and prayers,
>Emma

CHAPTER THIRTEEN

"Mom it's a good thing you weren't at Grandma and Grandpa's the last time I was over. Uncle Frank had caught a large snake and was showing it to the gang and me. I even held it."

Her mother shuddered at the thought.

Lydia cringed. "Oh, Ria, how could you! Snakes are so slimy and slippery."

"They aren't slimy at all. And they really aren't slippery. They just wiggle. They feel like, oh, rather like a piece of rubber, only nicer." She giggled at the comparison. "It is hard to say just what they feel like." Then with a sudden change of subject, she commented, "Uncle Philip Vincent Bartholomew Wallace the third still talks the same way even now. But, I'm ready for the next letter." She settled back to enjoy it while her mother and friend laughed.

Friday
October 13, 1916
Princeville, Nova Scotia
Canada

Dear Emma,

What a nice long letter you wrote. Lydia Ruth was quite delighted with the next "Ted, Fred, Larry and Jim" story. She is now asking for another one. I told her she would have to wait, for you couldn't spend all your time writing her stories. I can't believe Papa really did those things. Did Papa, Uncle Theodore and Uncle Lawrence really try to hang Uncle James? Edith said it's a wonder all four of them did live to grow up. I wonder if Mark would have been any different if he had brothers near his age. Perhaps someday Vincent's and Georgie's children will write stories about what they did. Though they may not have to if you keep writing them. I'll be sure to continue to save all these letters you are writing me.

Two snakes in the nests! Oh, Emma! I would have screamed too. I don't think I even would have waited for anyone to show up the first time. Mark and James laughed so hard about it all that I was obliged to stop reading for a time. Karl and Edmund seem to be getting on better together, and now you know a little of Karl and Kirsten's former life. Has Karl told you any more? Where on earth did Karl learn arithmetic so well? If he was only in school six weeks, it doesn't seem to me as though he would have had much of an opportunity to learn at all.

Are the children liking the new school? Who is the teacher? Is Georgie still as excited about school as he was before? Mark would like to know if Vincent and Georgie get into as much mischief at school as they do at home.

I don't see how your Uncle Philip could write all that on one post card. His writing must have been very small. Do you think he really will join the "Escadrille Americaine?" It sounds rather frightening to be in a machine in the sky high above the good earth. Why people want to fly like the birds, I don't know.

A new family has moved to Princeville. The house they live in is actually not truly in Princeville, being farther west along the coast than even our house, for our house is on the westernmost edge of the village. The Perkins family consists of Mr. Perkins (he is away at war), Mrs. Perkins (a thin, pale faced woman with an anxious look in her eyes and who is heavy with child), and six children. The oldest, Ruth, is thirteen years old! The closest girl to my age since we left

Tennessee! She is medium in height, thin and quiet. The second child is a boy, Thomas. Tom is only ten, although he looks at least twelve. He is a good-hearted boy despite his rough ways with strangers. It is quite apparent that his mother and sisters trust his judgment most of the time. He is undoubtedly the man of his family. The next one is seven-year-old Grace. Grace has trouble speaking and stutters and mixes her words up when she talks, consequentially, she is very shy. She seems to be of sweet temperament though. Anna is five. She speaks not a word of English but neither does Grace nor either of the other young ones. Hannah and Joseph, ages two and three respectively, finish the Perkins family. Both have large eyes and timid manners. Ruth speaks English better than anyone in the family. Tom understands more than he can speak, while Mrs. Perkins has a very limited knowledge of the language. They come from Quebec and speak French.

Ruth told me that they have moved around quite frequently. She and her mother do sewing when they can, and Tom does odd jobs. She said they moved here because Tom thought they could afford the rent. Nobody in the village thought the house could be rented, it is so old and set off by itself. The roof leaks in several places, some shutters have come off, and the whole place has a very dilapidated appearance. The Perkins' had been in the house for a week before anyone in the village knew it! Tom and Ruth came to try to find work, and since our house was the first one they came to, they stopped here first. Mama invited them in, asked several questions and ended up packing a basket with food as a welcome gift. Ruth was able to get work with Mrs. Lawson who is the town seamstress, and Tom found odd jobs around.

The next day being Friday, Mama, Lydia Ruth and I went to call on our new neighbors. Ruth and I got along well, and I believe if I am patient enough, I can win the little ones, for I do speak French. Mama speaks it as well. No one else in our family except Papa can speak or understand more than a few words of it. Lydia Ruth can't understand a word in French and yet she talked to the three youngest anyway. Grace stayed mostly out of sight behind Ruth or her mother. Oh, Emma, pray for Mama and me for none of the Perkins are Christians, and they are in such need of a Helper!

I had just written that last sentence yesterday when I was interrupted. There was a knock on the door and there stood Ruth and Tom, looking scared and worried.

"What is the matter?" I asked.

Ruth told me her mother needed help and begged me to come. What was I to do? Edith was in town, and Mama was with Grandmother. Mark was off somewhere with James, hopefully chopping wood. I couldn't leave Lydia Ruth at home by herself with Andrew, even if he was asleep for the time being. I had to think and act quickly.

"Tom, go to Mr. Stanly and tell him your mother needs Dr. McNeel right away. Lydia Ruth, go . . . no, wait a moment." I saw Heather Morris walking by. "Heather," I called, "can you please run to the Stewarts and see if Evelyn can come and watch Lydia Ruth and Andrew for me right away?"

She ran off to return a moment later with Evelyn. I knew I could safely leave the two little ones with her as she is a reliable girl. Leaving a note to be delivered to Mama, I hurried away with Ruth.

When we arrived rather breathless from running, we found Anna, Joseph and Hannah sitting on the old porch, sobbing. Anna wailed that she didn't want her mama to die! Poor little ones. They had never seen their mama sick like this. We only paused a moment to reassure them before going inside.

In a back bedroom, we found Grace and Mrs. Perkins. The child was nearly beside herself. I set Ruth to start a fire and Grace to fill the kettle. Oh, Emma, I can't tell you what all happened. I prayed as I had seldom prayed before. I was so thankful that Dr. McNeel had let me be there at the birth of the twins. All the same, I kept hoping Mama would come. I knew Dr. McNeel wouldn't be able to come yet, but I wanted someone else there. Ruth did what she could, but she was so worried, I'm afraid she was almost a hindrance at times. Grace just stayed crouched in a corner unless I needed her.

At last it was all over. Mrs. Perkins lay resting with her little baby girl beside her. Mama and the doctor arrived about the same time, nearly an hour after the baby had come. They named her Maria, though no one calls her anything but Baby, for now at least. Mrs. Perkins and Baby are doing well.

Now let me tell you about Andrew. He is sixteen months old and into absolutely everything! He is constantly on the go; anything he picks up must needs go into his mouth: bugs, sticks, rocks, sand, books, pencils, shoes, everything! Moreover, not only does it all go in his mouth, he bites it. Thankfully he hasn't been able to catch Lovey yet, though don't think he hasn't tried! One would get the impression that we never feed him, the way he tries to eat everything. The truth is, he eats more than Lydia Ruth ever did. He would eat all day if we let him. He doesn't talk much yet though he grunts and jabbers. The few words that he does say clearly enough to be understood are: "Mama," "no" (while his little head shakes back and forth) and "two more." Edith asked Andrew a few days ago if he wanted to eat.

Andrew said, "No," and shook his head vigorously. He then asked, "Two more?" For Andrew, "no," means yes most of the time.

He still has his dark hair, but his eyes are beginning to look more blue. Not only does Andrew toddle everywhere, he climbs. He climbs onto things, into things, over things, and under things. One day he actually climbed onto the dock and toddled toward the boats before anyone saw him. Thankfully, Sam Drinkwater was on the dock and caught him before he tumbled into the water. You can't take your eyes off of him for a moment unless he is asleep.

The McGuire twins are almost a year old. Now Rob

Roy is toddling around while William Wallace still creeps. They are both plump little things. I can't carry them both at once anymore. They still look strikingly identical. Only those of us who know them well can see the differences in them.

Six-year-olds Ross McIntyre and Henry Stewart are sick in bed with bad colds. They caught them playing outside in the cold rain several days ago. It is not at all warm here these days, and what the lads were doing out in the rain, no one quite seems to know. Mr. Morris saw them down on the beach playing. We are thankful neither of them got pneumonia. They are sick enough without that.

We had a letter from one of Mama's sisters in which she copied from Uncle's letter about what trench life was like. I thought of the boys when I read it.

You ask what trench life is like? In one word: hell! Words cannot describe it. You are always dirty; when it rains you are drenched as you stand in the sticky mud that at times comes past your ankles. The stench is utterly beyond description. You don't have time to bury the dead, the rats are constantly around and you dare not lose consciousness for even one minute. Your clothes are covered with lice. You can get rid of them about as easily as you can the flies by the pigpen back home. I don't know which is worse, the noise of bombardments or the unearthly stillness that falls sometimes. The barrages might mean death, but you don't duck any more, for you'll die just the same standing or ducking. They say you never hear the one that gets you. How would they know? They've never been hit. You soon learn to tell which shells will go over you and which ones won't. Just the same, the noise gets on your nerves. Many boys have been sent to the rear for shell shock. The shells aren't what bothers me. It is the quiet. You stand in the trench, knowing the enemy are coming, and yet you can see nothing, hear nothing. All is still and dark. Not a cricket chirps. Not a frog croaks. Not a bird twitters. There is no rustle of grass or leaves, for there is no grass or leaves to rustle. You know your comrades are on either side of you, yet you dare not move your eyes for fear the enemy is waiting just for that. You strain your eyes, trying to pierce the blackness. Finally the fight comes. Perhaps you are ordered over the top. Somehow you take another trench. What do you get for your pains? Nothing. It is worse maybe than the last one you left, perhaps with even some deadly gas in the bottom of it. And it may be a few days, or maybe only a few hours or minutes before the enemy drives you out again. You lose many comrades and you know that you might be next! That is what trench life is like.

I am so thankful that Papa is not in those trenches!

Oh, it has begun to snow! I wonder if the Perkins have enough wood? I'll have to ask Mark as he and James went to help Tom cut it. Perhaps I ought to go over and make sure they are all right. I should check on Mrs. Perkins and Baby anyway before the snow gets too heavy. Emma, pray that I'll have an opportunity to share Christ's love with the Perkins family. I'm sorry this is so short. Give my love to everyone.

Your affectionate cousin,
Maria

"Oh, Mom, don't we have time for just one more letter?"

Mrs. Mitchell shook her head. "I'm afraid not if Lydia has to be home by 5:00, for the next one seems to be quite long. Besides, I really don't have much voice left."

Both girls groaned and sighed. "Thanks for reading them to us, Mrs. Mitchell," Lydia smiled.

Returning the smile, Mrs. Mitchell gathered the letters and departed leaving the two friends alone. A silence fell on them to be broken when Mrs. Mitchell opened the screen door again and putting her head out spoke.

"Ria, don't forget the gang is going to be here on Monday, so I won't be able to read any letters that day."

"That's okay. I think I have an idea of who to write about anyway. But, Mom, where can we work?"

"Perhaps you can work at Lydia's house."

"My mom is going to be gone all day on Monday. She was hoping I could stay here until Dad can pick me up after work." Lydia looked worried.

"I know, Mom! We can work at Corporal's house! I almost know he would let us. I think he was listening to the letters from his yard for a while today. Don't you think he would?"

"He might. Why don't you run over and ask? If it won't work, you'll just have to do the best you can here."

"That would be a disaster if they are all coming." Ria protested and then laughed. "Come on Lydia, let's go ask him. He mentioned some forgotten heroes earlier, and I want to see if I'm thinking of the same ones!"

Corporal gave ready assent to having the two girls work at his house. Ria was a favorite of his, and more than once he had "rescued" her from the gang. Any friend of Ria's was more than welcome to join her. Ria loved spending time at Corporal's home. He seemed to be all alone and almost never spoke of his family or his past, yet she knew it was never far from him. She had seen a faraway look in his eyes on many occasions though it vanished when she spoke. He had told her his family had all died, and he was alone except for friends like her.

Ria's idea of who to write their report on met

with both Corporal and Lydia's approval. In fact, Lydia and Ria spent the remaining time they had talking over their report with him. By the time Chris was ready to accompany them in escorting Lydia home, they were eager to get started.

Both girls worked diligently on their report Monday afternoon, and when Lydia's father came to pick her up, they were quite pleased with their progress.

"Of course we'll have to wait until Mom reads more of the letters before we can really finish it."

Lydia nodded. "My mom said she would like to come over if it was all right."

"Can she come tomorrow? Oh, Lydia, that would be fun! I do hope she can."

"Mom," Ria queried with her foot on the bottom step of the stairs. "Why won't Corporal talk about his experiences in the war or even his family?"

"Things like that are difficult for someone to think about sometimes. Grandpa doesn't talk much about the war. Things happened that he would rather forget. Perhaps that is how it is with Corporal."

"He doesn't even talk of his family that died, but I know he thinks of them, for sometimes he just sits and stares at the picture of them."

Mrs. Mitchell looked thoughtful. "Ria, it is often hard to talk about the hard things that have happened to us. Perhaps his family died while he was gone to war or maybe in a tragic accident."

"I've often wondered what happened to them, but he looks so sad when he looks at the picture that I haven't asked.

"That's a good idea. If he wants to tell about them, he will. Now, you had better get off to bed. I don't want you falling asleep in school tomorrow."

CHAPTER FOURTEEN

The following afternoon found Mrs. Smith in a rocker on the front porch of the Mitchell home listening with a face as interested as the two girls on the porch swing.

Wednesday
November 8, 1916
Codell, Kansas
USA

Dearest Maria,

I just got your letter, and I wanted to write to you now. I shudder at the thought of the trenches. Whoever thought of having them to begin with? I'm thankful America isn't in the war. Have you gotten any letters from England lately? We just got a rather long one from Grandma and Grandpa Foster, and they said to send it on to you. So I am enclosing it. Grandma tells about more zeppelin raids only this time they were over London. But I will let you read it. She doesn't tell much about the others. Perhaps we'll get a letter from someone else. Maybe they did write, and the boat they were on was torpedoed. The boat the letters were on, I mean. It could have happened if they were on a British ship. Or just about any other ship. Did you hear about the German U-boat that sank three British ships, one Dutch ship and one Norwegian ship off the coast of Rhode Island last month? None of the crewmen were lost, and it brought several U.S. destroyers over there. I had no idea German U-boats were so close! Do you think there are any near Nova Scotia? If I had time, I would worry about you. But, of course, even a U-boat can't sink the land.

Oh, the elections are over now. Daddy and Mama voted for Charles Evans Hughes, and he won! He was the Republican choice. I didn't pay much attention to the elections. I know that President Roosevelt didn't end up running. Mr. Hughes didn't exactly say we would go to war, but he wants to be prepared just in case it happens. President Wilson had a slogan that was "He kept us out of war." I sometimes wonder if he would have ever led the nation to war if it came to that or if he would just try to talk his way out of it.

There are only fifteen days until Thanksgiving, if I count today, which I should as it is still morning. The children are at school, and the little girls are playing in the other room. Daddy has the boys all out working on something outside. I think Mama is still mending. I was helping her, but I'm afraid I was talking too much. I was thinking of all the things I was going to tell you and saying them aloud to help me remember them. Mama finally started laughing and said,

"For mercy sakes, Emma, go write that letter. If you wait much longer, you will have so many things to say, you'll run out of room again."

So I came here to write. Here, is at the desk in the parlor. Last time I ran out of room, and I didn't have any more paper, so I just had to stop.

I was going to tell you we loved "trying" to read Alan's letter. And "trying" is about right. It took several readings from different ones before we understood it all. We did enjoy it. If you send any more of his letters, please leave them in Scottish. Daddy always looks forward to hearing from Uncle Frederick's letters. Speaking of Uncle Frederick, I have written the "Ted, Fred, Larry and Jim" story you asked about. I don't know if I'll have time or room to include it in this letter, but if not, I'll try for the next one. I am going to send the four "Ted, Fred, Larry and Jim" stories that I have written so far to Grandma and Grandpa. Daddy thinks they will enjoy them. How many have I sent you?

In answer to your question about Vincent and Georgie in school, yes, they do behave. At least they have so far. They know that if they get in trouble at school, they'll get in trouble at home. The teacher is Paul Kingston. He isn't married, and Carrie said he is rather quiet. She likes him and thinks the other children do too. That is good as it makes--

Oh, I don't know what I was going to say. A neighbor stopped by and told Daddy that rumors in Codell are that the election results are still not certain. I don't know how that could be. Why would the newspapers say Hughes had already won if he hadn't? If Mr. Hughes didn't win, that would mean President Wilson would stay president for four more years. I don't know if that would be good or bad; I don't pay much attention to politics.

So there's a new family in Princeville, and a girl your own age, well close to it! That must be such fun. We are all praying for them and you and Aunt Amelia. Have you made friends with the younger ones? Are any of them going to school? Now you have a namesake. What does she look like? I miss having a baby around the house. I can hardly wait until spring. Rosalie is definitely not a baby anymore. She is three and a half years old!

I completely forgot until now to tell you that Montana now has a woman Congressman in the U.S. Senate! I think her name is Jeannette Rankin or something like that. She is the first woman to ever be elected to Congress. I believe she is a Republican. Isn't Montana where you have an aunt and uncle living?

Little Andrew is growing up quickly. He sounds like so much fun! Rosalie certainly never put things in her mouth as you say Andrew does. Maybe Andrew will be like Vincent and Georgie when he gets older. I can almost picture him leading the McGuire twins into mischief as they all get bigger. Hopefully they won't try what Daddy and his brothers did. Daddy said he doesn't think they ever did the same thing twice. They still managed to get into enough scrapes as it was.

Yes, I do think that Uncle Philip, if he is able, will join that flying group. He has always been ready to try anything new, Mama said. I think it might be rather exciting to fly in an airplane someday. Perhaps I shall get the chance before I'm old and gray-headed. Though by then I might have too much sense to want to.

There hasn't been much happening here. The weather can't decide if it should be cold or warm. I wish it would make up its mind. I am ready for a fire in the fireplace and the cozy times we all spend together around it in the evenings. Karl and Kirsten have never experienced the pleasure of our family evenings in the winter. David asked Karl if they (he and Kirsten) had ever had a large Thanksgiving feast. Karl shook his head and asked,

"What do you have?"

Then you should have seen his face as David and Edmund tried to list everything we have on Thanksgiving. After they couldn't think of anything else to add, Karl looked from one to the other then scoffed,

"You don't have all that at one meal."

"Oh, yes we do," David assured.

Edmund added, "You should see our plates on Thanksgiving! Really, you almost couldn't see them last year."

I don't know if Karl really believes them or not. It will be delightful to see what he thinks when we sit down to eat.

Well, here it is after dinner and this still isn't done. I had taken this letter into the kitchen where I could write a sentence now and again as I made dinner. When Daddy and the boys came in, it was still sitting on the end of the table. Edmund picked it up and read it.

"To see if it was all right," he told me. After he had

read it, he said it was "rambly."

"I know it is, but I don't have any longer stories to tell her."

"Humph," he grunted sliding into his seat.

After the blessing, when everyone was eating, I turned to him and said, "If I could think of anything interesting to tell her I would."

"What about you and Carrie?"

"What?" I wasn't sure just what he was talking about.

"In the kitchen last week?" he prompted.

"Oh Edmund, not that," I protested.

"She would probably find it quite entertaining."

"But I don't want to tell her that," I began.

David interrupted. "Why not? You tell on us."

"But this is different," I tried to argue.

Edmund cut me short. "If you don't tell her . . ."

"What, will you write the story for her?" I teased. You know how often Edmund writes you.

"I just might," he replied unexpectedly.

Before I could say anything David said, "I'll help."

"So will I," Karl added.

There was only one thing to say, and I said it. "All right, I'll tell her." You might wonder why I didn't just let the boys tell it. Well, they all had that look in their eyes, and I knew they would probably make it all sound worse than it really was, though it was bad enough, and so as not to be too humiliated, I'll just write it myself.

Carrie and I were making supper. I have forgotten what day it was. All were outside except the two of us. Carrie was tired and very distracted with the multiplication tables of seven and eight. I was also tired and my mind was somewhere else. Where it was, I can't recall, but it wasn't on supper. Neither one of us was paying much attention to what we or the other one was doing or had done. I know, that means disaster. We were making biscuits, stewed chicken and vegetables. Not a hard meal you might think; we didn't think so either. When it was about ready, Carrie rang the dinner bell. The little girls had already set the table so when all were in and ready, we could eat.

As Edmund sat down, he nudged me and whispered, "Just what <u>are</u> we having?"

I didn't have time to reply. David asked the blessing, and Daddy began to serve. It looked all right. The smell seemed slightly different, but I thought that might just be my imagination. Georgie, I think, was the first to taste the chicken. He chewed it really quickly, got a drink and blurted out,

"What did we feed that chicken 'fore we killed it?"

"Why?" Daddy asked.

"'Cause it doesn't taste good."

Everyone began tasting it. It was indeed terrible. There was a sweet and yet bitter taste to it. I didn't know what I had done. Someone tried the biscuits, but they were completely unfit. The only thing that tasted all right were the green beans. I was nearly in tears. What had happened? Mama was cautiously tasting the chicken and biscuits, thoughtfully chewing each bite.

"Carrie, how much salt did you put in these biscuits?"

Carrie looked bewildered. "I don't know."

Mama nodded. "Emma, did you salt or sugar the chicken?"

"Salt, I think, Mama."

"What did you thicken it with?"

"Flour."

Mama looked at us a moment and then began to laugh. She laughed and laughed, and before long almost everyone was laughing. I didn't feel like laughing. What was so humorous about a ruined supper? Mama finally managed to say between chuckles, "Oh, girls! Where was your common sense tonight? Here Carrie has salted the biscuits so much I don't know if the dogs will even eat them. And Emma! You sugared the chicken and thickened it with soda!" Then she laughed some more. "Come, girls. Let's clear this away and find something more suitable to eat."

There you have it. I don't know how Mama could laugh over it all, but she still chuckles when it gets mentioned. Nothing like that has ever happened before and hopefully it never will again! I don't know why the boys wanted it sent to you, but it's done now.

Now, as I really can't think of anything else I was going to tell you (though I probably will as soon as I send this off), I'll copy the "Ted, Fred, Larry and Jim" story for your entertainment. This one takes place only a week or so before the "Robin Hood" story.

It was a rainy day, drizzly and dreary, at least for Ted, Fred, Larry and Jim. They were tired of playing inside. There they must be quiet, for Little Maggie was taking a nap.

"Please, Mama," Ted begged, "may we go outside? We'll wear our mackintosh and rubbers."

"And hats," pleaded Fred.

Mama looked wearily at the four restless boys. It was so hard to keep them busy inside. "All right," she consented at last. "If you promise to be careful and not to go too far away."

There was an excited chorus of "We won't," "We will," "Where's my hat," "Thanks Mama,"; a mad scramble for boots, hats and mackintoshes, and then the four Foster boys were outside at last!

"Now, what shall we do?" Jim asked, stomping in a puddle and watching with delight as it splashed about his boots.

"Let's go there," Ted pointed to a small cluster of trees. "So don't 'stirb Little Maggie." Ted never bothered speaking in complete sentences all the time when he was just with his brothers. Why should he? They didn't care, and they knew what he meant.

Once among the trees, Jim again asked, "What shall we do?"

All four were silent, thinking. "Well, could play War of the Roses," Ted suggested slowly.

"No," Fred disagreed.

"We could play we're fighting for Prince Charlie in Scotland," was Larry's idea. Ted shook his head.

"Those Scottish people talk funny anyway," Fred pointed out.

"What if," Ted began, "just play soldiers. Lots can happen. Just make it up as we play."

That seemed like a good idea to the other three, and it was quickly decided that a nearby stump would be headquarters. Everything went on wonderfully for an hour or so. Battles were fought and won, injured were made well, and a whole militaristic air pervaded the yard. Eventually though, Ted and Fred longed for a little more excitement. Larry, they decided, would be a captured prisoner of war. They tied his hands behind him and blindfolded him. Then his guard, Jim, ordered, "Forward march."

Larry marched forward. Somewhat hesitantly it is true, for he was wondering and hoping he might not run into a tree. At last Jim told him to halt.

"He's an enemy soldier all right," growled a voice that sounded somewhat like Fred's.

"How many men were in your army?" questioned General Ted.

"I don't know."

"Larry," Fred burst out. "You aren't supposed to say that. Either say you won't tell or just don't talk."

"Okay."

"How many men in your army?" General Ted said again.

Larry didn't answer.

"I asked you a question, enemy soldier," roared General Ted. "Now you had better answer me!"

Larry trembled a little. Ted sounded really mad. Should he tell him? Fred said not to, and Larry really didn't know how many men there were supposed to be in the enemy army. No one had told him. Oh, how he wished he wasn't blindfolded. Then he heard Jim make a little noise as though trying not to laugh. That gave him courage, and he said, "I won't tell you nothing!"

"The im . . . prudence of him!" Fred exclaimed, believing he had the right word. "We cannot let it go unpunished, General."

"I should say not! He will face a firing squad at dawn tomorrow," was the grim answer of the deep-voiced General.

Suddenly it was dawn, and Larry was led away.

" Now, Larry," Ted told him, "when we fire our guns, fall down dead."

"But I want to still play," he begged. "Can't I play anymore?"

"'Course, you'll be someone else."

That sounded fine to Larry, so when the three boys went "bang," he fell down, right in a mud puddle from which he was promptly extricated and told he was great. That was the first of many firing squads. Larry was shot several more times as was Jim, and even Ted and Fred tried it. Finally even that became rather dull, and they all paused to think of something new to add.

As Ted looked around, his eye chanced to fall on a long piece of rope. "What could . . . use that for?" he mumbled more to himself than aloud. "That tree . . . just the thing!" Then to the others, "Let's have a spy come and hang him."

Fred thought that would be great fun. Larry and Jim weren't so sure. Past experience had taught them that they would most likely be the victims. Their hesitation however was unnoticed by their brothers. They were busy already getting the new idea ready. Fred climbed the tree and Ted tossed the rope to him.

"Ted," Fred called down, "let's just put the rope over the branch so we can pull the spy up."

"Okay," Ted agreed. He was busy fastening a noose at the other end.

Fred scrambled down the tree and asked, "Who's

going to be the spy?"

"I can't," Ted said, "couldn't pull me up."

"Me either," Fred added quickly.

"Well, Larry's too fat. Never get him up," Ted noted. "Have to be Jim."

Now, Larry really wasn't fat. He was only stockier than his brothers. Sometimes, like today, Larry was glad about it, but at others times he wished he were as lean as Ted, Fred and Jim.

"Why me?" Jim quavered.

"'Cause only small people like you can be spies. They can hide better."

"Oh," Jim wasn't too sure about this whole idea.

"Now, Jim," Ted instructed. "We'll close our eyes. You hide. Then try and sneak past us."

Jim tried, but Fred saw him, and he was captured. After a "trial," he was "sennenst" to be hung. Ted put the noose around Jim's neck, and then he and Fred grabbed the rope behind him.

Just then Larry burst forth, "I don't want to play this anymore."

"Or me," Jim added.

"We have to hang our spy first," Fred said.

But Larry wouldn't help. On the count of three, Ted and Fred pulled the rope, and Jim was soon dangling between the tree branch and the earth. Jim's hands weren't tied, and he desperately tried to pull the rope off his neck.

"Boys! Let go now!" The sharp command startled the hangmen, and they let go of the rope. Jim fell with a thud to the ground and lay still. Papa hastily tore the rope off his neck and helped him to his feet. After quickly making sure he was all right, Papa looked at the other boys.

Larry whimpered, "I didn't want to play it."

Ted and Fred squirmed miserably under the stern gaze of their father's eyes which had now turned a steel blue. All was silent save for the pit, pat, pat of a light rain on the leaves of the trees. At last Papa spoke. His voice was quiet.

"Larry and Jimmie, go to the house and get into dry clothes. You are both soaked to the skin in spite of your mackintosh, boots and hats."

The two little boys turned to obey, both wondering if they were in trouble. Then they heard Papa speak again. His voice was still quiet, but stern. "Theodore, Frederick, come with me." As Larry and Jim reached the house, they looked back and saw Papa leading the way toward the woodshed. What happened in there Larry and Jim never knew, but never again did Ted or Fred suggest they play hanging anyone. And for quite a while afterwards they only had pretend enemies. Thankfully Jim suffered no harm other than a few bruises about his neck.

And there is the story. I hear the school children coming, so I think I will close.

With much love and prayers,
Emma

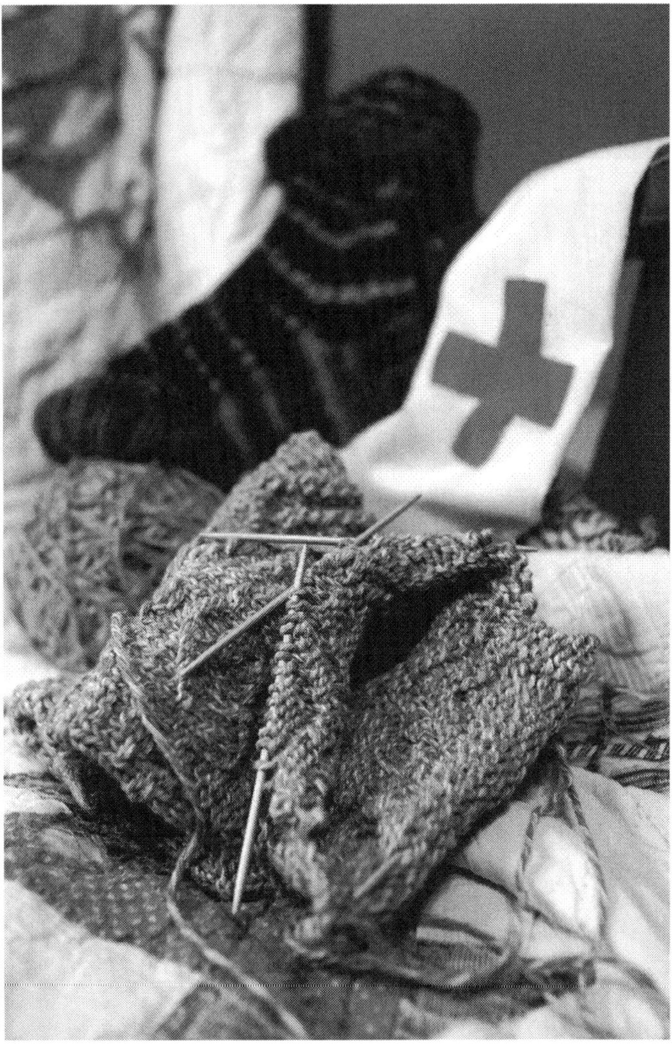

CHAPTER FIFTEEN

A relieved sigh was heard across the porch as the story ended.

"How could they do that?" Ria was indignant. "They could have killed him!"

"My father said many times that it was a wonder to the entire town that all four of them lived to grow up. God was certainly good to our family by protecting them in their youth as they did enough crazy things to kill them all. If that had happened, we wouldn't be sitting here today," Mrs. Mitchell remarked thoughtfully.

After a moment of silence, she continued reading.

Friday
December 1, 1916
Princeville, Nova Scotia
Canada

My Dear Cousin Emma,

This is an entirely new place from which to write you. I am in Pictou. I came with Edith today to help at the Red Cross. You see, Mabel and Amelia Burn couldn't come, and Edith asked me if I would go with her and Sheena McIntyre. It has been quite an interesting experience. If you'll believe it,

I have never been to the Red Cross headquarters here in Pictou. Oh, I have helped at home knitting socks and such but have been too busy to come into town with the older girls. The place has been simply swarming today. I can look up even now that it is getting late and see a few people still at work. The last Christmas packages for the troops have been sent out now. I imagine you are wondering why I am writing and not helping. The only reason is that I have finished my assigned tasks. Edith and Sheena both have some other things to attend to, and I have been left to my own devices for the time being.

Your letter was a pleasure, as always, to read. All were silent and quite riveted as I read the last "Ted, Fred, Larry and Jim" episode. When it was over and Jim was safe and unharmed, Mark exclaimed,

"I can't believe Papa tried to hang his own brother! Didn't he know what would happen?"

I don't see how they could do such things either! Think of what they are all doing now; Uncle Theodore is working in some intelligence group or some such thing, Papa is serving as doctor and surgeon in France, Uncle Lawrence is a Kansas farmer raising food for the country, and Uncle James is fighting somewhere for England. Quite a change occurred in each life. Speaking of changes, I have a story to tell you.

This took place only last week. It was a beautiful winter day. The snow was a dazzling white under the sun's bright rays. The sky a pale blue with white wisps of clouds scattered here and there. The air was cold and crisp. I was outside. It was too lovely to stay indoors. The children were in school, and everything was so quiet and peaceful. Even the sea was fairly calm; the gentle sound of the lapping waves added only to the delightful sense of tranquility. The snow crunched under my boots pleasantly as I wandered along. I didn't really have any particular place I was going; I simply wanted to get outside. Therefore I wandered, enjoying each moment alone. Thinking about it, I realized I had not been out in the snow alone yet this winter for more than a few moments. Eventually I found myself near the Perkins' home. Pausing, I was debating with myself whether or not I should stop when the door opened and Ruth appeared.

"Oh, Maria, have you come to visit us? Do say you will stay!" There was pleading in her voice.

That decided me, and I waded through the last snowdrift to the porch. The kitchen felt quite toasty after the outside cold. Mrs. Perkins greeted me with a smile. Almost before I knew it, I was bereft of my wraps and settled in a chair with Baby in my arms before a bright fire. Ruth sat on a stool at my feet while the young ones clustered on the floor about us. Even Grace was there. It has taken much time and patience, but at last she no longer hides when I am there. Tom sat nearby whittling. Mrs. Perkins had taken up her sewing, and all looked and felt so pleasant.

"Maria," Anna said softly. "It's almost Christmas."

"Yes, it is," I smiled. "I love Christmas time, don't you?"

Joseph tugged on my skirt. "Tell story? Yes?"

I smiled again. Joseph did like stories. So did the others. "What should I tell about?" I asked, shifting Baby to the other arm.

"A Ch . . . Ch . . . Christmas one," stammered Grace in a voice scarce above a whisper.

At that moment I knew the only Christmas story worth telling was the very first one. The sun shone in brightly at the window as I began. I told it all as interestingly and yet as simply as I could. They sat spellbound as I told of Mary and Joseph, no room at the inn, the stable, the shepherds and angels, the star and the wise men from the East. I told why Jesus had to come and ended with the story of the cross and the resurrection. There had been no interruptions during the entire story, and even when it was over, no one was inclined to break the spell that seemed to have fallen over the little group. I prayed silently. Mrs. Perkins, I noticed, had dropped her sewing sometime before and now sat staring into the fire heedless of the tears which trickled down her pale cheeks. Ruth also looked into the fire. On her face was a look of distress and awe mingled with a longing which made it quite a study. A log fell apart, breaking the silence and sending a little shower of sparks up the chimney.

"It is getting late," I said quietly. "I must be going or Mama will worry."

Rising, I laid Baby gently in her bed and put on my wraps. Mrs. Perkins remained motionless, apparently deeply lost in thought. The younger children remained still as well, though their eyes followed my every move. Ruth went with me to the door. As I laid my hand on the door knob, she whispered,

"He did that for me?"

"Yes."

"He loved me that much?"

"Yes."

"Does He want me?"

Again I answered affirmatively. She appeared almost unable to grasp that fact. Not another word was spoken by her as I opened the door and again stepped out into that wonderful world of glistening snow.

I went home thoughtful. Would the seed I had sown bear fruit? That evening I shared with the others what had happened, and we spent some time in prayer for the Perkins family before bed. That night a snowstorm came up, and the next morning I wasn't able to get to the Perkins' again as I had hoped.

On Sunday, after the service at church, Ruth came to me and whispered,

"I did it. I gave myself to Him, and He took me!" Her eyes were aglow with a new light and her smile was radiant.

Oh, Emma, words can't express the joy that filled my heart over those words! Mrs. Perkins too, has said, "Yes" to the Lord Jesus!

After telling you that, everything seems commonplace

now, almost of no importance.

Who did win the Presidency? It might have been mentioned in the papers, but I haven't read the papers for some time. Were the rumors right? How could they be?

Your letters are always so bright and cheery. Do thank Edmund, David and Karl for me, for making you tell me what you and Carrie did. So your mind still wanders sometimes as it used to, does it? That story had the entire village chuckling. No, I didn't tell it, it was all Lydia Ruth's doing. She and Edana McIntyre went from house to house, unknown to the rest of us, and at each one, Lydia Ruth sat down and immediately told the story of how her cousins made supper. The story must have been well told by her, for when Mrs. McLean asked Mama about it, the facts were correct. Lydia Ruth is becoming quite the storyteller. I can just picture the boys all laughing, and you, Emma dear, are probably wondering why you ever listened to them in the first place and have resolved never to listen . . .

Mrs. Mitchell turned the page over and then began looking around. "I don't have the rest of this letter. Did I drop it?"

Both girls began to look. "I don't see it anywhere, Mom. Maybe it is somewhere else."

"It must be. Hmm," Mrs. Mitchell looked at the girls. "I can go on and we can search for this later, though it's doubtful that we'll find it, or we can stop."

"Oh, please go on," Lydia begged.

Sunday
New Year's Eve, 1916
Codell, Kansas
USA

My Dear Maria,

I have decided to be different with this letter and write

it in two years. Right now it is a little past eleven o'clock at night. All is quiet here save for the crackling fire and the occasional low voices of the boys. The little boys are in bed as are the little girls. Carrie is asleep on the sofa. We are to awaken her a few minutes before the new year. Mama and Daddy are both sleeping, at least I think they are. I haven't seen them for several hours. It is rather dim here in the front room. The lamp near me is lit so that I can write. There is another light on, but it is turned down low. The boys are gathered near the fireplace. This is the last of the year, Maria. In less than an hour it will be 1917! The year 1916 will be history forever. What does this new year hold? Do you ever long to know what will happen in the days and months ahead and yet dread to know at the same time? That's how I am feeling right now. What will I be doing at this time next year? What will we all be doing?

Edmund just came to see if I was writing anything worth reading and said, "Emma! The next year hasn't even begun! Don't go wondering about the end of 1917 when we haven't even started the first of its 365 days!"

All right, I'll write about something else.

Let me see. Oh yes, President Wilson did win the elections. We were rather disappointed. As I understand it, California hadn't counted all their votes by the time the eastern papers went to press, and at that point it looked like Hughes had won. It wasn't until Friday that Wilson's victory was sure. It was a close race. We shall see what Wilson does this term.

I was reading your letter aloud to everyone, but when I reached the part about Lydia Ruth telling that cooking story, I refused to read it aloud. I stopped in some confusion as I saw where the sentence led. Edmund said I turned red, but Mama said it was only pink. Anyway, I tried to find a safe place to begin again. I turned to the last page but alas, I dropped that other page, and who do you think picked it up? That is right, it was Edmund. He was in a teasing mood that night, for instead of handing it back to me, he picked it up, moved farther away from me, found the place and began reading. It would have amused you, could you have heard the laughter and teasing that went on. Daddy finally put a stop to it all and let me finish the letter. Oh yes, I can laugh about it all now. And their teasing never really bothered me, but don't let Edmund know that.

Only fifteen minutes until next year!

I should tell you all about our Christmas. But where and when should I start? The usual things happened throughout the first part of December, except for trying to secretly make gifts for everyone. That can be rather hard, both thinking of gifts and making them, since there are eleven people in our family. This was Karl and Kirsten's first real Christmas.

Karl said they "never did nothin' back where they lived. Nothin' worth mentioning any ways."

It was so funny to walk around the house and see someone suddenly whisk something under their apron and try to look innocent or to have a door shut in your face while someone called out,

"Just a minute, you can't come in yet."

Even the barn held secrets. There the boys, big and small, would station themselves for hours allowing none but Daddy to enter. My favorite place to work was in the attic, pardon me, the garret. Way in the back near the chimney is a little place I cleared among the boxes and old stuff stored there. There is a window, one of the two which are supposed to lighten the attic, which has a seat in front of it. I washed the window so it was clean. There I spent many hours working on Christmas gifts. I could also see the barn from the window and could keep an eye on who went in or out.

Only three minutes until the new year! Carrie is awake now. Karl said he's never stayed awake until another year. Now only one minute!

Happy New Year, Maria! Now I ought to put a new date on the letter.

Monday, January 1, 1917

How fun! Have you ever had a letter written in two years? I haven't.

Oh, David just said it is snowing! Snow just minutes into the new year! We are going to do something. I'll write more later. Don't worry, we won't get into mischief as this is David's idea.

Good morning, Maria! Yes, it was morning when I stopped, but after we came in, we all went to bed. I really did intend to write your entire letter last night, but I didn't know David had an idea. Seeing though that I didn't get it written, I'll try to finish now. Let me tell you what we did as you are most likely wondering.

Quietly we all got our coats on and slipped outside. David had a lantern and led us out to the orchard. Carrie clung to my hand shivering with excitement. Where were we going? What did David have in mind? Not a word was spoken until we were all gathered under an old tree.

"Here is the new year," David said setting the lantern down and looking around.

"Looks rather like last year to me," commented Edmund.

"But it wasn't snowing last year," reminded Carrie archly. She turned her face up to the sky and squinted against the cold flakes.

"Now," David whispered, "let's each think of something we would like to do this year. I'll write them down and at the end of the year we'll see if any of our wishes came true." That was rather a long speech for David. He pulled out a small piece of paper and a pencil stub. "Karl, can you hold the lantern? Thanks. Let's start with the youngest. Carrie?"

Carrie thought only a moment before saying, "I want a brother or sister to share my birthday."

"Perhaps Georgie will. If he had two birthdays a year, maybe it would make him bigger." (Edmund was referring to Georgie's latest idea. He knows he is older every time he has a birthday, so one day he asked if he could have two birthdays a year. "That way I'd grow faster.")

We all began laughing but quickly hushed as the sound of it seemed twice as loud in the still quiet darkness around us.

"Karl?"

Karl was quiet for some time. "I want to stay here with Kirsten." He spoke so low that we had to strain our ears even in the stillness to hear him.

"Karl, we couldn't manage without your help. You and Kirsten are part of the family now, and I for one, don't want you ever to leave!" Edmund had placed his arm across Karl's shoulders as he spoke.

"I agree," David said. Carrie and I nodded. Karl wants to stay! Never before had we been completely sure he really liked it here.

"Emma?"

"David," I exclaimed softly but with pretended indignation. "Edmund is younger than I am. Just because he is taller, doesn't mean he has become older."

David bowed. "I beg your pardon. Edmund, it seems to be your turn."

Edmund didn't even pause to think. "I want to be as quick at arithmetic as Karl is."

Then it was my turn. What would I say? I couldn't think of anything at first. "I want to do something I have never done before."

Edmund just couldn't resist the chance to tease. "You could hold a snake." He made sure he backed to the other side of Karl as he said it. I let it go. Perhaps I would hold a snake this year, just to show him I could if I wanted to. I don't think I want to though.

David spoke then. "I want to buy a farm."

"Why?" Carrie asked.

"Isn't there enough work here?" added Edmund.

The lantern light shone on David's thoughtful face. "There's plenty of work. One reason is that I want to see if I can do it. I won't know unless I try. I'm almost seventeen, and I want to know if I really could do it."

"Do you want one as big as this?" I questioned. I was sure he could do it if he wanted to.

"Well, not quite," he smiled. "This is rather large to start on."

"The land isn't even all cleared," Edmund remarked.

"I know, but Daddy has been talking about clearing another section of it this year to plant more wheat."

"That will be a job!"

We lapsed into silence. Carrie yawned.

"I'm getting cold."

We all were. Quietly we made our way back to the house, put out the lights and went to bed. I didn't want to get up when it was time. Remind me to not stay up until next year again.

We are rejoicing with you over the Perkins family! Has Tom made a decision yet? Would you pray for Karl and Kirsten? Neither one has, that we know of, accepted Jesus Christ as Savior. Karl is silent when we have family prayers. He has such control over his emotions that one can never tell just what he is thinking. As for Kirsten, since she doesn't speak, it is always a guessing game about her thoughts. She seems to have no fear of any of us now and even appears less afraid of those we see regularly in Codell. One thing Kirsten does not fear is animals, of any kind. Big or small, she makes friends with them. I have seen her outside with bread crumbs in her open hands and birds landing on them to eat it.

Did I finish telling you about Christmas? I don't think I did. Our celebration began really on the 23rd. Mama and I got up very early to make figgy pudding as a surprise for Daddy. It was hard to make it quietly so he wouldn't wake up. When at last it was in the oven, Mama and I went back to bed. However, I couldn't sleep. I was so worried something would happen to it. Carrie woke up a little more than an hour before Mama and Daddy usually arise. On seeing that I was awake, she crept into my bed where we could whisper. It wasn't long before one of Carrie's best ideas occurred. Silently we dressed and slipped downstairs skipping the steps that creaked. While Carrie set the table and decorated it with pine cones, candles and pine branches, I filled the wood boxes and brought in water. I then laid things out for breakfast. We had just finished all we could do when we began to hear stirring from upstairs. With beating hearts and stifled giggles, we put out the lights and crept out of the room. We didn't dare go upstairs for fear of running into someone. Going instead into the cold front room, we huddled together behind the door and waited. We didn't have long to wait. Daddy's steps were heard followed by Mama's.

"Now, what . . . ?" we heard Daddy exclaim. "Helen, you didn't need to do all this. You should have been resting."

Mama's soft voice replied, "I didn't do this. Perhaps it was Emma. See, the wood box is full and there is water. One of the boys must have gotten up."

Carrie could scarcely keep back her giggles. We heard the boys begin descending the stairs slowly. They no sooner entered the kitchen when they were asked,

"Who got up early and brought wood and water in and started the fire?"

All denied having done it or even knowing about it. Carrie and I could wait no longer, and we too entered the kitchen trying not to act suspicious.

"Did you girls . . ." Daddy began, but was interrupted by Carrie saying gleefully,

"Happy twenty-third of December!"

Merry voices soon filled the room as Carrie and I explained. When Daddy found out it really was figgy pudding in the oven, he urged the boys to get the chores done quickly. Daddy loved the figgy pudding. There was none left after breakfast.

Later that day, all of us except Mama went out to find a tree. We found just the right one. Once it was up in the front room, we decorated it with strings of popped corn, cookies, candles and pine cones. We put up the crèche that all of Mama's brothers had made her the first Christmas she was married. It is a special part of Christmas each year. Mama knows who made each piece. Though some of it isn't done as well as others, it is still special. Uncle Philip Vincent Bartholomew Wallace III was only seven when he carved a sheep. That piece has always been my favorite. When I was little, Mama said I wanted to carry it everywhere and would kiss it each night before bed since I wasn't allowed to take it with me.

Sunday, being Christmas Eve, we had two special services at church. One in the morning as usual and the other at night. I love coming home in the dark after the Christmas Eve service. Even though there was no snow, the stars shone so brightly. We sang Christmas carols all the way home. It was late when we got to bed. That didn't matter the next morning when Georgie woke everyone up at 4:30, by bellowing a tune as loud as he could. Of all the songs he had to choose, "Jolly Old St. Nicholas." We all woke up, and since it was impossible to get anyone back to sleep, we just got up. Daddy got the fire started in the front room while we dressed. When he called us, there was a stampede as the younger ones raced down the stairs. I hope you don't expect me to tell you everything we did. It was a delightful whirlwind of a day. Presents, chores, feasting, another church service, singing and celebrating. We were all so tired by evening that there was no complaining when Daddy sent us all off to bed early.

The children had a delightful holiday from school. Today they started back again. Mama is doing well. She is busy sewing little white gowns. I have been doing most of the housework. Everyone keeps busy here.

We all laughed at the five boys in the snow. Are there really only four boys in the village school? I'm glad Tom seems to be making friends. We never would have thought of playing tug-of-war in the snow!

"That must be referring to the page that is missing," Mrs. Mitchell commented before continuing.

What a good idea. If we get enough snow, we'll have to try it. We were hoping the snow that started last night would continue, but so far it hasn't done more than dust the ground. We are hoping for enough snow to go sledding.

I must not have told you the "Ted, Fred, Larry and Jim Play Chimney Sweeps" story. I will try to remember to put it in another letter.

I must end as I have things to do.
With love,
Emma

CHAPTER SIXTEEN

Saturday
January 27, 1916
Princeville, Nova Scotia
Canada

Dear Emma,

A happy New Year to you as well. I am sitting at the desk in the parlor. A bright fire crackles cheerfully in the fireplace. The lights are lit though it is still early afternoon, for it is cloudy out, and I can't bear a gloomy room. The room is full. There is a village meeting in process, and as I was tired, I volunteered to stay home and watch all the children. And all the children I got! Except the Perkins children as Mrs. Perkins didn't attend the meeting. Some of the children could have been left quite safely at home, but none wanted to miss joining the fun. They haven't seen as much of me this winter since I haven't been in school. You are asking why I volunteered to watch all the children if I was tired, aren't you? Also how I can possibly write with them all here? To tell you honestly, I get more rest with all the village children than I do with only Lydia Ruth and Andrew. For one, Lydia Ruth has someone else to chatter to besides me, and furthermore, this gives twenty other pairs of eyes to watch Andrew. Right now all are seated, except Andrew and the McGuire twins, listening to Lydia Ruth tell a story of something she did last year when we were at P.E.I. Even William Campton and Arthur Morris, thirteen and twelve, are listening, though they seem to be having a difficult time keeping straight faces.

I did sit down last week and begin to write this letter. However, I didn't get more than the date written before I was called away. That being a story in and of itself, I will do my best to tell it.

I was about to write your letter when suddenly the front door slammed, and I heard Edith exclaim, "Why Jenny, what is the matter? You're all out of breath! What has happened?"

"I . . . don't . . . know," panted Jenny. "Where's . . . Maria?"

Edith called me, but I had already heard and entered the hallway.

"Oh, Maria . . . you must go . . . quick!" Jenny was breathing hard. It was obvious she had come as rapidly as she could.

"Go where? Jenny, take a deep breath. Relax. Now," I began again as she tried to do as I instructed. "What am I needed for and where? Start again."

Jenny drew another deep breath. "I don't . . . know what happened. I was outside with Elizabeth when someone, I think it was Mr. Stewart, shouted for me to get you and to hurry." She had begun slowly but spoke more rapidly as her breath caught up with her.

Without another word I snatched my coat and hurried out. There was no need to wonder where to go. The group around the Drinkwalter's house spoke plainly. No sooner had I arrived on the outskirts of the crowd, then someone caught my arm and urged, "Hurry, inside!" and I was hustled up the steps and in the door. Still thinking of what might have happened, I glanced around the room. No one appeared hurt. There were Mr. McLean and David standing by a blazing fire with damp clothes. Before I had time to more than notice that fact, I found myself being hurried into another room. There in bed, looking as white as death, lay Sam.

"What happened?" I gasped as I noted his blue lips

and felt his icy hand.

"He fell in the water," Mr. Stewart said quietly.

"He must hae slipped on something," volunteered Steve. "I donnae ken what unless it hae been some ice."

"It was Douglas McLean and his lad that pulled him out," Seth added.

"How long was he in there?"

Sam's eyes opened and hoarsely he croaked, "N . . . n . . . nae lang." He was shivering with cold. "Th . . . th . . . they were pulling me out . . ." He began to cough.

"One of you get that fire going!" I ordered. "This place is cold enough to give a well person pneumonia. Bring more blankets. Mr. Stewart, will you please fill a kettle and put it on to boil? We need some hot water bottles too. And some tea as soon as it can be made."

Just then a soft, pleasant voice said, "Whisht! Noo donnae fret yerself, lassie, I will take care o' the tea my ain self."

Gladly I left the tea in the capable hands of Grandmother. Almost before I knew it, the tea was ready. Hot water bottles were tucked under the blankets and the room began to grow warmer. Grandmother sat by the bed and fed Sam the tea. I stopped and watched a moment, noting that a little color was back in his cheeks, and he wasn't trembling as much. Knowing I could safely leave him a few minutes, I slipped out of the bedroom.

"Hoo is he?" Steve asked.

"He's getting warmer." I replied. Mr. McLean and David still stood near the fire. "You are both wet!" I exclaimed softly, noticing for the first time just how wet they really were. "You should go home and put on dry clothes before you get sick."

Mr. McLean smiled. That warm, quiet smile that reminded me of Alan. "Ah, Lassie, we were but awaiting for ye to ken hoo he is. Donnae fret ye aboot us. We'll be gangin' hame in a wee bit. Will the puir maun be a' right?"

I hesitated. Would he be all right? Was he only

chilled? What would Papa do? "I hope so." was all I could say, though I thought, 'Dr. McNeel would know better when he arrived.'

I asked Mr. Stewart if Mama knew where I was. None were sure, but David said, "I'll gae and tell yer mither for ye."

"You will do no such thing!" I protested! "Do you want to be sick too?" I did not want two people ill at once on opposite sides of town in winter.

"I'll be yer caddie, Maria."

I turned quickly. Duncan stood near the doorway, hat in hand.

"Is there onything else I suld or suld nae be telling her?"

Frowning in thought I wondered if there was some way I could write a note. As though he could read my thoughts, Seth said, "Thae be paper and pen in the top o' the desk ower there."

The note was written, and Duncan left to deliver it.

"Please," I begged Mr. McLean and David, "go right home and put on dry clothes. And have some hot tea."

"Donnae fret ye, we'll be gangin' hame noo."

Thus assured, I slipped quietly back to the bedroom. There wasn't much anyone could do but wait, for Sam had fallen asleep. Grandmother left me sitting by the bed alone with Sam. I was praying as I was sure the others were too. I wasn't worried for I expected Dr. McNeel soon. The room was quiet; the only occasional noise was made as more fuel was added to the fire in the stove. It was some time later, when it was quite dark and a lamp had been turned on dimly, that I began to notice that Sam seemed to be breathing with more difficulty. I felt his pulse; his hand was burning to my touch. Glancing hurriedly around, I spied Grandmother asleep in a chair. In a moment she was wide awake and hurrying out for some water. Mr. McIntyre must have been in a room nearby for he came in almost when Grandmother left.

"Can I help, Maria?" he asked softly.

"If only Dr. McNeel would get here quickly! We need him right away!"

"Lassie," he whispered, "no one could safely gae to Pictou for him tonight. There is a storm outside."

"No," I groaned, leaning my head against the wall. All strength seemed to leave me as I realized that Dr. McNeel would not be coming! I had been counting on him. For the first time I noticed the howling of the wind outside. What was I to do? I have never felt so alone and helpless. A hand was placed on my shoulder.

"Ye are nae alone. Duncan is waiting fer ony thing he can do. I will send him out to tell the others to be praying."

Scarcely noticing what he said, I tried to recall what Papa would have done, but I could think of nothing. What was I to do? Sam was very sick, and we couldn't get Dr. McNeel! I didn't know what to do. Mr. McIntyre spoke again. He must have returned; I hadn't heard him.

"What would Dr. McNeel be doin' right noo?"

"I don't know!" I wailed. This was too much for me. I was no doctor. I couldn't do it. "I can't do it!"

"Aye, Lassie, ye can."

I shook my head wearily.

"Maria," the deep voice was calm and sure. It had a feeling of strength. "Mind, the gude Lord hasnae left ye alone. What would yer faither be tellin' ye to do?"

Papa. I looked down at Sam's flushed face, noticed the restless movement of his hand, and suddenly I could almost hear Papa telling me what had to be done. I was afraid no longer. The Lord was with me.

All that long, weary, stormy night and the next, we battled for Sam's life. The storm raged outside, and no one could get in or out of Princeville for days. On the third day, the fever was down and Sam awoke, conscious. During those days I hardly slept or ate. After I saw Sam fall into a real sleep, I slipped out of the room for a little rest, leaving Seth sitting by his brother's bed.

"Hoo is David?" I heard one say softly.

"Aboot the same, I think," was the reply.

David? Sick? He was indeed sick, and I was soon at the McLean's. He had been out in the storm trying to keep a path clear in front of the Drinkwalter's. He wasn't nearly as ill as Sam had been, but enough to keep me busy going from house to house between the two. David received a good scolding from several people including myself for his foolishness.

It was only last night that I got to sleep at last in my own bed at home. Sam and David are by no means fully recovered, but they are on the mend. Oh, I will be so thankful when this war is over and Papa is home to stay! I enjoy being Papa's helper, but I don't want to be a doctor.

Evening

The children played several games with me before the meeting was over. Then they scattered to their homes through the snow. As soon as Mama and Edith arrived, I hurried off to check on Sam and David. Both are improving. David is growing impatient to be up and about, though what he wants to do in this weather, I'm not sure.

How wonderful that Karl wants to stay! We are still praying for both Karl and Kirsten. Keep Tom in your prayers. As far as I know, he is still fighting. Ruth said he hasn't been sleeping well. When I can be spared from the sick beds long enough, I intend to go visit the Perkins. It has been nearly two weeks since I have seen most of them. Mark and James have been there regularly to help get wood and have reported that Tom is, to use their own words, "a grouch." I do want to see Baby. She is still so small.

Emma, yours was the first letter I have ever seen or heard of which took two years to write. Well, was written in two years anyway. That must have been enjoyable. I was much too tired to stay up to the new year. I'm sure Karl's wish will come true, but I don't know about the others. Of course if you were to take Edmund's advice you could ensure that your wish came true. My wish would be that this war would end and Papa would come home! Surely everyone is getting tired of this fighting. Papa has been gone now for over two years! Lydia Ruth is now five years old. She doesn't really remember Papa, having been not even three when he went away. I nearly cried when a few weeks ago she came in the bedroom where Edith and I were talking and climbing up on the bed said,

"I wish I had a real papa, not just a picture-papa. Jenny only has a picture-papa like us. But Edana, Anne an' Ida have real papas. Even Caf'rine has a real papa an' she's only free."

"Oh, Lydia Ruth," Edith said gently, "you do have a real papa. He is just far away right now."

Lydia Ruth nodded soberly. "Just like Jenny's papa. He went away too. She said he's in heaven. That's far away 'cause he can't never come back. Is that where my papa is?"

"No!" Edith exclaimed hurriedly. "Don't say that, Lydia Ruth. Your Papa is in France, that's only across the ocean. Remember the letter he wrote you before Christmas?" Lydia Ruth thought a minute before nodding. Then she slipped off the bed and skipped to the door when she stopped, turned around and blurted,

"I guess he just forgot the way home."

I struggled to keep from crying. Edith wiped away a tear or two as well. And Andrew has never known Papa!

Maria

Dear Emma,

Maria would have written more I am sure, but as she was almost asleep, I sent her to bed. I told her I would explain to you the abrupt ending and get the letter in the mail. All these days of nursing and caring for the sick ones have simply worn her out. Dr. McNeel should be able to come tomorrow unless we get more snow. Your letters are such a delight and cheer to us; we will look forward to your next one with eagerness. Please give everyone our love.

      Ever your loving,
      Aunt Amelia

CHAPTER SEVENTEEN

>Saturday
>February 24, 1917
>Codell, Kansas
>USA

Dear Maria,

I have done something I have never done before! I was a little nervous, but I did it. Surprisingly, I enjoyed it. But there, I haven't told you what I did. No, on second thought, I will wait. I have to begin at the beginning as it will make a better story. It all seems unbelievable and funny at the same time.

It began in January, the last Saturday of the month to be exact. It was late afternoon. Edmund and I had just returned home from a lovely stroll to the creek and back, and I was about to start supper. Edmund had gone to help with chores. There was a knock on the front door, and I hurried to answer it. Mr. Holt and Mr. Jansin were standing on the porch. Cordially I invited them in. Daddy was in the barn with the boys. Mama came in the room with the girls.

"Carrie, run out to the barn and tell Daddy he's wanted, will you?"

Before Carrie left, however, Mr. Jansin spoke up. "We really came to talk with Edmund also."

Carrie nodded and hurried out of the room. I wondered what they wanted with Edmund. Mama was no doubt wondering that as well, but she asked about their families while we waited. Rosalie and Kirsten tired quickly and skipped back upstairs. I knew I should go start supper, but what was Edmund wanted for? I didn't want to leave until I knew. Right then Daddy and Edmund walked into the room. After pleasant greetings were exchanged, Mr. Holt spoke.

"I'll come right to the point. As you know, we represent the school board for the new school, and we are in need of some help. You see, early this morning Mr. Kingston stopped by to tell me he had just received a telegram and had to leave at once. He wasn't sure when he would be able to get back. Well, that leaves us with no teacher. We have tried everyone we could think of, but no one has been found who can teach this week."

We all listened in silence. Just what did they want?

Mr. Jansin took up the story. "We checked the Codell school records and found that Edmund had a very high grade. What we would like to know is if you," here he turned to Edmund, "would fill in as teacher for a few days or until we can find another substitute, or better still, until Mr. Kingston returns. Will you?"

Edmund stared from one to the other. Unbelief, and I couldn't tell if it was terror or dismay or a little of each perhaps, swept across his face. He opened his mouth to answer but nothing came out. Edmund was actually speechless! The clock ticked loudly as we all looked at Edmund and waited for his reply. At last he managed to stammer, "Me? I . . . I . . . I don't know anything about teaching school. Why not David or . . . or . . . or Emma? She could do it."

Mr. Holt grinned. "Oh, come now, Edmund, teaching a small school like this can't be that bad. We had thought of David, but his record wasn't as high as yours, nor was he in school last year, and it is also plain that he's a farmer."

"As for Emma," Mr. Jansin smiled at me. "Her record was as high as yours, but we thought since the school term was begun with a man teacher, it would be best to continue with one."

Edmund was still extremely hesitant and doubtful. The talk continued, Edmund protesting and Mr. Holt and Mr. Jansin pleading and coaxing. At last they wrung from Edmund a reluctant acquiescence to try to teach, but only until someone else could be found to do it. Mr. Holt and Mr. Jansin soon left leaving a dumbfounded Edmund still standing in the middle of the floor.

"Why did I say yes?" he moaned. "I don't want to teach any school! I was glad to be done with school and now . . ." His voice trailed off. "I'm no teacher. I'd rather work all day in the barn or fields."

I laughed at his pitiful expression. Mama laughed too. "Come on, Edmund, surely it won't be that difficult."

Edmund only shook his head.

"Well," Daddy clapped him on the shoulder, "you aren't starting tonight, so come out and help finish the chores."

All that evening and all day Sunday, Edmund looked nervous and at times actually petrified. Never had I seen him in such distress.

"Lucy, I can't teach!" he confessed to me Sunday night out on the porch. "If you only hadn't been such a lover of your studies, I wouldn't have had to study as much which would have kept my record lower which means I wouldn't be in this mess!"

I shook my head at him with a smile. "You'll do just fine," I told him. "Quit thinking it will be a disaster. You know it won't be."

"Humph," was all the response I got.

Monday morning dawned beautiful. The younger children were quite excited about the day. The boys especially were eager to leave for school. At breakfast Daddy told them that if they got into mischief at school, they would certainly hear about it when they got home. Edmund hardly ate at all.

"If I live through the day, perhaps I'll feel more like eating tonight," he muttered, miserably pushing his plate of scarcely tasted breakfast away from him. He left right after breakfast and family prayers.

It was a long day waiting at home. I kept wondering how it was going at school. At last Kirsten came and tugged at my skirt. She and Rosalie had stationed themselves at the window to watch.

"Are they coming?" At her nod I hurried to the door. Carrie, Vincent and Georgie were racing to the porch. I saw right away that something amused them. Almost as soon as they saw me, Carrie burst forth,

"Oh, Emma, Edmund isn't a teacher!"

"No, he isn't," chimed in Vincent.

"And Emma," Georgie added, his eyes sparkling, "it wasn't a bit like school."

"I hope you all behaved yourselves and tried to help." Daddy had entered the room with Mama. Heads nodded.

"But where is Edmund?" I questioned, for I saw no sign of my twin.

"He's coming. I think," Vincent said.

Grabbing my coat, I set off to meet him. I was about half way there before I saw him. He was trudging slowly along as though he didn't care if he ever reached home, hands in his pockets and head bent, staring at the ground. The sun shone brightly but Edmund didn't notice. He didn't seem to notice me either as I fell into step beside him. It wasn't until I slipped my hand through his arm that he looked up. Then he burst forth.

"I told you I wasn't a teacher! I told them I couldn't do it. It was worst than . . . than anything. I'd rather slave in the hot summer sun or clean out the barn all day than spend half a day teaching again! I knew it wasn't a good idea, and I was right. I'm not teaching anymore! They can find another teacher or close the school until they do. I don't care because I'm not teaching again. That's final. It's over. I'm done. No more!"

I gazed at Edmund in surprise. What had come over my twin? He had never acted quite like this before.

"Was it really that bad?" I asked softly.

"Emma." Edmund stopped and looked right at me. His voice was very solemn. "Today has been the worst day of my life. I forgot everything I had ever learned. I will never ever teach school again. I don't care if President Wilson himself were to ask me, I'll not do it anymore."

"What about what you told the school board?"

"I told them I would try it, and I did. I sent a note home with Fred Jansin for his father. It explains."

I said nothing more. There wasn't anything to say. Edmund was in no mood to be teased or questioned about the day.

It was late that evening when Mr. Holt and Mr. Jansin again came to the door. They looked worried. Try as they might, with pleading and begging, Edmund remained adamant in his decision to never teach again. Mr. Holt looked at Daddy.

"I don't know what we are to do! We need a teacher. David." He turned suddenly to David who stood leaning against the door frame.

"Don't look at me, sir," David interrupted. "I'm no more a teacher than Edmund. The one you need is Emma."

Before I could say anything, Edmund promptly agreed with him. "Emma would make an excellent teacher." Even Karl and Daddy were nodding, and Mama smiled in agreement.

"Could she handle the bigger boys?" Mr. Jansin questioned somewhat doubtfully.

"She can sure handle us," Edmund assured.

Mr. Holt and Mr. Jansin exchanged glances. "Emma?" Mr. Holt asked slowly.

I looked at Daddy who smiled and nodded, and at Mama who likewise smiled and nodded. "I'm willing to try," I said simply.

"She'll do more than try," Edmund grinned for the first time since Saturday evening. "She'll do it!"

And so, that is how I came to be teaching school.

Well, there is a little more I should add. I had a delightful first day. It did seem so different to be up in front and not sitting near the back, but it was a pleasant feeling. Mr. Kingston returned the following week but only to resign, get his things and leave. I am not sure why he left, but he is gone. When I was asked if I would teach the rest of the school year, I said I would be most happy to.

Edmund said, "I knew you could do it. I told them so from the first, but they didn't believe me."

He walks me to school each morning or rides with me as sometimes we go by horseback. After school he comes to walk or ride home with me unless I choose to walk home with the children. Maria, I never dreamed it was such fun to teach a school. I have fifteen children in all grades. Georgie and Sarah Smythe are my only first graders. There hasn't been anything exciting about school to tell you of yet, but I'm sure something will come up. The other day at home I told Georgie to do something, and he answered, "Yes, Miss Foster." I don't think he even noticed.

Can you believe Georgie is seven years old now? David turned seventeen last month, and Kirsten will turn seven next month. Did you realize that between just our two families we have at least one birthday every month? Kirsten's birthday is the fifteenth of March. Mama calls her our "sunshine girl" as she is always smiling around the house. She and Georgie are only three weeks apart in age, yet you would never guess it just by looking at and watching them. Georgie is tall, loud and always active. Kirsten is tiny still, looking as though she were almost six not almost seven. Since Kirsten can't talk, she is naturally quiet. She smiles all the time here at home. I don't remember her ever being grumpy while Georgie has days when he won't smile at anything. Kirsten and Rosalie are the best of friends. They share a bed, and at night I love to look at them sleeping. One sweet face surrounded by long blonde hair on one pillow while on the other pillow curly brown hair frames a round face. Rosalie has a way of making everyone she sees smile while Kirsten continues to cling to us and hide her face from strangers.

Oh, Maria, did you hear about the dog sled race that happened the end of last month? It was from Winnipeg to St. Paul. That is a five hundred mile race and in bitterly cold and snowy weather at that! The race began with eleven teams on January 24, but only five teams finished on February 5. There was one American in the race: Fred Hartman. He didn't win, but according to the newspaper clippings my friend Mary sent me from Minnesota, he was the favorite. His dogs got into a fight at the start and his lead dog was killed, leaving him with no choice but to be the leader himself. I'll enclose the clippings for you as Mark and James might enjoy them.

Are Sam and David completely well now? Your stories are getting better with each letter. I didn't realize there were so many in Princeville who speak Scottish. I knew the McLeans and Grandmother did, but I didn't realize the Drinkwalters and McIntyre's did too. Are they the only ones?

Everyone else seems to be getting snow but us. We haven't had any snow to speak of yet this winter. We've had flurries and dustings but no snow to play in yet. It is cold enough today for snow only it is sunny, and the weather here doesn't change as fast as in Nova Scotia. Uncle Lance and Aunt Ester in New York have had snow, and Grandpa Wallace who lives back in Tennessee wrote and said that he had snow. All the children at school are hoping for snow.

The U.S. has broken relations with Germany and Austria as of the 3rd of this month. Does this mean war? It was because of Germany's resumed unlimited sub warfare. It doesn't matter what country the ship is from anymore; if it enters the war zone it'll be attacked. This war sure has spread from some archduke getting killed in 1914 to involving so many countries in 1917. When and how will it end? Oh, Uncle Ian wrote and said the U.S. troops have been recalled from Mexico. They have been there a long time.

Did you know that Buffalo Bill died on January 10? Mama remembers getting to see his Wild West Show when she was young. Buffalo Bill was seventy-one years old the papers said. Think about it, he grew up here in Kansas.

I must end now. This is one of the two nights I don't have papers to check, and Edmund wants me for something. Perhaps my next letter will be longer, as I should have some news for you by then. I won't write until I do.

Love,
Emma

"Mom, I didn't know you taught school? And you were only fifteen! Can you imagine having a teacher only two years older than we are?" Ria turned to Lydia in astonishment. "They would never do that now."

"I only taught for a little while, but I did enjoy it. Now, do you want me to read the newspaper articles? Maria still had them folded here in the letter."

Every head nodded, and with no further word they were begun.

Sherburne County Times in Clear Lake
Thursday, 1 February, 1917

The dog team race from Winnipeg is not coming up to expectations in the matter of speed. It was confidently expected that some of the teams would arrive in St. Paul by Wednesday, but it is now estimated that it will be Friday and possibly later before they reach their destination, being still further hampered by the storm of Tuesday and yesterday.

Unless the storm interferes too much, it is believed that the leading teams will make St. Cloud by today. The local committee will be notified when the leading teams leave that city, and will notify by phone any who wish to be apprised of the hour. The committee has obtained permission from the authorities to ring the fire alarm bell about 20 minutes before the teams arrive in the village; this will give notice to all who wish to see the teams go through an opportunity. There will be no stops made here as the road from St. Cloud to St. Paul is the 'home stretch' and every minute is valuable.

Latest reports are that the teams are between Alexandria and Sauk Centre and handicapped by heavy snowdrifts.

Sherburne County Star News from Elk River.
Thursday, 1 February, 1917

...The dogs have had rough going in Minnesota, as the track has not been well packed. Nevertheless they have averaged fairly good time. There were seven leaders in the race bunched at Fergus Falls Tuesday and it is believed they will remain close together the balance of the trip. Hartman, the American driver who lost one of his dogs, and was behind, made up the lost time and passed the other contestants Tuesday night and yesterday morning was about 19 miles ahead of them.

Signs indicating the trail to St. Paul were received at Elk River last week and put up by Marshal Clark. The trail through this village follows the Jefferson Highway and the drivers will have little difficulty in keeping on the right track.

Sherburne County Times
Thursday, 8 February, 1917

The much advertised dog team race came to an end Saturday at St. Paul, Albert Campbell being the winner, arriving shortly after 12 o'clock, Hartman, the favorite, arriving about 5 o'clock. Hartman had the lead several times but his dogs were in bad shape.

Four of the teams went through Clear Lake Friday, arriving about 1:50 p.m. and stopping ten minutes; Hartman arriving just as the leading teams pulled out. Hartman plainly showed the terrible strain he was under, his feet, hands and face were frost bitten, his exhausted dogs laid down upon the depot platform and required much urging to take the trail, but, after a lunch of sandwich and cup of coffee he pluckily 'hit the trail' again and at Becker was only a few minutes behind the leading teams.

One of the largest crowds that Clear Lake has seen for a long time braved the cold, (25 below zero) to see these plucky contestants and their teams. About 75 came over from Clearwater, many of them being pupils of the public school, a recess having been given for the occasion. Many were present from Haven, Palmer, Santiago, and more would have come in had the roads been in better condition and the cold not quite so intense. It was plain to be seen that Hartman was the favorite.

Sherburne County Star News
Thursday, 8 February, 1917

As was the case everywhere else along the route of the race, Elk River people were intensely interested in the big dog race, which reached its climax when the leading team reached Como Park, St. Paul, shortly after noon last Saturday. Several hundred people were on hand here late Friday night to see the dogs come in and most of time stood about in the cold for several hours watching the dogs and the drivers.

All day Friday people had been on the watch for the dogs and the dog race was the main topic of conversation notwithstanding the crisis in international affairs confronting the nation. It was reported early in the forenoon that the dogs had already reached Clear Lake, and would make Elk River late in the afternoon, but that proved to be a false report and it was later learned that the teams could not reach town until some time in the evening.

On account of the drifted condition of the roads the drivers finally took to the railroad right-of-way, where the going was considerably better, but none of the distance from St. Cloud was made in good time and it was nearly ten o'clock when the four leaders finally reached Elk River. They were greeted by cheers by Elk River people, but nothing compared to the welcome received by Hartman when he pulled in some time later.

Hartman, the American driver, who had gained sympathy of all along the route, was behind when the leaders reached Elk River. A number of schoolboys, Clayton Swanson, Harry Olson and Harry Bell, went up the tracks a few miles to meet him, accompanied by Mr. Hide, one of their instructors. When Hartman came in it was seen that his dogs as well as himself were in a bad way, but when questioned Hartman said he was going to St. Paul.

All the drivers were taken care of at the hotel or restaurant and all went to bed to rest up, while their dogs were taken care of at the baggage room of the depot. Shortly after two o'clock Hartman arose, harnessed his dogs and left for Anoka, hoping to steal a march on his opponents and gain a lead which would bring him into St. Paul the winner of the race. But the other four drivers were tipped off by a local man who was on watch for them, and they all immediately harnessed their dogs and started off down the track.

Saturday was a day of business before pleasure for the winners of the first four places. From the minute they were aroused in Elk River in the early morning hours and were told that Hartman was on his way they wasted no time as they did Friday. The dogs felt the lash when they lagged. It was a case of attempting to shake off the others but the teams were so evenly matched that only Albert Campbell with his splendid blacks was able to open a gap. They whirled on through Anoka, Fridley and New Brighton without delays of longer length than they found necessary. They knew the struggling Hartman was behind them and 'club traveling' was over. Albert Campbell finished at 12:44 o'clock; Grayson at 12:49; Metcalf at 12:49:20 and Gabriel Campbell at 12:49:40. Hartman arrived about four hours later, but though he was the last man to arrive he was given an ovation by the immense crowd of carnival celebrators who had remained to see the plucky American come in.

CHAPTER EIGHTEEN

Tuesday
March 27, 1917
Princeville, Nova Scotia
Canada

Dear Miss Emma Foster,

    A school teacher! What a change it must be to be back at school where suddenly you are the teacher. I am sure you make an excellent teacher. Poor Edmund. I did feel so sorry for him, yet I laughed as well over the story. The idea of him teaching school was ridiculous. I'm afraid I would feel the same way he did were I ever asked to teach school. Now Edith, on the other hand, would be quite a success. She seems to have what it takes to handle a room full of children and teach them. I can handle a room or even a house full of children playing, but teaching is another story. Mama is wondering how Aunt Helen is managing without your help. Lydia Ruth says she wants to go to your school, and do you tell "Ted, Fred, Larry and Jim" stories there? I don't think she understands just who those boys are.

    This past Saturday I was longing to go outside. The air was enticing. Clean with a breath of spring in the wind, and the sun was shining. I knew it might snow that evening, but then the only clouds to be seen in the pale blue sky were piled high far up north. It was warm for March. I stood gazing out the open door at the sun sparkling on the sea, debating with myself about taking the little ones for a walk, when Mama's voice interrupted my thoughts.

"Andrew!" I heard her exclaim, followed almost immediately by a pleading, "Maria."
Hurrying to the kitchen I beheld Mama with flour and dough all over her hands (for she was making bread) trying to keep Andrew, who had climbed onto the table, from getting covered with flour. I picked him up just in time to save the dough from his grasping little fingers.

"Maria, if you're not busy, could you take him out? He seems to have cabin fever, for he is into everything today."

I told her I had just been thinking of a walk. Then, calling Lydia Ruth, we put on coats and hastened outside. Andrew, delighted to be out in the wonderful free world, ran as fast as his sturdy little legs would carry him, straight down to the docks. One of these days he is going to end up in the water. I wonder what he would do? But this time, Lydia Ruth and I, though we followed a little more slowly, caught up with him. Turning back up the hill, we were accosted by children's voices shouting for us to wait for them. Mrs. McGuire asked if I would mind taking the twins too, as she was trying to bake and she couldn't watch them at the same time. Soon the noisy bunch were gathered around, clamoring to know where we were going.

"Where do you want to go?" I asked.

Several places were suggested, but when one of them mentioned going to the Perkins', there was an instantaneous shout of "Yes!"

I only had to nod to send the entire crowd racing up the hill to the winding path among the pine trees. I brought up the rear with the three little laddies. Each is so very different from the others. Andrew, always adventurous, must climb every stump and rock in sight if it is at all possible. Rob Roy is a steady little laddie, plodding straight ahead despite the fact that the path turned. William Wallace has an inquiring mind. Every rock, stick or object in his path must needs be picked up or at least stopped and looked at. Thus I was almost continually running to bring Andrew back to the path, turning Rob Roy at each turn in the path and trying to urge William Wallace on. When the other children were lost to sight, I caught William up in one arm and Andrew in the other and, herding Rob before me, hurried as fast as little Rob's legs would go. We reached the children who had paused to wait for us, and I set the laddies down to catch my breath.

Six-year-old Ross McIntyre came to me and begged to be allowed to take his coat off. I shook my head saying, "It is still too cold to be without your coat. You may unbutton it, but leave it on." Well, I knew that were one child to take off his coat, all would soon have their coats off, and not only would they be off, but they would most likely be left along the path. It might seem like it was spring now, but those clouds in the north could bring snow before nightfall. Due, therefore, to the winding of the path and the slowness of the littlest ones, it was some time before we all reached our desired goal.

It was somewhat surprising to find Mrs. Perkins out in the little bit of level ground before their house, cutting the children's hair. Ruth and Baby were not in sight, and I assumed they were in the house. The children were all silent and seemed suddenly to have turned shy. Mrs. Perkins greeted us warmly, however, in her halting English and then began to talk to me in French. She had some questions about a part of Scripture that she didn't understand. As I vividly recalled Edith and me asking Papa about that exact passage several years ago and the somewhat lively discussion that followed, I was able to share it with her. We grew quite interested and forgot everyone else. Consequently neither of us noticed the children. It was only when Ruth came out and exclaimed in surprise that I remembered the children. Glancing around, I noticed many trying not to giggle, holding their hands over their mouths and nudging one another. Mrs. Perkins discovered first that she was no longer cutting her own children's hair. She had cut four others and was on the fifth child when the joke was discovered. How the children shouted with laughter. Even shy little Grace giggled.

"Children, children," Mrs. Perkins scolded, pretending to be quite upset. The mirth of the children was too infectious not to join in. It was some time before we all calmed down. Leaving the children under Mrs. Perkins' eye, I went inside with Ruth to see Baby.

Baby is nearly six months old and very sweet. She is almost bald, with only a little light fuzz on her head. Her eyes are big and blue, and she is quite a solemn little lassie. She is small, not thin, only rather delicate.

Not long after, William Campton and Arthur Morris came to say that the storm in the north was coming faster than expected, and we should all hurry home. Stepping outside, I gave a whistle through my fingers, shattering the still air with its shrill tones. Papa had taught me that years ago, and the children all knew what it meant. They came running from every direction. Checking quickly to make sure they were all there and accounted for, I gave the order to head for home. With shouts of "Good-bye" ringing through the air, we trooped off, William carrying his namesake and Arthur carrying Rob. I had Andrew.

Upon reaching the village, everyone scattered so rapidly that I couldn't be sure they all were home. Therefore, leaving Mark, Lydia Ruth and Andrew at home, I made my way around the village checking each of the children's homes. As I neared the end of the village, down by the pier, I paused to watch the fishing boats come in. The north wind was growing colder, and the sun was setting. I tied my scarf about my head. Almost unconsciously I began counting the boats.

"That larger one is the Drinkwalter's. There is Mr. McLean and David. It looks like they have Theodore Burn with them. Mr. Stanly's boat is there with him and Mr. Morris and Robert. Mr. Stewart and Mr. McGuire are over there, and that last boat has to be Mr. McIntyre and Duncan." I just love to watch the boats dock when the sky is almost white with coming snow. A few flakes began to silently fall. Turning slowly, I checked the last few houses and then paused once more to enjoy the panorama of peacefulness. Perhaps I can paint it in a word picture for you. It won't be quite the same as if I was out there right now and seeing it, but it will give you a glimpse anyway.

I was standing slightly above the village near my house. Looking northwest I could see the rocky cliffs and hear the muffled crashing of the waves at their base. Even the sea seemed hushed. It stretched out to the north in seemingly endless grey until it disappeared in the darkening sky. Turning east a little bit, I could see the light from the lighthouse at Pictou. The beam flashed far out to sea. On the gently sloping hill on my right were the village houses, their windows glowing with friendly welcome within while the snowflakes fell silently without. To the south, the dark pine trees looked even darker against the white sky. The wind blew gently through the branches with a soft sighing. Just turning a little more west was my house. The lower windows were lit, and smoke rose from the chimney. All was still. The waves lapped softly at the boats down at the dock, the whisper of the wind in the pines was so soft I almost had to strain my ears to hear it, and the waves by the cliffs gave just a soft constant sound. The delicate, wet flakes melted as they quietly landed on my upturned face. The sun had completely disappeared, and the darkness grew deeper. I don't know how long I stood there with my face uplifted, eyes squinted against the snow and thoughts far off in France, but when Mark called, I started and quickly went in to supper.

Emma, you'll never believe what Lydia Ruth did a few days ago. She cut her hair! Her long brown hair is now short. It is only a little past her shoulders. She said she didn't get it cut at the Perkins, so she just had to do it herself.

"Mama, I didn't cut it that short, the scissors did. I wanted it longer, but the scissors just cut it way up there," she explained.

"You shouldn't have scissors; they are not toys and will cut wherever you have them," Mama rebuked her soberly.

Mark said to thank you for the articles on the dogsled race. We hadn't heard a word about it which is not surprising as all have been stuck in Princeville because of the snow. The articles were read and reread by nearly every lad in the village, young and old alike. I can't even imagine what it must have been like out on the trail in those storms! I get cold just thinking about it. Mark, James and Charles Campton thought it would be great fun to ride in a dog sled. If there were dogs here, I'm sure it would have been tried.

With it being winter there hasn't been much else of interest going on. One delightful thing about all the snow is that Edith has been at home much more. When she and the girls couldn't go into Pictou to the Red Cross, they met in each other's homes to knit and talk. Since I am no longer in school, I have been able to join them. I don't know how many pairs of socks we knitted this winter, but I know it was several dozen. Mark wanted to know why we had to knit so many, and Edith replied,

"Have you ever noticed how hard boys are on their socks?"

He grinned somewhat sheepishly as just that morning he had complained that the socks Edith had darned only last week had a hole in them.

I didn't realize our families had a birthday every month. Be sure to give Kirsten a birthday kiss from us, and wish Carrie a happy birthday as well. I'm sure that by the time you get this letter, there will be another cousin, so please kiss the newest member for me. Mama, Edith and Lydia Ruth all send a kiss as well, and Mark said I could send one from him too. I'm sure Papa would send one as well, if he knew. Oh, remember when Rosalie came? I do wish we could all have been there this time.

I simply cannot picture David as seventeen! Which reminds me, Emma dear, that you have not told us all about everyone for quite some time. You have told somewhat of Karl and Kirsten but not for a little while. I want to be able to picture everyone as they are now.

To answer your question, yes, David is well. Sam hasn't regained his usual health yet, but Dr. McNeel thinks that it won't take long once it warms up. Grandmother has helped much with nursing Sam. She seems to consider all of us her children and grandchildren.

Oh, Emma, we have heard all these things about the "Zimmerman telegram" but what was it exactly? What did it say? There have been such conflicting reports, and no one is quite sure just what to believe. Is it true that President Wilson has armed all the U.S. merchant ships? Has he declared war? Is Mexico siding with Germany? If the U.S. is at war, will Uncle Lawrence join the army? Will David go? I'm sure you've heard about the Russian Czar Nicholas II abdicating. Now what will Russia do? With the Germans sinking so many ships, I don't know how America could get soldiers over to France if she does join. Enough of that talk. I hope you have some answers for us.

Emma, Tom has been converted! You should see him now. He whistles about his work and is so cheerful. We are still praying for Karl and Kirsten.

I look forward to your next letter.
Much love,
Maria

Mrs. Mitchell smiled at the girls as she folded the letter up again. "It certainly brings back a host of memories to reread these old stories."

"Mom, I can't believe you could write like that! You could write a book if you wanted to."

A gay laugh sounded on the spring air. "Ria, if I had wanted to write a book, I would have tried it a long time ago. I would much rather just stick with letters."

"Your cousin writes just as well as you do, I think." Lydia commented. "That must have been so delightful to finally have a girl her own age to talk to. And they spoke French," she smiled at her mother.

"Now, if I have some help in the kitchen, we should be able to read a few more letters before supper."

"What! Oh, Mom, are they staying for supper? Oh how wonderful!" Ria bounded out of her seat to throw her arms impetuously around her mother and almost smother her with kisses. "Let's go start right now!"

With much laughing and chatting, they entered the house to begin preparation.

"Ria, only set the table for six people tonight."

"What about the boys?"

"Don't you remember? It is Phil's birthday and the whole gang is eating over there."

"Who is Phil?" Lydia questioned, setting glasses on the table.

"He's a cousin. He is really Mom's cousin, but he is about the same age as Ed. He is Uncle Philip Vincent Bartholomew Wallace III's son."

"Does he have the same name?"

Ria giggled. "Uh, huh, only he is the fourth and everyone calls him Phil. He doesn't like being called by his full name. He says it sounds as though he were in trouble all the time. It is easier to say Phil anyway."

While supper was in the oven filling the house with mouth-watering smells and teasing the appetites of those who caught whiffs of it, the two girls had followed their mothers outside and were again waiting for the next letter.

Home Fires of the Great War

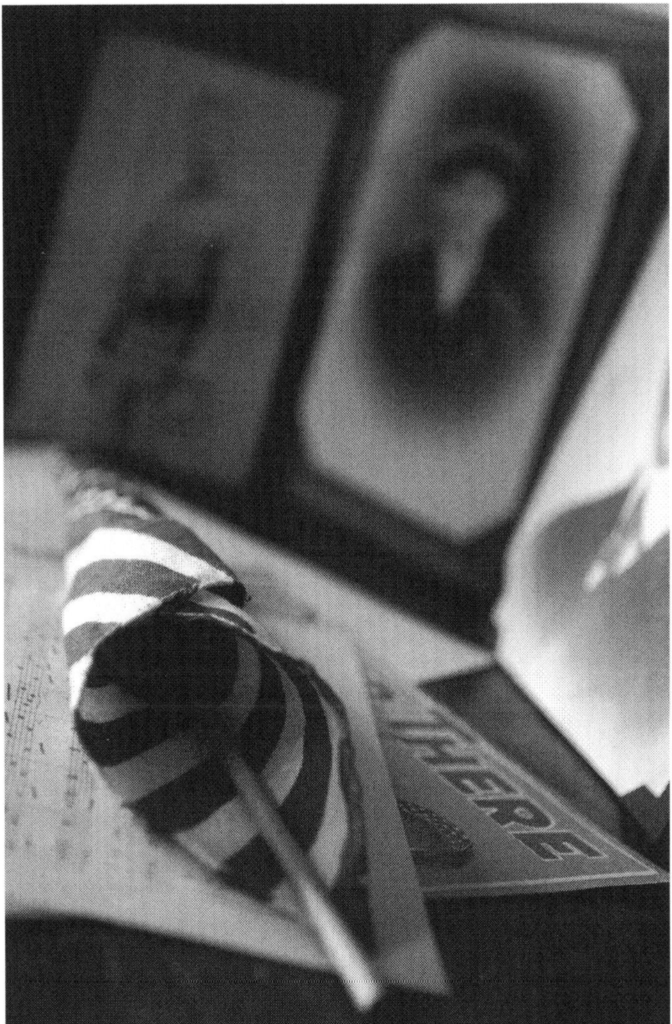

CHAPTER NINETEEN

Sunday
April 29, 1917
Codell, Kansas
USA

Dearest Maria,

I don't know where to begin. What do I tell you about first? Do I start with the most recent and go back, or do I begin in March and go forward? Oh, dear, there is just so much to tell, and I don't know where to start! Yet here I am wasting paper. I'll just tell you all at once and then tell it all more fully later. It's a girl, and Daddy is off to war! There! Now I will begin in March.

It was Wednesday evening, the fourteenth. Mama was looking tired as we all sat around the fire talking.

"Emma," Daddy asked suddenly, "do you think you could take Kirsten and Rosalie to school with you tomorrow?"

The young ones looked up in surprise. Kirsten was old enough to go to school, but Rosalie wasn't. What was Daddy thinking of?

I smiled at Mama and replied, "Of course. Kirsten, wouldn't you like to go to school tomorrow on your birthday?"

Kirsten looked a little worried.

"You can sit in the very front row and watch and listen," I told both little girls. I knew I wouldn't have to tell them to be quiet.

Rosalie smiled, gave a little wiggle and nodded her head. She was quite willing to go to school, and after a little time, Kirsten too seemed willing.

The next morning, in the flurry of getting ready for school and taking the little girls, none of the younger ones noticed that Mama wasn't around much. She was there to tell us all good-bye, and that was all. All eight of us left the house together. No, I didn't count wrong. Edmund and I rode off together, and Karl walked with the others to make sure the little girls were all right. He would then ride Jessie home, and after school I would walk with the children.

At school, Rosalie became friends with everyone before school had even started, with her quick, bright smile. Kirsten clung shyly to Carrie's hand after Karl left, until I placed her and Rosalie at a desk together, with Georgie across the aisle. All went smoothly, even with two little guests. Mr. Holt stopped by "just to see how things were going," he said. I couldn't keep from thinking about Mama throughout the day and actually dismissed school a little earlier than usual.

Papa was waiting on the porch for us when we arrived back home. He was smiling broadly.

"Did you have a good day at school?" he asked Kirsten, swinging her up in his strong arms.

She smiled and nodded, giving him a hug.

"I have a surprise for you," Daddy said.

"For me?" Rosalie asked kissing him as he picked her up in his other arm.

"It's for everyone," he replied, "but especially for Kirsten as it is her birthday."

Kirsten's eyes grew big with wonder.

"Have the boys seen it already?" Carrie wanted to know.

"Yes," Daddy said as he led the way upstairs after we had deposited our books and lunch pails on the table. The little boys were eagerly asking each other what the surprise was. At the top of the stairs, Daddy hushed the chatter and spoke low,

"Everyone be quiet now." He led the way to Mama and Daddy's room. Carrie and I exchanged excited glances. Softly Daddy opened the door, and stepping in, beckoned us to follow. Mama lay in bed looking pale but quite happy. The little bundle nestling at her side was gently picked up by Daddy and carried over to Kirsten. Kirsten was looking almost frightened at the sight of Mama in bed, but as Daddy came over, she looked curiously at the bundle. Kneeling in front of her he drew back the blanket and said softly,

"This is your new baby sister. She is especially yours because she shares your birthday."

An inarticulate sound came from Kirsten, then she sat right down on the floor and reached her arms out for the baby. Daddy carefully laid the baby in her eager arms. Kirsten's face fairly glowed as she gazed at the little face among the blankets. The little boys crowded to look. They were soon satisfied.

"It's just a baby," Georgie said.

"Yep, but you were a baby once," Vincent replied.

"Not like that," countered Georgie.

"Yep. No hair at all," Vincent retorted.

We heard no more, for they both ran off to play. Rosalie, Carrie and I sat on the floor by Kirsten to look at our new sister. Now the family was even, five boys and five girls.

"What is her name?" I asked.

"Evelyn Margaret," Mama answered. "Isn't she sweet?"

"Evelyn," Carrie said softly. "That sounds like too big a name for such a little baby."

"We can call her Eva," Daddy began, but Rosalie settled it all.

"Evie, Dis is my Evie."

And so Evie it has remained. Kirsten was quite reluctant to give her up to anyone else's arms, so at last I slipped away, knowing I'd get to hold her later. I'd hold

Evie, you understand. Everyone loves little Evie. She has light brown hair, only a little, but at least she isn't bald as Georgie was. Or was it Vincent? Perhaps it was both of them. I am hoping Evie's hair will remain brown, like Daddy's. She is becoming quite round and plump.

That was the 15th of March. What else besides Daddy leaving is there to tell? Carrie had a birthday. But you knew that. I did give her your greeting. If I have room in this letter, I'll tell you all about us. It has been a long time since I have done that. Now I should tell you the war news. I will try to answer your questions to the best of my ability.

War was declared before Carrie's birthday, but I think I had better start before that. I don't have a copy of the Zimmerman telegram. I think Edmund might have cut it out of the paper, but that was either the end of February or the beginning of March. I don't remember when the papers published it, and I don't have any idea where it would be now. I can tell you basically what it said. Germany told Mexico they would help them regain all the Texas territory (which by the way goes from the border of Texas and Mexico up into Kansas and over to the Arizona-California border) if they would join them as allies and declare war on the U.S. I suppose that was to keep us out of Europe. Well, it didn't work that way as the U.S. had found out about it through the English, and since we, the U.S. and Mexico, had just gotten our differences worked out, I don't think Mexico was eager to stir up more trouble. I'm sure you can imagine how indignant we Americans were over the whole thing. What with that telegram and the unrestricted sub warfare, everyone has had enough. Even President Wilson. The declaration of war passed the Senate 90 to 6 on the 4th, and on the 6th of April, 1917, the House passed it by 373 to 50. It is war. It is hard to believe at times. How long will it last? The patriotic feeling is everywhere around here. Everyone is singing George M. Cohan's latest songs, "You're a Grand Old Flag" and "Over There." Mostly the latter one. Here are the chorus words:

> Over there, over there,
> Send the word over there
> That the Yanks are coming
> The Yanks are coming
> The drums rum-tumming ev'rywhere
> So prepare say a pray'r
> Send the word, send the word to beware
> We'll be over, we're coming over
> And we won't come back till its over, over there.

It doesn't sound as well without the music. The music is what really makes it a song worth singing. Everyone has been singing it or at least humming or whistling.

Daddy had been thinking and praying for quite some time about whether or not he should go over to France and fight. You know he grew up English, and all three of his brothers are doing something for the war. When the talk about the U.S. joining first started, Daddy read every newspaper article and had long talks with Mama about going. David is too young to go, thankfully. Well, he could sign up, but Daddy says seventeen is too young. Besides, he has to stay and run the farm while Daddy is away. It was a full week after the U.S. declared war that he sat down with all of us older children and Mama and talked about enlisting. He told us he felt that he had to go now that we were truly in the war. We stayed up late that night talking. It is hard, but we are willing that he go and fight for our freedom. The following Monday, the 16th of April, Daddy went to Plainville and enlisted. Since he had a family and a large farm, Daddy didn't have to leave until the 24th. That gave us a little more than a week together with him. I will see if I can tell you about the day he left.

There was no school that day. I don't think I could have taught even if there had been school. I was so glad it was sunny and bright. A rainy day would have made it doubly hard. All were out on the porch waiting. Mama was in the rocking chair with little Evie in her arms. Edmund, Karl and I were perched on the railing, and David leaned against the pillar. The little boys sat on the floor without so much as a marble to roll. Carrie and the little girls were on the porch swing.

Daddy came out and looked at us all. He looked so tall and handsome in his new uniform. No one said a word. We all just looked at Daddy, and he looked at us. I was trying to etch his picture in my mind so I would never forget it. At last Daddy spoke.

"I know I can trust that the home fires will stay burning while I am away.

"David, I leave the farm in your care. You know enough to run it well. Edmund and Karl will help you. And there are friends you can go to for advice if you need it. If you think you can clear more land and plant more wheat, go ahead. I trust it all to you. I also leave the family in your care. Be the man of the family. There are several men in this family for which I am thankful, but you, as the eldest, are in charge. Take care of your mother and your sisters. I leave Carrie to your special care; defend her, help her and be her confidant.

"Emma, my joy, I know you will be your mother's right hand while I am away. If you are asked to teach next year, and your mother can get along without you, you have my blessing. You have done a wonderful job so far. Keep being my brave, bright eldest daughter and be sure to write to me often. Take your problems to Edmund if you don't know what to do. Help with the younger ones.

"Edmund, I leave Emma in your special care. Be her knight to defend her, advisor and counselor in difficulties, friend and companion in joys and sorrows. Help David with the farm. Give your advice freely, but don't expect it all followed. Help guide your younger brothers in the way they should go. Share any concerns with your mother, and keep the house cheerful.

"Karl, you may never know how thankful I am that

the Lord brought you and Kirsten to our home. Always know it will be forever your home. I can leave now knowing that with your help, the farm will continue to run smoothly. I place Kirsten in your special care. Continue to be her defender and leader. Help anywhere you can. Go to David, Edmund or your mother for advice. Keep up your studies and remember your Creator in the days of your youth.

"Carrie, my princess, help all you can around the house and in the garden. Keep an eye on the younger ones. Go to David, Emma or Mama for advice, counsel or comfort. Be bright and cheerful. Always remember you are my princess and God's princess. I leave you in David's care.

"Vincent, you must be a man now and help all you can. Obey your brothers and Emma as you obey your mama and me. Be a good example for Georgie to follow. Think before you do things, and be a brave, cheerful soldier until I come home. I leave Rosalie in your care. Always guard her and take care of her. Watch out for her and help her.

"Georgie, honor and obey your mother, brothers and sisters. Be helpful, don't complain about your work, but do it cheerfully and well. I leave little Evie in your special care. Don't tease her, but protect her. Remember you are my little soldier and defend your home. Send me some stories from your "Farmhouse Garret" that I may know what is happening around home.

"Kirsten, my sunshine girl, keep your smiles bright and spread sunshine everywhere while I am gone. Obey Mama and Karl as well as the others. Help your mama with Evie. Remember, she is your special sister. Georgie is her defender, but you are her nurse, sister, friend, and helper. Be a helper to Emma, Carrie and Mama around the house and don't neglect the animals. Help Rosalie and be cheerful.

"Rosalie, my little flower, be obedient and sweet. Help Mama and Kirsten with Evie. Keep everyone happy with your smiles. Learn to write your letters so that you can write me a letter.

"Evie, my baby," Daddy picked her up and held her.

"I'll miss you, but grow up sweet. Don't worry, for you have lots of people to love and care for you."

Evie, who had been looking at Daddy, suddenly yawned a big yawn right in his face. Everyone laughed then and felt more cheerful.

"Helen, I leave you with ten fine children to take care of you, the farm and each other. Don't worry about me, but pray. Children, respect and obey your mother. I'll be thinking and praying for you all every day I am away. Now, may the Lord bless and keep you all.

"David, are the horses hitched up?"

"Yes, sir."

"Let me read you a few verses I read this morning before we go." And after handing Evie back to Mama and pulling out a small Bible, he opened it and read:

"'For he maketh sore, and bindeth up: he woundeth, and his hands make whole. He shall deliver thee in six troubles: yea, in seven there shall no evil touch thee. In famine he shall redeem thee from death: and in war from the power of the sword. Thou shalt be hid from the scourge of the tongue: neither shalt thou be afraid of destruction when it cometh. At destruction and famine thou shalt laugh: neither shalt thou be afraid of the beasts of the field: and the beasts of the field shall be at peace with thee. And thou shalt know that thy tabernacle shall be in peace; and thou shalt visit thy habitation, and shalt not sin. Thou shalt know also that thy seed shall be great. and thine offspring as the grass of the earth. Thou shalt come to thy grave in full age, like a shock of corn cometh in his season. Lo this, we have searched it, so it is; hear it, and know thou it for thy good.' Job 5:17-27"

Then we all piled in the wagon and headed off to Plainville where Daddy would board the train for the training camp. It was a quiet ride at first, but soon we began to sing. We sang every patriotic song we could think of. At the station were many other families, some with sons in uniform, others it was the father leaving. As the train was about to pull out, Daddy leaned out the window, waved and shouted above the noise,

"Keep the home fires burning 'till I come home!"

And then he was gone. And we went home. At least he isn't going overseas yet. It is so different without Daddy. You know what it is like, only you have been without Uncle Frederick for several years.

Oh, I almost forgot to tell you something that happened before Daddy left. This will leave you on a more cheerier note.

It was Saturday the 21st. The little boys had been outside playing before breakfast. Kirsten and Rosalie had gone outside as well. When breakfast was ready, Carrie rang the dinner bell. Soon Daddy, David, Edmund, Karl and Vincent came in and washed up.

"Where are the little ones?" David asked.

"Outside somewhere," I replied setting a pitcher of fresh milk on the table.

"I hope they come soon, because I'm hungry!" Edmund exclaimed eyeing with delight the hot biscuits Mama was pulling from the oven.

The door opened and Georgie came bounding in declaring, "I'm hungry enough to eat all the breakfast myself." And he sat down and reached for a biscuit.

Mama quickly stopped him and sent him to wash up.

It wasn't until we were all seated at the table that Daddy noticed Kirsten and Rosalie were missing. Where one was the other usually was, so we asked Georgie where Kirsten was.

"I don't know. Can't we eat? I'm starving!"

"Not until the girls are here." Daddy told him firmly. Georgie does like to eat. Just when the older boys and Daddy were going to go look for the missing ones, the door flew open and a frightened little voice said,

"Oh, Daddy, come help her quick! Karl, she's stuck, and I can't get her out!"

We turned and stared in astonishment. It was Kirsten,

and she had just talked!

"Please Daddy!" she sobbed clinging to him, her hands and dress covered with dirt and her face streaked with tears. "She can't get out."

"Show us where she is, honey," Daddy said. "Boys."

The older boys and Vincent were already on their feet and heading to the door. I followed at Mama's nod. As I left the porch, I heard Georgie ask,

"Can't I eat now?"

We followed Kirsten out to the orchard where the little boys had tried to dig a hole to China last year. Then we saw Rosalie, buried up past her waist in the hole and sobbing bitterly.

"What happened?" Daddy exclaimed, not waiting for an answer as he ordered, "Boys, go get some shovels. It's all right, Rosalie, we'll get you out."

The boys soon returned and everyone set to work at once. They had to be careful so as not to hurt Rosalie. When she was asked if she was standing or sitting, Rosalie replied, "I's not. I 'tuck." Her tears had stopped when we first began to remove the dirt around her. Kirsten said she was standing, and the work continued. It was quite some time before she was at last free, for the dirt wasn't loose, having been watered and then drying somewhat. Vincent had been sent early on to tell Mama what had happened. At last Daddy picked up Rosalie, and we all set off for the house. Kirsten clung to Karl's neck as he carried her in his arms. After the girls had been washed and had on clean clothes, we sat down for a late breakfast.

It was only after we were all through that Daddy asked, "All right, what happened to Rosalie? Georgie?"

All eyes were on Georgie for he looked guilty.

"I didn't mean to scare her. She wanted me to do it," he began.

"Do what?" David questioned. "Let you bury her in the dirt?"

"No, I didn't bury her. I just planted her so she will

grow. She wanted to grow big, so I planted her. That is what we do in the garden," he protested as he saw amused looks pass between us.

It was hard to keep a straight face then, but when Mama began to laugh, it was impossible. Even Rosalie giggled now that she was safe. After the laugh was over, Daddy soberly explained to George why you can plant plants but not people. And so, that should give you something to smile about.

You painted your word picture very well. I could picture it all. I can't picture Lydia Ruth cutting her hair! I have kissed Evie for all of you. Oh, I was going to tell about each of us, but as this letter is so long anyway, I will save that until the next one. Remind me in your next letter.

Much love,
Emma

There were several sniffs as the letter ended, and Mrs. Smith shook her head.

"I don't see how you could write all that about your Papa leaving. It touches my heart. I do not remember my father at all, but I know I never could have written that," and she wiped her eyes again.

Mrs. Mitchell wiped a few tears of her own away as she responded, "I don't see how I did it either. Perhaps I was feeling so patriotic at the time that the full force of his leaving wasn't on me yet. It was certainly hard on all those who had to stay behind as their loved ones marched off to war."

CHAPTER TWENTY

Thursday
May 17, 1917
Princeville, Nova Scotia
Canada

Dearest Emma,

I am sitting on the window seat in our room. Lydia Ruth has long since been asleep, and even Edith seems lost in slumber. The moon is shining brightly in the window, and as I "had not one bit of sleepness in me," to quote Lydia Ruth, I thought I ought to start my letter to you. I see a light shining out in the yard from Mama's window downstairs. She must still be up. Perhaps she is writing to Papa. We got letters from him a few weeks ago. He is doing well. He said he was not exactly in the front lines, but he wasn't so far back as he had been. His letters didn't say much about his work, mostly they were to each of us. Oh, at times I miss Papa so much I don't think I can stand it another day to be away from him! Sitting here in the stillness of night with the stars twinkling brightly in the heavens and the moon sending forth its silvery light to dance on the gently rolling waves, makes it hard to imagine what it must be like over in France right now. What would it be like to be living in France? Or even in England with the bombings. I do wish I could get a letter from someone in England. Have you gotten any letters from there recently? But oh, how I long for Papa! When I am really busy, it isn't so bad.

I haven't told you yet that more lads are leaving here

for the war soon: Duncan McIntyre, Robert Morris, and possibly Theodore Burn. Poor Theodore. He is torn between wanting to go fight with his father and brothers and staying home to care for his mother and sisters. He is also engaged to a girl in Pictou. If he goes, that will leave Edward Campton and David McLean as the only young men in the village. Any older than me anyway. The others are much too young to join. A letter came from Finlay saying they were headed for the front. It wasn't long, but I don't have it with me to copy it for you.

I know how hard it must be for your family with Uncle Lawrence gone. Where is he training? Will you get to see him again before he leaves for overseas? How is everyone doing now that Uncle is gone? Emma, don't ever try telling me again that you can't write your feelings in letters. You may not be telling only your feelings, but you seem to be able to capture everyone's feelings. We all had tears blurring our sight while reading Uncle's last words. How could you even see the paper to write about Uncle leaving? We are praying for you all. At least Uncle isn't going over to the front lines yet.

I was so surprised to hear of Kirsten talking! Does she still talk? I wonder why she never would talk before. What caused her to stop talking to begin with? Mama wondered if Karl or Kirsten have told you anything else about their former life. They have been with you a whole year now. I got out your letters the other day and reread them. I still laugh at Georgie and Vincent's pranks. When I read your last letter about Georgie planting Rosalie, Edith laughed until the tears rolled down her cheeks. Does he ever make the same mistake twice, or does he learn from them? Poor Rosalie. Does she trust Georgie any more? I don't think I would, at least not for quite a while.

Oh, how I wish I could see little Evie! That is such a sweet name. I got out the scrapbook that has the picture of Rosalie in it as a baby. She was darling. If Evie looks like her, no wonder Kirsten loves her so much, plus the special fact that she shares her birthday. What do David, Edmund and Karl think of Evie? We couldn't help smiling over the little boys' reaction.

I know there is more to tell you than just war news and about your letter. Here is some village news. Mrs. Stanly had a baby! A little boy. Now at last Mr. Stanly has a son to carry on the family name. After three girls this little laddie's arrival has caused quite a stir. His name is Archibald after his father. I suspect he will be called Archie though. He has red hair and dark eyes. Florence, Edie and Ida just adore their little brother. He was born two days ago. There hasn't been a baby in that family for five years.

Emma, the kittywakes are back! The cliffs are covered with nests. I haven't seen any babies yet, but it won't be long now I am sure. The children were remembering a few years ago when James broke his leg trying to climb the cliffs to look at the nests. Was that really two years ago? There haven't been any broken bones since that time. Some sickness and new babies but not bones broken. Mark volunteered to try breaking a few for me when I made that observation earlier this week, but I declined the offer. I seem to have plenty to do without adding purposeful injuries.

I have been going at least once a month with Edith and the girls to Pictou to help out at the Red Cross. I don't see much of the city, but the drive there and back is so restful and beautiful. I don't even think I could paint a word picture of it for you. When you and Edmund make that trip up here after the war, you'll see what I mean.

You ought to see the fishing boats right now. They have been newly painted, polished and repaired. This morning as they went out to sea, the sun was just coming up, casting its golden rays across the sea, changing it from dark somber grey to a glorious sparkling blue and green. The wind was blowing, and the small waves crashing against the ships were crested with white that glittered and gleamed as the sun rose higher in the cloudless sky. Each ship was silhouetted against the brilliant horizon. I was so enthralled by the exquisite scene before me that I stood there motionless until the last ship was lost to view. How I remember standing down at the docks with Papa watching the same ships leave in the mornings. As I turned reluctantly away, I suddenly felt a longing to play what I had just seen on my violin. I didn't go back down to the docks, but I stood on our porch and just let the music whisper and soar from the strings. Mama came and stood beside me listening.

"You were playing the ships leaving this morning, weren't you?" she asked softly.

"Oh, Mama, did you see it too?" I asked, for she had stayed at home as I walked down to the docks to see Mark and James off with Mr. McLean and David.

"I saw it all just now as you played. It is going to be a beautiful day," she added. "Just look at that sky!"

It was indeed lovely. Deep rich blue with not a cloud to be seen. The wind was from the south and brought with it warmth and life. The birds sang madly from the trees, sky and rocks. Kittywakes called to one another from the cliffs. Flowers swayed in the breeze, and the few little insects that have ventured so far north this early in the year, jump and fly here and there among them. It was a day to be outside. Some washing was done around the village and it soon snapped gaily on the lines. I spent most of the day down at Grandmother's helping her with her spring cleaning. She hadn't gotten around to it yet. I washed windows, scrubbed floors and beat rugs. Once the house was clean, Grandmother and I sat out in the warm sunshine and did nothing. Emma, do you know the pleasure of working hard for hours and then just sitting and doing absolutely nothing? I haven't done that for ever so long. There seems to always be something more to do even if it is just watching children. I still love to watch the children, but occasionally it is just pleasant not to have anything I must do. After at least three quarters of an hour of just sitting, soaking up the sunshine and taking deep breaths of the fresh salt air, Grandmother began to tell about her life. She told stories I had never heard. There we sat until the boats came in, and the sun began to sink in the western sky. Now perhaps you will understand why I wasn't tired tonight. Mama's light has just turned off, so it must be getting late. The moon isn't as bright as it was earlier. I am beginning to get sleepy, so I think I will try to finish this tomorrow in the morning. Sleep well.

Friday,

I hope you slept well, Emma. I know I did. I didn't go watch the ships this morning as Mark wasn't going fishing. He tells me I really ought to go out on the ships sometime, and then I can tell you all about it. He insists I could learn to handle a boat and ought to learn how, for who knows when I might need to know how to do it. I might enjoy being out on the sea. Perhaps someday I will go. Would you like to hear about it if I did?

But I can't spend all my time and paper in "everyday nothingness-ess-es" to quote Lydia Ruth again. When I asked her what that meant, she replied,

"It means not like a story. We don't do story things much, just everyday nothingness-ess-es, and they don't make stories." She shook her head quite decidedly over that fact. "But," she added after thinking a moment, "Emma and Georgie and Rosalie and Kirsten make stories. They do lots of stories." She sighed a little sigh. "Not like us."

There was a story worth telling you about, but Lydia Ruth wasn't a part of it. It was several weeks ago now as it was still April when Mark, James and I went to visit the Perkins. The boys were going to help Tom cut some wood, and I went to help spring clean the house. I do so love spring cleaning! Ruth and I were washing windows. One on the inside of the house and the other on the outside. Little Hannah, who is only two, came outside wanting to help me. She is so small that the top of her head just barely reaches the bottom of the window ledge. I thought for a moment and then brought a chair out on the porch for her to stand on. Inside, Anna, five years old, was helping Ruth. It all happened when Ruth and I moved to the other side of the house leaving the little girls working on the lower half of the last window on the front side. When a sudden cracking sound was heard, I paused to listen. There were a few more cracking noises, a thud and a wail from Hannah. Dropping my rag I hurried around the corner of the house. Hannah was standing on the porch gazing up at the window crying.

"Hannah," I asked in French, "what happened? Where is your chair?"

Hannah looked up at me and replied dismally, "I standing on it. No big no more."

She was indeed standing on the chair as I discovered after a closer look. The problem was that the porch was rotting, and the chair legs had gone through the floor. I'm not sure how Hannah had managed to stay on the chair, or if she got back on it after it had fallen. Once I was sure she was all right, I tried to pull the chair up. It was stuck. I couldn't budge it an inch. Ruth, Anna and Joseph came out, but even with our combined efforts, we couldn't move it. It was such an odd sight to see that chair stuck in the porch, that I couldn't keep from laughing. We called Tom, Mark and James to help, but when that failed, we were forced to leave it. And there it still sits, awaiting the time when someone can free it from its imprisonment. I know it wasn't much of a story, but it was something out of the ordinary. Ruth said that at least it was covering up the holes in the porch.

There really hasn't been much of interest to write about. In a few years, when Andrew is older, I might be writing some stories about him as you do now about the little boys. I think those stories will include William and Rob and most likely Archie.

I must end now as I promised the children that when they got out of school today I would take them up to the cliffs and tell stories. I see them coming out of the schoolhouse, so they should be here in just a few minutes.

Farewell dear Emma, until next time. We are all

praying for you. Please kiss Evie for me. Don't forget to tell me all about everyone. Have I told you about us in a while? Not that there is much to tell. The children are coming!

>Love always,
>Maria

Outside the sun was beginning to set in a rosy pile of clouds in the western sky. Birds chirped and twittered their good nights while crickets joined in the chorus with their songs.

In the kitchen, Mr. Mitchell pushed back his chair and sighed. "It was all delicious, but I really don't think I could eat another bite. Could we save the dessert for later?"

"Mom, could you read just a few more letters while we wait for dessert?"

"I don't mind, if that is what our guests would like. They might be tired of listening to stories of long ago." Mrs. Mitchell smiled.

"I wouldn't mind in the least as that is about all Lydia talks about at home." Mr. Smith smiled affectionately at his daughter.

Mrs. Smith nodded. "I also enjoy them."

Ria didn't need her father's nod to excuse herself and return with the box of letters.

>Friday
>June 15, 1917
>Codell, Kansas
>USA

Dear Maria,

We have had several letters from Daddy! He is doing well, he says, though he misses us. He hopes to get a leave of absence before he is shipped out. He is in Camp Funston here in Kansas. I don't know if he will be shipped to another training camp before being sent overseas or not. Oh, he said that Uncle John (Mama's middle brother from Colorado) is there at camp too! His letters haven't been long, but he writes often. He sent us a schedule of sorts with his meals even listed. I thought you might like to see it, so I will copy it now.

5:45 stand reveille

6:20 march to breakfast: cantaloupes, cornflakes with sugar and milk, fried liver and bacon, fried onions, toast and coffee.

7:30 day's drill begins

5:45 flag lowered

7:00 p.m. lectures

10:00 lights out

Some time in there was dinner and supper. He didn't give times for those but he did tell the menu.

Dinner: beef a la mode, boiled potatoes, creamed cauliflower, pickles, tapioca pudding, vanilla sauce, iced tea and bread.

Supper: chili con carne, hot biscuits, stewed peaches and iced tea.

I don't think it sounds very appetizing. At times I almost feel guilty eating our delicious meals when I think of Daddy without it. But of course, as Edmund has so often said, "Just about anything will taste good when you're really hungry." I'm sure it is better than what they will be getting over in France. Daddy said the uniforms aren't very comfortable. They are wool and the collars itch. He said most of the men don't like the hats. Some say they wish they could meet the one who designed them in an alley on a dark night. We miss him, but things are going well here, even without him.

You should see the new area of land that the boys are clearing. It is very large, and they are doing it all themselves. Now that school is out, Carrie and I have taken over most of the daily chores around the house and barn so the boys can all work in the fields. Kirsten and Rosalie are both very helpful for little things. They now gather all the eggs and feed the chickens. Mama, Carrie and I have been at work on our garden. It is just as large as it was last year. Kirsten and Rosalie have been a great help in it as well. Vincent and Georgie have spent more time this year helping out in the fields with the big boys than helping here in the garden. That is all right though, for the boys needed some extra help.

Now, before I forget, let me tell you about everyone. I think I will start with Evie as she is playing on her blanket here on the porch beside me. Besides, I think I always start with the oldest.

Evie is already nearly three months old. Well, actually, now that I think about it, she is three months old today! Her hair is darker than at first, in fact, it really does look black. She is plump, round and rosy. She sleeps well and loves to be cuddled, but her favorite thing to do is talk. She jabbers away at any and all times. She giggles, crows, squeals, grunts and in general, makes as much noise as she can. You should hear her and Edmund in the evenings! The two of them carry on the most animated conversations you have ever heard from two persons, one of whom is only three months old. She is talking right now and oh, she rolled right off her blanket just now. I had forgotten to mention that she can roll over.

Rosalie is growing up. Her face is beginning to lose its baby look. She still is quiet but full of smiles for everyone she sees. Her hair is quite a ways past her shoulders and still curly. It has lightened up somewhat, looking more blonde than brown. She looked so cute this morning as Carrie tied a large rose colored bow in her hair to match her dress. She and Kirsten were going to Codell with Mama. She is still best friends with Kirsten. Rosalie isn't very tall yet, and she still likes to sit and snuggle on someone's lap.

It is hard to believe that Kirsten is three years older than Rosalie at times, for she is so tiny. People look astonished to find out that she is seven. Kirsten has continued to talk after that first time in April. She doesn't talk much, but she is no longer silent. Her long blonde hair had to be cut not that long ago as it became tangled in a piece of farm equipment. It is still down to the middle of her back when it is braided though. Kirsten's blue eyes seem to have a new sparkle in them when she is with Evie. I heard her telling Evie that she was the very first real birthday present she had ever had. I wanted to cry. Her affection for Karl hasn't lessened any though she willingly gives the rest of us a share. Her cheeks are rosy, and she seems to delight in the farm work.

Georgie may only be a month older that Kirsten, but he is nearly a head taller. If Vincent doesn't start growing soon, Georgie will pass him in height. He is just like Daddy in so many ways. Both when Daddy was a boy and now. He is stockier than Vincent, though both are the same height. He seems always in some scrape or another, tumbling out of trees, falling off the horses or cows, getting battered and bruised by his latest escapade. And if he isn't the one getting hurt, it is someone else. He doesn't usually do the same thing twice except for falling out of trees and off the animals. But in spite of all that, he is a hard worker once he sets his mind to it. He loves to work out with the big boys and gets into less mischief out there. David and Edmund did have a little difficulty with him not obeying, but only for a few days.

Vincent has really grown up. He isn't the leader of the mischief now. He has grown quite conscientious and is a hard worker. He doesn't try to get out of work now and is nearly as dark from the sun as the older boys. All that being out in the sun has lightened his hair so that it is now as light as David's. He is still outgoing and is almost always cheerful. He has taken his responsibility about guarding the house quite literally, for he and Georgie, when they aren't busy with work, will march around the house with their pretend guns or hide in the trees and bushes watching for enemies. They are so cute, though I wouldn't dream of telling them so.

Carrie has grown since last year. She is only half a head shorter than I am. She has spent so much time outside that her face is covered with freckles. She is getting darker as the summer moves on. The garden is her special care this year, and she thrives in it. She and David have become quite close as Carrie can't go to Daddy anymore. She always was close to David, but since Daddy left I think she needed to feel David's protection even more. She is wonderful with the little girls and Evie. She still rides Jessie as much as she can.

If you were to see a picture of Karl as he was last year compared to what he looks like now, you would have a hard time believing it is the same person. When he came, he was thin, pale, and sullen. Now he has broad shoulders, a sun-darkened face, hair that has been nearly bleached white, and an open cheerful face. He has grown considerably and is fast becoming a man. I don't know what we ever did without him. He works hard all day long and never complains. He still doesn't talk much and almost never about their old life in New York, yet I don't think he's forgotten about it. I wish at times he would tell us about it, for there are some things I wish I knew. Karl, Edmund and David are great friends. They work well together at anything.

As for Edmund, he is now at least two inches taller than I am, much to his constant delight. He is so dark with the sun that with his dark, straight hair he could almost pass for a Mexican. The only problem he would have is that he doesn't speak Spanish. He still teases us all good-naturedly, and we like it. He is so cheery that no one can be dull when he is around. Now don't get me wrong, he can be serious and even stern at times if the need for it arises. I don't know what I would do without my twin. If something bothers me, I know I can always go to him and talk. He will usually solve it too, for nothing is very big.

David is a real man now. He runs this farm as though he has done it for years. He is more serious than before but is ready to laugh with the rest of us. He is dark also from the sun. He is not the tallest, but I think he might be the strongest, but don't tell Edmund I said that. David really hasn't changed that much.

Mama is still bright and cheerful, ready to laugh and smile. I know she misses Daddy, but I have never even heard her sigh because he is gone. Perhaps it is a family trait since she has relatives and ancestors who fought in the Spanish war, the Civil war, the Mexican war, the War of 1812, and the Revolution. I think some even fought in the French and Indian war. I do know that she finds great comfort in her Bible. She also goes about the house singing. And when Mama sings, usually everyone else who hears joins in. Once Mama had been in the kitchen with Carrie and me, and she was singing. She went outside to bring in the wash and left us singing inside, but soon the little girls were singing on the porch, and then all the boys began out by the barn, so there was music everywhere.

Oh, I did forget myself. I don't think I have changed much. I do more housework than before as Carrie is out in the garden most everyday. I spend a lot of time writing to Daddy. I will start a letter to him on Monday, write a little each day, finish it on Sunday and mail it on Monday. Then I start all over again. I am no taller and am not darkened by the sun much, as I don't work in the fields. I don't think that Daddy's leaving made me grow up any. Perhaps it did, and I just don't notice it.

But that is the family now. I refuse to tell you about all the dogs, cats, chickens, horses, cows and all the other animals that inhabit our farm. I will leave that for Georgie and the "Farmhouse Garret." He said he was ready to start the paper as soon as he got "that letter maker."

"What is a letter maker?" David asked.

"You know, it makes the letters for the newspapers."

"Oh, you mean a press."

Georgie looked exasperated. Didn't anyone know what he meant? "I don't need a press 'cause I can do all the pressing myself. I want the thing that does the letters."

No one was able to convince him that what he wanted

was really called a press. The boys finally gave up trying. That is one thing about Georgie, when he once gets an idea in his head, it is hard to get it out.

I did so enjoy your letter. I do want to hear all about your time on a fishing boat. You see I am taking it for granted that you will follow Mark's advice and go out one of these days. Did you know that I have never been on a boat in my entire life? Unless you count the little raft David and Edmund built years ago to ride around the little pond. I have never seen the ocean either. Edmund and I really will have to pay you a visit after the war. I do hope and pray it ends soon.

That reminds me. Did you hear about the draft? All men ages 21 - 30 had to register on the 5th of this month. Not everyone likes it, though some boys will even lie about their age because they want to go over and fight. We know a boy in town that did that. He isn't more than seventeen, but he registered and is headed out for training. General Pershing landed in France on Wednesday the 13th. That was just the day before yesterday. The papers are full of war news now. It has suddenly become very important to the American people. Of course the U.S. troops haven't fought in any battles yet. The news is mostly about preparing for war, buying war bonds, saving things for the troops, and things like that. This war is real. It may all be fought over the ocean, but it is going to affect us here at home as well. And not just in missing those off fighting either.

Oh, to sit and do nothing! What a delightful thought. I might dream of such a thing, but I don't think I will ever be able to do it. Not until I am an old lady anyway. I always have something to do. This is the closest I come to it, and I am writing while I keep an eye on Evie. We really spring cleaned the house after Daddy left. Mama said it was to keep us so busy that we wouldn't have time to become sad about his going. She was right. There was no time. From almost the moment we got up in the mornings until we just about fell exhausted into bed at night, we worked.

We did so laugh about that chair. Edmund said that

surely Mark, James and Tom could fix the porch so it wouldn't fall apart. So Lydia Ruth thinks we live stories, does she? Well, I might have to think of a story to tell you now so as not to disappoint her. I love her quaint words. The other evening when Rosalie was cuddled on David's lap just before bed time, she said,

"Mama, my tireds have all gone away, an' I can't find them."

"Who have gone?" David asked, greatly puzzled.

"My tireds," was the reply.

Kirsten spoke up then. "I think she means that she isn't sleepy and doesn't want to go to bed."

Rosalie gave a great big yawn and nodded. "My tireds . . . all . . . gone." Her eyes closed, and she was asleep.

That wasn't much of a story, but, Lydia Ruth, anything can be a story if you write or tell it like one. There really isn't much to tell. We are all so busy with work and so tired at the end of the day that I haven't had the time to write down many things that happen. I will try to do better next time. I must end now and start supper. The boys will be in after a while and not too happy if there is no supper. Give my love to everyone.

Always yours,
Emma

Home Fires of the Great War

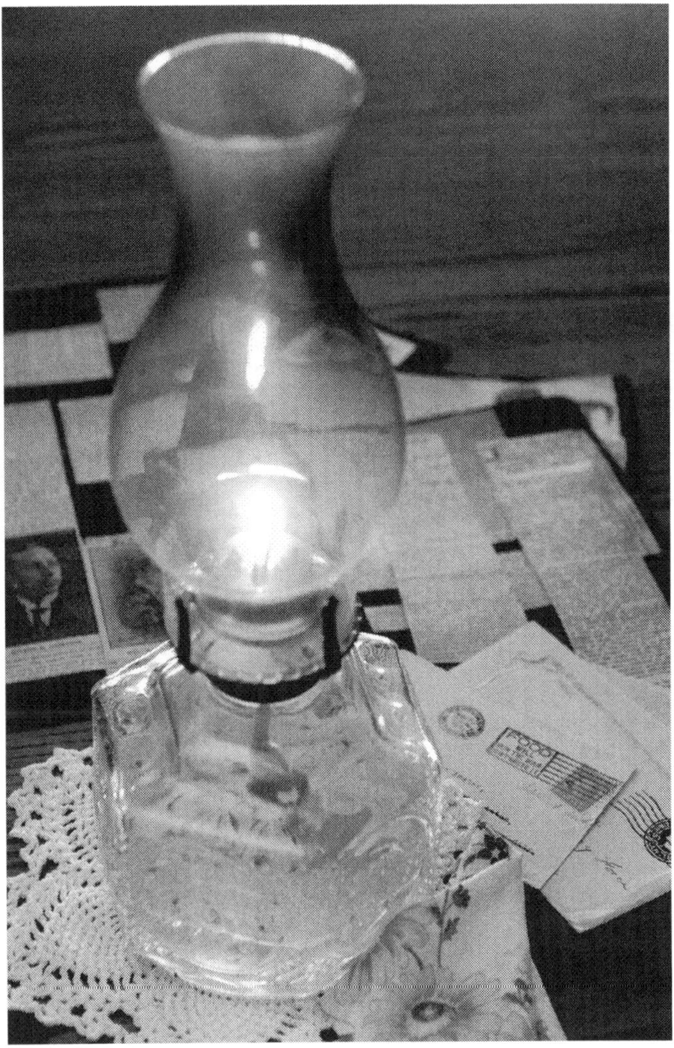

CHAPTER TWENTY-ONE

Tuesday
June 26, 1917
Princeville, Nova Scotia
Canada

My Dearest Emma,

    I know it is not time for me to write to you yet, but I wanted to start this letter now and hopefully write a little in it each day I am gone, as well as in Papa's. Yes, I am going away. Not very far, for it is only to Halifax, but I am going with the Camptons. I don't know how Mama came to consent to my going, but she did. Edith is nearly as excited as I am myself. She has told me more than once that I needed to get away to a different place and come back cheerful. I know I haven't been as cheerful these last few weeks as I should be, but it was rather hard. The Perkins are gone. They just up and left. No one knows where they went or if they will ever return. I can't even write to Ruth for I don't know where they are. They didn't even say good-bye except for a note Ruth left me tucked in a crack of the door. She and I had become such good friends, and I think all the little ones, even shy Grace, were used to me and accepted me. It has been hard still to believe they are gone, and I find myself walking up towards their house before I remember. I do wonder where they went. Will I ever see them here on earth again? It is a comfort to know that I will see them in heaven.

    All that and I haven't even started on the trip. I must

go and assist Edith who is packing up my things. I will write more later.

Thursday,

We are in the train on the way to Halifax now. Mr. Campton is reading the newspaper and Mrs. Campton her book in the seat across the aisle. Anne is nestled beside me asleep. At least I think she must be asleep, for she hasn't stirred for ten minutes. Edward has the other three in the seats before me and is beguiling them with a story. It must be an interesting one, for I catch intriguing bits of it now and again. We went as far as Pictou yesterday as we left home in the afternoon, and we had some shopping to be done. However, here we are on the train. It is hard to realize that I am truly on my way to Halifax without my family.

I haven't written anything for the past half an hour. I was thinking of when Papa left. We didn't go to Halifax to see him off, we only went to the train station at Pictou. Papa rode on this very train and saw these same fields and trees. Perhaps he even sat in this very seat! Oh, Emma, that thought has set a thrill through my whole being!

Sunday, July 1

Here we have been in Halifax for nearly three and a half days, and I haven't written a line. We are staying at the Carleton House which is at the corner of Argyle and Prince. The Revere Hotel is right across from the railway station, but none of us cared to stay there as it would have been much too tumultuous. As it is, the Carleton House has enough noise for me with it being on a corner in the middle of the city. We saw what will be the Prince George Hotel. It hasn't opened yet, or we might have stayed there. Halifax is so very different from Pictou. It seems busy all the time. Mr. Campton and Edward have been absent from us most of each day on business, but the rest of us have enjoyed ourselves. We have wandered quite about the city. We are so used to walking that it hadn't occurred to us to take a cab. I do believe we have been in more shops these last few days than I have ever been in my entire life! Elizabeth and Anne have stared wide-eyed at all the displays in the windows. William and Charles, who are now at the manly ages of fourteen and eleven, have been excellent escorts. We are constantly reminded of the war here, for everywhere we see "Buy War Bonds" signs. War news is all over the papers everyday. Each night everyone is required to draw their shades when it grows dark, partly for fear of attracting any German subs and partly so that no spy can signal the enemy. The penalty for violating it is up to five thousand dollars and/or five years of imprisonment. You can be sure that no lights are shown from our rooms.

We went to church this morning to St. Paul. I have heard that it is the oldest church here.

This afternoon has been spent in quiet. I had no idea that a city could be this bustling on the Lord's Day. I am feeling rather homesick now for the quiet peacefulness of our Sundays. To be honest, I do miss my family more than I dreamed. But for some reason I feel closer to Papa. Is it because I know this was the last city he saw as his ship left the harbor? Is it because I am a little closer to France no matter how small that little may be? I don't know. We are going down to the docks tomorrow. Even Mr. Campton and Edward are going. They don't have any engagements until the afternoon, so we will go down first thing in the morning. The girls are asking me for a story, and I have noticed that the boys seem no longer interested in their books. Until later.

Monday evening,

We did go down to the docks early this morning. It was so quiet. We saw and heard no one until we had reached the waterfront. The city was asleep. I don't think anyone here knows what a sunrise looks like, for no one seems to arise until long after the sun is shining. All the ships in the harbor were a glorious sight. Together we stood on a pier and watched a ship leave port and head out into the channel.

I watched, suddenly seeing not that ship but another one. One full of Canadian soldiers and a very special doctor. How had it looked? So far away was I as I gazed after that ship disappearing on the horizon that I gave a start when someone touched my arm.

"Do you care to still accompany us?" Edward asked with a smile.

I hadn't even noticed they had left, nor had anyone noticed my absence until they had stopped at the next dock and Mrs. Campton asked me a question.

"I'm sorry," I said apologetically as we turned and left the dock, "I didn't hear you leaving."

Edward said softly, "Your mind was on another ship that sailed a few years ago, wasn't it?"

I nodded. We didn't speak again until we reached the rest of our party.

I just can't tell you, Emma, what it felt like being down there and seeing all those ships and men at work. There was one ship flying the Stars and Stripes. There were ships from France, Belgium, England, and I don't remember where. We saw soldiers on guard so that no German ship or sub could come unnoticed. We could see clear across the harbor to Dartmouth. McNab's Island, which we could also see, divides the channel into two parts right at the mouth of it. We stopped at all six piers this morning though some stops were necessarily brief. Mr. Campton told us that each one was around 1,250 feet long and 360 feet wide! Can you understand why I can't really do them justice in telling about them?

For our midday dinner today we stopped at the Corona Café. I had spring chicken with steamed potatoes, creamed carrots and ice cream for dessert. I don't recall what everyone had, and you wouldn't be interested anyway. My dinner was so large that Charles helped me finish it. That lad could eat all day, I really do believe, and still be hungry in the morning. Mr. Campton and Edward had to leave us after we had dined, so we visited a few more shops before returning to our rooms. We haven't purchased anything here except a few war bonds and stamps. With signs everywhere, it is really hard not to buy them.

    Wednesday evening,

I have a little time to write now, but as we are leaving in the morning, I can't write for long. Today we were able to visit the Halifax Citadel. We spent nearly the entire day there. The lads truly enjoyed the experience and are still talking about it as I write. I am going to do my best to tell about it, more for the boys' sake than yours, Emma. Not that I think you won't enjoy it, but that the lads will enjoy it more.

The Halifax Citadel, which is named Fort George, was first built by Governor Edward Cornwallis back in 1749 or there about. It was built along with a few other small forts to guard the harbor from the French who had a fort up on Cape Breton. Though at the beginning the fort wasn't very large as it is today, it was very important in helping to protect British trade routes. In 1820, the fort that now stands here was begun. The old fort was completely leveled and the new, star-shaped Halifax Citadel began to appear. It was thought at first that the new fort would be completed in a year, but it wasn't until 1856, twenty-eight years later, that it finally was finished. The fort itself is in the shape of an eight pointed star. Looking at it, it is easy to see why it took so long to build. The walls are all stone, and there is a large ditch, rather like a moat only not filled with water, all the way around the fort. One thing that you may find interesting is that inside the fort is a large mast which makes it appear as though a ship is inside the fort. The mast with flags is used to signal other forts and, I'm not sure, but perhaps it is used to signal the ships as well. We saw the cannons, the barracks, rifle galleries and even a schoolroom for the children of the officers living in the fort. Emma, would you like to teach in a fort? Mrs. Campton, the girls and I didn't go all over the fort as Mr. Campton, Edward and the lads did. We did get to see the firing of the noon cannon. I am sorry I can't do a better job at describing the fort, but I don't have more time right now.

Tuesday, July 17,

It is time I finished this letter. It has been sitting here on the desk since I returned nearly two weeks ago. Let me see if I can finish the trip.

The ride to Pictou on the train was uneventful except for the fact that Charles managed to enter a different car than the rest of us, thus causing his mother great fright in thinking that we had left him. She was all right after he came casually strolling into our car after we had started, remarking,

"The seats where I was are pleasanter than these. Care to try them?"

Once back in Pictou, we visited the lighthouse there before driving back to Princeville. It was delightful to be home again. The quiet and peacefulness were even more noticeable and alluring after the noise and confusion of Halifax. I have spent most of my waking hours out of doors, usually with the children, but occasionally by myself or with Grandmother.

Now before I send this letter off, I have one other thing that I must tell you about. I will assure you at the beginning that everything turned out all right, thankfully, but it was frightening.

I was outside watching the three little laddies, Andrew, Rob and William. The other children were scattered around the village playing hide-and-seek. I wasn't paying any attention to them as I had enough to do keeping an eye on my charges. I wasn't paying attention that is until I heard cries of "Lydia Ruth! Where are you? You can come out now! Lydia Ruth! We give up."

As Edie came by, I asked her what was going on. She said that they couldn't find Lydia Ruth anywhere. Everyone was running around hither and thither looking in the places already looked in by someone else. There was no order or reason in their searching, and some places that I thought could be used by Lydia Ruth weren't even noticed. I had no doubt that she had either fallen asleep or just wanted them to look longer for her. The idea that she could be in danger or hurt never crossed my mind. When I could stand the hurry and scurry no longer, I whistled, and the children all came running.

"Where is she?"

"Do you know where Lydia Ruth is hiding?"

"Will you help us find her?"

Everyone talked at once, and I had to whistle again before they fell silent. I told them I didn't know where she was but thought it wouldn't be too hard to find her. I divided everyone up and assigned areas for each group to look.

"Look in, under and around anything than could by any stretch of the imagination be used as a hiding place for Lydia Ruth."

Everyone scattered. I expected it to only be a short time before someone called "found!" but the minutes passed. I was beginning to wonder where she could have gone. Suddenly a shout from the docks startled me. Leaving the little boys playing happily in the dirt by Grandmother's house, I ran down to see what had happened.

Mr. McIntyre was looking out to sea and asking who had untied his boat. All the children were gathering, and each denied having even touched the rope. All at once a dreadful thought struck me, and I grasped Mark's arm with a gasp, "Lydia Ruth!"

Mr. McIntyre looked at me, at the children, and then out to sea again. "Arthur, gae tell your faither he maun hurry so. William, we maun hae Mr. McLean, an' David, Mr. McGuire and Mr. Stanly. Donnae be lang!" Then turning to Mr. Stewart who had come up, he said softly, "I's warrant the lass is in the boat. We donnae hae muckle time."

Before anything else could be said, Mr. Morris hurried up with Arthur, to be joined quickly by the other men including Mr. Campton and Edward. Everything seemed to be in slow motion, dividing the men and lads into the remaining boats, telling the rest of us to wait and pray, the fishing boats then heading slowly out to sea in search of one lone craft.

Mark had gone with the ships as had James, William, Charles and Arthur. I turned dazedly away from the docks after the children. Grandmother called us all to her house where we knelt together before it and prayed. When we arose, Ross McIntyre came to me, and slipping his small hand in mine, said quite confidently,

"My faither will find Lydia Ruth. No one can hide from him."

I had to smile at his faith. By this time everyone in the village knew that Lydia Ruth was thought to be in a fishing boat that had slipped from its moorings and drifted away. Mama didn't faint or cry but stood gazing out to sea without speaking as the sun seemed to crawl towards the West. Edith and I stood beside her equally silent as the long minutes turned into hours. The entire village was subdued, and everyone waited, well knowing the many things that could happen to one little lass alone on the sea.

I don't remember who it was that first sighted the returning fishing boats, but soon we all saw them, their white sails against the growing dark of the eastern sky. There was one ship ahead of the others, and Mrs. McLean observed that it was the Drinkwalter brothers' ship. No sooner had it docked than Steve called out to us,

"Gin yer look'n for the bonnie wee lassie that went to sea for to find her faither, we hae fetched her hame."

He hardly had time to finish speaking before Mama, Edith and I were down on the dock each reaching eagerly for Lydia Ruth. The other boats docked, and Mark joined us. Every one talked at once, and it was completely dark before we all at last managed to return home. It seems that Lydia Ruth had climbed on the boat to hide. Somehow the boat came loose and drifted off. Lydia Ruth, on finally realizing that the boat was no longer near shore, came out of her hiding place and looked around. On seeing nothing but water, she remembered that Papa was on the other side of the water and thought of how glad he would be to see her. She had no doubt that she would be there by dark. It was Sam Drinkwalter that noticed the McIntyre boat, noting also that no one was steering it. The three brothers were quite surprised on reaching the stray boat to find Lydia Ruth calmly sitting and singing to herself. Seth told me,

"The Lass was nae pleased wi' us when we wad nae let her sail ony mair and took her to oor ain boat."

It is to be hoped that Lydia Ruth has learned a lesson and will never get into a boat by herself again.

I truly must end this now.
                Much love,
                  Maria

Ria and Lydia met in school the following morning in eager anticipation of the afternoon. "I can hardly wait!" Ria whispered.

Lydia nodded, "Me either!"

"Maria, Lydia, how is your report coming? Have you decided on that special person to write about?" Miss Bryant paused beside the two friends in the hallway. "You haven't mentioned anything to me, and you only have one week left."

"Oh, yes, Miss Bryant. We have decided. Is it all right if we don't tell you until we do the report for class? You see this is a very special report and . . . well--"

Miss Bryant smiled. "Of course you may keep it a secret if you want and if you can. Which of you is going to do the oral report for class, or have you decided?"

"I am. I like talking more than writing, so Lydia

is working on the written one," Ria squeezed her friend's hand as their teacher laughed. It was well known that Ria Mitchell liked to talk.

CHAPTER TWENTY-TWO

Out on the porch of the Mitchell home, quite a group had gathered. Mrs. Mitchell with the box of letters in her lap, Mrs. Smith in a rocker much like the one occupied by Mrs. Mitchell, Ria and Lydia, and Corporal. He had been persuaded to join them and hear for himself these wonderful old letters that Ria kept talking about. Besides that, he wished to find out about the heroes whom the two friends were honoring with their report.

Sunday
August 19, 1917
Codell, Kansas
USA

Dear Maria,

It is a quiet day today and very hot. We are all returned from church, and not much is going on. The older boys are all asleep here on the porch where a slight breeze can be felt. Mama and Evie are resting up in Mama's room. At least I hope they are, Evie has been very fussy today which is not like her. Mama thinks it is the heat. I can understand that. Even here in the shade it is hot. I'm not sure where Vincent and Georgie are. I do hope they aren't into some mischief. They both seem to be full of something these days. Why just this morning during church, but wait, you might want this as a story.

All was quiet in the church. The rustle occasioned by all being seated after singing had died down. The pastor arose and began to speak. He hadn't spoken for more than five minutes when Edmund nudged me with his elbow. I glanced over at him, surprised by this unusual action. He inclined his head slightly to the right where Vincent and Georgie sat with David and Karl on the other side of them. I looked over just in time to see David reach across and grasp Vincent's arm with one hand and Georgie's with the other. Then I bit my lip to keep the scream down that rose in my throat, for Georgie had a live mouse that was evidently intended as dinner for the snake Vincent was holding! David, with a stern face, but with hidden mirth twinkling ever so slightly in his eyes, rose and still with a firm grasp on each arm, led the little boys out of church. There were gasps as the three walked down the aisle and out of the door, and I thought I heard a few little squeaks, whether from the mouse or from someone trying to suppress their screams, I couldn't say. Karl, I noticed, was looking straight ahead. I could tell he was fighting with himself to keep his gravity, for he looked almost sullen. Edmund couldn't quite keep his mirth down, for he had to cough a few times and looked closely down at his Bible. Carrie, on the other side of me, hadn't noticed a thing until David was taking the boys out, and looked at me questioningly. As for Mama, she turned at the sudden disturbance by her eldest, but the people and hats were in her way, and she couldn't see. It was probably a good thing for Vincent and Georgie that she couldn't, though I'm sure David did quite as well. This whole thing struck me as so like a "Ted, Fred, Larry and Jim" story that it was some time before I could get my mind back to the sermon. Eventually David returned with two very sober and extra quiet boys who sat down meekly on either side of him and didn't move until the service was over. Thankfully no one mentioned the episode, though I'm sure it will be talked about in homes and around town for weeks to come. The stories of Vincent and Georgie are the delight of some in Codell who never forget to tell the latest one to anyone willing to listen. Now I know what Grandmother must have felt like.

Edmund, Karl, David and I couldn't keep it to ourselves either, and as soon as we could after dinner, when the little boys were out in the barn and the little girls were with Carrie picking flowers, we told Mama. She looked horrified and heartily approved the chastisement David had inflicted on the miscreants. After it was all told, Mama began to see the humorous side of it, as Edmund had all along, and began to laugh. Instantly we all joined her and peal after peal of laughter rang through the room until it was hushed by Evie's cries. Mama told me to write that story down and send it to Daddy as she was sure he was capable of doing the same thing as a boy. I have and thought you would also like to laugh about it.

Now you can see why I hope the boys aren't into mischief. David doesn't think they will do anything else, at least not today. I don't know what we will do if this behavior keeps on. Edmund said he was glad he didn't have to deal with the boys for he most certainly would have laughed.

Telling that story has reminded me of another "Ted, Fred, Larry and Jim" story that I have yet to tell you. I found it in the desk the other day with a note to copy it for you. And so before I forget, let me bring it out and copy it now.

This should be the first of the stories instead of the last as they are the youngest in this one. Ted is eight, Fred seven, Larry five and Jim four. Maggie wasn't born yet.

There wasn't much happening that day. The four boys had finished their chores and were trying to find a way to occupy themselves. It would have to be out of doors, for Mama was cleaning the house.

"What we going to do?" Larry asked, rolling down the grassy hill.

"I don't know," Fred shrugged. "But we have to find

something."

Jim rolled down the hill after Larry. He didn't know what to do either. Lying on his back he gazed at the sky. "I wish I could fly," he said to Larry.

Ted had remained silent, thinking deeply about something. Fred noticed a look come over his face that meant he might have an idea.

"What are we going to do, Ted?" he urged.

"Well," Ted began slowly. Larry and Jim left their hillside to come hear. "We become chimney sweeps." This was spoken in slow dramatic tones and immediately impressed the boys listening as the very thing to do.

Larry was the first to wonder how they would sweep the chimneys.

"Oh, we can get a broom. I think Mama has two. But we can't tell her what we are doing as it will be a surprise."

Fred looked puzzled. "Won't she find out as soon as we climb in the chimney?"

"Won't start with ours. Hmm, I know, down at the edge of town, you know, where those old ladies just moved. It would be good to start with theirs."

"Why?" Jim asked.

"Oh, because," Ted replied, "because we should help them."

Fred nodded. "Yes, we should help them. Let's go."

"I'll go get the broom," Ted called over his shoulder as he ran to the house. Soon he returned with an old almost fallen apart broom. "Mama said we could have it!" He eagerly informed his brothers.

It was with great rejoicing and many plans that the four Foster boys set off down the street to the house at the edge of town.

Upon arriving, they quickly found that no one was home. That fact didn't daunt them for long, and it was soon decided that a clean chimney would be a very nice surprise when they did arrive home. Little did they dream what the surprise really would be.

After looking around a little, Ted remarked, "Well, we can't climb up the chimney from inside, so we have to go on the roof."

The rest of the boys nodded and began looking for the best way up. Fred first noticed the tree and eagerly he and Ted climbed it. Larry handed up the broom and then with Jim, watched. Soon the two boys were safely on the roof and looking down the chimney.

"It's kind of small," Fred said a little doubtfully.

"Sweep the top part of it while I go get Jim. That way he won't get dirty."

Fred poked the broom down the chimney and moved it around in a vain attempt to get it clean.

"Come on, Jim, you get to clean this one because it is small."

Jim looked a little frightened and made no move to start climbing the tree where Ted was waiting.

"Come on, we can't wait all day," Ted urged.

It was with reluctance that Jim began to climb, slowly and with great fear. He got almost as high as Ted when he looked down. His face turned white, and he clung to his branch in terror. At Ted's urging, he only shook his head and began to cry.

Ted was disgusted. "Okay, then climb down and Larry can do it. He isn't scared of a little tree like this."

But Jim couldn't climb down, for he was much too frightened to do it alone. At last, with a great deal of help from Ted and Fred, who had finished his part of the sweeping, Jim was safely landed on solid earth once more.

"Now Larry," Ted ordered, "don't you go and be so frightened."

"I won't," Larry said confidently, for he loved to climb trees. True to his word, he successfully climbed up the tree and onto the roof. With Ted and Fred to help him, he clambered into the top of the chimney. With a great deal of wiggling and with pushes from both Ted and Fred, Larry managed to get down the chimney until just his arms and head showed above it.

"Here's the broom," Fred stuck the broom down a small crack between Larry and the bricks. When Larry tried to move it, he found to his great dismay that he couldn't move at all. He was stuck!

"I want to get out of here," he wailed to his brothers. "I don't like being in this."

"Larry," Ted began "you are already there, so just sweep the chimney; then you can get out."

"But I can't move!"

Ted and Fred exchanged glances, "Little boys can be so difficult at times." After trying in vain to persuade Larry to stay and at least try to sweep the chimney, they finally with great reluctance agreed to help him out. Ted never did like to quit something he had begun. But getting Larry out was a different story than getting him in. Pull and tug as they would, Larry remained firmly wedged in the chimney and couldn't be moved.

"I guess you'll just have to stay there until you get not so fat," Ted told him finally.

"I'm sure that after supper tomorrow you will be able to get out," was Fred's reassuring comment.

"We'll come get you tomorrow night."

Larry began to cry. "Don't leave me. I want to get out! Help me get out Fred! Please, Ted, don't leave me!"

Ted and Fred looked at each other. It would be silly to waste the rest of the day sitting up on a roof waiting for Larry to get thin enough to pull him out. There was nothing they could do now. And it might take days.

"Look, Larry," Ted said at last. "We can't sit here until you get thin. We would roll off the roof when we tried to sleep, and Mama would be worried. We'll come back later to check on you. You'll be all right for you can't fall off, and no wild animals can get you up here. We'll even do your chores for you."

And then, in spite of Larry's cries and pleas, Ted and Fred climbed back down the roof and down the tree. Calling up cheerfully to their stranded brother that everything would be all right, Ted, Fred and Jim left the scene of their latest escapade to find something more enjoyable to do.

For Larry, stuck in the chimney, time passed slowly. His feet began to feel strange, almost as though they didn't belong to him at all anymore. He couldn't move around and no one heard his cries for help. "I'm too fat," he thought to himself. "But I'm hungry, and now I can't eat for a long time. Oh, why did I say I would clean the chimney?" Tears began to roll down his dirty cheeks, and he cried until he was tired.

Towards evening, the two ladies of the house returned, neither one noticing the little boy stuck in their chimney. When they tried to start a fire inside, to their amazement it wouldn't burn, and smoke, instead of going up the chimney, poured out into the room. At last, after several equally fruitless tries, they decided that something must be stuck in their chimney. Great was their wonder and astonishment when, on going outside to look at their chimney, they beheld a little head sticking out of it. Being rather deaf, they were not able to hear Larry's pitiful cries which came hoarsely from his dry throat. Neither of the dear old ladies knew what to do. Having only been in the town for a short time, they hadn't yet made the acquaintance of "those Foster boys."

Meanwhile, Ted, Fred and Jim soon forgot all about Larry and his pitiful state in other games. When the supper bell rang, they hurried home, eagerly. It was after they were seated, that Papa asked,

"And where is Larry?"

"He can't eat tonight," Ted answered hoping that answer would satisfy.

Papa looked at Mama questioningly. "Is he sick?"

Mama shook her head. "I don't think so."

"Where IS he?" Papa asked again.

"Really, Papa, he doesn't want to eat," replied Fred with a glance at Ted.

"Boys, I asked you a question, and I want an answer. Where is Larry?" Papa's voice was growing stern, and the boys knew they would have to answer.

It was Ted who came up with the answer which he hoped would satisfy, for he didn't like to think of what might happen were Papa to find out what they had done. "Well, he is at the house at the edge of the village. You know, where those ladies just moved."

"Ted! He didn't invite himself to stay for supper?" Mama's voice was horrified.

Ted shook his head. "I don't think he did."

Papa and Mama exchanged glances. What could Larry be doing? "Why didn't he come home?"

"He didn't want to, I guess."

Fred added, "He really couldn't bear to leave."

Jim could no longer be kept silent by his brothers and piped up, "Larry can't come home for a few days maybe 'cause he's too fat. And he can't eat supper or breakfast or anything for maybe a year!"

A loud pounding on the door interrupted any further conversation. "Foster, did you know Larry is stuck in the chimney down at the Harris home?" was the somewhat startling sentence that greeted Papa as he opened the door.

"The chimney!" Papa waited to hear no more but with the neighbor rushed down the street. Mama hurried after them forgetting the other boys entirely.

Ted, Fred and Jim looked at one another then decided it was better to just stay there and eat.

Quite a crowd had gathered at the Harris home. It wasn't everyday one got to see a little boy stuck in a chimney. Larry's cries were pitiful indeed to hear for he kept saying that he didn't want to be a chimney sweep, and please don't leave him! Papa and several other men climbed onto the roof and after some difficulty, at last succeeded in freeing poor little Larry from his imprisonment. In spite of Fred's cleaning of the chimney, Larry was covered in soot.

Clinging to Papa as he was carried down the ladder,

Larry tried to tell what had happened, but he was so exhausted, that he didn't get very far. When he tried to stand, he found to his amazement and dismay that his legs wouldn't hold him, and he would have fallen if his father had not picked him up again. The doctor accompanied them home and after looking Larry over, he recommended a bath, a good meal, and a good night's rest. It was only after Larry was sleeping that Papa had time to speak to Ted and Fred.

Never again did Ted, Fred, Larry or Jim ever try to clean a chimney in that way.

I can see Kirsten and Rosalie out in the yard under a large shade tree with Carrie. She is usually with them on Sunday afternoons telling them Bible stories. David couldn't sleep anymore and has gone to check on Vincent and Georgie. Please pray for Karl. Something is on his mind. He is much quieter than usual and at times he seems deeply lost in thought. He is now fifteen and so unlike his former self.

I did so enjoy your last letter. A trip to Halifax sounds wonderful right now if it is any cooler than here. What a fascinating old fort. The boys were quite interested in your description of it. I can't imagine the noise of a big city. I think that Plainville is noisy, but I'm sure it would be quiet compared to Halifax. I don't remember ever staying in a hotel in my life. Not one of us does, except Mama. Georgie said he would write up, I mean down, your adventures in Halifax for the "Farmhouse Garrett," and here is a copy of it for you, complete with spelling, grammar and punctuation.

Maria's trip to halifaks
by Georgie Foster

in the begining maria went on a train to a plase, coled halefaks ther waz lotz of botes. to many to cout so Maria wokd around the sity a nuther famuly wuz ther to so tha ol wokd and wokd and went to ete at a res tront and had Chikin and stemd Putatoz and keritz and is Crem. That wuz gud tha so meny thengs to bi. but tha cudnt bi the thengs kuz tha didt hav ther muny and tha bot wor bons and stampz to fit the wor. it Wuz nis in halIfaks an tha viztd a fort namd george an it wuz a stor an thu gun wuz shot. tha had fun maria went hom agin and her Mama wuz glad to se her and so wuz edith and Mark and andrew and lidea Ruth. thu End. by Georgie Foster

I can't say that he has improved in his spelling much since last year. Hopefully he will in the next school term. He asked how to spell all your names except Lydia Ruth's. I suppose he thought that would be easy.

We get a letter almost every week from Daddy still. He doesn't say much about training, for it is always the same: shooting, marching, polishing buttons, digging, hiking, throwing tin cans to practice for hand grenades, shining shoes, cleaning guns, polishing buttons, shooting, marching . . . He did say that they somehow manage to fit in eating and sleeping somewhere. He misses us and said he misses hearing your letters. He hopes to get a leave of absence before he has to leave. I do hope he can. I miss him so.

The papers are full of war news. There has been some talk of peace, but how long will it be just talk? I wonder what General Pershing is thinking about peace? We have gotten letters from Uncle Ian, Uncle Lance, Uncle Philip Vincent, in fact from all of Mama's six brothers. You know they are all younger than Mama, but we haven't heard from some of them for quite a while.

Uncle Lance (He's the oldest, the one that lives in New York.) has been called up as he is with the National Guard at Camp Mills, New York, and is under the command of Colonel Douglas MacArthur. He said they call themselves the "rainbow" division because the men come from all over the country and have such different backgrounds. They are all from National Guard units he said.

Uncle David (he lives in Tennessee with Grandpa Wallace) tried to enlist, but was turned down for something.

Uncle John, as I think I mentioned before, is from

Colorado and enlisted and is with Daddy at Camp Funston. He wrote Mama and is eager to go over seas.

Uncle Ian is already over in France having gone over with the 1st Division. He said they haven't done any fighting yet, but the French are proclaiming them heroes already. He has heard talk of placing them in French and British divisions to "fill in the ranks," but General Pershing won't have it that way.

Uncle Michael has been drafted. He lives in Tennessee also, and is, or was rather, a clerk in a store with no military experience. He said he had never even fired a gun. He thinks it will be quite a while before they go over because "just about none of the enlisted or drafted men here know anything about fighting unless it is with fists." He is in Camp Gordon, Georgia.

Of course Uncle Philip Vincent is already over and has been in and out of the action since the beginning. He told us he had joined up with the French air force. It was only a brief postcard, so he didn't write much.

There was also a letter from Mary Jane. She said there was another air raid on London. It was the biggest one yet and there were 37 people killed in London. With Uncle James off fighting, Aunt Samantha and the children went to live with her parents farther north. Mary Jane didn't remember just where they had gone. Grandmother and Grandfather Foster are not living in London now either, having moved in with Aunt Margaret and Uncle Harris, at least for a while. Slough is still fairly close to London. She said she was going to write to you in a week or so, so you should be getting a letter from her before too long. She didn't say anything about Kent or Orville. I wonder how they are doing? Perhaps she will say something to you about them.

The wheat crop is doing better than even David hoped. The newly cleared land adds another five acres to the 375 that were already in use. You should see Carrie's garden. It is beautiful! Everything is producing well, and we should be well stocked for the coming winter. Right now with this heat it is hard to remember the cold days of winter.

Everyone here sat in breathless silence as I read of Lydia Ruth's boat ride. Georgie's eyes were so wide, and for once he didn't say anything. I think he was too surprised to find out someone else did something unbelievable. I shudder to think of what could have happened.

Now, as this letter is quite long and hopefully full of interesting news for you, I will close and see if I can pacify Evie for I hear her crying.

Love always,
Emma

P.S. One more story, Maria.

This evening, Edmund and I were out for a little walk when we came upon Karl standing all alone by the fence. Edmund asked him if he was all right.

Karl turned. His face looked troubled. "I don't know what to do."

"About what?" Edmund asked.

"About, well . . . about everything. I mean," Karl looked a little confused. "What, . . . why, oh, forget it. I'm just not like the rest of you." He started to turn away, but Edmund caught his arm saying,

"You can be like us, Karl, if you only will ask the Lord Jesus Christ to forgive you as He has forgiven us."

Karl shook his head. "You didn't have to live in the streets of New York. I did. I had to steal to get food to keep Kirsten and me alive. I've told lies, and if your dad had any idea what I was really like, he never would have let me come here much less say he trusted me."

I interrupted him. "Karl! Daddy is your father too. And he would love you no matter what you have done or what you do. Jesus Christ loves you even more than Daddy ever could."

Karl was silent, looking at the ground. I was praying, and I'm sure Edmund was too. At last Karl spoke again, his voice low and not quite steady. "Would Jesus really forgive me?"

"Yes. Do you want to ask Him to right now?" Edmund asked quietly.

Karl nodded and the three of us knelt in the gathering dusk out by the barn, and Karl prayed for the first time in his life. When we arose, there was a new look in Karl's face. A look of peace and well, I don't know what to call it, but you could tell he was no longer the same Karl.

I just couldn't wait until tomorrow to tell you, but now I must get to bed. I know you will all rejoice with us.

"Mom, Ted and Fred were just awful! They are worse than any of the gang."

"I agree they were quite something," Corporal nodded. "But I liked the mouse and snake in church story. I know if I had ever done such a thing, my father would have given me a dose of hickory tea that I never would have forgotten."

Mrs. Mitchell laughed. "If I remember right, that is what David gave the boys. I can tell you they never again brought a live creature to church, not even a cricket. Now, I have looked all over for the letter that should come next, but I haven't been able to find it anywhere."

"Yes," Ria put in, "we searched everywhere at Grandma's and couldn't find it. We even had the boys and Dad looking. I do wish we had it though." She sighed.

"But since we don't, shall we continue?"

CHAPTER TWENTY-THREE

Wednesday
October 31, 1917
Codell, Kansas
USA

Dearest Maria,

Daddy has been home for a visit this month! It wasn't a very long visit, but it was for a few days. He didn't even tell us he was coming. He said he received his pass and hopped aboard the first train out, and once in Plainville he hitched a ride with Old Mr. Carter. We didn't know he was coming and were in school! Were we surprised when we walked in the house and saw him! I thought something had happened when Edmund picked me up, for he had a big smile on his face and he wouldn't say anything. The exasperating boy!

I won't even try to tell you what happened that first evening. Just imagine twelve tongues going at once, for everyone talked and no one listened. That will give you a good idea of what it was like. No one wanted to go to bed, but Mama and Daddy couldn't be persuaded to let anyone stay up. I think they wanted some time together, just the two of them. I can't say that I blame them any. I had a dreadful headache when I went to bed from all the noise and excitement.

The next morning it was very hard to leave for school. I didn't want to go teach, and the children certainly didn't want to go sit all day in school. Daddy said we should all go, because he was going to go work in the fields with the older boys. Vincent and Georgie begged to stay and work, too, but Daddy wouldn't hear of it and sent them to get ready. Edmund took me to school as usual, telling me he would come pick me up afterwards. The morning went well, but that afternoon . . . Well, that is another story.

It was recess time, and all the children were outside. I wasn't out with them, as I had some things I needed to take care of. But there had never been any problem, and I didn't expect any. So it was a surprise when Kirsten burst into the schoolhouse crying, "Emma! Emma! Hurry!"

I looked up in astonishment. Never before had Kirsten called me Emma at school. I looked at her face and noticed it wore the frightened, almost terrified look that used to be so common on it. "Kirsten," I soothed, "calm down. Everything will be all right. What happened?"

"They are fighting!" she whispered tremulously, clinging to me in fright.

"Who are fighting?" I asked, starting for the door, noticing for the first time the sounds coming from out in the yard. Not waiting for an answer, I hurried out with Kirsten trailing behind.

The scene I saw was not one to inspire anyone, except with a desire to end it as quickly as possible. All the children were gathered around watching. Some, it seemed, were trying to stop the fight; others cheered on the combatants.

The children parted as I approached, allowing me to see Vincent and Frank rolling on the ground. "Boys!" I exclaimed, grasping an arm of each and jerking them apart onto their feet. "What is going on?" I demanded sternly.

Vincent looked somewhat ashamed, but Frank looked only mad. Neither one spoke. There was a stillness in the schoolyard. "Boys, go in to your desks." I spoke quietly. They departed in silence, and I turned to the rest of the children. "I want you to stay out here until I ring the bell."

In the schoolhouse, I questioned the boys and learned the whole story. Frank had been teasing, or rather taunting, I should say, Gretchen and Emil about being spies for the

Germans. Vincent had seen Gretchen in tears, moved closer and heard Frank's words. In his indignation over it, Vincent lost all thought of what he should do and simply put up his fists. That was all it took, and who knows how the fight would have ended if Kirsten had not come for me. I didn't feel as though I could punish the boys then, so I told them to remain after school and then rang the bell.

The rest of the day went by so slowly. In some ways I was thankful, for I dreaded what I had to do, but in other ways I wished it would go quickly so I could get it done with.

At last the other children had left, and I was alone with the two boys. I talked seriously to them for a few minutes and then picked up my ruler. It was the hardest thing I have ever done.

The boys left the schoolhouse very sober and quiet. After they were gone and I could no longer see them, I sank into my chair, buried my face in my arms and cried. Why did it have to be today of all days for this to happen? Did I do the right thing? I was so lost in thought that I scarcely noticed Edmund ride up.

"Are you ready?" his cheery voice sounded in the door. "Emma! What is it? What is wrong?" There was concern now as he hurried over to me. "Emma, what has happened?" he asked again, as I only answered with tears.

"Edmund, I can't go home," I sobbed out. "How will I ever face them? Oh, we shouldn't even have had school today."

Edmund was silent a moment then he said softly, "Lucy, just what is it that has happened?"

I looked up and saw only concern in his face. Didn't he already know? Hadn't he asked why Vincent wasn't with the others?

"Didn't you see the children?" I asked, choking over a sob.

"Yes," Edmund looked more puzzled than ever. "They were all walking home. They didn't seem quite as cheerful as sometimes, but what has that to do with anything?"

"Oh, Edmund!" I couldn't look at him and turned my head away. "There was a fight at school."

"Who?" When I didn't answer, he gently turned my face and looked into my eyes. I couldn't meet his gaze and turned away.

"Vincent?"

I nodded.

"Georgie?"

"No," I whispered.

"Tell me what happened," he ordered, perching himself on the edge of my desk where he could look at me.

So I told him. "How could I punish one and not the other? Vincent was in the right, but if I didn't punish him too, I'd be accused of playing favorites."

"Vincent might have been right in what he was defending, but he was not right in fighting at school. He should have come right to you and told you what was happening. I'm sure he understands that. Now stop blaming yourself. Dry your eyes and let's go home. I don't want to spend the rest of the day stuck in a school house." He handed me his handkerchief and stood up.

Just talking about it had made me feel better. The ride also helped, until we arrived home before the children. Edmund took the horses to the barn to unsaddle them, and I slowly entered the house. Daddy and Mama were both in the kitchen, Daddy in a chair with Evie on his knee, and Mama at work on supper.

"How was school today?" Daddy asked as I came in.

I looked at him. "Oh, Daddy!" I cried, running to him.

"There now, what is this all about?" He hugged me and then lifted my chin to look me full in the face.

I swallowed hard and blurted out the story once more. "I didn't want to do it," I said, "but I had to."

"You did what was right. Now, go wash your face and see if you can't find a smile somewhere. I think Vincent will tell me about it himself."

He was right. No sooner had the children come home, but Vincent went straight up to Daddy and told him what had happened. Daddy and Vincent were gone for a while, but when they came back, both were smiling and everything was all right.

I had a visit from Frank's father on the following Monday morning. He assured me it won't happen again. And it hasn't. Gretchen and Emil are settling in here, and after that first experience, the children have all accepted them. I see I didn't mention who Gretchen and Emil were. Their family moved here last month, and the children started school here the beginning of October. Mr. Straussmeyer is in a training camp ready to go overseas. Mrs. Straussmeyer and the children live with Mr. Straussmeyer's mother who, according to Gretchen, is really old and can only speak German. Both children speak German as well as they do English.

Daddy's visit was wonderful, but much too short. He had to go back on Tuesday. He doesn't have any idea when they will be shipped out. In some ways, I think it is harder now to have Daddy gone after he was home, than it was when he left the first time. Why is that? Perhaps it is because at first we were stirred by all the news of patriotism, and now the reality of it all has sunk in. Whatever the reason, it was harder to say good-bye. Perhaps it is also the fact that we know Daddy could be shipped over to France anytime now, while before, he was just going to a training camp.

I was so shocked to hear of Kent's death! Poor Mary Jane! This war is really becoming more and more real. How many blue stars now hanging in windows will be gold before the war is over? Will ours be gold? Maybe that is really the reason it was harder when Daddy left this time. Deep down inside, I wonder if . . . But I won't even think it.

Last week we had a bonfire one evening. It was a beautiful night for it. It was slightly chilly, a sure sign that autumn is here. There had been piles of brush from the acres the boys cleared earlier this year. All the large tree branches and such were split for the house, but there was still much left, and it was decided that a bonfire would be a good way to take care of it. It was on a Friday evening, so when we all had returned from school, David and Karl headed out to start it. Carrie and I helped Mama pack our supper in a hamper. Vincent and Georgie were wild with excitement, and I don't know what we would have done if Edmund hadn't stayed to help. At last we were ready and could set off. The fire was blazing delightfully when at last we reached it. The little boys would have run on ahead if Mama had not told them to stay with us. As it was, the three older boys had a difficult time keeping the younger two at a safe distance. Kirsten and Rosalie stared spellbound as the flames licked up the wood and brush. Evie seemed to enjoy it every bit as much as the rest of us did, for she talked and cooed, reaching for the flames and squealing when something in the fire snapped loudly.

It was a good thing we had packed an ample supper, for everyone ate ravenously. The fire continued to burn, and as the sun began to set, we drew nearer to enjoy its warmth since it was growing colder. David brought a stump for Mama to sit on, while the rest of us sat on the ground. Rosalie was soon cuddled on Mama's lap, staring somewhat sleepily into the fire. David sat with his arm around Carrie, and Kirsten lay curled up with her head in Karl's lap. Edmund and I were side by side, as you might guess, but Evie was in Edmund's arms, not mine. It was as much as he could do to keep her there, for she refused all efforts to cuddle and sleep and acted quite determined to get to the fire, if possible. Vincent and Georgie sat near Mama; their excitement over the novelty of the event had subsided.

"Look," I pointed overhead, "the first star."

All eyes turned to look and soon one and then another and then a few more stars began to show, twinkling with growing brightness as the sun sank lower and lower. All conversation ceased. Even Evie grew still as she realized that

Edmund was not going to let her have those bright pretty things. Into the stillness came the sound of a note being hummed followed by another note, and then Edmund began singing. That started it, and soon the air was filled with song. We sang any song we could think of, some sad and dreary, some light and cheerful, others calm and encouraging. Eventually we all fell silent, either overcome with sleep or a lack of voice.

"Would you four older ones please sing 'Keep the Home-Fires Burning for me?" Mama asked, looking into the dying flames.

David hummed a note, and then at his nod we began:

> "They were summoned from the hillside;
> They were called in from the glen,
> And the Country found them ready
> At the stirring call for men.
> Let no tears add to their hardship,
> As the Soldiers pass along,
> And although your heart is breaking,
> Make it sing this cheery song.
>
> Keep the Home-fires burning,
> While your hearts are yearning,
> Though your lads are far away
> They dream of Home;
> There's a silver lining
> Through the dark cloud shining,
> Turn the dark cloud inside out,
> Till the boys come Home;
>
> Over seas there came a pleading,
> "Help a Nation in distress!"
> And we gave our glorious laddies;
> Honor bade us do no less.
> For no gallant Son of freedom
> To a tyrants yoke should bend,

> And a noble heart must answer
> To the sacred call of "Friend"
>
> Keep the Home-fires burning..."

That last word "home" seemed to linger in the air around us as we ended. Someday, this war will be over. And if we aren't to meet here in our earthly home, we will meet in our heavenly one. The fire was not more than glowing embers with an occasional flame here or there. The cold could be felt, and though I had my coat on, I shivered.

Edmund glanced over at me before he spoke, "I hate to mention it, but it is getting late, and the wind is rather chilly to keep the younger ones out in it much longer. Besides, I don't think I could sing another note."

Mama gave a low laugh. "I'd be happy to go in, but I'm afraid I can't stir from this seat, for Rosalie is asleep in my arms, and Georgie is asleep with his head on my lap. I think Vincent might be almost -- if not all the way -- asleep, as well."

David gave Carrie a gentle shake to rouse her and then stood up. Karl was in such a position that rising for him would have been difficult without dumping Kirsten on the ground. Seeing which, David lifted Kirsten, and Karl stretched his cramped legs and stood up. I didn't want to move, and but for the fact that it was cold, I think I would have stayed right there. As it was, I knew I had to stand up, and it was with great reluctance that I did.

"Emma, take Evie, would you? I don't want to drop her when I try to stand up," Edmund requested.

I wasn't sure if she would stay asleep, but thankfully she did. Edmund took Rosalie from Mama. David managed to rouse the little boys enough to start them staggering for home and bed. Mama, Carrie and David with the remains of the supper, and Edmund, Karl and I with our sleeping sisters followed.

Once the kitchen was reached, Georgie, who never

had been fully awake, crawled under the table and laid down. No one could coax him to so much as stir, and at last Edmund and Karl moved the table so that David could take him to bed.

November 1,

I didn't have time yesterday to finish this, as I had many interruptions and couldn't stay up late, as there was school today. I see I didn't even mention that I was asked to teach again, but that much should be obvious.

I did enjoy reading about your birthday. It still seems rather strange to me that we can be sixteen. What is even more unbelievable is that Vincent will be ten at the end of the month! How can that be? I think the time is going by faster than it did when we were young. I understand and agree with your feelings completely!

Little Archie sounds so sweet. We certainly did laugh about those three little boys. Will they be another "Vincent and Georgie" or another "Ted, Fred, Larry and Jim?"

I know this isn't very long, but I have papers that must be graded, and this letter really should go with David and Karl who are going to town in the morning. Give my love to all.

    Ever yours,
    Emma

November 10,

As you can see, this letter did not get mailed by the boys in the morning. I was looking for something here in the desk today and came across this letter. I know I mailed something to you, for I gave it to Karl, and he assured me it was mailed. I do wonder what it was that I sent. Will you please enlighten me in your next letter? But, I should still send this letter.

Oh, I have to tell you that Georgie has given up his

idea of becoming a newspaper man entirely. It happened this way:

Yesterday in school, I decided to have a spelling bee. One of the "choose your team and toe the line," spelling bees. The children were all very excited, as we had never done that before. The sides were quickly chosen, and we began. Georgie was the second one up on his team, and I gave him the word "fox." He spelled it the same way he has always spelled it, "f-o-k-s," though goodness knows how many times he has studied it. He was the first one to sit down. His team groaned but continued on bravely and ended up winning. Later on in the day, we had a test in arithmetic, and Georgie answered every one correctly. I didn't know of the change in his decided career until we were all sitting around the supper table that evening.

"I have decided that the 'Farmhouse Garret' will have to have a new writer because I am going to not be a newspaper man ever again for my whole life," he announced abruptly.

"What brought about this change?" David questioned with a slight grin, for Georgie's manner was rather unusual.

"It's all 'cause I can't spell anything fit to be seen, and I can do that 'rithmetic right. I'm goin' to do numbers 'stead of letters from now on. And I've decided." The tone and manner of speech were so quaint that it was with difficulty that we kept a sober countenance. Several tried to talk Georgie into studying his spelling words a little harder before giving all writing up completely, but as far as he was concerned, he was through with spelling forever.

And so, I'm afraid that unless Georgie feels differently, you will never get to read any future issues of the "Farmhouse Garret."

Edmund and I are going to town in just a moment, and I will mail this myself. I wonder what I could have sent you.

Your bewildered cousin,
Emma

"What did you send, Mom?"

Lydia squeezed her friend's hand and whispered, "Be quiet and maybe we'll find out."

Mrs. Mitchell looked amused as she unfolded her cousin's answering letter.

CHAPTER TWENTY-FOUR

Wednesday
December 5, 1917
Princeville, Nova Scotia
Canada

Dear Emma,

It is a beautiful winter afternoon here. There is no snow, and the air seems mild for winter. The sun is shining brightly, and all is peaceful. I am writing here in the front room. A merry fire dances in the fireplace and makes the room delightfully cozy. Mark is at school but should be home soon. Edith and Lydia Ruth are knitting. I don't quite feel sure of what is being knitted, and I don't think I should interrupt and ask. They both appear to be concentrating very hard on their task. Andrew is with Mama at Grandmother's house.

I must tell you about that first "letter." Edith had brought it to me one evening after she had been in Pictou, and I opened it at the supper table. All were eagerly waiting for your news. I opened the envelope and pulled out some folded paper.

"It looks rather short this time," I remarked as I unfolded them, for there didn't seem to be as many as usual. I didn't say anything for a minute as I began reading to myself.

"Well," Edith prompted, "what does she say?"

I began to laugh. "I'm not sure what she wants me to do with this. It is a list of supplies for the farm, it looks like.

Here it says, feed for horses. Down here it looks like some part for a machine of some kind. Here is a note. 'Karl, check prices on cornmeal and flour,' I hope he remembered to."

"What?"

"Where is the letter?"

"Is this a joke?" were asked at once.

"I don't know what this is. Let me read some more. Here is a list of baking items. And here is another note. 'Would one of you please work with Georgie on his spelling when you return? Don't forget the paper for me, Emma.' I hope they didn't forget the paper."

Mark volunteered to work with Georgie though he said he wasn't going anywhere.

How we all laughed. I was sure some mistake had been made, but I didn't know what. Mark decided that you were being held hostage by some Germans and this was the only kind of note you could send out. "It must have a meaning somewhere," he insisted with a laugh.

When your real letter did arrive a few weeks later, Edith declared that no one must have worked with Georgie on his spelling and that is why he had changed his vocation. Oh, Emma, we are still laughing about it. I hope you didn't want those papers back? Karl certainly mailed what you gave him to mail, as it was your handwriting on the envelope. It was your own fault that it was the wrong thing. Emma, this story is known all over the village, and I might warn you, when you and Edmund come for that visit, it might get mentioned. Edith looked for those parts you needed, but couldn't find them anywhere in Pictou.

I must start on supper so will try to finish writing later this evening or tomorrow.

Thursday 13,

As you can see, I didn't write the next day, the 6th of December. That is a day that will forever be remembered here in Nova Scotia. It was shortly after 9:00 am when the quiet of the village was shattered by a dull boom, as of an explosion or some such thing, and the ground fairly trembled with the sound. Instantly the doors flew open all around the village, and everyone began streaming out to find the cause of it.

"What was that?"

"Did you hear it? What was it?"

"It sounded like an explosion!"

"The Germans must be attacking Pictou!"

"It's a zeppelin raid!"

The questions and guesses flew thick and fast, yet no one had any answers. Was it really a German raid on Pictou? If so, would we be next? The younger children stared wide-eyed, mothers were pale, and the lads were excited. The men held a quick conference and decided that some of them would head to Pictou to find out what had really happened. All volunteered to go, but Steve Drinkwalter declared that he and his brothers would be the only ones to go.

"If we a' whaur to gae, it wad leave nae one maun to guard the toon. An' ye maun a' hae guidwives, lads an' lassies an' hames. We hae naething. Donnae say ony thing. Seth, Sam, let us be aff noo."

No one could prevent them, and all were silent as we watched the three men depart. What would they find? No one knew. For several minutes, no one spoke. All was quiet save for the sound of the waves. Mr. Campton took charge and told everyone to go inside and wait. Mrs. Lawson, James and Jenny came with us, and I saw Grandmother go with the McLeans.

Several hours of anxious waiting followed. It was easy to imagine all sorts of horrors happening in Pictou. Had the Germans really attacked Canada? Was the fighting going to begin here? We prayed throughout the day as we waited and watched, listened and hoped. Mark and James occupied some of the time by planning impossible defenses for the village in which this house and the two of them would no doubt play large roles.

It wasn't until late in the day that Seth Drinkwalter returned. To the eager questions, he replied,

"It was nae a German attack. A ship blew up in the harbor of Halifax. The toon, frae what we can learn, is . . ." Seth hesitated.

"Is it gone?" Mr. Campton asked.

"Nae a' of it, but ilka report is worse than the one or. Sam and Steve hae bided fer to learn ony other news."

I know what you are thinking, Emma. Halifax is over ninety miles away and yet we heard the explosion. I can't tell you everything we did in the days and nights that followed. Almost all the men of the village left the following day to help the stricken city. The women stayed up most of the night gathering items that might be needed. The men actually couldn't leave in the morning as planned because a severe winter storm had struck in the night, and the road was nearly impassible.

Let me see if I can weave all the reports that have gone around into somewhat of a clear picture.

The French ship, *Mont Blanc*, was heading up the harbor loaded with tons of high explosives from New York. At the same time, a Norwegian ship, the *SS Imo*, was leaving port for New York. She was empty and traveling faster and in the wrong lane. The *Mont Blanc* signaled her several times to get out of the way, but for some reason the *SS Imo* refused. The ships collided and the *Mont Blanc* caught on fire. As the ship's captain knew what was on his ship, he gave an immediate order to abandon ship. I have heard stories that the crew all went across the harbor to Dartmouth and also that they landed in Halifax but couldn't make anyone understand their French; either way, there was a large crowd at the docks in Halifax to watch, for the force of the impact had sent the *Mont Blanc* straight for pier number six. The Halifax Fire Department was ready to try to put out the fire when at 9:05 the ship blew up. Never has there been a man-made explosion equal to that. It picked up rocks from the harbor floor and tossed them high into the sky from whence they fell in showers, along with shrapnel and splinters of the ship. The entire north end of Halifax was flattened. Hundreds were killed and thousands wounded. Windows were blown out as far away as 50 miles from the actual explosion. The force of the blast caused a giant tidal wave to wash, I don't know how far up, not just into Halifax, but also across the harbor into Dartmouth. The ship's anchor, which weighed 1140 pounds, was blown two miles away! With all those houses felled by the blast, fires started from overturned stoves in the destroyed buildings and quickly spread. Everything was in chaos. Rescue work was almost impossible in some places.

How do you shelter and help hundreds and thousands of wounded and dying, homeless and bewildered, terrified and frantic people? And as if all that wasn't enough, that night a blizzard struck with such fury as has not been seen for years! Is it any wonder that hundreds more have died? Help has poured into the stricken city in the last few days. Boston has sent ships loaded with medical staff and supplies, food, clothing and even glass for windows. I don't know how long it will take Halifax to recover, but I know it will take a while. The death toll is still unknown. The Lieutenant Governor's son, Lieutenant Eric Grant, was on leave from France, and according to the papers he said that "the sights here are worse than anything I've seen in the trenches." Worse than the front lines? What must it be like!

The men are still gone, and no one is sure when they will return. Everyone here is still in a daze about the whole thing. I can't write any more. Merry Christmas to you all. What kind of Christmas will it be for those poor people in Halifax? Homes destroyed, family and friends killed, wounded, blinded. My heart aches for them.

      Always yours,
      Maria

> Thursday
> January 24, 1918
> Codell, Kansas
> USA

Dear Maria,

It is nearly eleven o'clock at night, and I am sitting here at my desk in the school house. One candle is flickering in its holder near me; the flame's feeble light casts a dim glow about the room, though it does not pierce the darkest corners or even reach the door. In the darkness around the stove are the children, huddled beneath their coats, sleeping. The stove's warmth can only be felt much within a few feet of it, and here at my desk I can feel the cold drafts. Outside, the wind whistles and howls, blowing the snow into ever increasingly high drifts. Perhaps I ought to be trying to sleep, but as the stove will soon need replenishing, I won't try now. I don't think I could sleep anyway. So while I am up, I will tell you all about it. It will be a relief to talk to someone even if it is just on paper. I have plenty of paper and all night to write, so I can take my time and make this as long as I want. Or until I run out of candles.

Initially, there was no snow storm. Only a light dusting on the ground when we got up this morning. The sun was even shining a little through the clouds. I don't think any of us even thought of a storm. I know I didn't as Edmund and I rode to school. I told him I would walk home with the children today, so he took Jessie back after he built the fire in the stove and brought in a little wood.

"The boys can bring in more wood if you need it, Emma," Edmund said, dumping an armload down. "There is plenty out there."

"Enough for a blizzard?" I inquired laughingly. How long ago that seems! Was it only this morning?

Edmund laughed too and replied, "That all depends on how long the blizzard lasts. If you run out, you can always burn the desks." Then we both laughed again, and Edmund cantered away.

The morning passed by as usual. At recess it was snowing, but not hard, and the wind was calm. The children came in with rosy cheeks and sparkling eyes.

"Oh, Miss Foster," Mary sighed as she slipped out of her coat. "I just love the snow! I wish it would just snow for ever and ever!"

"If it did, we would all freeze to death," Vincent remarked cheerfully.

"I don't want to freeze," Mildred shivered.

"It would be so romantic to be stuck in a blizzard with the snow falling and falling . . ." Mary breathed dreamily, staring out at the snow.

"Dream on, little sister," John chuckled, "it isn't going to happen."

"But if it did--" Mary began again.

I interrupted, "That's enough of that kind of talk." I had noticed a few of the little ones looking anxious. Everyone settled into their seats, and lessons once more began. The snow continued to fall, but as the flakes weren't large nor were they heavy, I wasn't concerned. Though the wind had picked up some, it still wasn't strong.

Dinner time came, and with it a renewed talk of blizzards. I don't know who first suggested it, but almost before I knew it, everyone was saving part of their dinner.

"Just in case a blizzard does come," Sarah informed me with a giggle.

Even my sensible students, John, Carrie, Robert and Gretchen, were joining in. What could I do but go along and save part of my dinner, too? I thought of how Edmund would laugh when he heard, but he has laughed at me before, and it hasn't hurt me yet. We were almost finished eating when I suddenly felt a difference in the weather. Anxiously I looked out the window expecting to see, I wasn't sure what, but on the contrary, everything looked just the same. Then all at once, the school house was shaken by a violent gust of wind. Everyone looked up, startled. I felt instantly an overwhelming urgency to get the children home.

"Children, hurry," I commanded. "Get your wraps on. I'm afraid a storm is coming. Quickly now." I spoke as cheerfully as I could in spite of a growing fear that filled me.

Confusion prevailed almost instantly as the children rushed to grab coats, scarves, mittens and hats. I was busy helping Sarah get her coat buttoned when John called,

"Miss Foster, I can't see the shed."

I hurried over to look out the window. I couldn't see it either; in fact, I couldn't see anything. "John and Robert," I called, "come over here by the door. The rest of you children move back." I wanted to see if it really was as bad as it looked. With the help of the big boys, I opened the door. Stepping out on the step, I felt the cold pierce my coat all the way to my bones. The fierceness of the wind took my breath away. Straining my eyes as I would, not a single solitary thing could I see except the blinding snow. Turning, I stumbled back into the school room and again, with the boys' help, shut the door. For a brief moment I just stood there, catching my breath.

"Children," I at last managed to say calmly, "it's too cold and snowy for anyone to try to get home now."

There was a collective groan from the children.

"So, we will continue lessons as usual." I had to keep them from knowing how bad it really was if I could. At least the younger ones. I could tell that the older ones already sensed the seriousness of the storm. "Though, before we start lessons again, perhaps we ought to bring in more wood."

"We can't see the shed," John reminded me softly.

"If you had a rope, do you boys think you could find it and bring more wood in?" I glanced out the window then at John and Robert as I spoke.

"We should at least try before the snow gets any deeper," Robert assented.

"Do we have a rope?" I wondered, beginning to look around. A few minutes of searching showed that no rope was to be had. "All right, what can we use instead of a rope?

Everyone stood silently thinking.

"I know," Frank burst out, "couldn't we use our scarves? We could tie the ends together. Wouldn't that work?"

The others began to nod in agreement.

"That just might work, Frank," I praised.

Quickly, all the scarves were taken off or pulled out of pockets. I wouldn't allow John and Robert to add their scarves to the growing scarf rope in view of their soon venture into the snow. Not satisfied that our rope was long enough, we added pocket handkerchiefs, napkins from the lunch pails, and even a small doll blanket which Elizabeth found in her pocket. At last it was ready. The knots had been made as tight as John and Robert could make them, and the children thought we were ready.

"There is one thing more that needs to be done, children," I said. "We need to ask God to help us and to keep the boys safe."

Every head bowed, and I prayed. There was a moment of silence when I finished.

"Are we ready now?" Frank asked.

I glanced around the room and saw eager, nodding heads. For them, this was a real adventure.

"All right, let's begin."

The plan was for John to go out holding on to one end of our "rope" while I held on to the other end just inside the door. When John found the shed, he would tie his end of the rope to something sturdy, get an armload of wood and come back to the school house. Dumping the load at my feet, he and Robert would both go back out and get more wood. Meanwhile, the other children would take the wood and stack it against the wall. I kept the little ones away from the door and close to the stove. Everything worked as it was supposed to, and we now have a large supply of wood. Of course we have used quite a bit, for the wind is strong and finds its way in through the cracks and holes in the walls. We left our "rope" out in case we have to get more wood, but I pray we won't have to. John said there wasn't much left.

I have just put more wood on the fire. John had done it earlier, but now even he has finally fallen asleep. How strange and lonely it feels here. With the children all asleep, I can hear the wind even more. The creaking of tree branches, the rattle of the windows, the crackle of the fire in the stove, all seem to add to the feeling of desertion that has come stealing over me. I know I am not truly alone for Jesus has said, "Lo, I am with you always," and again, "I will never leave thee nor forsake thee." I am clinging to these promises.

A branch must have fallen, for I heard a sharp crack just now. I certainly hope that no one has tried to get to the school house. I don't know if it is still snowing or not. The wind is blowing just as strong as it was when the storm began. But I didn't finish telling you about the day.

By the time the boys had brought in the wood, they were very cold, and my hands were numb from holding the rope. Robert was almost gasping for breath, and even John was breathing heavily. Gathering around the stove, we sang a few songs while warming up, then I sent everyone back to their seats. We spent the rest of the day, not with the usual lessons, but with history quizzes, spelling bees, mental arithmetic drills and just about anything to keep our minds off the storm outside. We sang songs and told stories. I even told a "Ted, Fred, Larry and Jim" story. We told a continuing story where each person tells part of the story and then leaves it for the next person to continue. Only after it was quite late and everyone was tired and hungry did I think of supper.

Everyone brought out what they had saved. I am so thankful for whoever first thought of saving part of their dinner. It was a scanty supper all around, but at least we had something. All that long afternoon and evening I waited and hoped for someone to come to our aid, but no one did. When at last all hope of rescue tonight was gone, I helped the children move the desks and benches around to create makeshift beds by the stove.

It is after midnight now, I still have a long night ahead of me. What else can I write about?

David is now old enough to join the army. He is not old enough to be drafted, thankfully, and he doesn't want to go fight. Daddy is still not over in France yet, though we don't know when he will be shipped out. Uncle Lance, who is with the 42nd Division, is already in France. I think his division went over, or at least he did, in November.

Maria, we were so shocked to hear about the explosion in Halifax! I can't even imagine anything like it. And to think you heard it over ninety miles away! Do you have more reports on it? I'm sure the men from your village had stories to tell. I just can't imagine that it could be worse than the front lines. How long did the blizzard last? The entire north end of the city flattened! I just can't comprehend it all.

The time is just creeping by. It is not even half past yet. I can't tell if the storm is lessening or if it is my imagination. I am getting tired of this darkness. I want to light the lamps, but that would waken the children, and then I would really have problems on my hands.

We had a quieter Christmas. It was so very different without Daddy. Oh, on New Year's Eve, David came into the room with a piece of paper in his hand. "Come Carrie, Karl, Edmund and Emma, get your coats on, for we are going outside."

None of us could figure out why David was taking us all outside into the cold, but we followed. David always has a good reason for everything he does.

Once outside, we were led out to the orchard. David handed the lantern to Edmund and held up his piece of paper. "It has been a year since we all made a wish out under these very trees. Now let us see how many of us had our wishes come true."

"Oh, I had forgotten all about that," Edmund remarked. "What did I wish for, anyway?"

No one else spoke. David unfolded the paper and held it toward the light. "Carrie wished for a brother or sister to share her birthday. Sorry, Sis, but that didn't happen."

"That's okay. Evie shares Kirsten's birthday, and I think she likes it more than I would." Carrie smiled as she spoke.

"Karl wished to stay here. That wish has been granted fully and freely. We couldn't have done all we did this year without you, Karl."

Karl didn't reply in words, but the look on his face was adequate.

"Now, Edmund, you said you wished to be as quick in arithmetic as Karl. Are you?"

"Huh," Edmund grunted while Karl grinned. "Every time I think I'm nearly even, he gets faster. That means my wish didn't come true either." We all had to laugh, for Edmund can be so dramatic when he wants to be.

"Emma, yours was to do something you had never done before. Have you?"

I sighed, nodded and smiled. "Many things, and some I hope I never have to do again."

"I didn't know you held a snake," Edmund tried to sound surprised.

"Oh, be quiet!" I scolded, shaking my head at him. He is still such a tease. "I taught school, and I love it. I had never done that before." I was silent about those things I didn't want to repeat, and I think they all knew what I was thinking. I never want to say good-bye as Daddy goes off to war again.

"David, what did you wish for?" Carrie asked after a rather long silence.

"Me? Oh, I wished for my own farm. In some ways I rather got it, for I have to run this one. And I have found that I enjoy it. Of course it would be impossible without Edmund and Karl here to help."

We didn't each wish for something this year, for all the wishes are the same -- for the war to end.

Friday 25,

I must have fallen asleep after I had written that last part, for I was suddenly awakened by a noise outside. I listened. It wasn't the wind. Things were a little lighter, so I was sure it must be morning, though still very early. I sat still and waited. I heard it again. This time is was a little louder, and John awoke.

"What was that?" he asked, not fully awake yet.

"I'm not sure," I answered, getting stiffly to my feet. The candle had burned out, and it was cold. "Put some more wood in the stove," I directed.

John obeyed, and we again heard the noise. It was getting louder and nearer. Robert was roused, and the three of us looked at one another in the dim light. I wasn't sure if the windows were frosted over or if they were covered by snow drifts, but I couldn't see out of them. Without warning, the door crashed open and two figures covered with snow stood in the doorway!

"Edmund! Karl!" I gasped.

The light from the rising sun sparkled and glistened on the snow and lit up the schoolhouse. The sudden noise, commotion and light effectively awakened the rest of the children, and confusion reigned.

Edmund and Karl took charge and soon had everyone in the sleigh. We took all the children to their homes before heading for ours.

And that, Maria, is the latest news. I am too tired to write more now. I look forward to your next letter. Give my love to all.

> Love and prayers,
> Emma

CHAPTER TWENTY-FIVE

> Friday
> February 22, 1918
> Princeville, Nova Scotia
> Canada

Dearest Emma,

I have just put Andrew down for his nap and decided to take advantage of a quiet afternoon to write to you. Mark and Lydia Ruth are in school, Edith is in Pictou and Mama is at Grandmother's. Grandmother doesn't seem as well lately. I pray it is just the cold winter and that when spring comes, she will be better.

Your letter made me shiver as though I could feel the cold with you. I am so thankful you had not sent the children home before the storm hit, or you would have worried about them. Did anyone suffer from the effects of the day? Lydia Ruth wants to know what "Ted, Fred, Larry and Jim" story you told. Had anyone else come out to look for the children?

Let me tell you about us, especially the younger ones, as they have changed the most, and I don't believe I have mentioned them much in the last letters.

Andrew is quite a handful. He isn't at all like Mark was, calm, sensible, and deliberate, but is very active, gets excited about almost anything, and never seems to remember anything he's been told. He is only two and a half, yet he climbs better than Mark did at age five. The other day I found him on the fireplace mantle reaching for the curtains of the nearby window. I didn't wait to find out what he was going to do, I just pulled him down. I am looking forward to spring with eagerness, for then Andrew can run outside. In looks, Andrew is much the same, only bigger, and his hair is lighter. He loves playing with Rob and William, and the three of them can get into more mischief in five minutes than the rest of the village children combined! Now I know what you have been through, and poor Grandmother Foster!

Words are difficult to find at times when trying to tell of Lydia Ruth. She still looks much as she has all her life. She is certainly growing up, but in such unexpected ways. We never can be certain just what she will do next. I'm sure I mentioned before of her boat ride. That is a good example of her -- well, Edith calls it creativity, Mark, persistency, Mama, independence, and I call it carelessness. I must say though, that Lydia Ruth is very easy-going and sweet-tempered. I can't recall the last time she was out of sorts with anyone. Even when things don't go her way, she amiably changes to suit. When she is with her friends, if someone else wants to be in charge, she will cooperate cheerfully, however, if not, she will lead. She has also finally mastered knitting and has begun a "knitting 'ciety" with Edana, Anne, and Ida. She is very social and pays regular weekly visits to each house in the village, no doubt telling them the latest news from Kansas. She continues to talk as much now, if not more, than before.

Mark can be described in a very few words: tall, hardworking, studious and dependable. He does enjoy laughing over his cousins' pranks and wonders how they thought of them to start with. He and James are as inseparable as ever. Mrs. Lawson told Mama that "it felt almost as though she had two sons instead of one." Mama has said the same thing several times. I don't know what we would do without Mark and James.

I can hardly believe it, but Edith will be twenty years old in April. I told Mama I didn't see how that could even be possible. Edith is always busy. It is so difficult to tell about her; she is friendly, cheerful and energetic. She seems to always bring sunshine with her wherever she goes. Home would be mightily difficult at times were it not for her buoyant spirits. There is another side of her character, though, which I have glimpsed occasionally, but she knows where to go for help. At those times, I have seen her with her Bible, gaining the help and comfort she shares with others. Edith always includes me if I can be spared, and we so enjoy being together.

Now you expect me to tell you about Mama, don't you? I would if I could. She is the very best Mama in all of Canada, I am quite certain. Mama, Mark and I are the quiet ones in the family, while the other three do their best to stir us up. I just can't tell what Mama is like. I can't find the words to use. She is just the same as the last time you saw her only perhaps a trifle quieter with Papa gone.

I must tell you about helping in Halifax. I suppose I should have started with that, but some antic of Andrew, who is supposed to be asleep, made me tell of him instead. It was over a month and a half ago when we got back, but I'll try my best to tell of it.

When almost all the men of the village were already in Halifax, we received word that Red Cross workers were wanted. Thus it was that Mable and Amelia Burn, Sheena McIntyre, Edith and I set off with several other volunteer workers for the stricken city. Among those going was Mary Ellis, the fiancée of Theodore Burn. She, and if I remember correctly, two other girls had taken their V.A.D. (Voluntary Aid Division) training; the rest of us were all Red Cross workers. The ride to Halifax was such a contrast to the ride I had taken previously with the Camptons. Each of us wore a Red Cross arm band, and as we neared the city, we bowed our heads in prayer.

Never will I forget that first look as I stepped off the train. Was this really Halifax? I bit my lip and struggled with tears. Edith saw my emotion and put an arm around me. I didn't have long to think, for suddenly an army officer was ordering us to our posts in different hospitals. Edith, Mary and I were assigned to the Cogswell Street Hospital at first. The place was packed nearly wall-to-wall with the wounded. It had one hundred beds, yet I know that more than twice that amount were lying on the floors.

I can't tell you on what days things happened as it all runs together in my mind. Before long we were sent to the Camp Hill Military Hospital where I think we spent the most time. There were times that one or two of us were assigned to go to the slums to help there. A young man, Bernard Gow, was our escort to and from the slums several times. His father, Dr. Gow, worked some of the time in our hospital. Those dreadful houses! Almost every window in Halifax was gone. The only way to keep out the fierce cold was to board them up or cover them with blankets, sheets, paper, anything. Even the hospitals were that way, and you couldn't tell if it was night or day.

Oh, Emma, the suffering that took place all over the city is indescribable! So many were injured by glass and flying debris. Many, many were blinded, others had lost limbs. Most seemed to have lost at least one family member, many all of them.

I don't know who it was that first found out that I had nursing training. They thought I did anyway. The only training I have had was from Papa, and perhaps a God-given instinct when it comes to sickness. Anyway, I was then put full time on nursing. I worked alongside the "Green Cross" workers from the Rhode Island Hospital Unit. They were really Red Cross workers, but they had responded so quickly to the call for help that they had forgotten to bring red fabric for their armbands. Therefore, on the train to Halifax, they cut up the Pullman curtains from the train, which were green, and used them. Occasionally I caught glimpses of some of the men from our village or exchanged a few words with Edith, Sheena or one of the other girls.

One doctor I was privileged to work beside was Dr.

Dan Cox, a returned missionary. Once when I was soothing three small children, a young woman, and an elderly lady, Dr. Cox entered the room to check on another patient. I noticed he watched me until I had my charges asleep and then asked,

"Are you a V.A.D.?"

"No, sir," I replied.

He looked at me a moment before saying, "I wouldn't guess you were more than seventeen, yet you are as efficient and well trained as any nurse I have worked with."

"I am only sixteen, Doctor," I answered and watched his eyes widen in astonishment.

"Miss Foster, where did you receive your training?" was the next question.

"Only from my father."

"Is he here?" the question was eagerly put.

I shook my head and told him Papa was over in France and had been since we entered the war.

Dr. Cox's eyes softened, and his hand was placed on my shoulder. "You have been blessed with a very special gift from God, young lady. I pray you will always use it for His glory." With that, he quietly left the room. I never saw him again, for I was called away to another hospital.

I snatched a few hours of sleep here and there. Often I was so tired I couldn't think at all. When I could think, I wished for Papa. It was times like these that I longed, oh so much, for him. One thing I discovered about the covered windows was that you didn't know when it was night and so didn't know you were supposed to be tired. I would work until I could scarcely keep up and was ordered by one of the doctors to go get some rest.

The city had begun to rebuild before the end of December, though it will take months to again be the city it was. There are so many stories I heard; it would take a book to write them all down. Many of them were so very sad, but there were amazing and heartwarming ones as well. I will tell you a few of those.

A baby was found by some soldiers sleeping quietly in

the ash pan of a still warm stove. Evidently the fire, ashes and coal were removed by the force of the blast, and the baby was blown there in their place. To the soldiers' great astonishment, the baby was uninjured.

Another lady, who had been bathing her baby when the explosion occurred, was uninjured, but when the second alarm was sounded of another explosion, she only had time to wrap her baby in her apron and a small blanket before rushing outside. Some kind lady gave up her large muff to put the baby in to keep it warm. That kind act no doubt saved the little one's life.

I also heard of one doctor saving the life of another doctor. Dr. Thomas was trying to help all the people who were coming to him for aid, but he couldn't handle them all. When he suggested to some that they go to Dr. Chisholm who was a colleague of his, they informed him that he was dead. Dr. Thomas couldn't believe it and rushed over to Dr. Chisholm's office. He found Dr. Chisholm unconscious with a severed artery. After sewing up the artery, Dr. Thomas revived Dr. Chisholm and told him to try to get to a hospital. He did and is now doing well.

We were there in Halifax for several weeks. When at last we left, the men from Princeville came too. I was so exhausted and glad to be home. I love this little village! I couldn't sleep that night. I believe I was so used to days without much sleep that I couldn't relax. I lay in bed until I could stand it no longer. The sights and sounds from Halifax echoed in my mind and refused to leave me in peace. Finally, I got up and tiptoed downstairs and into the dining room. After carefully shutting the doors, I placed my violin on my shoulder and softly drew the bow across the strings. Sitting there in the dark, looking out at the peacefully sleeping village which was bathed in the moonlight, I let the violin tell it all. How long I played, I don't know. I do know that the moon had set before I finished. Upon returning to my bed, I fell at once into a deep sleep and did not awaken until late the following day.

That is the first time I have written about Halifax. Mama wrote it all to Papa after we had returned and shared experiences. I don't care to read over it, so I do hope everything is understandable. I have been interrupted several times by Andrew who I told you is supposed to be taking a nap, but he seems to think he should be able to get up after he has closed his eyes. He is finally asleep, and leaving him to Mama, who has returned, I am going to go visit baby Archie. He is growing so quickly.

Mr. and Mrs. Stanly are going into Pictou and will mail this letter if I ever will stop writing and get it in the envelope.

Please tell Georgie happy birthday for us. I just remembered that today is his eighth birthday!

Love always,
Maria

"Mom," Ria just couldn't keep quiet anymore. "Didn't your cousin become a nurse? A real one I mean?"

"She did. After which she married a young man, and they went together to China as missionaries."

"Are they still there?" Lydia's question was soft.

Mrs. Mitchell shook her head. "No, my cousin died two years ago in China. Her husband and children are still there though. I remember she told me that it was during that time in Halifax that she realized just how much nursing meant to her as well as sharing Christ's love with others."

A silence fell over the little group, each one busy with their own thoughts. Ria looked around. Mrs. Smith wore an expression of joy mingled with sadness. Corporal's eyes had that faraway look that Ria had seen so often. It pained her to see it now, and she asked for the next letter to be read.

CHAPTER TWENTY-SIX

Saturday
March 23, 1918
Codell, Kansas
USA

Dear Maria,

We all laughed about your description of Andrew. Just be thankful you don't have two such little boys or four of them! I told Edmund that I think I would like to have many girls and only a few boys when I get married. Boys can be such a handful. You should have heard him laugh! He fairly shouted with laughter; in fact, his merriment brought David and Karl over to find out what was so humorous. After the boys had their laugh out, I said,

"I told you boys could be difficult, and you have just proved that sometimes they can be impossible." I couldn't help smiling as I said it. That produced some merry teasing for a while.

Mama said Lydia Ruth reminded her somewhat of Edith when she was little. You didn't tell anything about yourself. I know how easy it is to forget to do that.

I suppose I should tell you what has occupied my mind for nearly two weeks, and even now over a week later I still find myself growing pale and trembling at the thought. I don't know if I can tell it without frightening myself, but perhaps it will make me less terrified if I see it all with the ending down in black and white. And so, here it goes.

It was a Tuesday, the fifth of this month to be exact,

that it all began. It was a beautiful day: warm and pleasant, and the sun shone from a cloudless sky. The children were lively. I could scarcely keep them in their seats until school was out. I did take pity on them and on myself by letting them out fifteen minutes early. They scattered like dandelion seeds on a windy day. I knew I would have extra time before Edmund came, so I set to work at once grading papers. I didn't want to have to do that when I got home. I was as anxious as the children to be out of doors. I was nearly through when I heard a step in front of me and felt a strange sort of dread as I looked up. It was not Edmund, but some stranger with unkempt hair, a rough beard and dark hostile eyes. My heart beat fiercely, and I remained in my seat. I knew I couldn't stand. For one terrifying moment, we stared at each other. Then the stranger broke the silence; his voice cut the air like a knife, although it was low.

"All right, pretty lady," he began, "where are those spies that you teach here in this dump of a school?"

I stared stupidly at him. What was he talking about? I thought he must be drunk, but there was no smell of liquor on him. Was he insane?

"Where do they live?" he snapped out.

"I don't know what you are talking about." I tried to sound calm and dignified, but I'm afraid it was an utter failure.

"Now don't give me any of that." His voice was full of hate. "I know you have two German spies here. Now just tell me where they live, or else."

German spies? Here? Then my mind grasped what he was saying. He was calling Gretchen and Emil German spies! How could he? I grew indignant at the very thought and stood up. "Sir, there are no German spies. All of these children are Americans, and so are their families!"

The man looked at me darkly, and something about his look sent a chilling, unknown fear down my spine. When he spoke again, his voice was low and seething with ruthless ferocity. "You have exactly eight days to decide what you will do. If you choose to tell me what I want to know, nothing will happen to you or to your family. But," and he leaned closer, "if you choose not to tell me, or if you should mention this little matter to a soul, you will be forced to watch the execution of your beloved brothers and see the complete destruction of your home. You will then be turned over to the government as a German sympathizer. The choice lies with you."

I couldn't say a word. I simply stared petrified as he turned and left the school house. How long I stood there unable to move or even to think, I don't know. At last I sank into my chair in a fit of trembling.

Thus it was that Edmund found me as he opened the door with a smile and a "ready to go . . ." He never finished his sentence, for with a cry of "Emma!" he rushed over to me.

"Emma, what is it? What happened?" he asked, his arms about me.

I couldn't answer. I could only cling to him tightly, as shudder after shudder shook me, and my breath came in gasps. At last I calmed down and gave a queer little laugh as I pulled away from him and saw the unfinished papers still waiting on my desk. "I meant to have these all done by the time you came," I said, beginning to gather them with hands that shook in spite of me.

Edmund hadn't said a word since he first questioned me. Now he put his hands on mine and held them. He looked into my face and spoke quietly, "Emma, what happened?"

Looking back at it now, I can see that I should have told him immediately what had happened, as it would have saved a great deal of fear, but at the time I was so terrified and bewildered that I didn't think rationally.

With another little, half-hysterical laugh I replied, "I didn't finish checking these papers. Now I'll have to do it at home."

"Emma, I'm not going to be put off like this. Now

what happened before I came? Did it happen during school, or was it after the children had left?"

I looked at him pleadingly while trying to pull my hands free. "I . . . I . . . oh, please, Edmund, let's go home." My eyes filled with tears, and I shuddered anew at the remembrance of my visitor. "I just want to go home," I said again.

He looked at me a moment longer then quietly released my hands. "All right," was all he said, but his look and the tone of his voice made me realize that this wasn't the end of it all.

We rode home in relative silence. Edmund talked about the farm and asked a few questions about school that could be answered with a nod or shake of the head.

The rest of that day and even the next morning are still rather hazy in my mind. No one questioned me, for which I was extremely grateful. I think I owe that consideration to Edmund. He and I left for school at the usual time. As we neared the school house, I felt that chilling fear again. Somehow I had to keep Edmund there until the children came. He didn't seem to be in any hurry to leave and cheerfully filled the water bucket, sharpened my pencil and did half a dozen other little things that I usually have the children do. It wasn't until I heard the first of the children arriving that I told Edmund I thought he could go. He looked at me closely and asked,

"Are you going to dismiss school early again?"

I shook my head. There was no way I was going to sit by myself in that school house and risk "the man" coming back. I managed to push the unpleasant thoughts to the back of my mind while I taught. After school was dismissed, I had Fred and Hannah stay to help me with a few things.

So the days passed. Edmund would stay at school until the children arrived. He never complained, but when I had him sharpen my pencil two days in a row when it didn't need it, he eyed me in puzzled silence. After school, I either started back with the children or managed to think of something that I needed help with and kept one or more of the children. But I never kept Gretchen and Emil. At home, I was silent and wouldn't answer any questions Edmund asked, though I wanted to so badly. I would put him off or change the subject. I just couldn't face up to it all. I felt at times that I was all alone. I did pray. I don't think I could have lived though those trying days without prayer. But I didn't know what to do. Well, actually I did know, but I was scared every time I thought of it. I couldn't betray Gretchen and Emil. And yet, how could I betray my family? It only occurred to me later that "the man" couldn't possibly have done what he said he would do without much help. Where he would have gotten that help, I don't know.

Tuesday of the following week came, and I hadn't seen any sign of "the man." I was beginning to think it was just a practical joke of some wandering tramp. So, that day I dismissed school and stayed behind. I was determined that this fear was ridiculous, and I wouldn't be a slave to it any more. I was telling myself that I was foolish to worry about it as I sat grading papers. When the door opened, I felt before I saw "the man."

"I didn't come for your answer yet. I'll be back tomorrow for that," he said. "I just wanted to remind you that it is either the lives of the German spies or your family. The choice is up to you." His voice was cold and brutal, and his eyes gleamed with hate. "Beware how you answer me." And then with no further words, he turned and slunk from the room.

It was no prank! This was for real! I had to get out. I had to think. I had to decide. Tomorrow was the last day. Would he come before or after or would he, oh dreadful thought, would he come during school? I gathered the papers in nervous haste. My trembling hands didn't help matters, but at last I stood outside by the door listening for the sound of the hoof beats which would announce Edmund's coming. It seemed like hours before I heard those welcome sounds.

Edmund drew rein and sprang off Comrade. "Emma, are you all right?" he questioned, taking my books and preparing to help me mount Jessie.

I nodded and looked away.

"Where is your lunch pail?" was the next question.

"I must have forgotten it."

"I'll go get it," he said, stepping away from the horses towards the door.

"No!" I fairly screamed. "Edmund, please!" I added at his look of astonishment. "Let's just forget it. Don't leave me. I mean, don't go back for it. I can use another one tomorrow. Oh please! Let's go home." I was fighting back tears of fright.

Without a word, Edmund mounted, and we turned our horses' heads towards home. I kept looking uneasily around, fearful that "the man" was near by. Edmund must have noticed my agitation, but he didn't speak of it. He simply rode right beside me and talked about the commonplace things of home. Each mention of one of the family was like an arrow in my soul. How could I betray them? I couldn't. How could I betray Gretchen and Emil? I couldn't. Round and round my mind whirled. I couldn't think. My head ached, and I was desperately tired with the whole thing.

Arriving at home, I reined in and dismounted in front of the house. I didn't want to see anyone, and I knew that on such a lovely day, almost everyone would be outside. I slipped inside and started up the stairs.

"Emma," Mama's voice sounded from the kitchen. "Do you have papers to check this evening?"

"Yes."

"If I can help in anyway, just let me know."

"I will." How sweet of Mama. Did she know something was wrong? I'm sure she did, but she didn't bother me; she only let me know she was there if I needed her. I entered my room, shut the door and sank into the chair by my desk. I had to think. I had to decide what to do.

In a moment I was up again. I couldn't think there. The little girls could come in at any time, and I wouldn't frighten them for anything. Where could I go? To the barn? No, the boys would be doing chores in a little while. In Mama's room? No, someone would come in. Up in the attic would be the perfect place. No one went up there, and away in the back by the window I would be safe from unwanted questions.

I ran up the stairs and was soon curled up in the window seat, and staring out at the yard. Mama was taking the clothes off the line. Carrie and the little girls were playing out in the sunshine. I saw Edmund stop near Mama on his way from the barn. They seemed to be talking about something. Edmund looked towards the house then back at Mama. I suddenly knew. They were talking about me. I saw Mama nod and watched Edmund move toward the house. Was he really coming to talk to me? Well, he could talk but I wouldn't. I couldn't. If he knew, he wouldn't even ask me. I heard his steps on the attic stairs. How did he know I was up here?

"Lucy," he began softly, using the name he seldom uses anymore as he sat down beside me on the window seat. "Something is bothering you. What is it?"

"How did you know I was up here?" I asked, wishing to change the subject, but Edmund wouldn't fall for that again.

"It's no use answering the Yankee way, Sis. I knew you were here because you weren't in your room. Now, what is the matter?"

I wouldn't look at him. "I . . . I can't tell you." I didn't mean to say it, but it slipped out.

"Why can't you tell me?"

"Because I can't. Oh Edmund, go away! I can't tell you!" I turned my face toward the wall and bit my lip to keep back the story that fairly burned to get out. I knew I would tell if he didn't leave. And oh, what would happen then. "Edmund, please go," I begged frantically. "I have to think. I can't tell you. Oh, please! Edmund, if you love me." I choked on a sob and twisted my hands in my skirt.

Once again, those strong hands of his were placed over mine, and he held them firmly. "Emma," he spoke tenderly, yet there was something about it that reminded me of Daddy and brought to mind his words, "Go to Edmund with your problems."

I listened.

"Emma, I do love you. That is why I can't stand by any longer and see you suffering alone. I have known something happened at school last week and again today, and I *will* find out what is going on." There was something very comforting in those words, "I *will* find out."

I drew a long shaky breath and leaned back against the wall. I still kept my face averted from Edmund, but I no longer tried to pull my hands free.

"Who told you not to tell?"

"A man," very softly.

"What did he look like?"

I described him as well as I could.

"Had you ever seen him before?"

I shook my head.

"What did he want from you?"

That was the question I had been dreading. I looked at Edmund in panic, then out the window and around the darkening attic as though I was afraid "the man" was there listening. My hands tightened convulsively on Edmund's, and I felt I could scarcely breathe. Edmund waited quietly, looking steadily at me and squeezing my hands. At last I began to speak. My voice was scarcely above a whisper, and each word seemed to choke me. I'm afraid I didn't speak very coherently, for Edmund had to question me for some time before he finally got enough to at least understand that he, David and Karl had been threatened with death for some information.

Steps were heard on the stairs. I suddenly gasped, in horror convinced that "the man" was coming. Edmund quickly put his arm around me and assured, "Emma, it is only Karl."

The relief was so great when I heard Karl's voice that I burst into tears.

Karl didn't come over to us but called from the top of the stairs to know if we were going to come down to supper. Edmund told him not yet, and Karl left us alone again.

I don't know how long we stayed there, Edmund questioning and me answering, but at last he was silent. "Oh, Emma!" he sighed at last. "Why didn't you tell me that first day?"

I didn't answer, and I don't think he expected one. I leaned my head wearily against the window pane to cool my hot cheeks. I was so tired. I just wanted to stay there. How could I go to school tomorrow? I thought it, but was too tired to ask Edmund. Neither of us spoke for several minutes.

"Come on, Lucy," Edmund stood up. "Let's go eat. I'm hungry."

"I don't want anything." All I wanted was my bed.

"Well, I'm not letting you go to bed without your supper, so come on. No more questions, I promise." Edmund can be very persuasive when he wants to be, and before I knew it, he had me downstairs and in the kitchen.

Mama greeted us with a smile and set before us plates of hot food. David and Karl were also there, but no one betrayed by word or look that anything was unusual. It was much later than I had thought, for the younger children were in bed. It was after some time that I remembered.

"I have papers to grade," I groaned aloud.

"These papers?" Karl asked, holding up a few that lay on the table in front of him and David.

I stared at them. "You didn't . . . you did! Oh, thank you both!" I smiled at them and then in spite of everything, or maybe because of everything, the tears began again. Mama came over, kissed me and sent me to bed. I don't think I was ever more ready to go. I slept well that night. Better than I had for a week, for the fear was gone. I thanked God that night and took courage. Edmund would do something. I didn't know what, but he would.

I only found out later that after I had gone to bed, Edmund told the whole story to the others. David and Karl were so indignant that they were ready for anything.

It is rather hard to tell you the ending, as it all happened so bewilderingly fast. Edmund took me to school as usual, telling me to stay calm, the Lord was with me and that everything would be all right. He left me and rode away home. At least I thought he had. I was nervous, but that chilling fear that had kept possession of me for so long was gone. I knew I had nothing to fear, for the Lord was with me. As I began preparations for the day, I sang. I hadn't sung for a week. I heard the door open, and I turned around. There "he" stood.

"Is there something I can do for you?" I asked.

"Now don't give me that," was the snarling reply. "I've come for your answer. Which is it going to be, the spies or your nice brothers?"

"I believe I will keep both," I answered quietly. "There are no German spies around here, and as for my brothers, you might have to take it up with them, but I don't believe they will cooperate with your little plan."

"The man" gave a wicked laugh and came a step closer. My hand closed on my ruler, though what I would have done with that, I'm not sure. At that moment the door quietly opened, and in walked David, Karl and Edmund, as well as the sheriff and one or two other men. I watched as the sheriff walked up behind "the man," who was calling me all kinds of names and making threats against anyone-and-everyone, grasped him by the shoulder and spun him around, saying as he did so,

"You are under arrest."

That really was the end. Everyone left, and the children arrived. The first ones looked wonderingly at the group leaving the school house, but soon forgot about it as school went on.

I feel so much better having told that story. I wouldn't write it to Daddy, as I don't want him to worry about us. You are the first person to hear the entire story from start to finish. Oh, Maria, what is the country coming to when we can condemn innocent people just because of their last name? This incident isn't the only time it has happened. In other places, the hatred is even worse.

I don't think I would have had the courage to go to Halifax to help as you did. I mean, I would have loved to help, but I don't think I could have stood to see the suffering all around. Everyone here listened spellbound as I read about your time there. I'm going to copy that and send it to Daddy. I sent him the first news of the explosion, so I think he would like to hear more about it.

Evie is now a year old. She toddles some, but not much. Her greatest ability is talking. She talks in complete sentences much of the time and is not shy of any one. Unlike Rosalie, who makes friends with her smile, Evie makes friends by chattering. I haven't heard Lydia Ruth talk for a long time, but I really believe that Evie can out talk her. There is such a difference in the house now. For so long, Kirsten and Rosalie would play without talking, but now that Evie is bigger, she more than makes up for any quiet of the other girls.

Kirsten is eight years old. She is still quiet but not nearly as shy. She is doing well in school. She loves helping Mama in the house, but her favorite place to be is with the animals. Rosalie is usually with her. Kirsten now gathers the eggs, and I don't think she will be bothered by any snake she may come across. She and Evie are so different, and yet they get along so well. I think Evie's favorite person is Edmund. She calls him "Demund" and tells him everything.

Vincent and Georgie have kept out of mischief for so long that I am beginning to get anxious that they will break out in some way soon. Edmund said he was prepared for anything. I just hope they don't do anything in school.

I must go now, as it is getting late, and tomorrow is

Sunday. Give my love to everyone. I'm sure Mama would send her love as well if she knew I was writing now, but she is already in her room. I have a suspicion about Mama. I don't know for sure, as she hasn't said anything, but I can't help noticing that she seems more tired than usual. And I don't think it is Evie's chatter.

Love,
Emma

Monday
April 22, 1918
Princeville, Nova Scotia
Canada

Dear Emma,

I could hardly read your letter without cringing in horror! What a frightening experience! Edith said you should have told him that you would do no such thing and to leave immediately. She probably would have done just that. Mark listened in silence and kept shaking his head.

"Why on earth didn't she tell Edmund? And why didn't he make her tell him sooner? What kind of a brother is he anyway?" were his exclamations.

Mama could only say, "That poor girl."

I think you will all enjoy Lydia Ruth's solution to the entire problem, "Emma shouldn't have 'smissed school that day then he wouldn't have come." With those insightful words she ran out to play in the sunshine. I read the story of "the man" to the village children who had been begging for some new story. My supply had run out. It is now all over the village, and when I last went to Pictou, I heard it mentioned there as well. Little stories go a long way.

I just love the spring. Don't you? Everything is so fresh and new. We still have cold days now and then, but the warmer weather is here to stay. The younger ones are nearly wild with spring fever. I thought it would be easier to watch

Andrew when he could go outside. How wrong I was. I am nearly worn out trying to keep an eye on him, not to mention the twins. Archie is nearly a year old and is already quite mobile.

Speaking of little ones, I see I haven't told you that there is a new little Campton. This wee one is a bonnie lassie with light hair and blue eyes. She was christened Mary. Everyone loves her, and she is called "Little Princess." I overheard William and Charles discussing her name with Arthur Morris and Mark and James. They were all in agreement that she was not "Bloody Mary," however, they couldn't decide if she was "Mary Queen of Scots" or Queen Mary, wife of William of Orange. If you haven't noticed, all the Campton children are named after kings and queens of England.

I should have told you in my last letter that David McLean is now at the front. Mr. Stewart was drafted three weeks ago and is also gone from the village. It has been very hard on Mrs. Stewart with Malcolm and Finlay and now her husband in the war. Several letters have arrived from the front, which no doubt you will be interested in. This first letter is from Duncan, and I copy it in its entirety.

"Sinsyne it is nae raining noo, I decided I maun write a letter. A letter to a'body. Havers! This war maun be ower soon for the Americans are so. They are a' braw maun an' are dour to win. I can nae understand muckle o' their gab. We are a' well an' wuss we were back in the hame toon. The food is food. Nae at a' ilk as food frae ony hame in the village!

David an' Robert are nae gude at writin' they say. I donnae think that is sae. Did ye ken sic daft excuses? Ony hoo, I am their caddie this time an' mind their greeting.

I can hear thae Americans singing. Sic voices. It is gude we hae them on oor side of the war. Nae because of their singing, ye ken, for David an' Alan sing muckle better, but their fighting is gude.

Nicht is coming an' wi' it, mair rain.
                    Duncan McIntyre"

This next one is from Theodore Burn. It is only a postscript at the end of one of his home letters, but it's for you.

P.S. I met a maun the other day. An American wi' the 1st Division. A braid shoouthered maun. He was nae a callant, yet we begude gabbin' o' oor hame an' families. The mair I heard, the mair I became sure that this maun knet o' the Fosters. An' it was sae. The maun's name is Ian Wallace. Is that name one that ye ken?

It must be your uncle, Emma. Imagine how strange that must have been.
I would so love to hear Evie. Lydia Ruth does most of the talking around our house, with Edith a close contestant. Andrew, though he is nearly three, still doesn't talk much. He grunts, points and says some things. He can talk when he wants to; his problem seems to be a lack of interest.
Edith is calling, so I must end now. I look forward to your next letter.
                With love and prayers,
                    Maria

"Goodness, Lydia! I had no idea it was so late! We must be getting home now. Thank you so much for letting my Lydia come over so often." Mrs. Smith arose as the clock was heard striking five.

"We love having her here. It gets rather lonesome with no other girls at times. I hope you can both come again. And you too, Corporal. You are welcome any time to come listen." Mrs. Mitchell held out her hand to her departing guests.

"I just might do that, I just might," Corporal agreed moving slowly down the steps and across the yard.

"See you tomorrow in school, Ria." Lydia waved to her friend.

"Hurry, Lydia! If we want Mom to read any letters before she has to leave, we'll have to run." So saying, Ria caught Lydia's hand and almost dragged her down the sidewalk. At the street corner they halted, gasping for breath, waiting for the traffic to stop. A sudden honking of a horn startled them both.

"Are you girls in a hurry or something?" The speaker leaned out of a truck and was regarding them with a merry face.

"Jack!" Ria exclaimed. "Can't you give us a ride home? We have to hurry. Please!" she begged.

"Sure thing. Hop in the back."

The girls wasted no time in obeying and were soon flying down the road in the back of the pickup.

Pulling to a stop in front of the Mitchell home, Jack called out, "Here you are."

"Thanks, Jack! You're wonderful!" and Ria leaned around and kissed him before jumping to the ground. Lydia stared in shock at her friend. Hardly had the truck disappeared down the street before she exclaimed,

"Ria Mitchell! How could you?"

"Oh, that was just one of my cousins," she replied carelessly. "He is Uncle Edmund's son. One of them, anyway. He has five sons. Jack is the second one."

"Almost everyone and their dog seems to be a relation to you."

"They are. Most of them, anyway. Come on,

let's go find Mom."

Mrs. Mitchell was found in the sewing room. "I didn't expect you home so soon." She looked up from the sewing machine.

"We wouldn't be, except that Jack brought us home," Ria informed her. "But he left. Can you read now, Mom?"

Mrs. Mitchell assented, and soon all were situated to their comfort, and the reading commenced.

Rebekah A. Morris

CHAPTER TWENTY-SEVEN

>Thursday
>May 30, 1918
>Codell, Kansas
>USA

My Dearest Maria,

I almost wasn't able to write to you this month. May didn't start out in a hurry, but it seems the closer it gets to summer, the faster the days fly. This is the first real break I have had for over a week now. If I sound somewhat incoherent, it is most likely because I am still rather bewildered.

Mama is doing better now and is resting. Evie, too, is quiet, which means she is sleeping. I verily believe that is the only time the child will stop talking. Mama says that even I didn't talk that much at fourteen months. No wonder Mama is so completely worn out! But there, I am not starting at the beginning. I will start with the last thing, as that is uppermost in my mind right now.

May 20 is now officially Cyclone Day here in Codell. This is the third year in a row that a tornado has come through on that day! This time it was later in the day than the two previous years.

The day was chilly, or rather, it was cold. The boys were all working with their coats on, and Carrie was worried about her garden. I had gone into town with Edmund that morning, and there was a lot of talk about cyclones. It appeared to be too cold for such storms that day, as we had heard that a hot, dry, sultry day was the kind that brought tornados. It was towards evening when David came in from the barn looking for Georgie and mentioned that it looked like a storm was brewing in the southwest.

"Probably just a thunderstorm, so I wouldn't worry about it," he said. "Where is Georgie?"

I hadn't seen him, but Evie saw him in a tree. David and Georgie were soon back in the barn.

We had finished supper, and the boys were standing around looking at the large billowing bank of clouds. The wind was picking up. David suggested we all go to the cellar since it was Cyclone Day.

"But I don't want to go there," Georgie protested. "I want to watch the clouds. No cyclone hit us last year, did it?"

"No," David admitted, "but it would be better to be safe than sorry. Should we go, Mama?"

Mama looked tired. I hadn't realized just how tired until then. She nodded. By then the wind was really blowing, and the rain was beginning to fall.

The three older boys hurried us all outside to the storm cellar. The wind was so strong that it took both Edmund and Karl to open the doors. David, with a lit lantern, first helped Mama down, and then came up so that the younger ones could go down. The dogs followed Vincent and Georgie down, as well.

"Kirsten!" Karl suddenly exclaimed. "Where is she?"

We all glanced around hurriedly. Where could Kirsten be? "I know she left the house with us," Edmund spoke confidently.

"Then where is she?" Karl snapped.

"Take it easy, Karl," David said gently. "We'll find her. The rest of you . . ."

He didn't finish his sentence, for I interrupted, "There she is!" and pointed toward the barn.

There she was, sure enough. Struggling bravely against the wind, holding something carefully in her apron, she pushed on. Karl dashed to her side, swept her up and staggered back to us against the wind.

David was the last one to descend the cellar steps. As he pulled the heavy door to shut it, the wind suddenly yanked it from his grasp and slammed it shut with a crash that startled all of us.

David stood for a minute staring blankly at the closed doors above his head. "Well, you needn't do it quite so hard."

Carrie gave a little forced laugh at David and then shivered. The cellar was dim and cool. I sat by Mama over to one side. David joined us. Karl had set Kirsten down beside Rosalie, and seated himself at her other side. Kirsten opened up her apron and displayed one of the barn cats and her litter of kittens. The little girls completely forgot the storm in their delight over the kittens. Karl was silent, looking now and then up at the doors and then over at Mama. Vincent and Georgie, never very far apart, just sat silently for once in their lives. Edmund sat with Evie on his lap. Evie wasn't quiet.

"Demund," she piped up looking at Edmund with a smile. "Ooh doe outyide?"

"No," Edmund replied, "it is too stormy to go outside."

"Tarl doe outyide?"

"No, Karl can't go outside, either."

"Emma doe outyide." Evie's little head nodded very confidently. She has gotten a funny little notion in her head that I can do anything and see everything.

"Emma isn't going outside, either."

"Me doe'n to doe outyide and doggie."

"You aren't going anywhere!" Edmund held her above his head as she giggled with delight.

"Demund doe yeep, den me doe outyide."

I smiled at her playfulness and was grateful for even a little bit of lightheartedness. The cellar seemed to grow colder as the sound of heavy rain on the doors could be heard, and I shivered involuntarily.

"Are you cold?" Mama asked, her own face pale in the feeble light.

"Only a little," I replied, wishing I could say otherwise.

David produced a few blankets from somewhere and called the others to come over. "If we all stay together it will be warmer."

Carrie sat beside me sharing the blanket David tucked around us. The others gathered around with Vincent and Georgie taking places together beside Mama. Evie's chatter ceased as the changes were made and the severity of the storm seemed to grow more intense with each passing second. Carrie clung to my arm, and I could tell she was frightened. I didn't feel too sure myself. A glance at the older boys' faces only confirmed my fears, for they were set, and I noticed that all three were stationed the closest to the doors. Thankfully, Kirsten and Rosalie didn't realize the danger as they happily played with the kittens under a blanket at Mama's feet. I looked at Mama. Her face seemed even more colorless, and her lips were pressed tightly together, while her breathing was rapid. I glanced imploringly at Edmund, not wanting to alarm anyone by speaking. He must have felt my eyes on him, for he turned to look at me. I gave a quick nod toward Mama. He glanced at her and nudged David who quickly took up a place almost behind Mama and said softly,

"Lean on me, Mama. Everything will be all right."

I don't know how long we sat there in silence listening to the sounds outside. I know it was late, for the little girls all fell asleep. Even Evie stopped talking and slept. Vincent and Georgie seemed to doze off and on. I couldn't sleep.

As the storm intensified, Karl began to sing "Jesus Lover of My Soul." I don't think I have ever mentioned what a wonderful voice Karl has. It is a rich baritone, usually though he sings tenor quite as well, and he can harmonize with any song he hears. I don't know where he got his talent. Since he has become a Christian, he sings much of the time

and each song is so full of feeling. He had reached the lines:
"Cover my defenseless head
With the shadow of Thy wings."
when the doors of the cellar were suddenly yanked open and hail, rain, branches and other debris where dumped in right where most of us had been sitting at the beginning. Then abruptly, the doors slammed shut once more and a thunderous crash was heard above them. The little girls woke in fright, and even Georgie buried his face against Edmund, who was trying to calm Evie. Carrie was sobbing in terror, and it was all I could do to hush her.

Mama was busy trying to calm the little girls, and no one noticed Vincent at first. He rose slowly and began to edge toward the pile of debris.

"Vincent!" I called, glancing up then and seeing him.

He didn't look back but quickened his pace.

"Vincent!" I called again.

Karl rose swiftly and was at his side in a moment. I saw him say something, but Vincent shook his head. Karl spoke again.

This time Vincent's reply was audible, his tones frantic. "No, I want to get out! I want to get out! Let me go!"

Karl tried to guide him back to the rest of us, but Vincent resisted. I wasn't sure Karl could manage him alone. David and Edmund could be of no help, for they were both occupied. All I could do was watch. Karl held Vincent's arms to his sides and spoke to him again. The storm was raging wildly, and I couldn't hear what he was saying. It took only a short time before they came back to us. Karl kept a hand on Vincent's shoulder or arm as though to reassure him.

"Let's sing," Karl suggested, and immediately David began "A Shelter in the Time of Storm." We sang on and on. I don't know how long the storm lasted. It felt like days. I was cold and stiff and hoarse by the time things were quiet outside. The little girls had fallen asleep again, lulled by the singing. Poor Mama looked so weary and wan.

At last Edmund stood up, placed Evie in Karl's arms

and moved with rather stiff steps to the stairs. Reaching the doors, he pushed to open them, but they wouldn't budge. Not even an inch.

"David, Karl, one of you come give me a hand," he called softly.

Karl arose after passing Evie on to me, and went to join Edmund. The door still wouldn't move. David went to their aid, but even with their combined effort, they couldn't raise them.

"There must be something on top of them," Edmund grunted.

"Let's try one more time." David wasn't ready to give up yet.

Together they heaved upward with such force that Karl lost his balance and fell. For just a moment he lay still on the cyclone's refuse heap, then slowly he stood. I couldn't see his face in the dim light, but I heard Edmund ask, "Are you all right, Karl?"

"Yes, I think so."

David, who had been looking at the closed doors, spoke, "I don't think it's going to do us any good to try any more. There is certainly something on top of these doors. All we can do now is to wait and pray for help."

I glanced at Mama. She gave me a slight smile, but it wasn't full of joy and rest as usual. I stood up, carefully holding Evie, and made my way over to the boys who were still gazing at the doors. Edmund came down the steps.

"Is she awake?" he asked, nodding towards Evie.

I shook my head. "I'm worried about Mama," I whispered.

"Why?"

"I don't know. Something just doesn't seem right with her. I'm afraid she . . . she's worrying about what happened outside."

David and Karl joined us.

"There is really nothing we can do, Emma," Edmund said. "Suppose we all go back and try to get some sleep.

Things are bound to look better when we are rested."

I don't think many of us really slept. I know I didn't. Every sound, however small, roused me to wakefulness. Was that someone outside? Would anyone come to our aid? It felt like days passed as we sat there in the dark, the lantern having been turned down to the faintest glow. I couldn't see more than the dim outlines of the others.

All at once, one of the dogs stood up and began whining softly; its wagging tail brushed my arm.

"What is it, boy?" David's voice was barely audible. "Edmund, do you hear anything?"

Silence for fully a minute, then unmistakable sounds were heard somewhere up above us. Those were men's voices I heard! The three boys sprang up and made their way to the stairs again.

"David! Edmund!" a man's deep voice called.

"We're down here!" both boys answered simultaneously.

"There's a tree on top of the doors. We'll have to cut it away before we can get you out. Are you all down there? Is everyone all right?"

"We're all down here, and I think everyone is fine."

"Just hang on. We'll get you out as soon as we can," came the voice again.

All the commotion had awakened the children, and they were eager to get out. Vincent especially was restless. When at last the doors were opened, he was the first one to scramble out.

The sun was beginning to come up, and the destruction was incredible. Half of the porch was completely ripped off the house. Many - but not all- of the windows were blown in. Fences were down and trees were uprooted. The ground was completely saturated with puddles of standing water. The chicken house was nowhere to be seen, nor were any of the smaller outbuildings. Thankfully, the barn was standing. Everything from dishes to branches, to boards and clothes were to be seen in all directions.

None of us had any words to express ourselves as we stood gazing around.

The men who had come were from Plainville. I didn't know them, but the boys did. One of them was a doctor. He told the boys to get Mama inside and make her lie down. The structure of the house was still strong and there were some rooms, they said, which hadn't been damaged. It must have been around that time that Karl was noticed limping. The doctor quickly discovered a bad cut on his leg caused, no doubt, by his fall earlier. He was also put to bed and his leg bandaged. Kirsten was reassured by Karl that he would be all right. The men said that all doctors had been called out of Plainville to come assist the injured. And as soon as The Plainville Central (that is the telephone central) learned of the cyclone, they roused all able men to come to Codell's assistance and rescue, as well as the surrounding areas.

The more we learned about the destruction, the more terrible it became. The papers reported ten people killed, scores injured and property damage in the millions! This tornado hit Trego, Ellis, Rooks and Osborne counties. Part of Codell is completely destroyed! The new school house that was built several years ago is a total wreck. The Methodist church and parsonage were destroyed, but Reverend and Mrs. Hall were out of town. The Stackhouse home just north of the church was demolished, but thankfully no one was injured. Mrs. Printz's home is no longer there. She was also gone at the time. The only thing left of the Pentecostal church is the floor lying nearby and the organ. Walt Murphy, the telephone manager, broke his arm trying to hold the office door shut. And the list goes on. Mrs. Adams and baby were killed. The Jones' baby was killed, and Mrs. Jones and three of the children are seriously injured. Mrs. Glendening's baby was blown from her arms but was later found unhurt. So many places are completely destroyed; houses, barns, stores, everything. We have so much to be thankful for! Though part of the porch was ripped off, the roof damaged and windows blown in, we still have a house and a barn. None of us were seriously injured, thank God!

That day was hectic. David and Edmund worked on fixing the roof, while the rest of us tried to clean up the rooms and some of the yard. Poor Karl was nearly distracted, because he couldn't help. And that night we once again spent in the cellar, as another storm had come up. That went on for several days: working hard during the day and then rain and storms in the evening and spending the nights in the cellar. Karl finally tossed aside all orders, got out of bed and began to help. When the doctor came, he threatened to send him to the hospital if he didn't keep off his leg. It was with much grumbling that he was forced back to bed. I finally convinced him that he could be a help there if he would watch Evie for me. I was nearly wild trying to keep up with her, take care of Mama and get meals ready, not to mention all the extra work I was doing. Vincent and Georgie have worked tirelessly, and even Kirsten and Rosalie have helped. Carrie is working on her garden. Mama was in bed until just this morning. She still doesn't really look herself, and I will have to see that she doesn't overdo it.

Edmund went into Codell yesterday and came back wondering if it will ever be built back. So much of it was completely decimated. He said that about half the town was destroyed!

That is enough about cyclones - or, excuse me - tornados. Surely I can think of some more pleasant family news to tell you. Rosalie is now five years old. We had a small party for her. It wasn't much, but she seemed to enjoy it. Speaking of Rosalie, let me tell you a little story of her and Kirsten. This is especially for Lydia Ruth.

It was back near the beginning of May, or perhaps it was the end of April. The little girls were out playing one afternoon with some of their dolls. I hadn't been paying attention to them, as I was busy with other things. Carrie was most likely in the garden and Evie, well I think she had gone into town with Mama and David. Anyway, as I said, the little girls were playing with the dolls. Rosalie came to me and whimpered,

"Emma, I want a baby."

"Go get your dolly, Rosalie," I told her.

"But my dolly doesn't be real." Her face was the very picture of despair.

Kirsten came over then and looked wistfully at me. "We do need a baby, Emma. Please." As though I could make a baby out of nothing just for them!

"Go get your dolls," I told them again. But they just shook their heads.

"I wish Evie didn't go with Mama," Kirsten sighed dolefully.

I nearly laughed. "Girlies, I can't make a real baby for you," I told them. "You'll just have to be satisfied with your dollies. Now run along and play, I must get back to work."

They slowly trudged out of the house.

When I next looked out the window, I beheld them happily sitting on the grass dressing what I thought were their dolls. I was turning away when a sudden shriek caused me to look again. Both girls were running after something. Whatever it was finally climbed a tree, and in spite of their coaxing, refused to climb down.

Don't think me a hard-hearted sister for not going to their aid, but I had to get the dinner out of the oven and ring the bell. Besides, they hadn't called for help. The boys and Carrie came in and washed up, but Kirsten and Rosalie didn't. We could see them, but no matter who called to them, they paid no attention. Finally Karl and Edmund decided to go out and get them. Vincent and Carrie wanted to see why they didn't come, and it ended up with all of us going, except Mama, David and Evie who were not home yet.

When we reached the tree and the little girls, Karl said, "Kirsten, it's time for dinner."

For answer Kirsten flung herself against him and sobbed out, "Save my baby!"

We looked at one another in astonishment. What was she talking about?

"Rosalie," Edmund began, "what happened?"

The tears were starting to roll down Rosalie's cheeks as she wailed, "Her baby run away and won't come down!"

No one seemed to know what to do. What baby were they talking about?

Vincent came to the rescue. "Rosalie," he coaxed, "where did the baby go?"

Pointing up into the tree, Rosalie said, "Up there."

We all looked up. There, at the very top of the tree, was something. As we gazed at it, a frightened little meow reached our ears.

"Is that a cat?" Edmund inquired.

"No, it's just a kitten," Kirsten cried. "And now it's stuck! Karl, can't you save it?"

Karl looked at the tree doubtfully. Those branches near the top were rather small.

Before he could say anything, however, Vincent had begun to climb to the kitten's rescue. He is so used to climbing trees, that in no time at all he had the kitten in his hands. Kirsten and Rosalie clapped their hands in glee. We watched as he soon came scrambling down.

"Where is my baby?" Kirsten asked breathlessly, as Vincent dropped to the ground and no sign of the kitten was to be seen.

"I think he left it in the bird's nest," Georgie began, but was stopped by a reproving look from Edmund.

"He's right here." Vincent began unbuttoning his shirt. "I put him down my back so I wouldn't squash him climbing down." At last the shirt was off and the kitten was in the arms of Kirsten.

"Vincent!" I couldn't help exclaiming. His back was covered with scratches from the sharp little claws of the ungrateful, rescued kitten.

"Come on," and Karl gently propelled him towards the house. "Something ought to be done about those. Emma?"

"I'm coming. Edmund, won't you please bring the little girls in to dinner?"

It was some time later that we all sat down for a late dinner. Mama, David and Evie had arrived before we were ready. Vincent never uttered one cry as the scratches were being washed. Edmund had to get quite firm with the little girls, for they wanted to bring all seven of the kittens they had put doll clothes on into the house.

The girls still dress some of the kittens up in their dolls' clothes, but there is one kitten who won't play with them anymore, but runs away and hides. Edmund says he doesn't blame it.

Oh, Maria, I have to tell you what we read in "The Literary Digest." You may have heard about the book drives that are happening here in the states. We are supposed to be sending books for the boys at the front, but some people are just using it as a way to get rid of books. They have sent books on how some professional woman preserves her beauty, how to do fancy needlework, how to care and feed infants and even the book, *How Women Love*! How can people be so thoughtless? It is simply absurd. Mama laughed so hard at the thought of Daddy or Uncle John trying to read about fancy needlework that she had tears in her eyes. Edmund said he always wanted to know how women love.

This letter is getting to be quite long. Thank you for sharing those letters with us. We long for any news from the front.

I must really end this, as there is still work to do after the storms.

Give my love to all,
Emma

Tuesday
June 18, 1918
Princeville, Nova Scotia
Canada

My Dear Cousin Emma,

We were all so pleased to receive your telegram! What delightful news! We are eagerly looking forward to your next letter, that we may hear more about it! I do hope you will write soon.

Your letter arrived several days after the telegram. How is Aunt Helen doing? I could almost feel the cold dampness of the cellar as I read. I am so thankful no one was outside when the cyclone hit. It does seem hard to believe that three cyclones hit Codell in three successive years on the same day and all in the evening! I don't wonder people call May 20th "Cyclone Day." Mama was very thankful that we don't have such storms here. All Lydia Ruth thought about was those missing chickens. She said to ask you, "Did you find those poor, little, cunning chickens anywhere yet?"

I wish I could have been there to help you and to nurse Aunt Helen. There has been no one here in need of my assistance. I saw Dr. McNeel in Pictou last week, and he again offered to let me come assist him. There are times when I would like to, but most of all I just want Papa home so I can work with him.

Andrew is three years old now. The older he gets, the more mischief he gets himself and the twins into. It was only the other day when Mama, Lydia Ruth, Andrew and I were over at the McGuire's. Mama and Mrs. McGuire were sewing while Jean, Lydia Ruth and I knitted out on the front steps where we could keep an eye on the little boys. Stephen had been allowed to go out on the fishing boat with his father that day, so he wasn't around. The McGuires live right next to Grandmother on one side and the Stewarts on the other. I had taken my eyes off the laddies for just a moment to help Jean, and when I looked up, they were gone. I couldn't hear them, so I knew they must be into something. We couldn't see them anywhere. Jean and Lydia Ruth joined the search. You will never guess where we found them. They were in the Stewart's kitchen happily throwing ashes from the stove all around and rubbing the floor with some of Grandmother's fine damask napkins! I have yet to figure out how they got the napkins or got into the kitchen to begin with. Life is certainly never dull around here anymore.

Many of the village children have grown older and no longer follow me around every time I take a walk. However, there are younger ones who are rapidly filling those places. Everyone still loves to listen to stories. Now that the days are warmer, we all enjoy sitting out in the sunshine and telling or listening to stories.

I suppose I must now tell you about my fishing trip. It wasn't my idea. It was Mark who persuaded Mr. McLean to ask me to go. The lads go out with him quite often, as both Alan and David are away. I really didn't think I could be spared, but Mrs. McLean volunteered to help Mama watch Andrew. There were five others besides me on the boat: William, Charles, Mark, James, and of course, Mr. McLean. I will say that though I have been around water for so many years and have even been on large vessels, never had I been on this small a boat, so far from shore, and with a load of smelly fish too. I was feeling rather out of place as we set off. The lads were all in high spirits as they set about different tasks. The motion of the craft, being smaller than I had before ridden on, was decidedly more noticeable.

I watched the receding shore line until I could no longer make out the houses. Turning my gaze to the wide expanse of deep blue water and azure sky, I felt a sudden longing to sail on and on until we should reach France. All noise of the busy lads working around me faded from my thoughts, and all I seemed to hear was Papa telling me again how he and Uncle Lawrence came across the ocean to a new life in America.

"Ah, Lassie," Mr. McLean's voice brought me back to

the present. "Ye maun be far away wi' that look in yer een. Be ye in France?"

"No, but I was far away," I answered with a smile.

"Don't let her get too far away, or she'll fall overboard," Mark teased.

That was the end of my daydreaming for the time being, the lads being eager to show me all over the ship and instruct me in everything they themselves knew. I'm afraid I am a slow learner when it comes to ships. It was the end of the day before I was finally able to state correctly each time which side of the ship was port and which starboard. The port is the left side of the ship when you are facing the front, and the starboard is the right. My lessons came to a halt when we reached our fishing spot. It is a puzzlement to me how they find the right place without any signs. It isn't like on land where you can mark a tree or memorize how the rocks look. It is all just one vast expanse of water which all looks the same; at least it does to my eyes.

Once the fish started filling up the bottom of the boat, I stayed out of the way as much as possible. I enjoy eating fish and will even clean a few if Mark can't get to it, but to have hundreds of fish flapping around my feet wasn't exactly the most enjoyable experience I have had. And they smelled! I am used to the smell of fish, but usually it is in moderation, being mingled with the smell of earth, trees, and flowers, while here it was entirely fish! I don't know why fishing is such an attraction, but Mark and James are delighted each time they can go out with someone. It must be in James' blood, as his father was a sea captain, but I don't know where Mark gets it.

Now, I know the boys are all wanting to know what kind of fish we caught, or rather the lads and Mr. McLean caught. They were fishing this time for haddock. Sometimes the village men will go out for cod, but they are usually gone for several days then, as they have to go to the Banks for them. The lads have all been asking Mr. McLean to take them to catch a swordfish this year, but I don't know if he will. I have heard that it is rather dangerous. On the way out to the fishing grounds, Mr. McLean was telling us about the halibut that he, Alan and David caught once. Did you know that a halibut has both eyes on his right side? His right side is brown or grey while his left side is usually all or mostly white. They are large fish. The one they caught was about five feet long! Larger ones have been reported.

"Maria," Mr. McLean called to me just before the ship was turned to head for home. "What do ye think o' a day fishing noo?"

"Well," I wasn't quite sure what to say, "it was certainly a new experience."

Mr. McLean smiled. "But ye donnae care muckle for the smell o' the fish."

He was quite right. I much preferred to gaze across the water watching the sunshine sparkle and dance on the waves, or watch the sea gulls and kittywakes soar and swoop overhead trying to forget what was down on the deck by my feet.

The sun was setting as we neared the docks. This was the first time I had seen the sunset from a ship coming into port. I didn't have much time to enjoy it, for there was much commotion as the lads brought the ship in and tied her. I was glad to be home once more with my feet on solid ground.

A letter from Papa came today. Pray for him, Emma, he is working so hard! But here is the part that will interest you:

A few days ago, I was busy with the wounded. They were bringing them in faster than the small staff could handle almost. I went from one patient to another. Those whose wounds could wait were moved, and those in immediate need were given attention as rapidly as possible. There are so few of us in comparison to these poor lads. I had done countless surgeries that day, the night before, and the proceeding day. I was well nigh spent, and as yet another man was brought in for surgery, I wanted to say he would have to wait, for I must have a rest. Maria, I am thankful you are not here to witness these trying scenes. With a prayer for strength, I bent over my new patient. His right leg had been blown off by a shell, but to my utmost surprise, I found him conscious and not only that but with a clear mind, for I heard him whisper,

"Hello Fred."

I paused to look at his face. It looked familiar. A pain-filled smile flickered briefly across his worn and haggard face.

"Jim!" I gasped.

The man nodded ever so slightly. "My ... leg ... is ... gone?" The question was calm.

All I could do was nod. I returned to my work, more determined than ever to help all I possibly could. At last there came a lull in the flow of wounded, and I slept for an hour before making the rounds of the wounded. I found Jim quiet and resting as well as could be expected. His one desire is to live and go back to England and home. Pray for him and me. I miss you all so very much!

Now you can pray for Uncle James as well. What will be the total of wounded and killed when this war is over?

Edith reminded me just now that I should get this in the mail, for the sooner you receive it, the sooner you can reply.

With love,
Maria

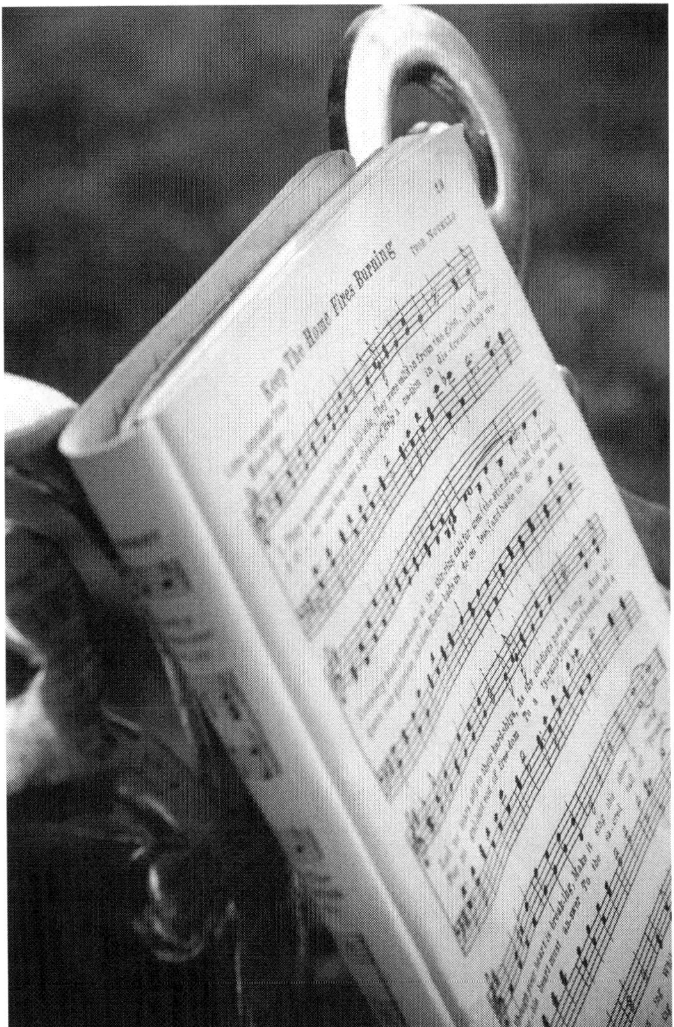
Keep The Home Fires Burning

CHAPTER TWENTY-EIGHT

> Thursday
> July 11, 1918
> Codell, Kansas
> USA

Dear Maria,

I don't know what kind of letter this is going to be, but I'm going to write it anyway. You see, Mama, David and the twins are gone to Tennessee to be with Grandpa, and I have to run the house. At least Karl and Edmund are here to help, or I'd never be able to manage. Evie is taking a nap, or I wouldn't try writing now. Thankfully the little boys are all out in the field, and Carrie has the little girls in the garden. It sure is different with Mama not here. They all left this morning. But I should start when the twins were born, shouldn't I?

They were born on June 6, as the telegram said. Oh, dear, Evie is awake, I'll have to write later.

> Evening,

All the younger ones are in bed now, so I should be able to write for at least a little while with no interruptions. I don't remember when my last letter was sent as so much has happened. Mama hadn't been feeling well ever since the cyclone hit. All that was just too much for her, and she was in bed for over a week. Even after she got up, she wasn't her usual self and tired easily. On the morning of the 6th, when she didn't come down for breakfast, I took a tray up to her, only to hurry rapidly back down the stairs to say,

"Karl, take the younger ones outside! David, go get the doctor! Carrie, go help with the girls, no stay here, or no go out, I'll call you if I want you. Edmund--" By that time I was rather flustered and told him, "do something."

Everyone did my bidding at once except Edmund. He just stood and looked at me.

"Edmund," I exclaimed in exasperation, "what on earth are you doing?"

He started chuckling and shook his head. "I'm doing something. You didn't tell me what, so I decided to look at you."

"Edmund!"

He responded with a chuckle and an, "Emma, Emma. You'll have to calm down or you'll be of no help at all to Mama."

I stared, astonished, then laughed and returned upstairs. He was right, and I knew it, but he can be so exasperating at times.

The doctor came with David, and late that morning the twins arrived. Now let me tell you all about them, as I'm sure you are longing to know. Telegrams aren't very good for long messages.

Franklin Wallace, or Frankie, as we call him, is most certainly the biggest. He was so at birth and has continued to be. He is more fussy than his twin and refuses quite often to go to sleep if he isn't being held. Though he likes to be held when he is sleeping, he fusses if he is held much while he is awake. That is certainly something new and different. I didn't know any babies were like that. His hair is brown - dark brown - and his eyes are dark. He has a round face and, would you believe it? A dimple! Mama said he looks like Uncle Philip Vincent Bartholomew Wallace III! Only he doesn't have a dimple. Uncle Philip doesn't.

Little Freddy is just that, little. He is so much smaller than Frankie even now, but the doctor says he is healthy. He seems nearly the opposite of Frankie in just about everything. His hair isn't dark but rather light; he doesn't have as much as Frankie, but at least he isn't bald like some others I know. He wants to be held all the time when awake, but will fuss and cry if he gets tired until you put him in bed. His face is more oval in shape, and though he too has a dimple, it is on the other side. I'm not sure just who Freddy looks like. Sometimes I can see some of Carrie, while at others I think of Daddy. His full name is Frederick William.

Oh, the joys of having babies in the house again! I didn't realize how much I missed having a baby around. Evie hasn't been a baby for many months. With all her chattering, you would think she was nearly three years old, when in actuality she is really not quite sixteen months.

Well, Edmund is yawning quite dramatically, and Karl is standing in the doorway looking first at me and then at the clock. I think they are trying to tell me to quit writing and get to bed so they can do the same.

Sunday 14,

I was going to write more on Friday and then again on Saturday, but it didn't happen. I had no idea it could be this difficult to run the house with Mama, David and the twins gone. I thought it would be easier with no little distractions, but it isn't. In the first place, Evie has not wanted to take a nap. But if I let her stay up, she is not very happy later. I think I will have to start having Edmund tell her to take a nap, as he did today. She started to fuss, but when he told her to stop, she did. And he's the one who said I could handle anyone. It seems that I can't handle Evie. When Rosalie was little, she used to fall asleep wherever she happened to be. All we had to do was pick her up and put her in bed.

Things are quiet here today. I am so thankful for a day of rest! Life would be miserable without it. Carrie is writing a letter to Daddy now with the little girls watching. I told Karl and Edmund to be prepared for an outbreak from the little boys, for I noticed the restless look in Vincent's eyes this morning, and Georgie has been too good for the last several weeks. And if they both -- well, we shall see. I am just rambling now, so I think I'll write another time.

Wednesday 17,
I was expecting it, and it came. It happened last evening, but I was too busy and distracted to even attempt to write then. Now you can have the story.

Vincent and Georgie had been out in the yard after supper catching lightning bugs to put in a jar. Since they do that most evenings, I thought nothing of it. The little girls were outside too. When Edmund called them all in for bed, Vincent and Georgie ran upstairs at once in such a hurry that I knew something was up. As Edmund was busy listening to Evie explain why she couldn't go to bed and convincing her of the contrary, I asked Karl to go see what was up. He came down a moment later saying that both boys were getting ready for bed, and nothing seemed wrong except that they seemed a little more excited than usual about it.

"That's what I was afraid of," I moaned.

"What is?" Edmund asked, coming into the kitchen then.

Before I could reply, Vincent and Georgie came bounding down the stairs to say good night. Once they were safely back upstairs and in their room, Edmund looked at me.

"Do you think something is not quite right?"

I nodded. I wasn't sure what, but there was something in the air. The three of us sat and pondered in puzzled silence until the little girls came to say good night. Still wondering, I followed the girls upstairs and tucked them into bed after listening to their prayers. Pausing irresolutely in the hall afterwards, I glanced towards the boy's room. Perhaps I should look in on Vincent and Georgie.

Softly I turned the doorknob. I was unprepared for the lightning bug that flew unexpectedly into my face. I screamed. I couldn't help it, Maria, I really couldn't. Then I noticed that the room was full of the insects, flashing here and there about the room. I was speechless. It wasn't until Edmund and Karl's steps were heard in the hall and Carrie's voice sounded asking what was happening, that I spoke.

"Vincent and Georgie! What . . . why . . ."

The door was flung wide open. Edmund's gasp of astonishment was clearly heard.

"Yet me yee!" Evie demanded, pushing against my legs.

I glanced down. There was Evie in her nightdress, and at their open door the other girls were gathered in wondering silence.

Of course by this time, the lightning bugs were flying down the halls and into other rooms.

Edmund ordered the boys to start catching them. The girls helped too. In fact, we all were catching the flying lights. At one point, Karl caught Georgie coming inside with a pail in his hand.

"No, Georgie," I heard him say firmly. "There are to be no toads or snakes to help catch these. Take them back outside at once." I shivered over the thought.

At last we had the majority of the insects back in the yard. I didn't feel like writing that evening. Once we had the children back in bed, Edmund, Karl and I sat down wearily in the kitchen. We looked at each other, and Edmund began to laugh. The thought of us all chasing those insects all over the house was too much. After we had a good laugh, I went straight to bed. I'm afraid I didn't sleep very well, and I am still finding the little creatures in unexpected places. Edmund dealt with the boys this morning, and I hope it won't happen again.

Saturday 20,

Here it is Saturday already, and I find I still haven't told you why Mama, David and the twins are gone. It was on the 10th that a telegram came from Uncle David telling Mama that Grandpa was ill and to come at once if possible. With Mama being the only daughter and not having seen

Grandpa for many years now, she really felt that she should go. That day, she talked with us five older ones. Carrie was included. It was decided that David would go with Mama as escort and leave the farm in the hands of Edmund and Karl. There was talk of having Edmund or Karl go instead, but Mama didn't want to separate Edmund and me nor Karl and Kirsten. Carrie is growing up and said as long as Edmund and Karl would be home, it was all right if David went. The younger ones were told that evening. Kirsten looked worried until Mama assured her that Karl would stay behind. Evie wanted to go too. Edmund told her she was too big to go. Her eyes opened wide and after a moment she smiled and started chattering as usual. Surprisingly, it was Vincent and Rosalie that had the hardest time parting with Mama. Kirsten tried in every way she knew how to comfort Rosalie and dry her tears. As for Vincent, he wouldn't wave as the train pulled out of the station and then was moody all the way home. He was irritable and out of sorts until Edmund took him aside and had a long talk with him.

Tuesday 23,

Mama and the rest are coming home tomorrow! How I long to hold those little babies in my arms again! Everyone seems in high spirits tonight. Edmund and Karl have them all outside playing something. I don't know what, but from the sounds of things, it must be fun. I'll try to finish this after they come home, as it is past time the young ones were in bed.

Thursday 25,

Maria, I don't know if I can tell you this. They are home, but oh, Maria, pray for us!

It was mid-afternoon, and we were about to head to Plainville to meet Mama, David and the twins at the station. All, with the exception of me, were out back by the barn eagerly watching Edmund and Karl hitch up the horses to the wagon. I was inside taking care of a few last things.

Walking over to shut the front door, I noticed a boy on a bicycle coming quickly down the lane. Stepping out on the porch to meet him, I noticed he had a piece of paper in his hand,

"This the Foster place?" he asked.

"Yes."

"Got a telegram. Just sign here."

I signed and took the telegram with a beating heart. Who was it from? What did it say? Was it about Daddy? Was Mama delayed? With the last question, I suddenly tore open the paper and read the few lines it contained. They burned themselves into my memory. Even now I can see them every time I close my eyes.

"Helen, Captain Lawrence Foster of the 89th division has been reported missing in action. Will write soon - John"

I stared in shocked horror at the paper. The whole room seemed spinning, and I caught at the door frame for support. This couldn't be true! There must be some mistake. Not Daddy! I looked wildly around the empty room. My first impulse was to run outside and tell everyone. But I couldn't. They were all so eager and excited. I just couldn't spoil Mama's homecoming. Everyone had been looking forward to this day, and now it was ruined. But I wouldn't tell them. With a choking sob in my throat, I ran, half blinded by tears, to the safety of my room. After fastening the door securely, I flung myself on the bed, my face buried in the pillow. Missing! The word brought back a memory. Once I had asked Daddy what "missing in action" meant. He replied, "Well, it could mean you were captured, or lost, or it could mean you were blown to bits and there was nothing left of you."

Daddy couldn't be . . . I just wouldn't let myself think it. He couldn't be! Though the tears coursed down my cheeks, I couldn't cry, . . . not yet. Someone might hear me, and then they all would know. Suddenly, there was a knock on the door, and Kirsten called,

"Emma, its time to go."

"I'm not going," I managed to say without crying.

"But, Emma," Kirsten begged, "you have to go! We're going to get Mama and the babies and David."

"Kirsten," I implored, "just go on. I can't go, and that's final. I have to make supper." I added the last as an afterthought, for it struck me that Edmund might come up if I had no apparent reason for staying. I fairly held my breath as I listened to her retreating footsteps. Oh, how I longed for them to leave so that I could cry without notice. Unknowingly, I crushed the telegram in my hand and tried to choke back the sobs that rose up. Then, just when I expected to hear the wagon leaving, I heard someone running up the stairs three at a time. It was Edmund. Why did he have to come up? Anyone else wouldn't be likely to notice the tears in my voice, but I wasn't so sure about my twin. A sharp rap sounded on the door.

"Emma, its time to leave." I bit my lip to keep back the sob that seemed to almost strangle me. "Emma, come on!" he ordered as I didn't reply.

"I can't come. I'm staying here."

"Are you sick?"

"No." Why wouldn't he leave me alone?

"Then I don't understand at all. You didn't say anything last night about staying home. Why won't you come?" He seemed bent on knowing the reason, but I couldn't and wouldn't tell him.

"Never mind why," I almost snapped. "Just go away or you'll be late." There was silence then and after a minute I heard him turn and go slowly down the stairs. I wanted to run after him, to beg him to understand and to forgive my impatience, but I didn't move. I just buried my face deeper in the pillow, for the sobs would come in spite of all my effort to keep them back.

Finally, I heard the longed-for sound of the wagon rumbling down the lane, together with the shouts and laughter of the children. I was alone at last. Letting go of the fierce check I had held on my emotions, I cried as I had never done before. Great tearing sobs shook me, and tears soaked the pillow. All the pent-up emotions from the last half hour, the weeks and months of nameless fears that had been suppressed for so long, came forth. In the midst of it all, I suddenly caught my breath; someone was knocking on the door!

"Lucy," Edmund called. "Open the door." Why was he here? How was he left behind? Why didn't he go with the others? I wouldn't open the door. "Lucy, what's wrong?"

"N . . . n . . . nothing," I stammered. I knew it wasn't true, but there was nothing he could do, for I wouldn't tell him.

"Emma, something *is* wrong. Now open the door!" his voice was quite firm.

"Please, Edmund," I implored, "just go away and leave me alone! I won't open the door. There isn't anything you can do." The last words ended in a sob. Edmund said no more, and I heard him walk down the hall to his room. Why did he have to stay? Why did the telegram have to come at all? Why did Daddy have to go fight? Why was there a war anyway? Why? Why? Why? Tortured by all the questions, my mind was in a turmoil and the whole world seemed crashing down around me. There was nothing to hold on to. I couldn't even pray except "Help, Lord!" and He did.

Right then, in the depths of my despair, someone sat down on the bed beside me, and a hand was laid on my shoulder. "Emma, what is it?" Edmund's voice was gentleness itself, and for a minute all I could do was cry. "Lucy," he pleaded, "won't you tell me?"

I would tell him. I couldn't bear it alone any longer. Sitting up quickly, I thrust the crumpled bit of paper at him and buried my face in my hands. I couldn't stand to see the look that would come. The silence that followed seemed an eternity before it was broken by a deep sigh, then, "Oh, Emma!" It was all he said then, but he put his arms around me and drew me to him. Leaning my head against his chest, I cried violently. He said nothing, but just feeling his strong arm around me and his hand stroking my hair brought comfort. When at last I grew calmer and my sobs were less violent, Edmund began to speak softly.

"I will never leave thee nor forsake thee . . . The Lord is my refuge and strength, a very present help in trouble, therefore will not we fear . . . In the Lord put I my trust . . . The Lord will be a refuge for the oppressed, a refuge in times of trouble . . . In my distress I called upon the Lord and cried unto my God: He heard my voice out of his temple, and my cry came before him, even into his ears . . . Trust thou in the Lord . . . The Lord is with me . . . The Lord hear thee in the day of trouble . . . The Lord is my Shepherd; I shall not want. He maketh me to lie down in green pastures, . . ."

As his voice went on reciting verse after verse, I began to relax. At last, drawing a long, shaky breath, I looked up at my twin. He looked down at me and asked softly, "Do you want to talk now?"

I nodded and sat up. Edmund handed me his handkerchief, as mine was soaked. "I didn't want to ruin the day," I began.

"When did it come?"

"When you were all outside. And then I just couldn't go."

"Why didn't you tell us?" he questioned.

"It would have ruined everyone's day."

"Is that why you wouldn't talk when I came to the door the first time?"

I nodded. "Why did you stay? Now it's ruined your day too."

"I stayed," he said gently, "because my sister needed me. I could tell you were upset, so I simply sent the others on and stayed behind."

It dawned on me then for the first time that the other children had gone to Plainville without Edmund or me. "Edmund! How could you send them on?"

Edmund smiled a little. "Karl can handle the horses as

well as I can. You know that. Besides, Kirsten is in the wagon, so you know he will be careful. I don't think he'll have any problems."

"How did you come in?" I asked. "I didn't want you in here."

"I know you didn't think you did, but you needed someone; I could tell."

"But how?"

Edmund continued, "Since you wouldn't open the door, I climbed out my window onto the porch roof and in your window."

"I didn't want to tell you! I wasn't going to, but ... now I've spoiled Mama's homecoming!" I began to cry again, and Edmund slipped his arm around my waist.

"Hush, Emma," he said. "It's not spoiled yet, but she'll have to know."

"Do we have to tell her tonight? Can't we wait until tomorrow?" I entreated with my weary head on his shoulder.

He nodded. After a minute of silence, Edmund drew me down on my knees with him, and we spent time in prayer. I prayed for Daddy. I just couldn't make myself believe he was gone. He couldn't be! As we rose from prayer, I drew a shuddering breath and put my hand on my aching head.

"Emma," Edmund instructed, "bathe your face and then lie down and rest."

"I can't," I protested, trying to appear like my usual self. "I have to fix supper."

"You aren't fixing any supper until you've rested." His voice had that firmness to it which does not get ignored. "Do you want Mama knowing as soon as she comes?"

The rest did make me feel better. Together Edmund and I prepared supper. I didn't know what Edmund had done with the telegram, for I didn't see any sign of it. The table was set and the food almost ready when we heard the wagon. I turned quickly to Edmund with a half-frightened look.

"Think about the babies," he said softly, "and smile."

We stepped out on the porch, and as Karl drew rein near the barn, we hurried out to greet them. Edmund reached the wagon first and lifted his arms for the twin Mama was holding. With a light kiss, he handed him to me and then helped Mama climb down.

"Freddie is getting bigger," I remarked, cuddling the little bundle in my arms.

"Yes," Mama agreed, giving me an embrace. Then she turned again to the wagon to get Frankie from David.

"Emma!" Rosalie called.

"Emma! Emma! Emma!" shouted Evie.

"Look!" Rosalie was waving something eagerly.

"Emma! Emma!" Evie shouted again, climbing on the edge of the wagon, and had not Vincent grabbed her skirt, she would have tumbled out.

"We got letters from Daddy!" Rosalie called above the noise of all the others.

I glanced in mute anguish at Edmund and then, not trusting myself if I stayed, I quickly put Freddie in his arms and darted to the house. I had only a moment alone, but that was enough, for when they came in, I had the oven open and was checking the supper. David hardly waited until the oven was shut before giving me an affectionate greeting.

"Friendly sister you are, running away like that without so much as a hello," he teased. "What are tears doing in your eyes? Are you sorry we've come home?"

I shook my head. "Opened the oven and looked in too quickly." I wiped the tears away with my apron.

Supper was a lively meal. I was glad I didn't have to talk much. The others did it for me. All too soon - for me at least - Mama began to open one of Daddy's letters. Quietly, as I was in the habit of doing, I began to clear the table. How thankful I was for that habit. No one seemed to notice my unusual emotion, unless it was Edmund. I scarcely heard a word that was read, for in my mind the words of that telegram kept repeating themselves over and over. I didn't talk much as the girls and I cleaned up the kitchen afterwards. Everything felt as though it took ten times as long as usual. Would the day never end? I felt as though in a dream. When would I wake up?

Standing later by the living room window as Mama put the children to bed, I fought back the tears that wanted to come. "Stop!" I ordered myself sharply. "You cannot cry now. Wait until you are in bed."

The older boys came in and sat down. They were all quiet. Each seemed busy with his own thoughts. Mama's step was heard on the stairs, and then she entered.

"This is pleasant," she said. "My four big children all together again. Were you waiting for me?" Her voice was light and pleasant.

I didn't hear the answer the boys gave.

"Emma," Mama called softly but cheerfully. "Aren't you going to come join us?"

I didn't answer nor turn from the window. I couldn't. She didn't know! Oh, poor Mama! How could she bear the news when we told her, as we would have to do eventually.

"Emma," Mama called again. "I want my daughter. Won't you come?"

Suddenly I could stand the strain of silence no longer. Turning, I gave Edmund one despairing look, then flew across the room to Mama. Sinking to the floor at her feet, I buried my face in her lap with a perfect burst of tears. For several minutes, no one said anything as I continued to cry, and Mama stroked my hair. I think most of them were too astonished to say anything. I don't cry before others unless I am strongly moved. I thought I had cried all my tears earlier with Edmund, but it seemed I hadn't.

"Emma," Mama spoke softly, soothingly, as to one of the little ones. "Tell us all about it."

"I . . . I can't!" I sobbed.

"Why not?"

"Because, oh, . . . I . . . I just can't!" I stammered.

"Boys," I could tell Mama was looking at Karl and Edmund. "What has happened?"

I checked my sobs, waiting for the answer that I just couldn't give, but Edmund remained silent.

"I don't know, Mama," Karl replied.

David spoke up then. "Ed, why don't you just confess since Emma can't?"

There was silence. I finally looked up and saw Edmund staring fixedly at the wall. His jaw was set firmly, and he neither moved nor spoke. Wiping my eyes, I looked up at Mama with a shaky smile.

"Don't worry about me, Mama. I'm all right now. But I'm glad you're home."

She smiled back, but said, "There is something going on that I don't understand, and before any of us go to bed, I want to know all about it."

I knew she meant it, and I wasn't sure if Edmund would tell. I knew I couldn't.

Edmund turned finally to look at Mama. "Can't you trust us, Mama?" he asked.

"Yes I can, or I would never have left you two in charge so long. I knew something wasn't right when you didn't come and meet us with the others." Quietly she reached out and took a hand of each of us. Looking first at me and then at Edmund, she said softly, "You've had bad news about Daddy, haven't you?"

How did she know? Edmund bowed his head in answer, unable to speak.

Mama gave a deep sigh, then spoke just as calmly as she had before, but very quietly. "Where is the telegram?" Without a word, Edmund pulled it from his pocket and handed it to her. Not a sound could be heard but the ticking of the clock as she read those lines. Not until David and Karl had also read it did Mama say anything, and then it wasn't to any of us.

"The Lord preserve thee in the day of battle. The Lord preserve thy going out and thy coming in. A thousand shall fall at thy side and ten thousand at thy right, hand but it shall not come nigh thee."

Mama didn't say much that night but sent us all to bed soon after.

As I stood upstairs near my bedroom door, David came over and put his arm around me. "Don't blame yourself for letting Mama know tonight," he whispered. "Even I could tell something was amiss, and she would have gotten it out sooner or later."

I looked at him gratefully and went off to bed. I had been blaming myself, but I knew David was right. Mama would have found out anyway before we went to bed. She always does.

I can't write any more. Pray for us, Maria. It can't be true. It just can't! Freddy is crying. Will Daddy ever see him or Frankie?

>   Always yours,
>   Emma

CHAPTER TWENTY-NINE

"Mom, you can't stop there! You just can't! What happened? Please read just one more!" Ria's voice was intense and eager. "Please, Mom!" Even Lydia looked longingly at Mrs. Mitchell.

That lady glanced at her watch, then at the girlish faces before her, pleading with every look of their expressive eyes. "I--" She was cut short by the ringing of the telephone.

The friends' faces fell, and they looked the keen disappointment they felt. Neither spoke, however, and in another moment Mrs. Mitchell returned. "That was your Aunt Louise," she began, addressing Ria. "She is running a little late, so she can't pick me up for another thirty minutes or so. That means--"

With a bounce of delight, Ria interrupted. "You can read another letter! Goody!"

"Hush!" Lydia shushed her. "Be quiet and listen."

Saturday
August 24, 1918
Princeville, Nova Scotia
Canada

Dear Emma,

Oh, how my heart bled and ached for you! I couldn't

read your letter to the others; Mark had to. I just can't tell you what I felt! The entire village shared your anguish, and the relief was very great when your telegram came through saying it wasn't so. Have you gotten a letter from Uncle Lawrence since the last telegram? I can't even begin to imagine what you must have felt like during the time of uncertainty. I wrote Papa all about it. I am thankful anew that he is with the medical corps not in the front lines! Even so, I worry. I know I shouldn't, but sometimes I can't help it. When will the war be over? It has been almost four long years since Papa was home. I feel at times as if I really can't wait another day to see him! I know you feel the same way about Uncle, though he has been gone for only sixteen months.

The other day I had to be doctor and nurse to a sea gull. Little Catherine Morris found it. She is five now, but so tiny and delicate that she seems to be only three, except when she talks. She discovered it along a rocky cliff. The bird wouldn't let her get near it to pick it up, so she sat down and watched it. No one knows how long she stayed there. It was suppertime when Heather came to ask if I knew where she was. Usually I do know where the children are, so it was only natural for her to come ask. But this time I didn't. Mark, James, Edith and I joined in the search. No one in the village had seen her all afternoon. Mrs. Morris was growing worried, as Mr. Morris was out fishing and Robert is in France. We called and called, but Catherine wouldn't answer. At last James ran up to me and said he and Mark had found her. I followed at once, almost afraid of what they had found. It was with great relief that I saw Catherine sitting safely beside Mark. She refused to leave until "the puir, wee, sick birdie" was caught so it could be made better. After some difficulty, the lads succeeded in catching the gull. Catherine was tired, and I carried her back home. I asked her if she had heard us calling for her. She told me yes, so I asked why she hadn't answered. Her reply was, "The puir, wee, sick birdie wad hae been sae afraid an' wad hae gang away. He truly wad hae, Maria. Hoo wad ye hae made him better if he wa' gang?"

As you can see, Catherine speaks Scottish as well as - if not better than - some of the others. Perhaps it is because she is with her mother so much and Mrs. Morris speaks it as fluently as Grandmother. I love listening to them converse. It does take more effort to follow the conversation than if it were between some of the others. I love the sound of the Scottish tongue.

Safely back at home, Catherine wouldn't eat her supper until she had watched me set the bird's wing and Arthur had given it some fish. Mrs. Morris told me the next day that Catherine had pleaded to have the bird in bed with her that night. I'm not sure what Mrs. Morris would have done if Heather hadn't told Catherine that the bird might hurt himself more if she were to accidentally knock him out of bed while she slept. Then Arthur put in his bit of advice by telling her that for a bird to have to sleep in her bed would be like her having to sleep in a big pile of sticks. Mrs. Morris didn't know which reason persuaded her, but she agreed to let it sleep somewhere else.

Tell Kirsten and Rosalie the sea gull's wing healed very nicely, and he flew away to join his friends once more. Catherine claims that it comes back to the docks for fish every day, but as there are always quite a number of sea gulls there, no one is certain it is truly the same one.

Here is a story that should cause you to smile. I don't recall exactly when this took place as it was several weeks past. Mama, Lydia Ruth, Mrs. Lawson and Jenny had gone into Pictou with the older girls leaving James behind with Mark. I was quite busy all day watching Andrew, the twins and Archie. Most of the other children were outside with me, as well. When time came to make supper, I asked Mark and James if they would watch Andrew. I could send the rest of the children home. Instead, Mark offered to make supper with the help of James. I was hesitant to accept his offer, for he had not done much cooking. Finally their earnest pleas caused me to yield, though I did so with reluctance. I made them promise to call me if they needed any help. When thirty, then forty minutes had passed with no call from the lads, I grew nervous. What if something was going wrong and they were too busy to call me? What if they had called me but I hadn't heard because of the children? Edmund, don't laugh. I feel sure Emma would feel the same way were you to undertake the task of making supper yourself.

At last, when a full hour of waiting had passed with no call, I determined to go and see how things were progressing, just to reassure myself. That is when a problem arose. The only children who were with me still were the younger ones, and I couldn't very well leave them in charge of the four little laddies. I could either take them all with me or not go. Thinking over all the problems of taking the children with me, for you must know that we were past the village with no houses nearby, I decided to stay and trust the lads with supper. No sooner had I decided when a question came to me; if the lads did call for my assistance, how would I manage to give it with all these young ones? David, do stop laughing, and Aunt Helen, it was truly a perplexing problem. I may be almost seventeen, but I didn't feel like it then.

It was about that time when I decided that I should start herding the children back to the village. I say herding, as some don't follow very well. That is when I ran into yet another difficulty. Catherine wanted to be carried, as she said she was tired. The other young ones followed my directions and headed for the path. I had decided not to go back by way of the cliffs since I had no older ones to help me. All at once, Archie decided that he didn't want to go with us and turned in the opposite direction. Usually, Archie is a very sweet and easy-going laddie, but if he gets an idea in his head, it is nearly impossible to get it out. I called to him, but he moved right along. Ida ran after him but couldn't bring him back. That is when I noticed Andrew and Rob starting to climb a fallen tree. The tree was very old and rotting, and I didn't want anyone getting hurt. William, whose hand I was holding to keep him from stopping too often to look at things, had started crying for some reason. Archie was still persisting on not returning with Ida. Ross, Henry and Stephen started a wrestling match, Edana and Anne were pulling on my skirt trying to get my attention, and I didn't know who to take care of first. At that moment, who should suddenly appear but Grandmother!

"Havers! I's warrant ye suld hae some help wi' a' thae wee littlins, Lass, ye look forjaskit! Isna that sae?"

I nodded wearily.

"Ye just gae an' bring baith the lass an' the laddie back so an' I'll bide wi' these a wee."

Gratefully, I set Catherine down, let go of William's hand and started after Archie. It ended with me carrying him back, as he refused to walk. When I returned to the children, Grandmother had them all around her singing "The Campbell's Are Coming." We made it safely back to the village with no other difficulties, thanks to Grandmother. I really don't know what I would have done without her.

Mark and James managed to fix supper without my help, and though it wasn't made the way Edith, Mama or I make it, it was better than I had thought it would be. Edith said, "It has a unique flavor which is no doubt the specialty of the Mark and James cuisine."

I took my violin outside a few weeks ago and played for two hours. It wasn't my intent to play for so long, but requests kept coming, therefore I kept playing.

Last evening, Edith and I sat up and talked with Mama for quite some time. We talked about so many things. One of the things we talked about was when Mama met Papa back in Tennessee and the years we spent there with you. She usually doesn't tell many stories, but she told us of the time when Edith and David decided to go west. She said they packed some clothes and a few sticks of candy in their wagon and made you, Edmund and me pull it. She said we were nearing the edge of town before Uncle Lawrence and Papa found us. Edith said she remembers that just a little.

She couldn't have been more than six or seven years old at the time.

We all laughed about those lightning bugs in your house. Mama said to tell Edmund she hopes he wasn't too hard on Vincent and Georgie, for she distinctly remembers a time when he brought a jar full of crickets into our house and let them go in the room where baby Mark slept. When asked why he had done it, he replied, "So they can sing Baby Mark to sleep."

Mama said it was weeks before they got rid of all the crickets.

How I wish I could hear Evie talk. What does she think of the twins? Edith asked who Evie looks like. It sounds as though Edmund must be very busy looking after you and Evie. Does Kirsten do much with her, or is she with Rosalie all the time?

We had some news from the front. It was not cheery as usual, but we had already learned of it from the newspapers. I'll copy them anyway, as I have room. This first is from Alan.

So I lie in bed in a hospital. Donnae fret yerselves. I's warrant this shouther wound is naething. Dr. Foster wad hae told me gin it were. Malcolm is in the bed beside mine. Puir braw maun! He is wounded in the leg. Hoo he maun dree frae a' he hae been through. Ye ken, I's warrant, that Finley deid. He deid a laochain! I kent the lad wad gie his a' gin he maun. Malcolm was wi' him at the end. I donnae ken hoo lang for the smoke hid them. The doctors say Malcolm drees frae shell shock as well as frae his wound, for he lost muckle blude. Pray for him. I maun nae write muckle mair noo, for the nurse is gabbing o' calling Dr. Foster.

Donnae fret aboot me. The Gude Lord is still wi' me.
Alan

Now here is Papa's side of the story.

"I'm sure you have read of Finley's death in the papers. I am thankful that Malcolm and Alan are in the same hospital I am, as my presence seems to be a comfort to Malcolm. He is suffering from shell shock, exposure, and loss of blood from a gun shot wound in his leg, as well as pieces of shrapnel in many places. However, I am afraid what is worse is that he is reliving over and over his brother's death. From what Alan has said, Finley risked his life to save Malcolm and then died right there in his arms. Pray for them all. Alan was a witness to some of it as well. I have had Alan moved to a cot next to Malcolm, as he has had the most success in calming him when I am busy elsewhere, which is most of the time.

Alan's shoulder is, I am afraid, going to keep him from going back to his regiment for some time, as it is going to take quite a long while to heal. As soon as possible, I will be sending both of them to a hospital farther from the front. Alan seems to have a suspicion of it and appears to be trying to force his shoulder to heal more rapidly. He is a brave lad and the nurses say they never hear a word of complaint pass his lips."

Edith and Mama send their love. The others would do the same were they here to send it. Kiss those sweet babies for us.

All my love,
Maria

CHAPTER THIRTY

Monday
September 30, 1918
Codell, Kansas
USA

Dear Maria,

Nearly all are sick here with this dreadful influenza! Karl and I are the only ones who seem to have resisted the sickness. Edmund was the first to come down with it some time ago. I can't keep track of the days anymore. They all blend together stretching out with no end in sight. Edmund tried to hide his illness but was ordered to bed by Mama and me as soon as we noticed. Only after begging her to think of the twins was Mama persuaded to let me nurse him. I think it was the next day that Vincent and Carrie fell sick. A few days later Georgie, Rosalie and David also took to their beds, to be followed by Mama and Evie. Kirsten took care of the twins and tried to stay away from the sickness, but it was no use. Within two days she and both babies were ill. From then on it has been a nightmare. Days and nights run together without end. The sun hasn't shone for such a long time that I have nearly forgotten what it is like.

The doctor comes every day. Dr. Pierson was so over worked that his nephew or some relation of his, a Doctor Mitchell, has come from Stockton to help him. It is Dr. Mitchell that comes here. When I first saw him -- how long ago that seems -- I didn't think he could even be out of medical school. He told Mama he had already had the flu and couldn't get it again, when she told him she was afraid he would get sick. At least that is a comfortable thought.

Edmund is on the mend, thank God! He was allowed out of bed yesterday morning for a few hours. He doesn't have much energy, but he is getting better. Carrie, Vincent, David and Georgie are better. David didn't have it as hard as some of the others. Evie and Rosalie are over the worst, the doctor thinks, but Mama, Kirsten and the babies are still very sick. The doctor looks grave after seeing them.

Oh, Maria, everything is so hard! A neighbor has been doing the chores since David took sick. I don't know what I'd do without Karl! I feel so helpless, so useless. I am tired all the time. Sleep doesn't rest me anymore, and I don't want to eat though I make myself do it, for I won't get sick! I can't get sick! I have sung songs and told stories until I could hardly speak. I have walked the floor for hours with the twins or Evie in my arms, I have almost forced food down sick ones who didn't want to eat, bathed fevered faces, smoothed blankets, turned hot pillows, and I don't know what else. When will this nightmare be over? I don't have time to even read the Bible. I pray all the time, but God feels so far away. My prayers don't seem to go beyond the ceiling. A fog seems to have enveloped me, and I can't find my way out.

It has been a few days since last I wrote. I have just come back from a funeral. Freddy is gone. Our sweet, darling little Freddy! Uncle Frederick's namesake. Edmund came down to the kitchen where I was and sank down at the table, burying his face in hands that shook.

"What is it?" I asked him, and he told me. Without a word, I went upstairs. There in his little crib lay Freddy. He looked asleep. His thin face wore a peaceful expression. Gently I picked him up and kissed him. I didn't cry. I couldn't, as there were no tears. Poor Mama! She doesn't know. Today he was buried. Before I took him away, I carried him to each bed and let each one kiss him. Dr.

Mitchell and I were the only ones at the cemetery except for old Joe who digs the graves and keeps the place up. Edmund was still not allowed out of the house, and Karl and I couldn't both be gone at the same time. All the children who knew what was happening cried as we left. Even the older boys. But I still couldn't cry.

There on that gentle hill, I knelt with the little freshly made grave before me, the cold winter wind blowing against my face, and I wished for the tears that refused to come. I felt frozen inside. Numb and desolate. There were no flowers to place on Freddy's grave nor were there any brightly colored leaves. Only a miserable drizzle that began to fall as the doctor helped me into the automobile, and we went home. Home to sickness and tears.

It doesn't seem real. Nothing seems real anymore. The doctor said Frankie is better. Why did God take Freddy and not Frankie? Oh, Maria, Daddy will never get to see Freddy! Will Daddy ever see any of us again? I feel alone, shut in from the world. Is there still even a real world out there? I see no one except the doctor and those here in the house. Is there anyone still alive outside of this house? Are you still alive? Oh, how I long to get out of this fog, away from all this darkness, sickness and death! Why can't I cry and ease this heavy burden that is pressing my heart? The ache will not go away and there is nothing I can do! Why can't I find rest in sleep? I can't even pray and find comfort, for God seems so very far away.

Here I have sat for over an hour staring at nothing, trying to realize that Freddy is not upstairs with Frankie. The doctor just came and told me Kirsten is over the worst and to go get some rest. Rest? What is that? I will go up and see how everyone is. I might write more later.

I will try to write more now, as it is the only thing that helps relieve me somewhat of this dreadful ache. It was a long, hard night. Evie took a turn for the worse and nothing would settle her down but to be carried in my arms. She didn't care where I went as long as I kept walking. Karl tried to take a turn, but Evie cried so that, I just kept her. She is better now, and Doctor Mitchell hopes she is really mending. Doesn't he know? Oh, Evie, I can't lose you too!

Now Mama is the only one who hasn't gotten any better but rather has grown steadily worse. Oh, what will we do? She can't die! I won't let her! But I can't do anything! I've never felt so helpless in my life before.

I couldn't write anymore yesterday as I sat here in the kitchen until dusk. Not thinking, not praying, just sitting. It was only when I heard the neighbor setting the pails of milk on the back porch that I got up.

There is no change in Mama. Edmund is getting stronger. Carrie and Vincent were allowed up this morning. David got up yesterday. Poor Georgie! He is so restless and yet doesn't have the energy to move much. The others are improving little by little. But Freddy! Why did God take you? Why can't I cry? My heart is heavy, and my eyes ache dreadfully and yet there is no relief in tears. What if Mama should . . . no! She can't! I won't let her! The doctor has come again.

Oh, Maria! Maria! How I wish you were here! Will you even get this letter? Karl tried to persuade me to go to bed, but I can't. It wouldn't do any good, for I cannot sleep. Oh, Daddy, where are you? Do you know what is happening? Are you sick? Oh, if only I could not feel so forsaken and forgotten. Pray for me, dear Maria! Pray. If only the sun would shine. If only I could cry and sleep.

I hear footsteps on the stairs. They sound like Edmund's. Not as he used to go down the stairs, flying, but slowly, step by step. He used to run up and down the steps three at a time, but now it is so very slow. What is he coming to tell me? I am afraid, oh, so very afraid!

Maria,

Emma requested that either Edmund or I tell you that Mama is better and send this letter to you. I think before I send it, I will add a little to relieve your mind. The dawn is breaking in the east, with a golden sun at last shining through the clouds. Mama is better. Her fever is gone, and she knows us. Thank God! She still doesn't know about Freddy, so pray for her and us.

The doctor came out of Mama's room last night and told me she was better. I had just tried to persuade Emma to get some rest, but with no success. Doctor Mitchell was quite concerned about her, and with Mama better, he said that Emma must get rest. Edmund went down, and after nearly three quarters of an hour, he came back with Emma. She went straight to bed, asking only that we tell you Mama is better and send this off. Do pray for Emma. The doctor hasn't seen her yet, but I am afraid she is ill. I dare not mention this to anyone else, but she is so worn out with care and worry, that if she is ill, well, it will be a long illness I am afraid. And I don't want to think how it might end.

I must get back upstairs. I left Edmund and David on watch, but it is time David was back in bed. When they are both well enough to take care of things, I am going to bed and sleep for a whole day.

Keep praying!
Karl

"If I have time after I get ready, I'll read this last letter of 1918 to you. It looks really short. And neither of us wrote it. It looks like Edmund's handwriting. While you wait, why don't you work on your reports. You only have six more days to get them finished."

Since Aunt Louise wasn't there when Mrs. Mitchell came down, she pulled out that last letter of the year and sat down to read.

Tuesday
November 12, 1918
Codell, Kansas
USA

Maria,

As Emma is still not quite well enough to write to you, I have taken it upon myself to do it for her. I realize that it is your "turn" to write, but as I so seldom write (have I ever written you an entire letter before?), I concluded that it would be permissible to so carelessly interrupt the flow of letters lest you should begin to fret over the silence. Not that the silence should bother you, as it was you who were to break it next. But to forever dispel any worries you may have had, I now write this letter.

In all seriousness, though, Emma was fretting that you would worry over her last letter. I didn't see it, but from the state Emma was in when she must have written it, I can well imagine and understand her concern. Karl did say he added a note that Mama was better and asked you to pray for Emma. We are thanking God for sparing her. There were days when the doctor held out no hope for her life. She was so completely worn out that she had no will power left to fight the disease. It was only by God's great goodness that she is alive today! She is still very weak and not her usual self, but I think she is gaining. Also, now that the armistice has been signed, ending the war, I think it won't be long before she is up and teaching school again.

Everyone else is up and doing well. It was difficult for us all to get used to the fact that there is only one baby now. Mama took it better that we had thought. She said she knew, even when she was so sick, that he was gone.

Evie's tongue certainly doesn't seem to be affected by her illness. Emma has been in her own room ever since she took sick so that Evie wouldn't bother her with constant chatter. That chatter has been a help, now and then, in entertaining the younger ones.

If you can believe it, Karl never took sick. He says he

doesn't remember ever being sick in his life. I told him he should become a doctor, and he wouldn't have to worry about anything that was "catching." He wasn't interested, however. He'd rather farm.

It is snowing here. The flakes are large and fat, the kind that stick and stay to cover everything in white. I don't know if we can keep Vincent and Georgie inside today or not. Perhaps the doctor will come and take pity on us and let them go outside for even an hour!

I don't think we'll find it hard to be thankful this Thanksgiving with all on the mend and the war over. Now we just need Daddy home. I have thought of another thing I am thankful for and that is that I don't have to write letters very often. I remember now why I don't write. How on earth Emma can think of enough things worth writing about to fill so many pages remains a complete mystery to me. I haven't written nearly a fifth of what she would write, yet I can't think of a single thing more to say. So I'll end.

         Your cousin,
         Edmund.

P.S. I guess I won't end it quite yet. I just found out that Emma wanted to send part of a letter to you, so I had better copy it. I don't even know who it is from, but she has the place marked. Why you would want to read about this, I don't know, but here it is.

I can't say I expected to be loading train cars with food and other supplies still. I thought I would be at the front long before this. Lest you think that this is an easy job, let me inform you of what we sent out just today and add that the order came for it all at 8:15 this morning, and it was all on its way ten hours later.

    1,125,000 cans of tomatoes
    1,000,000 pounds of sugar
    600,000 cans of corned beef
    750,000 pounds of hash

150,000 pounds of dry beans

You couldn't guess how many freight cars it took. Only 457 of them. I tell you this army takes a lot of work to keep it going. Never again will I make the mistake of thinking that the garden back home would feed an army. I know better now. And I didn't mention all the other supplies that have to be sent out day after day. The work is never done here in the S.O.S. (that's Services of Supply).

There, it is in. Don't blame me if you aren't interested in it. I was just following orders. Not that she knows I'm writing.

Edmund

The next day the girls spent all afternoon writing their reports.

"I don't think anyone else will be doing a report on this," Ria remarked once, looking up from the paper before her. "Aren't you glad Corporal suggested it? I don't know if I would have thought of it if he hadn't mentioned something that started me thinking and listening."

Lydia nodded her head in agreement but spoke not a word.

After another few minutes, during which Ria stared into space and played with her pencil absentmindedly, she spoke again. "Don't you want Mom to keep reading the letters until those at war come home?"

Again Lydia nodded.

Ria sighed. "I wonder who came home first?" Then, as if to herself, she added, "I just know something really grand is going to happen--"

"Ria, if you don't get to work, we'll never get to find out because we have to get this done first."

After that, no sound save the scratching of pencils across paper was heard.

Rapidly Ria raced down the stairs, nearly colliding with Ed halfway down.

"Whoa!" he exclaimed, catching her. "What's going on? Is the house on fire?"

"No, Lydia is here! It is Saturday, and we are going to finish our reports and hopefully have time for Mom to read some more letters." So saying, she dashed down the remaining steps, through the hall and into the living room where she seized her friend and whirled around the room.

"I'm just so excited that I had to do something!" she explained flushed and laughing as she sank at last into a chair.

Lydia was too bewildered to say anything for a moment. She was growing used to her friend's exuberant ways, though they still startled her occasionally.

To work the girls went with such intense interest and determination that they were finished within an hour.

"There," Lydia sighed. "Now we just have to rewrite them at home. Or," she corrected herself. "I have to rewrite this one, as it is to be handed in. Do you suppose it will matter what your copy looks like, since you are going to read it?"

"I don't know, but it wouldn't hurt, I suppose, for me to copy it just in case. But we can do that later. Come on, let's go find Mom."

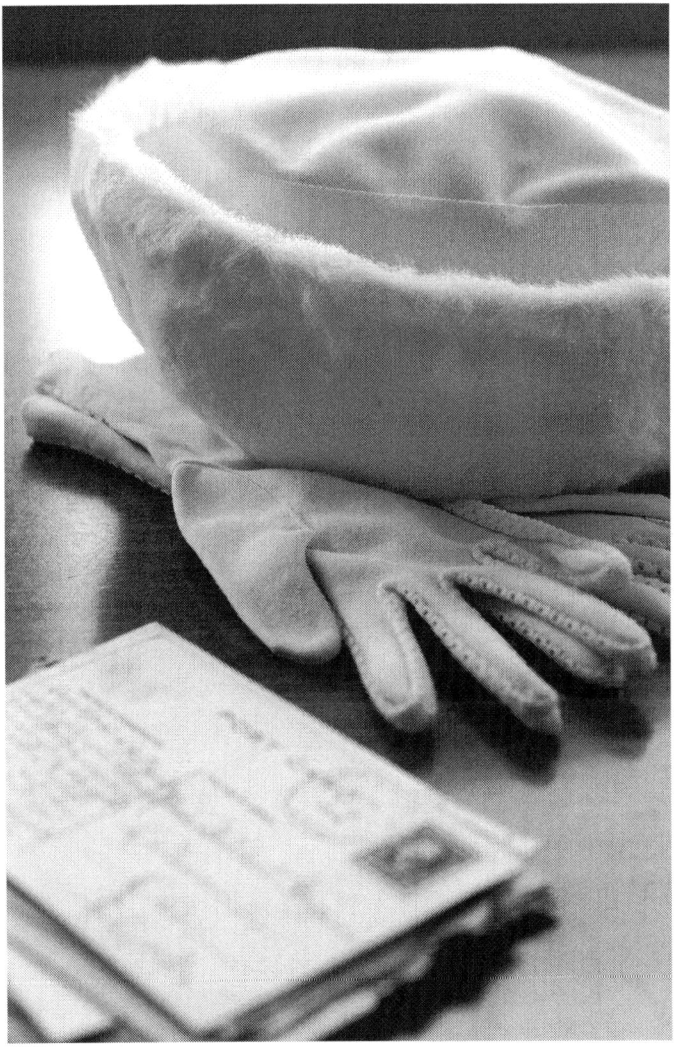

CHAPTER THIRTY-ONE

"Please, Mom, can't you come read some more letters to us? We finished our reports except for rewriting them, and there is over an hour before Lydia has to go home."

"Let me get these cookies out of the oven first." Mrs. Mitchell opened the oven door and pulled out a pan of gingersnaps. "Here you are," she placed one on a napkin for each of the girls. "You can be my taste testers and see if they are any good."

The girls expressed great satisfaction with their treat, and then the trio settled themselves on the front porch to read.

Wednesday
January 1, 1918
Princeville, Nova Scotia
Canada

My Dearest Emma,

I really don't know what to write about first. My heart is full of sorrow, thankfulness, heartbreak and relief. I meant to write this yesterday while it was still December, but I didn't have an opportunity.

Our hearts ache with you in the loss of dear little Freddy. It is comforting to know, isn't it, that he is "safe in the arms of Jesus." How can those who know not of our loving Savior find any comfort at all with the loss of a loved one?

And the war, that dreadful, terrible war is over at last! Papa and Uncle Lawrence will come home! I hope it is soon that they return. What could keep them away? Mama tells us not to get our hopes up that he will be here soon, for the army is sometimes slow. I pray it won't be slow in this.

Edmund, thank you so much for your letter, and the postscript. It came at the right time to cheer me. Also to relieve my fears regarding Emma. I know what it feels like when nearly everyone is sick. That is why I haven't written until now. I know it has been a long time since I have written. Wasn't it August? Four months with no letter from me, and now I don't know what to write. I am too tired to think of four months ago at present. So I will just do my best.

Mabel Burn was the first to become sick here, and it wasn't until Dr. McNeel came that we found out it was influenza. We had dreaded it coming to the village and hoped and prayed we would be spared. It was no use trying to keep the children quarantined, though we tried. The sickness spread slowly at first, then it seemed to gather strength, and before long, almost the entire village was down. After Dr. McNeel had been here a few times, he left me in charge, as there was too much sickness in Pictou for him to get away. You know what little there is that can be done. At one time, the only ones not sick were Mama, Mrs. Stewart, Mr. McLean, Elispeth McIntyre, William and Elizabeth Campton, Seth Drinkwalter and me. Every house was stricken.

Grandmother is gone. The very first one, but sadly not the last. Wee bonnie Mary Campton died shortly after Grandmother. Our little village princess is gone. Catherine Morris is also gone. She was a delicate child, but I thought she was rallying and going to make it, when she had a relapse and was gone before I knew it. Steve Drinkwalter, the oldest of the brothers, died too. Mrs. Stewart was the last to go.

The poor Stewart family! First it was Finlay and now Mrs. Stewart. Mrs. Stewart never seemed to fully recover from the shock of losing Finlay. Mr. Stewart and Malcolm are still in Europe. Evelyn and Henry are nearly orphans right now. The McGuires have taken them into their home for the time being, but I don't know if they will stay there.

It has been nearly a week now since the last ones were pronounced well. There really was no Christmas celebration here this year. I have spent the last six weeks or more going from house to house trying to minister to the sick. How I longed for Papa with every step I took, every drop of medicine I gave. Oh, Emma! I want Papa so badly! I feel like a little girl whose dearly loved Papa has gone from her for the first time.

I am tired. I don't think I will write any more right now. I am going to go cuddle Andrew and Lydia Ruth and tell them all about Papa once more.

Saturday, January 4,

It has been several days since I wrote the above, and I think it is time I finished it and sent it to you.

We celebrated Lydia Ruth's seventh birthday yesterday. Yes, I know her birthday was on the 21st of December, but she was still somewhat sick then, and Mama and I were much too tired to plan anything. It was just a quiet little tea party. Just our family and James and Jenny. James and Mark served us, and even Andrew tried to help. It didn't last very long, but I think Lydia Ruth enjoyed it.

I would tell you about everyone, only they are all so unlike themselves now that it would be no use. Everyone here in Princeville is pale and thin. It doesn't help any that it has been cold and snowy the last several days, either. No one wants to be outside much. We just don't have the strength. I am looking forward to spring now with double interest: Papa coming home and warm weather. I do love the blazing fire in the fireplace but long intensely for the warmth which the sun brings.

I know we must have done some things that were worth writing about before this dreadful sickness came on, but I can't remember what they were. I do have a few letters that I will copy for you from Papa and others, as I can't seem to fill up the pages with home news. Perhaps after I do that, I will be able to think better. Edmund, I have also wondered how Emma can remember so much to write about. I love reading her letters. Don't you? I know you read them, for she has told me so.

Here is the other news. This first is from Papa.

Alan was brought in on the 11th of November. The day of the armistice. I'll never understand why the officers didn't order a cease-fire until eleven o'clock when the armistice was to go into effect. As it was, there are many wounded and dead who didn't need to be. Don't worry about Alan; he will be all right. The wound was in his shoulder again as it was the last time. His spirits are in no wise affected by his wound. The only thing that is difficult is to keep him from trying to play his bagpipes. There are several American lads in the beds near him and at least one of them has a fine voice. If Alan can't have his pipes, he at least can sing. We have had concerts at all times of the day and, I am afraid, the nights. I know you will keep praying.

I have heard that I may be shipped to England for New Years. How I wish I could spend this Christmas and New Year at home with you all!

This next one came on a postcard. It wasn't addressed to anyone, but his handwriting is so small that it was hard to read.

The war is ower! I's warrant it will nae be lang or we are aince mair hame in bonnie Princeville. Hoo we a' wuss to be there noo. I want to gae out in the boat an' fish aince again. To wear claes that hae nae lice in them. Havers! What a thought! An' aye, I wuss to eat as mony sally lunes as I can. Ye heard nae doubt about Alan getting wounded. I'll bide a wee wi' him gin I can an' suld they let me, I'll bring him hame.

David

Emma, I just now realized that it is the year 1919 and not 1918, as I dated the beginning of this letter. A new year. A year with the war over! Last year in January I was in Halifax helping after the explosion, and you were stuck in the school house during the snowstorm. This year, or rather last year, has held so many things: births and deaths, war and peace, sickness and health. And yet, isn't it a wonderful thought that our Heavenly Father knows what each day holds before it happens? Mama read a verse to us this morning about a thousand years being as a day to Him. I don't think I could face this new year without His promise to hold my hand.

I must end now, as it is growing late. May the Lord whom we serve bless and keep you and your family in His tender care this year. This is the last year before the 1920's!

All my love,
Maria

Saturday
February 8, 1919
Codell, Kansas
USA

Dearest Maria,

You'll never guess who is here! No, it isn't Daddy or Uncle Frederick. You'll never guess. He showed up on Wednesday with . . . But let me tell you the story.

There was a sudden pounding on the front door just as we were sitting down for dinner, and before anyone could reach it, the door was flung open and in walked someone.

We heard David, who had gone to answer the door, gasp some unintelligent words, and then there in the doorway stood Uncle Philip Vincent Bartholomew Wallace III! No one said anything for a full minute, I do believe. We all just stared. Even Mama made no move. At last, Uncle Philip broke the silence.

"Well! My own lief sister, methought would fain welcome me back from the land far distant, though my unexpected return be egregious--"

He got no farther, for Mama suddenly found her voice and cried as she threw her arms around him,

"Philip, Philip! How did you? When . . . ? Oh, I just can't believe it is you! After all these years!"

"Nonetheless, lief Helen, it is I. And I have brought my wife with me."

"Your wife?" Mama turned in astonishment to see a shy, blushing young woman with nut-brown hair and hazel eyes.

"Jennie, this is my one and only sister. The best sister in the world -- I beg your pardon boys," as he bowed to David, Edmund and Karl, "your sisters are the exceptions to my claim, I am most certain, though one is apt to forget others when introducing the very dearest women on earth to each other. Jennie, as I was saying, this is Helen."

Long before Uncle Philip had finished his introductions, Mama greeted Jennie -- Aunt Jennie, I mean -- with warmth and affection.

"I declare, Helen," Uncle began again, "I was going to introduce the children to their new aunt, but I find that if I essayed to do so, I would no doubt blunder terribly, for the only one I am sure of is Emma, for she could look no more like her than if she were the only one. So you must introduce me as well as my wife."

Before Mama could reply other than with a laugh, Evie spoke up. She, of course, was the first of us children to find her tongue.

"Who is you, Mister Man?"

Uncle Philip picked her up as he replied, "I, mon petit mademoiselle? I am your Uncle Philip Vincent Bartholomew Wallace. The third one to bear that grand and honoraire name. And who, if I might be so bold as to enquire from so charme a damselle, are you?"

Evie just giggled.

"Boys, bring two more chairs, and Carrie, set two more places, please. Now," Mama said when the chairs and places were set, "do sit down, and I will introduce the children, though I am astonished that you can't recognize more than Emma!"

"Mon lief, do recall that the years past have been near half a dozen since I last beheld any of them. These la jeunesse are now men and women. The years may have kept me young, but they have not done so with these offspring of yours."

Mama introduced us all, and Uncle Philip was, or at least pretended to be, perfectly astonished. Kirsten would scarcely look at either Uncle Philip or Aunt Jennie and wouldn't say a word. Rosalie smiled shyly and whispered a hello. Vincent and Georgie stared. When Mama asked Uncle how he managed to get home so soon, he replied,

"The war was over, the fighting done, and there was no need for prolonged lingering. I wanted to return to America to show my wife, and so I came. We caught the first shark out of port. We did stop a day or so to see Father but then headed out here. I simply couldn't wait longer for a glimpse of your dear face mon cher soeur, especially when I produced my wife."

Yes, Maria, he talks just like that, only he adds more dictionary words as well as throwing in French words and phrases now and then. Mama's face glowed with joy at having him home, but I know when Daddy comes home, it will be radiant. Uncle Philip limps now and then, a reminder that his leg isn't quite what it once was. Evie adores him and wants to play with him all the time. She hasn't deserted Edmund, but I think Uncle is a close contestant in her affections. Carrie was very quiet around him at first as she was only seven when he left and doesn't really remember him. But Aunt Jennie has completely won both her and the two little girls. Of course Frankie is doted on by both Uncle and Aunt. Aunt Jennie's father and three brothers all headed to France at the first opportunity, and since she had no mother or sisters, she headed over too. She worked as a Red Cross nurse in France, and that is where she met Uncle Philip. As soon as the war was over, they were married by the closest chaplain, and they came on to America. I don't know how they got here, but Uncle has a way of getting what he wants. Don't worry, what he wants is usually a good thing. Aunt Jennie is from Boston and makes quite a contrast to Uncle Philip. She is quiet and genteel and very much a lady, though there seems to be a spark of spirit in her, too, that is usually not seen but comes out at unexpected times. Uncle adores her, and the rest of us love her too.

Evie can't quite say their names, so she calls them "Untle Man an' Aunt Dennie." You should have heard her talking this morning with Uncle; he is a match for her impossible questions. She was on Uncle's knee as usual when she asked,

"Untle Man, does oo know mine Daddy?"

"I most certainly do, mon petit."

Evie nodded her head, "Den I tink oo tan 'tay here. But," and she tipped her head sideways and looked puzzled, "Aunt Dennie not know Daddy. Why oo not bing Daddy home? He done dit losted."

Uncle answered right away. "Ah, mon petit, your father is far too egregiously keen for inamissibleness to be juxtaposited his mind. Have no doubt, he shall return."

While the rest of us sat and stared at Uncle Philip, trying to figure out what he had just said, Evie nodded with a grave face and replied, "Yes, I tink de eggs are missin'."

Uncle Philip and Aunt Jennie are staying here until they can buy a home of their own. I think Uncle is looking in Plainville. He said he has lived as long as he cares to away from us all and that he must live nearby.

That has all happened within the week. Now I must go back in time for more things to tell about. I nearly fell out of bed in shock when Edmund announced that he had written you a letter. Was it more than two paragraphs? I suppose it must have been or it wouldn't have interested you. What on earth did he write about? He said he told you I was better. I hope he did more than that.

I could start with Christmas, but we didn't do much, at least nothing interesting. I can't wait until Daddy comes home. I know how you feel. Mama and Uncle Philip have been asked over and over when Daddy is going to get home, but neither one has an answer. Uncle said that he was sure some troops would get stationed in Germany for a while. Oh, I hope and pray that Daddy isn't one of them! But if it isn't Daddy, it will be someone's father and husband or perhaps a brother or son. Oh, I don't like war. But I am so proud of Daddy and Uncle Frederick, Uncle Philip, Uncle Ian and all the rest for going to fight for their home and country.

Speaking of Uncle Ian, we got a letter from him last year, and it has been sitting here on the desk waiting for me to send part of it to you. The letter was dated October.

Well, I tell you I think I've just done the most astonishing, as well as possibly the most amusing, thing in my life. I have just captured my oldest brother! Yep, I captured Lance right there in the French village. I was just following orders. Our boys of the 1st are laughing yet. General Pershing had issued orders that the 1st was supposed to capture [blacked out]. Unbeknownst to us, however, the "Rainbow" Division had already captured it, and we ended up capturing them. Even their headquarters with the commanding officers fell into our hands. I'll never forget the look on Lance's face when I shouted for the group of men to surrender...

                Ian Wallace of the 1st Division

Here I am rambling on about war and other things of no "conkweeance," as Rosalie says it, and you are waiting, as no doubt the rest of your family is too, for a story. This story should give you something to laugh about for a few days.

It was a few weeks ago on washday, and it was bitterly cold out. There was no snow, and it was only slightly overcast. Mama, Carrie and I spent the morning in the kitchen washing clothes before Carrie and I took them outside and hung them on the line. There was a wind blowing, so we knew they would dry at least a little before freeze-drying. That day was a very busy day. After the laundry was washed, I made bread and a dozen other things, I do believe, then started on supper. The boys, all five of them, were outside somewhere. I don't know where, but they weren't around the house. When supper was almost ready, Carrie looked out the window and then called me over. I looked, glanced at Carrie, and we both started laughing.

"It sure would be a sight," I agreed, "if it worked."

"Let's try it."

I was agreeable. We had to have Mama's help, or it wouldn't work. "Carrie, go ask Mama if she can come help us, but be sure to keep the little girls, especially Evie, out of the kitchen, or it will spoil everything."

Carrie nodded and slipped away, to return a moment later with Mama looking mystified.

"What is it you want to do?"

When it was explained to her, she first looked out the window and then at us; after a moment she began to chuckle and then to laugh. I hadn't seen her laugh that much since I don't know when. She finally managed to tell us to hurry and get them.

Carrie and I threw our coats on and rushed outside, trying to smother our laughter in case the boys were in the barn. We worked rapidly, partly from cold and partly from the pent-up excitement of what we were about to do.

Returning to the kitchen, we saw Mama hadn't been idle. The three of us worked at a feverish pace, choking back the giggles that rose in our throats. At last all was set, and Carrie rang the bell. We had let the little girls see our work as we were finishing it, and Kirsten added the finishing touches to it. All were told they must keep quiet and let it be a surprise. Oh, what a surprise it was!

I wish I had a picture of their faces for you. It was even better than I had thought it would be, for they came in one at a time. I don't know if I can describe it all to you or not. Let me try. First the door opened and Karl stepped in.

"The others are . . ." His face grew blank as he stared around the kitchen. "What--"

Edmund was the next victim, and he fell right into the trap. Leaning over the stove to kiss me, he suddenly gasped in shock and straightened in bewilderment.

Before his brain had registered what he had seen, David and the little boys entered.

"Mama-- Oh, I'm sorry," David began. "I didn't know we had company." Then he too looked puzzled, and his hand went to his head as he frowned.

Vincent stepped across the kitchen to give Mama a hug and then gave a cry of alarm. "Evie is going to fall--"

You are puzzled by their responses? That is because I can't tell you just what the kitchen looked like, as I was laughing too hard. However, I'll do my best. The laundry had frozen outside in strange shapes, which gave Carrie the idea in the first place. We set them around on the chairs and in front of the stove and things like that. To give them even more the appearance of real people, we stuck brooms, mops, dusters and even knitting needles with a ball of yarn on the top down the neck of each dress or shirt. Then we put hats or something on them. They were so queer looking. One "man" had his sleeve bent as though his hand was reaching for his hat. One of my dresses was at the stove with the mop, and that is what Edmund almost kissed! Evie's dress was placed standing up in her chair and when Vincent saw it, it had thawed enough that it just collapsed. Kirsten added a pair of glasses to one lady and a handkerchief to another lady with her hand to her face and a few other such things.

We had all been watching the boys through a crack in the door, and after "Evie fell," we couldn't keep back our mirth any longer. Coming into the kitchen, we were just in time to see Edmund turn instinctively to catch "me" as my dress suddenly collapsed and the mop fell. The boys caught on to the joke and began to laugh too. As each "guest" collapsed, our merriment increased. Oh, Maria, I wish you could have seen it! When our last "guest" "fainted from the heat," as David so candidly put it, and we could speak again, Carrie and I removed the laundry while the boys washed up. As you may suppose, supper was very lighthearted that night.

So you see, Vincent and Georgie aren't the only ones who think of amusing things to do.

Can you believe David is nineteen years old now? Georgie is almost nine. Do you recall the time we were supposed to paint the barn and ended up playing Indians? We were talking about that the other day. Karl and Kirsten couldn't believe we would do such a thing. The little boys don't remember it at all.

Edmund just asked if I had told you about going sledding. No, I haven't yet, but I'll change that now. It was near the beginning of January when the snow came. Not enough to trap us in the school house again, but enough to go sledding. There is a perfect hill near our home. Now don't get any ideas that I stayed at home and took care of the little ones. We all went. Even Mama and Frankie! I know that some people think that Kansas is a large flat field, but that just isn't so. We do have hills and even trees. The boys made the track by sledding the first few times, and then everyone had turns. One time, Edmund and I were going to go down together when Evie begged to go with us. David dropped her in Edmund's lap, and Karl gave us a push. We were about halfway down when we suddenly ended in a snow bank! I don't know what Evie had done, but somehow

Edmund forgot to steer for a minute. We weren't hurt and quickly tramped back up for another try. This time, we did it without Evie.

Let me see, was there anything else of interest to tell you? I'm sure there probably was, only I can't remember it. I think that nearly always happens. Perhaps I ought to go ask each one what I should tell you about. No, that won't do, for either the letter would be packed with not much interesting, or it would never get sent. I really should start keeping my journal again; that way I could remember the interesting things.

It is warm outside today for February. Even if it is just the beginning of February, I love these mild days. Aunt Jennie is going to go with us into Codell in a little while. You ought to see the town! People have moved away and stores are closed. Ever since the last Cyclone Day when much of it was destroyed, no one seems interested in rebuilding. I wonder if it will die completely?

I really must end this. Give my love to all.

                Ever yours,
                Emma

CHAPTER THIRTY-TWO

Tuesday
March 11, 1919
Princeville, Nova Scotia
Canada

Dear Emma,

How I laughed over your letter. I could just picture the boys faces when they saw your company. Edith wants to know if you are sure Edmund didn't actually kiss the mop. I don't believe we have laughed that much over a letter for a long time. That is a story that is going all over the village. I was surprised to find it had been Carrie's idea. For some reason I had the feeling that Carrie was quiet and never dreamed of doing things like that. I do think it was a wonderful idea though. Mark and James are no doubt thinking of trying something similar when next the clothes become frozen on the line. That might not be for a while, for the weather is warming up somewhat. It is certainly not spring yet, but the bitterness in the air seems to have lessened.

Mama was speechless to hear that your Uncle Philip is married, for she remembers hearing him say more than once that he would only marry someone just like his sister. And then he would add that there was only one Helen, therefore, he would not marry. It doesn't sound as though your new aunt is like Aunt Helen. Is she? Are they still living with you, or have they found a place of their own? At least you won't have to try to decipher his handwriting any longer.

Reading your letter made me wish for Papa's homecoming all over again. I have a letter from him that I must put in for you. I am going to do it now before I fill up these pages with other things.

"Being here in England again gave me such a longing to go back home that I applied for a ten day leave, and much to my surprise and delight, I did at last receive one. I headed out on the next train for London. The train made several stops at different stations, and as it was pulling out of one, a voice which sounded strangely familiar asked if the seat beside me was taken. I turned around to find that my own brother Lawrence was standing beside me! I can't describe the surprise and delight to find that he, too, had received a pass and was headed for London! Need I mention the fact that we talked the rest of the trip? When we arrived at the house, who should we see out in the front yard but Margaret! She didn't recognize us at first, but when she did, I'm sure her voice was heard far away. Nearly all were there: Father and Mother, James and his Samantha with their four young ones, and Maggie and Harris with their two little fellows. The next day brought Theodore and Nancy up from Dover with the younger three. Mary Jane said she would write to both you, Maria, and to Emma. What a time we had there those ten days. I didn't know how much I had missed everyone here until I saw them again. I wished I could have had you all here with me but rejoice that each day is one day closer to when I will be home! I long more than ever to get back to you all.

"One evening, Mother brought out a long letter which Emma had sent to her and read a few 'Ted, Fred, Larry and Jim' stories which she had written. I can tell you the room rang with laughter over those stories. To tell you the honest truth, I don't remember the chimney sweep episode, but as Mother does, I'm sure Larry didn't make it up. I must say that Emma's story writing ability has greatly improved. Ted and I have some not-so-good memories of the sequel to the spy hanging which took place in the woodshed. Father had a very strong arm, as we recalled. Those stories brought to mind many another adventure we four lads had, and stories were told and discussed for hours. I could relate a few where Lawrence and James were the instigators. That was after Theodore and I grew out of the role. Mother and Father had so many stories of us four that I'm sure it would fill a book. The young ones listened in wide-eyed amazement at some of those stories.

"All too quickly, the ten days passed, and now I am back with the wounded, waiting for ships and orders and all such things. I see I didn't mention that James is doing quite well. Their house was destroyed in an air raid, so they are staying with Mother and Father. Margaret and Harris are still in Slough though they are up in London quite a bit."

So you see, Emma, your stories have been a source of great entertainment on both sides of the Atlantic. Did Uncle Lawrence tell about his leave? I'm sure he did. Did he give more details than Papa? If he did, I hope you will share them with us. Sometimes I think that Uncle Lawrence is more of a story teller than Papa. Perhaps that is why you are so good. It would have been such a delight to be in England with everyone, don't you think?

One day in early February, I had a pile of your letters out on my bed rereading them when Edith joined me. We took turns reading them aloud. I don't recall what year it was, but one time you told about St. Valentine's Day and how it came about. Edith and I thought it was a quaint idea. That night, after Andrew and Lydia Ruth were in bed, Mama, Mark, Edith and I set to work and created enough cards for each child in the village. On the evening of the 14th, the three of us crept out after dark and slipped them under doors. None of the cards were signed, as we didn't want it known who had made them. There was much talk the next few days about them. Edith had had the forethought to make sure we each had one as well. I wonder if St. Valentine's day will ever become popular again.

Yesterday, Lydia Ruth did an astonishing thing. While I straightened up our room, I heard Mark suddenly exclaim,

"Ouch! Lydia Ruth!"

Leaving my broom in the middle of the floor, I stepped across the hall into Mark's room. "What happened?" I asked.

"She just bit me," Mark reported, showing his arm, which indeed held little teeth marks.

"Lydia Ruth!" I exclaimed in my turn. "What made you do a thing like that?"

Lydia Ruth stared at us wide-eyed for a moment and then with a quivering chin and tears in her eyes, she whimpered, "I just never bited anyone before, and I didn't know what it was like. I'm sorry."

After Mark and I exchanged perplexed, but at the same time, amused glances, he gave Lydia Ruth this advice. "Next time you want to try something like that, try it on yourself."

Lydia Ruth looked at him and then, before either of us could stop her, she bit her own arm and burst into tears. Knowing I couldn't keep from laughing, I simply left the room leaving Mark to comfort Lydia Ruth, which he did. Life is never dull with little ones, is it?

I just looked up and realized why it is dark. A snow storm has begun, and the lamps have not been lit yet. All are home this evening, and Mark now has a blazing fire in the fireplace. Edith is telling a story. It has to do with the village, so I will finish this later.

Friday, March 14,

As you can tell, several days have passed since I first began this letter. We were completely snowed in on Wednesday, not leaving the house at all. We told stories, I played the violin, and we talked about Papa. Andrew had to be amused, though for the most part, he amused us. He has discovered that if he can get one of my pencils in his possession, he can write on things. Mama and Edith spent a quarter of an hour up in the attic before they finally discovered an old slate and a slate pencil for him to use instead. That kept him busy for over an hour. Before he would "write," he crawled under a small table which was barely large enough for him. He seems to enjoy cramped quarters. Even when he sleeps, he will curl up in a ball in the corner of his bed. Perhaps his search for small places is what leads him into everything.

The sun is shining today, though the snow is still on the ground at the present. With the mild breeze off the sea, it won't stay around for long. Oh, Emma, you should see what I can see looking out the window. Bright, dazzling snow covers the village as though it were a layer of frosting. I see several children out building snowmen. It appears that Arthur Morris and William and Charles Campton are beginning a fort. I don't see Mark or James anywhere at the moment. The azure sky is nearly cloudless except on the horizon where they billow in great soft heaps of ivory, tinged here and there with sunlight. The sea is a mixture of mousy gray waves tipped with white lacy foam as the breeze stirs them. The village houses are a sharp contrast with their crimson sides against the snow, sky and sea. Smoke spirals upward from the chimneys to be blown into wispy puffs and then disappear. You may not think so, with what I have just told you, but spring is in the air. I can feel it and smell it when I step out the door. Spring! Glorious spring! Spring means warmer days, flowers, insects, days spent outside, kittywakes and most of all, Papa coming home! Surely they won't make him wait much longer. I love the spring. When you and Edmund come for that visit, you must come in spring. Speaking of spring, I am reminded to send a birthday greeting to Carrie as well as to Kirsten and Evie. Give them all a kiss for me and tell them I wish I could give it in person

Edith told Mama and me that she, Sheena, and Mabel might as well wear yellow ribbons now.

"Why is that?" Mama inquired.

"Why, Mama, don't you know, we are considered 'old maids' since we are all nearly twenty-one and not one of us is so much as engaged." Edith burst forth into laughter, most likely at our faces.

"Why a yellow ribbon?"

"Mama, to show that our lovers are far, far away. So very far, that we don't know them."

Mama and I joined her in the laughter this time, yet there seems to be truth to it. Amelia is engaged, you know. Did I ever tell you that? Now that I think of it, I don't believe I did. She has been engaged for nearly two years. She said the wedding will be as soon as he comes home.

Speaking of home, I see Mark trudging up the hill. It must be nearly time to eat. Give everyone my love. We will look forward to your next letter. And, Emma, do start that journal again.

Lovingly,
Maria

Thursday
April 17, 1919
Codell, Kansas
USA

Dear Maria,

I am outside enjoying the beautiful spring day. It is a little warm in the sun, but the shade is quite pleasant. The boys are all off in the fields, even Vincent and Georgie, as school is out. Carrie is at Uncle Philip and Aunt Jennie's helping with their garden. She loves working in gardens. The three little girls are busy helping Mama with something, and Frankie is sleeping. Can you believe he is ten months old already? I have so many stories to tell you; I hope I have enough paper. I didn't realize I was running so low until after Edmund and Karl came back from town. But here I am writing nothing of interest and wasting paper. I did start my journal again as you requested, and now I have loads of things to say.

You won't believe it, but the unbelievable has happened, Maria. It happened on Monday. Edmund and I quarreled and wouldn't speak to each other for nearly an entire day! We've had quarrels and arguments all our lives, but never one that lasted this long. It wasn't really a quarrel, I suppose; Edmund just teased me a little too much, and I got angry. It was all over a silly thing anyway. Doesn't it seem strange, Maria, that the silly, unimportant things are the ones most likely to cause problems? This was all about a city boy we had met only once. I didn't like him and said so to Edmund later. His name was--

Mrs. Mitchell broke off in the midst of her sentence, and the color on her cheeks deepened into scarlet. "I don't know if I should read this to you or not," she began.

"Oh, please, Mom, don't stop. Who was it?"

Mrs. Mitchell glanced towards the front door as though to make sure no other ears could hear. With a look of mixed mirth and shame, she answered. "It was . . . your father."

Ria couldn't keep back her surprise. "Dad? You didn't like him?"

"Not at first, but here, let me read my feelings."

His name was Christopher James. I only know because that is what his mother called him. His brothers and sisters all called him Mitch. He was older than us, and there was a city air about him. I didn't like it. He was polite and everything, but he looked like he didn't know what real work was. He definitely isn't someone I care to know more about.

He looks like a "Mama's boy." Anyway, Edmund took a fancy to him. I don't know if he really liked him or just thought he might be interesting. As I said before, I didn't like him. We were out in the barn alone when Edmund found that out and began to tease. He was in a terribly ornery mood, for he actually told me I would probably marry him! The idea! I said quite indignantly, "I wouldn't marry him if he were the last man on earth! I'll never marry a city boy!"

Edmund just laughed and continued to tease until I had had enough.

"Edmund!" I fairly shouted, "Don't you ever dare mention Christopher James Mitchell to me again!" I was fuming. "And I will never, ever marry a city boy!"

Edmund looked indignant. "Can't you take a little teasing?" he asked crossly.

"A little teasing?" I stormed. "That wasn't teasing! Now just leave me alone."

"Fine, I will," he growled and stomped off to the field, while I ran to the house.

Well, that's what it was all about. I spent the morning moody and silent. When the boys came in from the fields for dinner, I didn't even look at Edmund. We sat side by side as usual, but we didn't speak or look at each other. Thankfully, Georgie and Evie kept up an almost incessant chatter, so I didn't think we were too noticeable. I did see Karl and David exchange glances as they watched Edmund. In the afternoon I kept very busy. It was refreshing not to have school to teach. Mama asked me when Edmund and I were going to go get the rest of my things from the school house and lock it up for the summer.

"Oh, sometime," I told her. "I don't know when."

"You could go today," she said looking keenly at me. "I'm sure David would be willing to spare Edmund for a few hours."

I shook my head and kept my eyes on the weeds I was pulling. "I don't want to go back to school today."

Mama said no more, but I had a feeling that she knew.

That evening, Carrie and I made supper, and hardly a word was spoken. We both seemed lost in thought. Only when the three little girls came in did the talking come too. Evie just can't keep quiet! I really don't know if she knows what quiet is. David and Vincent came in first when Rosalie rang the bell, with Georgie just behind. Usually I would have asked where Edmund was, but I didn't today. When David came back from washing up, he looked at me a little strangely but said nothing. Edmund and Karl came in just then, and without a word to anyone, Edmund went to wash up. Karl paused to speak to Kirsten and Mama. Supper was a quiet meal. Georgie was too hungry to talk much, and Mama made Evie eat before she talked. As for Edmund and me, neither of us said a word unless we were spoken to. I hardly ate. I could tell Mama, David, Karl and Carrie were watching us though not appearing to. I wanted to burst into tears, but I couldn't. By the time supper was finally over and the kitchen cleaned up, I wasn't angry anymore, only miserable, but I didn't know if Edmund felt the same way. I took the broom and went to sweep the porch, though it really didn't need it. As I stood leaning against a pillar and watching the sunset, the verse "Let not the sun go down on your wrath" came to mind. How I longed for Edmund. Right at that moment an arm went around my shoulders, the broom was taken from my hands, and I was led off the porch away from the house. I knew without looking that it was Edmund. How he happened to be there was this way.

He had been wandering restlessly around the house ever since supper was over. He was sorry, too, but didn't know if I would forgive him yet. He wasn't even sure where I was. On entering the living room for the seventh time, Mama suddenly handed him my shawl saying, "Take this out to your sister."

David looked up from the newspaper and ordered, "And don't come back until you two have made up, please."

"Amen!" Karl added emphatically.

"Now get," Mama gave him a push toward the kitchen.

In silence, but together, we walked over to the pasture fence.

"Edmund," I started.

"Emma," Edmund began. Then we both laughed, but my laughter quickly turned to tears. I had never had such a miserable day. Edmund dried my tears, and we climbed on the rail fence. There we sat and talked, watching the sky. It was so beautiful! The sun had set, but the sky wasn't dark yet. We watched as the stars began to come out and the moon rose. Edmund had put the shawl around me as it grew chilly, but we just didn't want to go in. After all, it had been nearly a whole day since we talked, and we had a lot to say to each other.

It was David's voice that startled us when he asked, "Haven't you two made up yet, or are you planning to take all night?"

We both laughed a little sheepishly. "I didn't know it was late," Edmund said, jumping off the fence and turning to help me down.

"Only about 11:30," David answered.

I gasped, "Surely it's not that late!"

"It is," assented David, "so be quiet when you go in."

As I quietly got ready for bed in the dark, trying not to waken the girls, Carrie sat up and questioned sleepily, "Do you have a twin again?"

"Yes," I whispered back and smiled to myself as I climbed into bed.

Edmund and I headed over to the school house on Tuesday morning, and who should we find stuck in a mud hole in front of the school but Christopher James Mitchell in his automobile! I stole one quick glance of disgust at Edmund before dismounting and walking to the school house door. I gave a cold, barely civil nod in return to the stranded motorist's greeting, entered the school and closed the door sharply behind me. Now, Maria, don't you go and lecture me on my impolite behavior. I know I was rude. I also know I deserved the lecture I received from my twin on the way home, though I pretended not to even hear it. Maybe someday I'll laugh about this. Perhaps when I am happily married to a farmer! And if you are wondering, yes, Edmund helped get his auto out of the mud puddle. I didn't come out until it had gone, along with its driver.

Peal after peal of laugher rang out from the porch. Neither of the girls could speak for several minutes, and even Mrs. Mitchell had tears in her eyes from her mirth.

"Does Dad know that you didn't like him at first?" Ria queried when she could speak.

"Oh, I am sure your Uncle Edmund informed him of that fact. I don't believe he has ever mentioned it to me, but I can't imagine Edmund keeping such a thing to himself."

Oh, I must tell you about Evie. It would have been laughable if it were not so pitiable. We have, or rather did have, a black rooster whose name was Nighty. I believe Georgie named him, not that it matters. Nighty was mean. His favorite past time seemed to be terrorizing any person, with a few exceptions, who was outside. For some reason he never chased David, Edmund or Karl. Any of the rest of us were fair game as far as he was concerned. He was treacherous. If you turned squarely around on him and started walking toward him, he would turn tail and leave, but the moment your back was turned, he would be running straight for you. It got so bad that the younger ones wouldn't go outside without one of the older boys. That rooster was the only one Kirsten couldn't tame. Evie loves to be outside, but was terrified of Nighty. She would run screaming to the house or to the nearest person if he so much as looked at her. Finally Edmund had enough of it. One day he caught Nighty, who had just chased Evie inside, grabbed his legs and snapped his head against a fence post before tossing him behind the barn.

When Evie heard the news she ran outside at once and shouted, "Nighty's dead! Nighty's dead!"

Kirsten and Rosalie were much quieter upon hearing the news but also took immediate advantage and spent the rest of the day playing happily outside.

A day or two later, Evie was outside playing and singing, "Nighty's dead! Nighty's dead!" I was in the kitchen with the older boys when a sudden, shrill, terrified scream came from outside! The boys sprang to their feet in an instant, knocking over their chairs as they did so.

"Nighty's comin' af'er me!" Evie's holler sent us all into action. At once we rushed for the door. Edmund was first. Leaping off the porch he sprinted across the yard and scooped up Evie in his arms. I stared from the safety of the porch. There indeed was Nighty. His head was hanging down at a grotesque angle from a broken neck, and he was staggering straight for Edmund.

"That beast!" Edmund exclaimed. "Here, David, take Evie, and I'll deal with him." That was easier said than done, for Evie refused to let go of Edmund. Try as they might, they couldn't get Evie to leave Edmund. Meanwhile the rooster was coming closer and closer. Evie's screams again rent the air, and Edmund gave up to the inevitable and said, "One of you can do it, and make a good job of it!"

David caught the luckless rooster and Karl grabbed a hatchet. In another minute, the rooster was without his head. Unlike the other butchering of chickens they do, the boys didn't let go of this one for some minutes after his head was off. If you don't know chickens, they run around like crazy for a little bit after their heads have been chopped off.

Nighty would most certainly have headed straight for Edmund and Evie.

Evie was still clinging in terror to Edmund's neck and crying, saying over and over, "Nighty's af'er me! He is!"

"No, Evie," Edmund soothed. "David has him, and Karl is chopping off his head. He won't be after you any more."

"But he comes back!" Her face was buried against his neck while her legs were wrapped tightly around his waist. She was shaking and trembling.

Mama and I hurried over, but even with our combined effort, it made no difference. Edmund was the only one she wanted then, and it took nearly a quarter of an hour for him to just get her calmed down enough to raise her head.

He took her to see that Nighty was really dead, and then they watched as he was buried. Still, it was almost a full hour later before Evie would let go of Edmund's neck. She refused to go outside alone for two days after that, and will never go anywhere near where Nighty is buried, probably fearing that he will somehow come out of the ground and chase her. She has regained most of her courage by now, though she still looks warily at the barn when she passes it. The other way she was affected is that she dislikes any and all chickens. No longer will she go with Kirsten to feed and gather the eggs. She wants nothing to do with them. I can't say that I blame her, can you?

Before I look in my journal to see if there is anything else of interest left to tell you, let me answer your letter. Yes, we did hear from Daddy. He did most certainly write more. I'll copy it here for you, so you can have the rest of the story.

"And now let me see how well I can turn my story telling skills into writing. I know I can't do as well as you, Emma, but I will see what I can do. It should be better than nothing. As soon as the war was over, I applied for a leave to go to England to visit Grandma and Grandfather. To my utmost astonishment, it was granted right away. And I always thought the army was slow. I took immediate action and hopped aboard the first train headed for the coast, and then when I had crossed the channel I headed for London on the first train. The first car I entered was full, so I moved on to another one. As the train began to move, I spied an empty seat.

"Is this seat occupied?" I questioned of a soldier wearing the rank of medical captain, who was gazing out the window.

He turned, and I think he was going to reply, but instead he just stared. I know it was rather rude, but I stared too. I wasn't sure if my eyes were playing tricks on me or not, for there in the seat was my brother Frederick! I couldn't tell you what I said then for I was completely dumbfounded. I did sit down, and as the wheels went clickity-clack, we began to talk. Not just a little talking but a whole barrage of talk. To our surprise, we soon found out that I knew almost as much as he did about his family, and likewise, he knew about mine. I must say that Emma and Maria are such excellent correspondents that we could talk intelligently about the little commonplace home life events that have taken place in our absence.

Before we were aware of it, the train stopped in London, and we detrained. Neither of us cared to wait for a conveyance, so we walked. It was a glorious day for a walk. The sun was shining, and the smell of London was in the brisk, cold air. Personally though, I would have preferred the smell of the farm back home.

During the walk, Fred turned to me suddenly and remarked, "You had best polish up on your British accent or the folks will be thinking you're a Yank."

"I am a Yank now," I replied with a strong British accent, "and don't you forget it."

We reached the house at last and found Maggie out in the yard. I called to her, and she gave a scream and threw herself into my arms, but no sooner had she caught sight of

Fred than she decided to leave me for him. She couldn't make up her mind which of us to hug, so she took an arm of each and in the midst of laughing and crying and calling to those in the house to "come look what she found," she led us to the door. I cannot describe the greetings which followed. I think you can imagine them if you try. Remember that Fred and I hadn't been home for nearly seventeen years! We found to our great satisfaction that not only were Maggie and Harris there, but Jim and Samantha were there as well. Not to mention the crowd of young ones. I never could get everyone's name straight.

Oh, the supper we had that night! I can't even begin to tell about it. I had only dreamed of such a supper since I left home. Talk was continuous around the table that night, and we conversed for hours. At last we went to bed. The beds! A real bed that was soft, with a down pillow for my head! It was pure luxury after what we had at the front. And my favorite part was not having to get up when the bugler sounded Reveille, for there was no bugler! Oh, the delight of it all! I could go on and on about that bed and no bugler, but I no doubt have you all in fits of laughter already.

It was the next morning, late morning I suppose it was, that I was in the parlor alone when I heard a great bustle in the hall and a masculine voice saying,

"Mother, is everything all right? We caught the first train this morning . . . What is going on?"

And Mother replied, "Just step into the parlor a minute, and it will all be explained."

The door opened and Ted walked in. Then came the amusing part, for he didn't know who I was.

"Ted," I said at last, as he stood in puzzled silence before me, "do you intend to ignore your younger brother's return home after seventeen years? Really, I thought better of you." I spoke with as much Yank to my speech as I could.

He was astonished beyond words for a moment when he did finally recognized me. "Larry!" he gasped, and then Fred walked in.

I heard Mother say later to someone, "Now what have I done sending for Ted. Those Foster boys are together again, and no one knows what they will do next. They always seem to be in one scrape or another when they are together."

What we did this time was talk. Ted, Fred, Jim and I. Maggie flitted in and out, not wanting to miss anything, but busy with other duties. I think it was that evening that Mother got out the stories. Oh, I forgot to mention that Nancy and the children had come with Ted. The stories were the "Ted, Fred, Larry and Jim" stories that Emma had written and sent. Everyone enjoyed them greatly. Not everyone remembered them all, but Ted and Fred remembered some of them afterwards. Papa laughed so hard the chair shook as Mother read about Robin Hood.

"I will never forget the sight of Larry's hair or lack of it," he chuckled. "How you all managed to survive to grow up is a miracle."

Other adventures were brought up and told. Did I ever tell you the story of when we decided to go on a crusade? Or the time Jim and I put Maggie on the train? It wasn't just Ted and Fred who came up with ideas. Jim and I came up with just as many ourselves, though we never tried to hang anyone. You all should have heard Ted and Fred moan over the remembrance of that story. I declare, Emma, if you were here and could listen to your grandmother tell those stories, you would have enough to fill a book. But on second thought, perhaps it is best to not tell too many stories of what we did.

All too quickly the ten days passed by. The luxury of remaining in a soft down bed as late as I wanted, talking for hours with my brothers, romping with the young ones, eating more than my fill of Grandmother's marvelous cooking, all came to an end, and Fred and I boarded the train back to our regiments."

And then Daddy talks about other things. He was right, he did have us in fits of laughter. No one could picture

Daddy lying around in bed or caring what he slept on. I did so want to be there too. He never did tell us those stories he mentioned. Perhaps he will when he comes home. I'll have to ask him. Little did I realize when I wrote those stories that "Ted, Fred, Larry and Jim" would one day sit around listening to them.

Now on to other things. I wish I could box up some warm spring air and send it to you. It is at times more like summer here than spring. I much prefer to have spring and then summer and not summer mixed in with my spring. It is only a few days short of being a month until Cyclone Day. I can't help wondering what will happen. Now why did I think of that?

I don't really remember much about St. Valentine, but I do remember the cards I saw at Grandma Conway's. Perhaps Andrew will become a writer, and he can take over the "Farmhouse Garret." David was asking Georgie about that the other day. He still declares that he can't and won't write. I certainly hope he does better in spelling next year than he did this year.

I don't want to, but I must end this, as this is the very last of my paper. I know Edmund is going to tease me about it. He just doesn't understand about writing letters full of interesting things. I told him I'd most likely use it all up. He thought I could get at least three letters out of it. Much he knows.

                Out of room,
                    Emma

CHAPTER THIRTY-THREE

Friday
May 23, 1918
Princeville, Nova Scotia
Canada

Dear Emma,

Papa hasn't come home yet, but nearly everyone else has. Every day we are expecting to hear from him saying when he is coming. So far nothing but, "I still don't have orders to come home and don't know when they will arrive." Seeing the returning men makes it difficult to wait for our turn. How can the army still need him? The war is over, and troops are coming home daily now, I am told. Oh, how I miss him! Forgive me, Emma dear, for complaining. I know it won't do any good to sit here and fret because Papa is delayed. How thankful I am that he is coming home! We received word that Mr. Stewart died in a French hospital in February. Poor Evelyn and Henry! To lose father and mother and brother. Malcolm is home, though. That is a comfort. He has suffered from shell shock, but he seems to be doing fine now. He is much more silent than I ever remember seeing him. Perhaps he is remembering. I heard that he witnessed his brother Finlay get shot and then had him die in his arms just moments later. He has been through so much already, and to come home to find his mother and father had died and he wasn't with either, must be hard. No wonder he is silent. The children had been staying with the Burns, and even now when Malcolm gets too moody and silent, they will go back to Mabel. We have all rallied around them and tried to help, but at times it feels hopeless.

Not all homecomings were as sad. Let me tell you of a few. At this point no one had returned from the front, and while we waited eagerly, no news had reached the village indicating a return. It was quite early in the month. A beautiful spring morning was dawning, and life was beginning to stir. All at once the skirl of a bagpipe was heard coming over the still air. It was a gay, lilting march full of life and joy. Mark, always eager to learn the latest news, dashed to the window.

"It . . . it's Alan! And David! They are coming! They're home!" Mark's shout brought us all, not to the windows, but the door. We weren't the only ones. All across the village, doors flew open and eager people, young and old, poured out of the houses to welcome the first war heroes home. It was Alan, right enough. No one plays the bagpipes like he does. And yes, there was David beside him. The music came to a sudden halt as Mr. and Mrs. McLean came out of their home.

"Mither, we're hame!" Alan called out, and the next minute he wrapped her in his arms. David was in his father's embrace, and the crowd cheered. After a few moments of greeting were exchanged among the now reunited McLean family, the questions began to fly.

"Have you seen Robert?"

"When is Theodore coming?"

"Any news of Malcolm?"

"What about Duncan?"

"Where's Papa?"

"When did your ship come in?"

"Did you walk all the way?"

At last with a laugh, Alan raised his hand for silence. "Eneuch, eneuch! Hoo can we ettle to answer a'bodys questions a' at aince? Nae, I hae nae een ony one. I had eneuch wark to keep my een on this callant," and here he nodded in David's direction. David merely grinned. "But, donnae fear, they cannae be far behind us."

With cries of "welcome back!" and a few hearty hand clasps, the crowd dispersed to leave the McLean family to enjoy their reunion in peace.

The next to return only a few days later were Theodore and Malcolm. Their return was expected, for Theodore had wired ahead that they were enroute when they reached Halifax. That was a sweet and yet sad homecoming. Evelyn cried until Mabel gently led her away for a little while. I know Theodore is planning to get married soon. Amelia's fiancee returned a few days later. I have heard talk of a double wedding. What a charming idea, don't you think? Amelia told Edith that they were going to wait for her father to come home before either wedding took place.

Last week, Edith, Sheena McIntyre and I were in Pictou to do some needed shopping. Sheena left us for a moment to check on something inside the store we were passing. We continued strolling on a few steps when we heard a scream behind us. Turning, we beheld Sheena struggling to release herself from the embrace of a young soldier! Before either of us could do more than stare, an officer of some rank grasped the soldier roughly by the shoulder and sternly ordered,

"Let go of that lady! Is that the way you treat young ladies now that you are back in Canada? You are a shame to the uniform you wear!"

The soldier merely looked up and remarked with a smile, "Och! Ye can nae be expectin' me to treat mine ain sister ilk as a' other lassies, can ye? An' when I hae nae seen her for mony lang years."

At those words, Sheena ceased to struggle and gazing up, gasped, "Duncan! My wee lad! Hoo ye have changed!"

It was indeed Duncan McIntyre, though I would never have known it, for he has changed indeed. He left a lad and has returned a man. For one thing, he is taller. When he left, Sheena was still slightly taller than him, and now he towers head and shoulders over her. He is dark and broad shouldered, and there is an air of confidence and ease about him that certainly wasn't there when he left. How many years ago was that? I beg your pardon, Emma, you are most likely not interested in those things.

The officer, satisfied that Duncan was no longer a disgrace, departed. Quite a crowd had gathered watching the two, who were completely oblivious to it all. After several moments, Sheena suddenly pulled away from his embrace with a gay little laugh and said,

"Come lassies, this stranger has taken up eneuch o' my time for the present. We really maun finish oor shopping an' start for hame or--"

Edith cut her short. "We are not going any where until we welcome this 'stranger' back home," and she held out her hand with a smile.

Duncan took it. "Edith Foster. Ye haenae changed a bit."

"Jest listen to the maun! Sic compliments. Wad ye say ilk to Maria?" And Sheena nodded towards me.

I held out my hand, and Duncan took it but stared at me. "Sheena," he at last exclaimed. "Ye maun be joking. This isna Maria. That was a lass, while this, . . . an' yet, aye, I do see the smile is ilk. Aye, it maun be." He shook his head in disbelief.

Edith and Sheena laughed, and my cheeks were hot. Thankfully, Duncan didn't continue to stare, but picked up his bag, shouldered it and said, "Lead the way, lassies, I follow."

We finished our shopping rapidly and were soon on the way home. Duncan and Sheena kept up, as Uncle Lawrence put it, a barrage of talk. Sheena is rather like Edith is many ways, for no sooner had we reached the village than she called out, "A'body! Duncan is hame!" which brought everyone out of the houses in a hurry.

We are still waiting for Mr. Burn, Robert Morris and Papa to come home. It is starting to feel as though the war really is over, seeing Alan, David, Theodore and Malcolm about the village again. And now Duncan. The children are in lively spirits, and it is as much as I can do to keep an eye on them. I am no longer the pied piper with a long trail of children behind me. I told Edith I feel more like a sheep dog trying to contain a group of unruly sheep. One thing that will keep them together is if I read your letters. The "Ted, Fred, Larry and Jim" stories are in demand again. I found that the lads just returned from war seem to enjoy your letters as well as the rest of the children, for I often find them stopping to listen.

Speaking of your letters, Emma, I felt so sorry for poor Evie. Lydia Ruth wants to know if "that bad, naughty rooster chicken stayed dead." Evie has much sympathy here for her troubles. Why didn't you get rid of Nighty a long time ago?

I am tempted to lecture you, but I will refrain, as I can understand your feelings. Tell Edmund I thought better of him than to tease you about such things! Mark is curious if you have seen the city lad again after he was freed from the mud puddle. Mark and James have decided that they will come visit you before too long. There always seems to be something happening there. Edith told them that there is always something happening around here, only instead of hearing about it later, they are usually some of the ones doing it. That was a reference to a story in and of itself. I can't tell it like you would or even like Edith, but here it is:

It was two days ago when Charles, James and Mark disappeared for several hours. No one knew where they were. Around noon, William and Arthur began to look for them. They could find no trace of them. All the men were out fishing except Alan, who had to rest his arm. Mrs. Lawson was growing concerned, as was Mrs. Campton. Usually the lads tell someone if they are going anywhere. When the sun was an hour or so past noon, and no sign of the missing lads was found, Alan, William and Arthur set out to search the surrounding area, as the village had been covered thoroughly.

As there was nothing I could do, I agreed to take the four wee laddies, along with Ross and Henry as my helpers, for a walk. We set off, with Andrew leading the way. William and Rob stayed close behind him, and Archie followed at his own sweet pace. I told my helpers to stay with the other three while I brought up the rear. I was enjoying the peaceful afternoon. Archie was quiet, and I could hear the birds singing in the trees up above. Sunlight sifted down through the pine trees as we wended our way up a hill. Though unseen, the waves crashing against the cliffs could be heard. I had fallen into a reverie when a sudden sound of shouting caused me to snatch Archie up and hurry after the others. There, to my relief, I beheld the three missing lads. Relief quickly turned to dismay when I noticed that all three were covered with mud and were nearly knee deep in a large muddy pool of water.

"Mark! What are you doing?" I gasped.

"We are constructing a pool for the young ones to use this summer. See?" he pointed to a dam built at one end. "This will be clear in a little while, and we left places in the dam so that some of the water will go through which will make this not too deep."

I didn't have a word to say. It was a very ingenious idea. The small stream heading for the sea, once dammed up, made a small pool. Enough water ran out of the dam to keep the pool fresh, though it was very murky at the time.

Andrew and the twins evidently thought the idea a very good one, for with one accord they slipped down the muddy bank and landed with a splash in the pool.

I didn't know what I was going to do. It was only May. Not warm enough for swimming here, though it may be so down in Kansas. I kept a hold on Archie and told Ross and Henry to stay out.

"See, Maria!" James called out. "It doesn't even come up to Andrew's chin."

How was I to get all the lads home? They were evidently enjoying themselves. If it had been a warmer day, I would have let them all get in. As it was, I ordered them all out. Archie, who had been trying for the last few minutes to get to the water, set up a deafening howl when he found that he couldn't get there. I groaned. Andrew and the twins refused to get out. The older lads tried to help, but failed. At that most opportune moment, Alan, William and Arthur appeared through the trees, no doubt directed that way by the commotion. Alan gave a few quick orders, and everyone was out of the water. Jackets were wrapped around the wee laddies, and we all set off for the village. I didn't lecture or scold. There was enough of that when we reached home. Thankfully, no one has taken cold, and Mark and James reported that the water in the pool is nearly clear. The younger ones are waiting impatiently for warmer weather.

Alan's arm is doing much better. I see I have neglected to mention that bit of news to you. Alan had been wounded in the arm twice, and each time, he has failed to give it enough time to heal properly. When he reached home, it was doing well, but only a few days afterwards, he and David went fishing with their father. He overstrained his arm, and as a result, I was called. I protested that I was not a doctor, but Alan, with a twinkle in his eye, informed me that since I was the daughter of his doctor, I should be able to give some advice. I did... "Stop using it until it is completely well." I'm not sure he liked that verdict too well. He has followed the advice, however, and stayed home. I have let him use it some now, though not much.

It was such a delight to see the fishing boats heading out to sea this morning, knowing that many old hands were back on board. Mr. McLean took Mark and James as well as David this morning. Alan still uses his arm too much when he goes. Oh, I can't wait for Papa's return! Then I won't have to be doctor and nurse. You see, Doctor McNeel is growing too old to make the trip out to the village anymore, so we must go to him or do without.

Thank you for sharing Uncle's letter with us. He did give more details. Lydia Ruth wants those other stories of

"Ted, Fred, Larry and Jim." She said to please ask him when he comes home. Mama needs my help now, so I will end this. Give my love to all.
>Your loving cousin,
>Maria

CHAPTER THIRTY-FOUR

On Monday morning when Ria stopped by the Smith home for Lydia, she discovered that Mrs. Smith was planning on coming to listen to more of the letters that afternoon. The day dragged by for Ria. She felt restless and had a difficult time paying attention during school. At last the bell rang, and she was free. She didn't know what she was so excited about, but she gave a skip and tossed her dark braid over her shoulder. She didn't chatter as usual with Lydia, for her thoughts were a whirl of letters, reports and the feeling that something was going to happen.

Arriving at home, they found both moms enjoying the sunshine, having a merry chat over cups of tea.

In a little while, the letters were again pulled out, and Mrs. Mitchell read:

> Wednesday
> June 25, 1919
> Codell, Kansas
> USA

Dearest Maria,

Daddy is home! Home for good and always! Is Uncle Frederick home yet? I have at least three people telling me right now to tell it as a story. I had best comply, or they might write this letter for me.

I don't remember when it was that we received the letter saying that he was in the good old U.S.A. again. In fact, he was in New York. That must have been some time in early May. For days we waited and waited, growing more impatient all the while. Everyone wanted to go to town each day to see if a letter had come. We spent hours cleaning the house, weeding the garden, and generally straightening up the entire place. We wanted everything to be spotless for Daddy's arrival. At last, Karl drove into the yard one day waving something white and shouting, "It's come!"

He was practically mobbed with everyone trying to reach that letter. It was only when David called a halt that Mama was able to take the letter and open it. We waited in breathless silence, staring at her. A smile began to creep across her face until she couldn't smile any wider.

"He will be coming on one of the trains on the 30th. And, oh! That is tomorrow!"

Don't ask me to describe the commotion that followed. Everyone talked at once. The rest of the day was a whirlwind of activity. We would be leaving first thing in the morning to be in Plainville for the first train, and then we would wait until Daddy came. At last we managed to get the younger ones off to bed, and Mama and I collapsed into chairs and looked at each other.

"It's a good thing Daddy doesn't come home every day," I remarked. "I don't think I could live through many more such days."

Mama laughed. "I don't think I could either. As soon as the boys come in, we will all head to bed and try to get what sleep we can before tomorrow."

I nodded. I knew I needed rest, but I certainly didn't feel sleepy. I had a difficult time getting to sleep that night. I would doze off and then wake up all excited. The night dragged on. At last dawn came and with it, a renewed rush of excitement. If David, Edmund and Karl hadn't been so steady and calm, we never would have gotten ready in time.

As it was they made each of us do our chores properly and had the wagon hitched up before we were done.

All the way to town we talked and sang. Anytime Vincent or Georgie saw anyone, they would shout, "Daddy's coming home today! Daddy's coming home!"

At last we arrived. David tied the team to a hitching post, and we hurried to the station. There were crowds there. David took charge as Mama was much too excited to even think about us. I really think we could have climbed aboard the first train, and she wouldn't have even known. Edmund had Evie on his shoulder, while Karl kept a hold of Rosalie and Kirsten. I carried Frankie. Oh, Maria, he looked so cunning! Mama and I had made him a little soldier's outfit. We had also made Vincent and Georgie outfits. David kept a tight hold of their hands, for there was no telling what they would think of to do. Carrie stayed as close beside David as she could. The press of the crowd grew as the time for the first train arrived. Flags were waved and cheers were heard on all sides as it finally pulled into the station. We all watched eagerly, straining our eyes to see each soldier stepping off. Daddy wasn't there.

After the train pulled away for its next stop, returning soldiers to their homes, we all looked at one another.

"Well," I sighed, "how long of a wait until the next train comes?"

"About two hours," Karl replied, glancing at the paper he pulled from his pocket.

"Let's take a walk around town. I think everyone has pent up energy." Mama laughed as Georgie twisted this way and that striving to make David loosen his hold of him. Evie started bouncing on Edmund's shoulder until he set her on her feet.

We did walk. Some of us ran. It was difficult to keep track of all the young ones in a busy town like Plainville. I wouldn't want to live here; there is no room to play.

When the next train arrived, we were at the station, waiting. Again, we searched each returning soldier but didn't find Daddy. Another walk, this time to the wagon, where we ate our dinner. When the next train pulled into the station, every eye was busy searching. Suddenly Edmund called out,

"I see him!"

No one else was tall enough to see over the crowd before us. Mama must have caught a glimpse of him, for she started forward through the crowd. As the crowd parted for her, I too caught a glimpse of Daddy. He was looking around, and his face lit up when he saw Mama. Then the crowd closed in behind her, and I saw no more. David tightened his grasp on the little boys, for they were trying to worm their way past the crowd. Everywhere folks were shouting and cheering. A warning whistle from the train sounded, and the crowd swept us back from the tracks towards the street as the train moved away from the station.

"Stay together, and we'll wait by that lamp post," David called to us.

It was hard work getting to the lamp post, and even harder to stay there with the crowd pressing past us. There had been more soldiers on this train than on the two previous ones. Eventually, however, the press thinned, and we had room to look around.

"Edmund," I questioned. "Do you see Mama or Daddy anywhere?"

Edmund shook his head. "I was wondering what happened to them. It's as though the crowd swallowed them up altogether."

"Perhaps they headed back to the wagon," Carrie suggested.

"And then headed home without us," Karl chuckled. "I don't think Mama really knew we were still here."

"Even if Mama forgot us, I don't think Daddy would," I argued.

"I see Mama!" Evie shouted from Edmund's shoulder.

We all turned and there, coming from the direction of the wagon, were Daddy and Mama. Vincent and Georgie broke away from David's relaxed hold and raced for Daddy's arms. Carrie was only a step behind them. When Daddy released the little boys and Carrie, he picked up Kirsten and Rosalie, who nearly smothered him with hugs and kisses. At last they were set down, and it was my turn. The funny thing about all the greetings was that Evie turned shy. No one could understand it. She hid her face on Edmund and wouldn't even look at Daddy! She has never been shy of anyone in her life before. Frankie, nearly a year old, took an immediate liking to Daddy, especially his bright brass buttons, which he tried to eat.

The drive home was one of continuous chatter. Karl drove the horses as David and Edmund tried to keep the excited young ones from doing something rash. The excitement was even affecting quiet Kirsten and Rosalie. After we were on the way home, Evie forgot all about being shy and shouted with the rest.

Don't expect me to tell you about getting home and the day or so afterwards. It would be impossible. At least to tell in detail. Daddy was very impressed with the farm and all the work the boys had done. He praised Carrie's garden and went with Kirsten and Rosalie to look at their chickens. He listened as Evie told him about Nighty. She still won't go near the chickens. Vincent and Georgie got praised for their hard work on the farm. I didn't have anything to show him. I wasn't teaching school then, and I didn't have any garden. I had begun to wonder if I had really done anything while Daddy was away. It was then that Mama and Daddy came out of the house. Mama was saying,

"And if it hadn't been for Emma's hard work, this place wouldn't be looking like it is. She keeps everything running smoothly even if I'm not around."

"And if it hadn't been for Emma's wonderful newsy letters, I wouldn't have known half of what went on while I was away," Daddy added, giving me a kiss.

"She sure keeps us on our toes," Edmund remarked with a grin at me.

While David added with a chuckle, "She makes Edmund mind, which is more than I can do."

That caused a laugh. I never realized that just those simple everyday things can make a difference. But enough of that. Life has been different in a way now that Daddy is home. He doesn't talk much about the war. He is glad to be back. He works outside with the boys and comes in for meals with a smile. Mama's lightheartedness has returned, and the house is full once more with laughter and joy. The first week or so that Daddy was home, Vincent and Georgie seemed to forget how old they were and got into more mischief than ever. That is, until Daddy took care of them. They have settled down now much to my relief.

Let me tell you about everyone, as it has been some time since I have done that. Daddy and Mama are about the same. Well, I don't know when I last told you of Daddy, but I don't think parents change as much over the years as children do. Yes, I just called the older three boys, children. Wouldn't they put up a fuss about that if they found out! Edmund might read this if I don't finish writing it this afternoon, and then I'd never hear the last of it.

David is much the same. He is quiet in comparison to Edmund, yet he enjoys a good laugh. His face and arms are dark from the sun, for he spends most of each day working out in the fields. He hasn't grown any taller. The farm has flourished under his care.

Edmund is a head taller than David and broad shouldered. As you can tell, he still loves to tease. He, too, is a hard worker and is darkened by the sun. I have probably told you more of him than the others.

Karl is growing. I think he will catch up with Edmund before much longer. His hair is growing lighter by the day. I wonder why the sun lightens some people's hair and not others'? Of course I think David or Edmund would look rather ridiculous with blonde hair. I think Karl enjoys farm work even more than Edmund. He is rather quiet, more so than David, but he is strong. His shoulders are broader than

Edmund's. Karl is nearly seventeen now and doesn't resemble at all the street urchin Daddy and Mama brought home so long ago.

Carrie is a young woman now. She, too, is quiet. I am thankful that not everyone loves to chatter. She has a face covered with freckles, for she is in her garden nearly every day for hours. She enjoys baking with me, and though she much prefers to be outside, cleans the house and helps with the laundry. I suspect that she doesn't get mentioned much because her quietness makes it easier to forget she is around.

How do I tell you about Vincent without telling about Georgie? They aren't twins and don't even look alike, yet they are nearly always together. Where one is, the other is most likely to be nearby. They both are covered in freckles, and they both are growing like weeds. Mama and I can barely keep them in clothes that fit. Georgie is still a little taller than Vincent, much to his delight. Vincent doesn't seem bothered by it anymore, though he used to be. They are both hard workers, and they play just as hard.

Kirsten is still very quiet. The quietest one of the family, I might add. She has named each one of the chickens, and they come running when she calls them. She still favors Karl over any of the other boys, which is not to be wondered at. She tries to help around the house, but she can't manage Evie. Rosalie, on the other hand, is her faithful shadow. If Kirsten does it, Rosalie has to do it too. Rosalie's hair is still curly and long. Can you believe that Rosalie is now six years old? Has it really been that long since we have seen you? Maria, we really must do something about that.

But let me finish. I think I have told about Evie more than some of the others. She just can't go unnoticed when she chatters nonstop from morning until dark. She has brown hair which isn't really curly like Mama's or Rosalie's. It never stays in place. Even when I braid it, it will be a mess in ten minutes. Mama said if we let her wear an old ragged dress and play outside for a little while, she would almost pass for a lost child. Her cheeks are too round and rosy to make it really convincing, though. Now that Evie is two years old, she has begun to get into mischief. No sooner had we gotten the little boys almost finished with mischief, than here comes Evie. I'm sure the things she gets into will not be what the boys ever dreamed of doing. I'm sure you will be plentifully supplied with stories of her in the months to come.

Frankie is a contented little fellow except when he is hungry. Then he seems to think that everything must stop at once until he is full. His hair is darkening considerably. Daddy said he hoped it would be as dark as Mama's. I can't help but wonder what Freddy would have been like if he had lived. I can't write about that. This is supposed to be a happy letter.

As for me, I am myself and always will be. I certainly haven't grown nor done anything remarkable. I don't chatter nonstop, nor have a garden.

Let me see, what else was I going to tell you? Oh, tell Mark that Edmund and Karl have seen that city boy when they have gone into Plainville a time or two. Thankfully, Edmund has refrained from mentioning him to me again. I found out from an offhanded remark by Karl.

Yes, Lydia Ruth, the rooster is still dead. That reminds me that I haven't yet asked Daddy for those other stories. I will try to do that soon.

Maria, I had forgotten that you read my letters to the children. I do hope you have been careful of what you read. I'm sorry I don't have any stories this time except Daddy coming home. I'm sure there were some, but I don't want to go get my journal and see. Besides, I don't know where the journal is. I think Evie had it last. Or no, perhaps it was Georgie. I don't remember. Don't fear the journal isn't a private one. It is a family one in which anyone can write if they have a mind to. The only thing is that no one except me has a mind to do it. Such is the way of things around here. Daddy said it was good to have only one family recorder, or the stories might get mixed. I think Georgie was going to draw some pictures.

When Cyclone Day was coming, people began leaving Codell. No one really wanted to be there for the next cyclone. We were waiting for word from Daddy and didn't have any place to go anyway, so we stayed. Cyclone Day came, and we were all nervous. Our necks grew sore from watching the clouds and sky. As evening approached, we wondered if we should spend the night in the storm cellar. We decided not to, though many people did I heard. There was not a single storm in the area. No cyclone, no rain. We were so thankful. Perhaps now there won't be any more cyclones on May 20.

My cousin Margaret wrote me a long letter the other day. She is Uncle John's only daughter. Her brother Roger was serving as a mechanic in the 94th squadron. That is the Hat-In-the-Ring squadron with Captain Eddie Rickenbacker! He actually got to be there and work on the planes. Margaret said that Roger is home now and tells stories all the time about that squadron. She said he can tell you the name of each member and how many "kills" each had. Roger said the mechanics weren't treated as if they were of lower status, for each pilot knew how important good mechanics were.

Uncle Michael is now back in America, as is the rest of the "All American," Division including Sergeant York. I'm sure you have heard of him though and how he "captured the whole German army." At least a whole lot of them, anyway. I have forgotten just how many prisoners they had.

I really must end this. It is time to start supper, and if I don't want Edmund to read this, I must get it ready to mail now. I forgot, why did I not want him to read this? Oh, well, I don't have time to read it over and see. Everyone sends their love. I am looking forward to hearing about Uncle Frederick's arrival home.

Lovingly,
Emma

Monday
July 28, 1919
Princeville, Nova Scotia
Canada

My Dear Emma,

I just had to get away from everything to think. No, Papa is not home, and he doesn't even know when he is going to get here. How can they still need him in England? We need him here. Mr. Burn and Robert Morris are home, but not Papa. Why haven't they let him come home? I am so tired of waiting for him. We received a letter two weeks ago from him saying, he didn't know when he would get home. Thinking of that letter and everything else going on, I just had to get off somewhere by myself to think and write. I am so tired, and my head aches, and I want Papa. Oh, Emma, it is so very hard to wait! I feel like Andrew when he wanted his supper and it wasn't ready. I told him he had to wait.

"Mia," he whimpered, "I can't wait, 'cause I have lost all the bits of my patience."

I feel as though I have "lost all the bits of my patience."

Everything has been happening all at once, and I don't know what to think. Why does everything come at once and then for a long time there is nothing?

I am tempted to throw this paper away and start this letter again, but I won't. I am just overwhelmed by everything. It does help to write it down. You don't even know what is happening, do you? First, I have run away. Not for keeps, as Lydia Ruth would say, just for the time being. I wandered farther up the coast where no one is likely to find me soon. Here all is quiet, save for the waves and a few sea gulls, and they don't need me. The sun is shining from a slightly overcast sky, and it is pleasant to sit here and do just nothing. Of course I am writing this letter, but there is no hurry, and I pause quite often just to enjoy the stillness and peace.

I suppose my running away wasn't the first thing. Was

it days, weeks or months ago that it all started? Stephen McGuire fell off the dock striking his head on something, and had Arthur not jumped in after him right away and pulled him out, he would have drowned. Stephen was and still is sick, though he is much better. Mrs. McGuire is in bed also, only she is waiting for the arrival of another baby. It isn't supposed to come yet. I am not needed for that, so don't think I am. I have been over at the McGuire home every day taking care of Stephen and Mrs. McGuire as well as trying to be in half a dozen other places at once.

Jenny took sick only a few days ago, to be followed by Elizabeth Campton, Heather Morris and Edie Stanly. I have no idea what they have nor how they got sick. Dr. McNeel in Pictou died suddenly at the beginning of July, and the only other doctor there is some young one who tries to put all patients in the hospital. He won't come out to Princeville for anything. I told you we needed Papa. He also refused to give me any instructions in caring for those who won't go to the hospital, so I am on my own for the most part.

And as if that were not enough, Ross fell yesterday morning from some place-- I don't know the details-- and knocked himself out cold. I think he will be all right. Needless to say, I have been kept very busy. I don't remember when I last had a full night's sleep. I'm sure that has something to do with the throbbing in my head. I told Mama that I dread to go outside now, for every time I do, someone calls me. Oh, Papa, Papa, I need you. We all need you.

I don't know how long I have sat here, letting the peace and quietness fill and refresh me. I do know that I should work on this letter or it won't get finished. Surely there are more interesting things to write about than sickness.

Ah, I have not told you of the double wedding. Yes, it was Amelia and her John and Theodore and his Mary. It was a beautiful wedding but very small. No, John and Theodore did not wear their uniforms. They were sick of wearing them, Theodore told us. It sure is different in the village without them both. There is only one Burn child left unmarried, and I don't think it will be long until Mabel is married as well. She and Malcolm are engaged. When they are married, they will have Evelyn and Henry living with them. Evelyn is delighted with the prospect, and as long as they don't leave the village, Henry doesn't mind. I overheard him tell Malcolm that if they left the village, he would run away and come back and live with the McIntyre's. Malcolm just laughed and told him he wasn't planning to leave. Henry and Ross are as close friends as Mark and James. That leaves Edith and Sheena to be the old maids. Edith said there should always be one old maid in a village, so she might as well be that one. I don't think she is in any hurry to get married. I know I am not ready for her to leave.

I have forgotten to add that one baby has already been born in the village. The Stanly's have another girl. She was born on Mark's birthday. That means she is two weeks old. Her name is Lillian. Poor Archie, surrounded on all sides by girls. He doesn't seem to mind having a baby in the house, though. Florence is doing a wonderful job of taking care of the house, but it certainly has complicated things now that Edie is sick. We've kept her away from the baby and Mrs. Stanly. It is hard on Mrs. Stanly, and I think she would have been up and about already if Mr. Stanly and I hadn't objected. I didn't want to object, but I truly don't need any more to nurse. I do hope that whatever the girls have will not spread.

Let me tell you about Mark and

"Why did you stop, Mom?" Ria questioned anxiously.

"Well, I think we must be missing a page or two, for the words on this sheet don't connect with the previous ones."

Ria sighed. "Missing more of the letters."

"Can you read it without it, like you did before?" Lydia inquired.

Mrs. Mitchell, after glancing at the rest of the letter, nodded and began again.

and when she returned she remarked,

"Maria, I don't see what you find in nursing to so interest you. Why, when they are sleeping, there is no one to talk to."

I imagine you are having a delightful time with Uncle Lawrence home. Do give him our love. I almost envy you having him home. Oh, Emma please pray for strength to wait. I truly don't think I can go another day without a hopeful word. My verse this morning was, "Wait on the Lord, be of good cheer, and He will strengthen your heart, wait I say, on the Lord." I don't know if I quoted that just right or not, but that is what I keep repeating to myself. Why is it so hard to wait?

I must end this wonderful time of quiet and get back to the house. The sun is moving ever westward. I have been out here half the afternoon. I do hope no one calls for me tonight. I would so like to sleep peacefully once more.

Please do not fret over me, Emma. I'm sure that this fit of the blues will not last long. I really must end this. Give my love to everyone.

Lovingly,
Maria

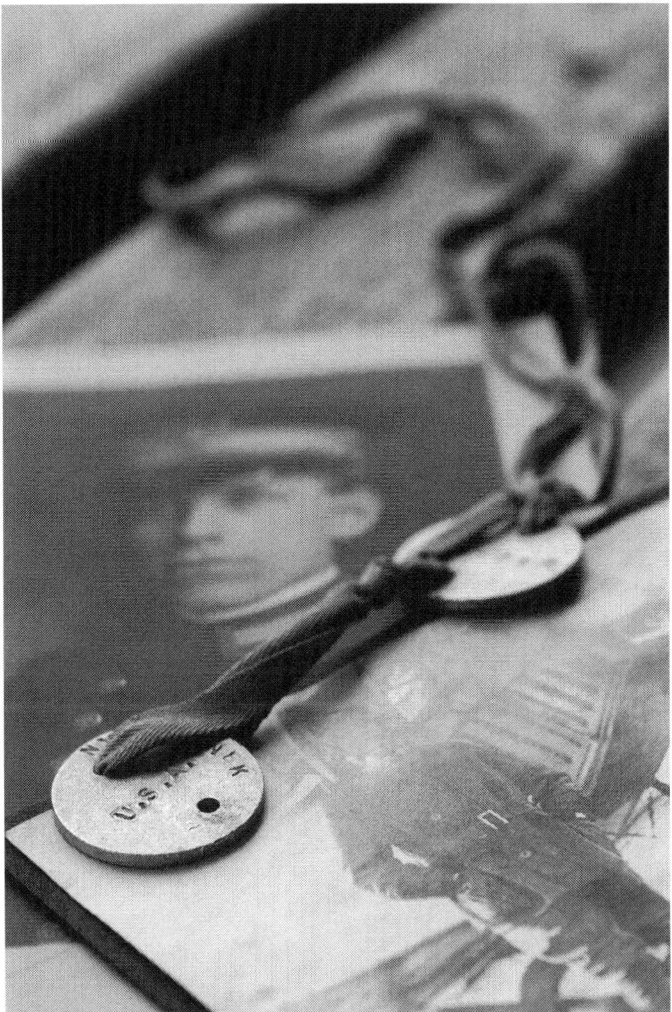

CHAPTER THIRTY-FIVE

Oh, Emma! Emma!

Papa is home! He is home! I can hardly believe it, but it is true. I can see him now as I look up, sitting beside Mama, with Andrew and Lydia Ruth on his knees. Mark is on the floor in front of him, and Edith is perched on the arm of the sofa next to him. He is home again! He is home to stay! No more worry of where he is. He is home! No more worry over missing letters wondering if he is ill. No more worry about him being overworked. He is home! Oh, I don't know what I am saying! You will understand I'm sure. I don't think I'll sleep at all tonight for joy. I don't even want to think about bed, even if it is growing a little late. Papa doesn't return home every day. Oh, how I've missed him! Every time I look up now, I can see him. He is really here. I was sitting on the floor by Mark, but I just couldn't wait any longer to tell you the news. I will get this ready to send tonight so that it can go out first thing in the morning when Mr. McIntyre goes to town. I want you to get this as soon as possible. I haven't even told you yet how it all happened.

It was a complete surprise. No one knew he was coming. He didn't even know himself at first. I don't know if I can tell it all quite right, but I have heard it so many times this evening that I might be able to.

Papa was in England not knowing when he would get home. He had just written us a letter saying that it might still be weeks or months even before he would be shipped out (they kept him very busy in the hospitals there) and sent it on the first ship home. The following day, Papa got orders to accompany the next troop ship home, as it had many wounded on it. That ship left only two days after Papa had mailed his letter. He decided not to telegraph us, as he didn't know how long he would be detained in Halifax. Upon arriving, he was relieved of his duties and dismissed! When he got his papers, he found that a train left for Pictou in twenty minutes. He was able to get his things and race across town to the train depot just in time. He said that he prayed the train would not leave before he got there. It didn't! And we never knew he was coming! On arriving in Pictou he was in such a hurry that he didn't stop to look for conveyance to Princeville but set off on his own. He said he enjoyed every minute of the walk.

No one was around to announce his arrival in the village, at least no one came out to see him, and he proceeded directly home without interruptions. All was quiet when he opened the door. No one could be seen or heard at first. Then Papa's quick ear noticed a tune being hummed in the bedroom. Mama didn't know anything until Papa had her in his arms and was kissing her.

"She gave a faint gasp," Papa said, "and turned as white as the letter she held in her hands. It was a good thing I held her, or she would have fallen."

Mama turns pink and laughs when he says that. She said it was because she had just received his letter saying he didn't know how soon he could come home, and it rather took her breath away to suddenly find herself in his arms. It was a little bit later when Papa asked where everyone else was. Mama told him Edith was out hanging up the laundry. Together they went out to the kitchen door. There was Edith, completely unaware of the surprise behind her until Papa cleared his throat. Edith looked around, gave a scream, and, dropping the clean laundry in the dirt, ran to throw her arms around him and laugh and cry at the same time. The laundry was completely forgotten until supper was being made this evening. Mama, Edith and Papa had no sooner gone inside than Mark returned with Lydia Ruth and Andrew. He had taken them for a walk. Mark didn't say a word after he cried, "Papa!" but wouldn't let go of him for at least a minute, Edith said. Lydia Ruth hung back rather shyly until Papa asked,

"Where is my baby girl?"

Then she replied with her usual truthfulness, "There is no baby girl here. I'm a big girl and almost grown up." Then with a dimpling smile she added, "But you can pretend I'm a baby girl."

Papa swung her up in his arms and kissed her while she kissed him exclaiming, "I have a Papa home now!"

Andrew was still unsure. Even when he was told it was Papa, he stood looking doubtful. Papa set Lydia Ruth on the floor and, getting down on level with Andrew, held out his arms with a smile and a, "My little son."

Andrew tipped his head to one side as though in thought and hesitated. With a sudden nod of his head, he walked into Papa's waiting arms saying, "Yes, MY Papa."

Everyone then talked at once and slowly moved into the front room to sit and keep talking. All at once Papa looked around the room and exclaimed, "Why, where in the world is Maria?"

Mama said I had gone to write a letter to you somewhere where it was quiet and asked Mark if he knew were I was. He didn't but ran off to go look. He returned, not having found me.

I had wanted to find a secluded, quiet place to write. Some place where the village children nor anyone else would be likely to find me, for I wanted to be alone for a little while. It had been a few long, hard weeks as I explained in the letter, and I wasn't feeling very well myself though I didn't admit it at home, for there is always much to do. I was tired, though I'm not any more, and I just needed some quiet, so I wandered farther away than usual. I wrote your letter and just enjoyed the quiet of the day. But the other letter says all that. Walking slowly home, my thoughts turned to Papa as they usually do when I don't have other things to distract me. I wondered when he would be home. As I approached the house, I saw everyone on the porch. Perhaps there is a letter from Papa saying when he will be home, I thought, quickening my pace. Suddenly I stopped short. Someone had stepped off the porch. Someone in uniform and someone who . . . I didn't wait any longer, but dropping everything, I ran with a cry straight into Papa's arms. I could only exclaim, "Papa, Papa!" as I clung to him, sure that I could never let go. He held me close, and I again heard that well-remembered and longed for voice talking to me. Tears rained down my face as I tried to look at him. I couldn't see him, so I hugged him again, laughing and crying, very much like Edith did, Mama says. I didn't want to let go, and even when Mark hollered that my papers were blowing away, I didn't care. Mark, Lydia Ruth and Andrew ran after your letter and gathered most of the pages. I know at least one page blew out to sea, and had not Mark grabbed his jacket, Andrew would have run off the edge of the cliff trying to catch it.

Once we all finally got inside, we just sat and talked. And talked and talked. All those years we had been apart. Nearly five years! We just couldn't leave Papa, and even when Edith and I went to make some supper, we couldn't stay away for long and kept returning until Papa laughingly said,

"I suppose I will have to go and stand in the kitchen if I want any supper tonight." He actually did go and stand in the doorway, watching us for a little while as Lydia Ruth set the table and Andrew sat on his shoulder.

And so there it is. And Papa sits here, here in this front room, home at last. I do hope the rest of the letter makes some sense. I haven't had time to put the pages together properly, and I don't know what page or pages are missing. I know it won't matter that much this time, as Papa is home at last!

With love and in haste,
Maria

Monday
September 1, 1919
Codell, Kansas
USA

Dearest Maria,

The weather is growing cooler, at least sometimes. More often than not, however, you would think it is the middle of July. Of course September has only just started, but I am more than ready for autumn. Every one is busy. School started today, and I am not teaching. With so many families moving, and the land that the school house was on having been sold, the children are going to school in Plainville. The Codell school isn't rebuilt after last year's Cyclones, or they would be going there. I am sure there will be times when I miss teaching, but I do love to stay at home. Rosalie has started school this year now that she is six. Kirsten seems much more sure of herself with Rosalie along. That leaves Evie and Frankie at home. Speaking of Evie, do I have a story for you!

It was only last week that it happened. It was a beautiful day, sun shining and a cooler breeze blowing from the north. Everyone was outside enjoying the day. Mama and Daddy had gone for a walk. Vincent and Georgie were somewhere, climbing trees, no doubt. Georgie has fallen out of at least five trees in the last two weeks. Thankfully he hasn't hurt himself yet. But that has nothing to do with the story on hand. Carrie was with David in her garden. I'm unsure what they were doing. I am not a gardener. The only things that grow for me are flowers and weeds. I don't plant the latter, but they grow anyway. Kirsten and Rosalie were playing in the barn loft with the kittens. Karl and Edmund had been together until I wanted to take a walk with Edmund. Karl was kind enough to take a hint and said he had something else to do. Have you noticed that Evie has not been mentioned? I also see I have neglected to say that Frankie went with Mama and Daddy. As I was saying, each of us thought that Evie was with someone else. That was a mistake. I should have known better that to assume that. But assume it I did. Edmund and I hadn't walked more than fifty feet when Karl's voice rang across the yard,

"Emma!"

Edmund sighed in exasperation. "You're always being called for some reason, Lucy," he complained. "And just when we're going to do something."

I laughed. "I'm sure it won't take long. I'll be right back."

Walking briskly to the house, I skipped up the steps into the kitchen and stopped dead in my tracks.

"No, no, Tarl!" I heard Evie exclaim and saw her push his hands away. "I mateing a pie for Demund. Don't oo touch it."

Karl glanced my way and stepped aside. Maria, I was speechless, completely speechless! There was Evie standing on a chair before the kitchen table with eggs, flour, salt, sugar, water and I don't know what else all over. She had a few bowls, pans and pie plates, and all were covered with whatever she was concocting. There were cracked eggs on the table, the floor and down her dress. She had a dusting of flour completely covering her from head to toe. She paid no attention to me until I at last found my voice.

"Evie! What on earth are you doing?"

Evie looked up quite calmly and replied, "I's mateing a pie for Demund. He yike them."

I bit my tongue a moment and glanced at Karl. He shrugged.

"Evie," I began again, suddenly inspired. "Did you ask Mama if you could make a pie?"

Evie shook her head.

"Then," I said, "you have to clean everything up, for you can't make a pie without Mama saying so." I reached for a spoon as I spoke.

"No, Emma!" And Evie slapped my hand!

"Evelyn!" Karl exclaimed, catching back her arm as she raised it to slap me again. "You are not supposed to hit. Now Emma told you to clean up." He let go of her arm.

Though I hadn't been sure of what Evie would do, I soon found out.

"No!" she cried. "No! No! No! I's dunna mate a pie!"

"Evie," I tried to interrupt, but she was beside herself.

"I not dunna stop! No, no, no!" With each no, she threw something across the room. Never had I seen her in such a temper.

Karl thankfully had the presence of mind to step outside and call Edmund, for I could do nothing with her. I was busy trying to keep the rest of the eggs from being hurled to their destruction by Evie's small hands when suddenly Edmund appeared.

"Evelyn Margaret!" his voice was stern, and he pinned Evie's arms to her sides. "What is going on?"

"I mate a pie an' I's dunna mate it!" She fairly hollered, struggling to get free.

"Evelyn, that is enough," Edmund's voice was still stern. "Stop."

Instantly she stopped. She stood still on her chair and tears began to trickle down her flour-dusted face. I looked at Edmund, and Edmund looked at me. I saw his mouth twitch. This was not a good time to laugh, for the kitchen was a disaster, and Evie really shouldn't be laughed at, for she had been naughty.

Edmund spoke quietly as he turned Evie to look at him. "Karl and Emma told you to stop making a pie, didn't they?"

Her head nodded.

"Then you should obey at once. They had a reason for

telling you to st--"

Evie's sudden burst of tears cut Edmund off short. She flung herself against him wailing, "I mate a pie for oo all my by yelf! Yike Emma mate all her by yelf! I mate oo a pie!" she sobbed again. "Oo yike pies."

"Evie." It was no use talking to her at that moment, for she sobbed out her grief of wanting to make a pie just for him as I had done and didn't listen to a word that was said.

For several minutes we stood and waited. Finally as Evie grew quieter, Edmund tried again, "Evie, I would love to have a pie from you, but until you are older, you have to have help. Perhaps soon Emma will help you make one."

"No, Demund, all my by yelf."

"Not until you are bigger," Edmund replied firmly, and Evie didn't argue anymore. "Now," Edmund went on, "there is a mess to clean up." He looked down at Evie and then at his own clothes, now nicely covered with flour and egg.

The cleaning up of Evie and Edmund was easy compared with the rest of the kitchen. Thankfully David and Carrie came in right then, and I sent Evie outside with Carrie to get cleaned up. Edmund left to take care of himself, leaving Karl, David and me to start on the kitchen. David cleaned the floor by calling in one of the dogs. One of the bowls on the table was filled with white grains of something.

"Is that sugar or salt?" I asked.

David tasted it. "Umm, well," he hesitated.

Karl tried it. After looking at each other, they nodded in agreement, and David said,

"Both."

I groaned. Yes, Maria, the entire bowl was filled with a mixture of sugar and salt. It was completely unfit for anything. I recalled Lydia Ruth's experience several years ago with flour, but this was ten times worse. We were still cleaning when Mama and Daddy came back. Mama took one look and remarked,

"Evie's doings."

I nodded grimly, but Mama started laughing. And as you know, if Mama once gets to laughing, we all join in. The kitchen fairly rang with laughter, which did make the rest of the cleaning a little less like a chore. Since that time, we have all kept a very close eye on Evie and her doings. Of course Evie isn't always into things, thankfully.

Frankie is starting to walk. He is still somewhat unsteady on his feet, but he keeps trying. He is so different from Evie, who talked; from Rosalie, who was content to sit and look around; and from Georgie who put everything in his mouth. Frankie has to touch everything. It doesn't go into his mouth unless he is hungry. It is so cute, for he will first touch whatever it is quickly as he stares at it.

Oh, the joys of having Daddy home again! I love hearing his voice at prayers every morning. Not that David and Edmund didn't do a fine job while Daddy was gone, but you know what I mean. He doesn't tell many stories of when he was over there, and the ones he does tell are the happy or funny ones.

Maria, your letter had me in tears when I first started it and realized that Uncle Frederick wasn't home. I couldn't even read it at first. I had to go to my room and read the entire thing myself before I dared to try reading it aloud again. And then your second letter was "just the gladdest thing," as Kirsten put it. I do hope you got the rest you needed. Was everyone in the village surprised to see Uncle, or had some of them seen him come home? I know what you mean about everything happening at once.

September 3, Wednesday

I suppose if I am ever going to get this sent, I must first finish it. I should have finished it on Monday, but I was needed to help Aunt Jennie. She hasn't been feeling well for the past several weeks, so Monday afternoon when Karl went to pick up the children from school, he dropped me off at Uncle Philip Vincent's, and I only got home this morning. No one would consent to me being anywhere else but home for my birthday, though I might as well have stayed there, for we have done nothing at all. True, they did wish Edmund and me a happy birthday, but that is it. I haven't even seen a sign of doing anything special. Eighteen years old, Maria. Can you believe it? I won't say how the time flies, for I must say that every time. It is still true, but I won't say it.

I just remembered, what is the newest McGuire baby? When did it come? Is everyone well now? Edith, Mama said that it was a little early to decide to become an old maid. She said it was all right to get married later if that is what the Lord wants. Have Mabel and Malcolm set a date yet? Where are Theodore and Amelia living?

Your letter did leave a strange gap and was rather mixed until I sorted the pages. The missing pages were still missing. Edmund says, "how can missing pages of a letter become un-missing." Well, I certainly don't know.

Maria, this is your uncle writing now as you might guess from the different handwriting. I saw this letter sitting here unfinished on the desk and thought I'd add a note myself. Edmund and Emma were kicked out of the house and told to go away. It is hard getting ready for their birthday surprise with them around. Well, that was some time ago, and we are ready and waiting for them to come back. I won't spoil the surprise but will let Emma tell you about it when she returns.

Tell your father I welcome him back to the American side of the Atlantic. Now, Edith, I hear you are planning on being an old maid. I just thought I'd tell you that your Aunt Margaret said the same thing, and within a year she was married. So I am expecting to hear of your engagement before long and won't be surprised in the least.

The sun is moving closer to the west, and there is no sign of the twins. Perhaps we had better send out a search party. I won't take up any more paper but leave it for Emma.

Uncle Lawrence

September 4, Thursday

Maria, I see Daddy decided to add a note to this letter. I'm sure he has roused your curiosity about Edmund's and my absence. I'll tell you what happened.

They really and truly did tell us to get out of here and to go away. We felt very obliging and left. I had been longing to get out in the fresh air, for it had rained the night before. Edmund wanted to escape from Evie for a time. That child can wear anyone out with her chatter. When we were ordered out of the house, they didn't tell us when to come back. We took advantage of that and set off for an adventure on our own. We didn't have any particular place we wanted to go, so we simply started strolling across the fields. We talked as we went and before we knew it, we were far from the house. I did make a suggestion that we should perhaps circle back around, but Edmund had a fit of obstinacy and wouldn't turn.

"They told us to go away, Lucy," he grumbled in mock disgust, "and I for one don't intend to give them the pleasure of doing that again for some time."

Naturally I wasn't about to go back without him, although I threatened to. We kept on going and then much to our surprise, we crested a hill and saw Plainville before us. Yes, Maria, we had walked all the way to Plainville without following the road. It had been a pleasant way.

"What do you say we stop in at Uncle Philip and Aunt Jennie's? Wouldn't they be surprised to see us. Uncle Philip would think it a good joke, no doubt."

"You are just wanting a ride back home," I teased.

Edmund made a face as he shook his head in denial.

Arriving at Uncle's, we found that no one was home. We sat down on their steps and rested. At last I broke the silence.

"Edmund, we really should start for home, as it is going to be dark before much longer."

Edmund agreed, and we set off back the way we had come. It was dark when we reached our yard. Lights shone out of the kitchen windows. Edmund threw open the door, and we stepped in. Everyone looked up.

"Where in the world have you two been?" Mama exclaimed.

"Only to Plainville, Mama. You told us to go away, but didn't tell us when to come home." Edmund looked and spoke so innocently that he had everyone laughing.

The surprise was sweet. The girls had baked us a cake, Uncle Philip Vincent and Aunt Jennie were there, and a special supper had been prepared, which wasn't much the worse for the long wait it had. We all had a merry time over the "surprise that surprised the surprise" as Vincent put it.

I must end and get off to bed. I hope you have as happy a birthday as we did. I'm sure you will with Uncle home. Give my love to all and kiss Uncle for me.

     Always yours,
     Emma

CHAPTER THIRTY-SIX

"We really must save these last few letters from 1919 for tomorrow, as we don't have time this afternoon to finish them all."

Mrs. Smith nodded in agreement. "Might I come back?"

"Of course! I'm delighted to share these stories with you as well as with your daughter. I used to read aloud my cousin's letters to the entire family. I didn't realize just how much I missed that until now. Now," she turned to the girls, "you have your reports finished, right?"

"Yes, Ma'am," they both chorused.

"Then we can enjoy tomorrow's reading with no thought of unfinished projects."

"Mom, I'm going to invite Corporal to come listen tomorrow too. That's okay, isn't it?"

Mrs. Mitchell smiled. "Of course it is."

When the girls stopped by the Smith house the following day to drop off Lydia's books, they found her mom waiting for them.

"I thought I would walk with you. That is, if you don't mind."

Lydia assured her they didn't mind in the least, and the three set off for the Mitchell home.

During the walk, Mrs. Smith's hand kept moving to her pocket as though to reassure herself that something was still there. The expression on her face puzzled Ria. No one talked much on the walk which was rather unusual, for Ria loved to talk. Today, however, her thoughts were busy. She felt that something was in the air; something was going to happen. She had been feeling that way for several days, but the feeling was stronger now than ever. Why she felt that way she couldn't have told except for the strange fluttery feeling of her heart. Something special just had to happen.

Arriving at home, they found Corporal sitting on the porch with Mrs. Mitchell, evidently waiting for them.

"Well, it's about time you showed up," he greeted Ria. "I was about to give up and go home."

She laughed. "I didn't think we were that late."

"Well, maybe not, maybe not." His smile was bright. Ria seated herself beside him while Lydia and her mom found seats on the porch swing.

"There are only three letters left. Shall we see what happens?"

Saturday
October 25, 1919
Princeville, Nova Scotia
Canada

Dearest Emma,

A very happy though late birthday to you as well. Everyone laughed so at you both leaving home. How far is Plainville from your house anyway? I remember it as a very long way, but that was quite a few years ago. Did Evie get to help make that cake? Oh, Emma, I can see you are going to have your hands full helping take care of Evie. How is it that

Edmund can get her to do anything, yet you can't? I always thought that you could get anyone to mind you. Do keep your eyes on her, for since she is related to Vincent and Georgie as well as to "Ted, Fred, Larry and Jim," she could think of innumerable bits of mischief, I'm sure. How Papa laughed imagining Edmund trying to eat a pie that Evie made "all her by yelf." Alan's comment when he heard that story was -- Oh, Emma, I have neglected to tell you the most important news!

Edith and Alan McLean are engaged! Are you properly surprised? Uncle Lawrence declared that such news wouldn't surprise him. Let me tell you the whole story, as it stands out very clearly in my mind.

Papa and I were outside one evening in August. Papa had been home for several weeks, and all the cases of illness had been taken care of. I was thoroughly rested now that Papa was home, and we were just returning from a stroll to the cliffs as we used to do before the war. We had been hearing the bagpipes for several minutes and stopped to enjoy them, when we saw Alan out on the rocks playing. After the song was finished, Alan came over to join us.

"You certainly have a touch with those bagpipes, Alan. I don't think I've ever heard anyone play like you do," Papa told him.

"Thank ye, sir. Aften were the times in the war that a' my hert langed for was to see wi' mine ain een aince mair this bonnie countrie. To see a gowden sunset such as that, the brae of the toon so wi' its canty hames an' play on the cliffs. Ye ken what I mean, sir."

"Indeed I do, Alan," Papa replied heartily. "If I recall correctly, you kept saying something to that effect when you were in the hospital."

Alan smiled, but there was a new look in his face, and his eyes seemed to glow with some feeling not expressed before. "I's warrant ye ken I spoke of other things as well?"

At Papa's nod, he continued. "I behove to say thae hae nae changed." He seemed waiting for Papa to reply, but for several minutes all was still. The waves dashing against the base of the cliffs was the only sound breaking the silence.

At last Papa smiled and held out his hand. "If you can win her heart, son, you can have her."

Alan gripped the offered hand and then hastily turned away.

Papa looked after him and spoke softly, "He's a brave lad, and I'd be proud to claim him as a son-in-law."

I looked at Papa in astonishment. "Papa--"

"Maria, don't mention anything about this to Edith. Let Alan do his own wooing. I think he can manage, don't you? He isn't one to let the grass grow under his feet."

I nodded, for I was too much surprised to speak.

There was no time for any grass to grow, for it was the very next evening that Alan came upon Edith and me out on the cliffs. He was in full Scottish attire and carried his bagpipes.

"Gude evening, Lassies. Gin ye hae a song ye'd like to hae played, ye hae but to say it aince."

Edith laughed lightly, "How did you know I had just been telling Maria that if some of those old Scottish ballads could be played right now, all would be perfect?"

When Alan asked if there was any certain one she wished for, Edith frowned and started humming a tune hesitatingly. As Alan began to play, Edith smiled and nodded. It was a dreamy tune, yet there was a touch of the wild Scottish flair that makes that music so enjoyable. No sooner had that song ended when he began another one followed by yet another. Edith sat still. Her gaze seemed to be on nothing particular, and her hands were clasped in her lap. I don't know if she saw the rosy sky with its velvety purple clouds lined with gold, or the sea reflecting some of the glory of the setting sun, but perhaps she did. So lost in the music was she that when I slipped away, she made no move, nor so much as stirred. Alan saw me, and his eyes smiled.

It was quite late when Edith came home that evening

with flushed cheeks and starry eyes. She said not a word to me until we were in our room, and Lydia Ruth was asleep.

"Maria," she whispered, standing by the window bathed in the soft pale glow of the moonlight. "Alan asked me to be his wife."

Softly I stole to her side. "Did you give him the answer he wanted?"

"Yes." The reply was scarcely audible. "I never even dreamed that it would really be true someday."

I wondered what she was talking about, but she told me before I could ask.

"I don't know how long I have felt this way. I used to wonder, but when he left for war, I knew I loved him. And when he came home, I knew it was still true. Only Papa had to be here first . . .." Her voice trailed off into silence; she squeezed my hand.

That is the whole story. Edith has a new spring in her step and a lilt to her voice. When Alan is not off fishing, he is most often here or somewhere with Edith. Alan wants to get married soon. There is no date set yet, but I have heard talk of spring.

I went into Pictou with Papa the other day, and everywhere the trees were brilliant in their autumn dresses of crimson, gold and brown. The days grow increasingly colder, and the men no longer go out every day to fish. School is progressing well here. Lydia Ruth is delighted to be back in school. The days are filled with housework and watching Andrew, Archie and the twins.

Speaking of the twins, the McGuire's have a little girl, much to Jean's delight. After twelve years of waiting, she at last has the little sister she has dreamed about. The little one's name is Marion. She is rather dark haired but has the bluest of eyes. She is small when compared to the size the twins were but not delicate.

Yes, everyone is quite well now. Papa has seen to that. The only thing I regretted was that I wasn't feeling well enough myself to help. That is what I have so longed for. I feel so free now just knowing that in an emergency I won't have to wait for someone from Pictou or do it on my own. Papa is home. It fills me with thankfulness every time I stop to think about it.

Mama just paused to ask me if I knew where Edith was. The last I had seen of her was several hours ago when she and Alan left for a walk. Mama says a storm is approaching, and she hopes they don't get caught in it. The wind certainly has picked up, and the sun is hidden behind slate-grey clouds. The sea is growing more restless each time I look at it. Mark is eating at the Lawson's this evening. Perhaps Alan will stay for supper.

It is now after supper; the storm is still raging, though not as fiercely. Edith and Alan came in just before the rain broke loose. Edith's hair was loosened and windblown, and she had Alan's jacket about her shoulders. Her gay laughter announced their arrival. It wasn't difficult to persuade Alan to stay. Papa built a roaring fire in the fireplace while waiting for supper to finish. Right now I am in the front room writing. Lydia Ruth is telling Andrew a story in front of the fire. Edith and Alan are cleaning up the kitchen. I was prepared to wipe the dishes as Edith washed them, but Alan took my towel. Mama and Papa are somewhere. I hear Edith's voice, so they must have finished and are heading this way.

We all sat around talking and telling stories for some time. Mark arrived during a lull in the storm, and Alan departed. It is growing much colder. A perfect night to snuggle under warm quilts. I wonder if we'll have snow in the morning. Papa asked if I was planning to write all night. I must end this now and get to bed, for it is quite late. Besides, Edith is ready to go up too.

Love as always,
Maria

Sunday
November 16, 1919
Codell, Kansas
USA

Dear Maria,

It is cold, cold, cold here right now. It wasn't this cold when we left for church this morning, nor even this cold when we headed home. By the time dinner was over, though, a bitter wind was blowing in fierce gusts across the fields from the north. We haven't had any snow yet. I do wonder if this is bringing snow with it. No one is outside. We are all gathered in the front room around a blazing fire. It is too cold in the bedrooms to think of staying in there. Frankie is asleep in Daddy's arms, and Evie has finally fallen asleep in Edmund's lap. That child could talk the hind legs off a mule, to quote Daddy. Carrie is reading her Sunday School book. Kirsten is reading hers to Rosalie. Mama is resting. Vincent is also reading and as usual, is completely absorbed in his story. As for Georgie, he is lying before the fire with his heels in the air. He can read very well now but refuses to write. As for the older boys, they are all reading or falling asleep. I think Edmund will be asleep long before I finish this letter.

We were all so happy about Edith and Alan! Tell them congratulations for us, please. Daddy said that Uncle Frederick had made a comment to him on the train about something that Alan had said. That is why he was expecting it. I guess that leaves Sheena to be the old maid, or is she engaged now, too? What does Lydia Ruth think of it all? I can't picture Edith speaking Scottish. Does she try?

It is almost Thanksgiving. We have much to be thankful for this year. Can you believe this year is about over? Next time I write it will be 1920! Carrie, Kirsten and Rosalie are going to help with preparing the feast for Thanksgiving. I'm sure Evie will "help" or hinder as much as she can. Perhaps we should persuade Edmund that it would be to the best interest of the feast if Evie didn't lend a helping hand. You know the saying about too many cooks. I think Evie would be the one too many'th. (I know that is not a word, but I thought I could take liberties as I'm no longer a teacher.) Mama will help when needed, but I plan on doing as much as possible without help. I do love baking and being in the kitchen. I just wish I had someone to shoo me out when it came time to clean up. That would be a welcome change. I wonder if I could talk the older boys into it now and then.

Just listen to that wind whistle! You can't hear it, for I can't describe it, but you can imagine it I know. It is a cold that goes right through you the instant you step outside. I think I'll stay inside, thank you. I get cold just listening to the wind. Karl put another log on the fire. I love listening to the pine and cedar logs snap, sizzle and pop as the flames lick at their sides.

Let me tell you a story that happened a few weeks ago. Thankfully it was warmer than now, or the results might have been different. David and Karl were in the back field working on something. I never was very good at remembering those details. Daddy and Edmund were working in or near the barn. Daddy needed to send a message to David so told Edmund to deliver it. If Edmund had walked, it would have taken quite a while, as the back field is a long way from the house. I was bringing in the clothes off the line and got a front row seat on what happened. Edmund climbed into the pasture where Jessie was grazing. The other horses were in a different pasture. Now, though Jessie is Carrie's and my horse, she lets anyone ride her and is as gentle as a lamb. We often ride her bareback when we are in a hurry. But, back to the story. Edmund crossed to Jessie's side and vaulted onto her back. Jessie lifted her head and started off at a word from Edmund. When I looked up a moment later, Jessie was standing calmly grazing while Edmund was clambering out of the watering trough! He was dripping with water and looked utterly bewildered. He didn't notice me as he squashed towards the house. I don't believe there was a single square inch of him that was not wet. I picked up the basket of clothes and followed. Stepping onto the porch after him, I heard Mama exclaim from in the kitchen,

"Edmund! What has happened to you? Are you all right?"

"I'm just a little wet," Edmund grumbled. "Jessie decided to dump me in the watering trough. I was supposed to take a message to David for Daddy, but I guess it will have to wait."

"What is the message?" I heard Carrie ask.

Edmund told her, and she slipped out of the door with her coat.

"Carrie!" Edmund called, starting after her. "You can't ride Jessie. She is in no mood to let anyone ride her." He paused on the bottom porch step. "Carrie, you'll just get hurt!" He might as well have called to the wind, for Carrie paid no heed.

She slipped through the fence rails and called Jessie. Jessie came at once, and in another minute Carrie was on her back and riding for the back field.

"Females!" Edmund snorted in disgust. "I'll never understand them."

"Maybe not," I told him, "but you had better get inside, get dry clothes on and warm up, or you will catch pneumonia."

"Hump," was all the reply I got as Edmund continued to watch the now distant form of horse and rider as they reached the crest of a hill.

"Edmund Foster!" I exclaimed. "Get inside! Your teeth are chattering!"

He turned at last and went in. Daddy shook his head when Mama told him what had happened and gave orders for him to remain inside the rest of the day. He did, thankfully. You will be wondering if he did get sick. Yes, but not really sick. He had a cold for a week or so and still has a cough. Maria, maybe you would have faired better as a nurse, for he was a perfect bear with me. But I am no nurse and know it. I'm sure I deserved some of his growls, but surely it wasn't that bad. Do all sick people act that way? I don't remember ever being so bad. I know Mama isn't, but she has had time to "grow all the way up." That is an expression of Georgie's.

Georgie wants absolutely nothing to do with the alphabet if he has to spell. As I mentioned earlier, he reads very well. His teacher in school told Daddy that Georgie could write if he put his mind to it. The problem is that he won't, or at least he wouldn't. Georgie is doing better in spelling now that Daddy has Karl helping him. Karl won't put up with imperfection when there is no reason for it. That must be why he is so good at all he does. The other evening when the children were all studying, I overheard Karl and Georgie.

Karl was speaking, "Spell fox."

"F-o-k-s, fox." Georgie simply refuses to spell it any other way even though he was been told time and time again that it is f-o-x.

"Georgie, spell fox."

"F-o-k-s"

"Spell fox."

"I just did," Georgie complained.

"No, you didn't," Karl spoke firmly but with none of the impatience that I would have felt. "What you spelled is not a word. Now, spell fox."

"F-o-k-s"

That went on for five whole minutes before Georgie finally spelled fox the correct way. He saw that Karl wasn't going to give up. He also knew from experience that if he wasn't finished with his spelling when it was bed time, he would have Daddy to deal with, and usually that meant a trip to the woodshed.

On Georgie's last spelling paper, he finally spelled fox correctly. I hope Karl is finally getting through to him. I don't think he will ever love spelling or writing, but at least he can spell fox. Georgie told me that he thought people should be allowed to spell words any way they wanted to. Can you picture what a disaster that would be?

Vincent has a new love, and that is reading. He is nearly always carrying a book around in his pocket to read in his spare minutes. He reads anything he can get his hands on, including the farmer's almanac. David has even found him doing his chores with one hand while he holds his book with the other and reads. Once he started reading at the table, but Mama quickly put a stop to that.

Kirsten and Rosalie love school. Kirsten had been rather slow in learning some things, but now that she has Rosalie to help, she is in the top five of her class. Of course it does help that Karl helps her when he is not working on spelling with Georgie. Now that the cold weather has set in, I'm sure there will be even more time for study. I think Karl would make a wonderful teacher, but he only scoffs at the idea.

"I'm not going to get stuck in a school house all day, Emma," he told me. "I'd hate it."

Evie has for the most part stayed out of mischief. We have kept a close eye on her, although she still manages now and then to come up with something. For the most part, however, she talks. Daddy asked her if she hadn't run out of words yet. She looked very thoughtful and serious for a moment, and then replied, "I not fink I have, 'tause I always detting more in me belly."

Georgie fell out of a tree and knocked the wind out of himself. He couldn't talk for a full minute, and Evie thought he had knocked all his words out. She gets such quaint ideas.

It has begun to rain and sleet. I can hear it hitting the windows. David, Karl and Vincent are heading out to check on the animals. Daddy is going to join them as soon as he lays Frankie down. Edmund was told to remain here, as he is still coughing. He doesn't like it, but he stays. He detests being shut up in the house. I hope for his sake that his cough leaves soon. Evie is awake now. We've had quiet long enough. Perhaps it is a good thing that Edmund stayed, for Evie wants to go outside to see the ice. Georgie is telling Kirsten and Rosalie a story of what he sees in the fire. It is hard not to laugh. Kirsten did interrupt him once to tell Rosalie that it was all pretend, because there is a dragon in the story.

The boys and Daddy are back in now. The younger ones are begging Daddy for a story. I'll end this now and join the circle around the fireplace to listen too. Happy Thanksgiving and Merry Christmas to you all!

> All my love,
> Emma

Home Fires of the Great War

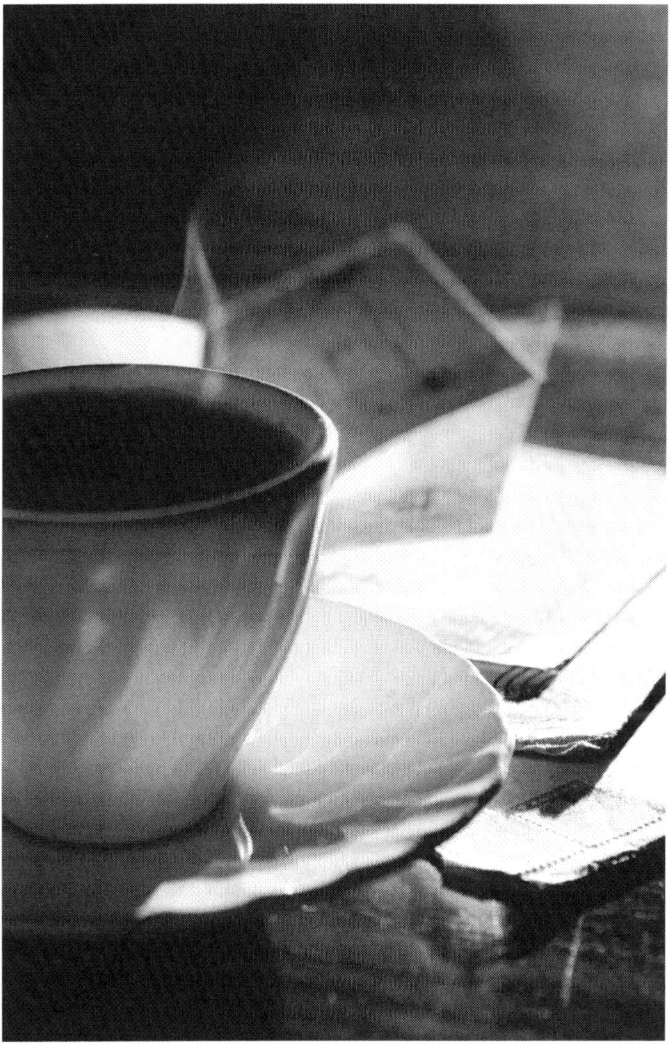

CHAPTER THIRTY-SEVEN

Wednesday
December 10, 1919
Princeville, Nova Scotia
Canada

My Dearest Emma,

A merry and happy Christmas to you. Christmas is nearly here. The first Christmas in five years with Papa home! The very thought is joy. Oh, how I've missed him during this festive season! Our house is trimmed with greens and holly. Smells of baking cookies fill the house now. Edith and Lydia Ruth are busy. Christmas is only fifteen days away. We are planning a regular Christmas feast on the first night of Christmas. The McLeans and Lawsons will certainly be invited as will the -- dear me, I have forgotten to tell you what happened in November.

It was cold and snowing quite hard the night it happened. Alan was spending the evening with us, and everything was cozy and warm inside. Mama and Papa were putting Andrew and Lydia Ruth to bed, as it was rather late, and they were both sleepy. Alan, Edith and I had just entered the front room when I thought I heard a knock on the door. I paused for a moment and listened. It came again faintly, but on hearing Mark's footsteps and the doorknob's rattle, I just waited.

"I hope no one has come for Papa," I remarked.

"M... M... Maria," I heard someone stammer. I knew that voice, didn't I? Where had I heard it? Then my name was again called, and I hurried out. There, completely covered with snow stood the slight form of a young girl. She coughed and gasped out my name again.

"Grace!" I exclaimed, for I finally recognized her voice. Hurriedly, Mark and I got her coat and hat off, and I gently guided her into the front room. Alan quickly set a chair nearer the fire, and Grace nearly fell into it. I could see she was exhausted and well-nigh frozen, but how did she get here? I hadn't heard from the Perkins since they left over two years ago. Were they all back? Where were they living? Why was Grace here? Before I could ask any questions, Papa came in. He must have heard the knock. Grace was coughing and shaking with cold.

"Edith, get a cup of tea. Mark a blanket. Alan, put another log or so on the fire, and Maria get her wet shoes and stockings off." Papa's orders were given rapidly yet quietly. Then turning, Papa left the room almost as swiftly as he had come.

As I knelt in front of Grace and began to remove her shoes, a broken, half-suppressed, French "No," caused me to look up quickly. In the light of the room I could see the white, scared face before me. As I drew off her shoes and stockings and rubbed her numb feet, I asked her gently in French what was wrong. I listened in silence to the pitiful, haltingly told story. Mark returned, and he and Alan tucked the blanket around Grace's trembling form. Edith had just entered the room with the tea as Grace finished. Quickly speaking to Grace in French, I stood up assuring,

"I will go right now!" then added in English, "Mark, get my coat, please. And my boots."

Mark turned to go, but paused as Edith exclaimed, "Why, Maria! Where could you go? You can't leave in this weather!"

"I have to," I replied, turning to go, but Alan caught my arm.

"Lassie, didnae ye ken it's snowing outside? Ye'd be lost fer sure by yerself."

I must go!" I pleaded, attempting to pull away from his grasp.

At that moment, Papa reentered the room, glanced at us all, and, taking the tea from Edith, crossed the room to Grace's side.

"Drink this," he ordered gently.

Breaking away from Alan's loosened grasp, I hurried over, for Grace was looking more frightened than before.

"Papa, she only speaks French."

Papa didn't even look at me, but spoke in French and held the steaming cup to her blue lips.

"Papa, I have to go! You understand, don't you?" I begged. For a moment, all was still. Papa glanced at me, and I could read the questions in his eyes. I realized then that no one knew what Grace had told me. I explained as well as I could.

Tom Perkins was hurt. Grace thought it was bad. The baby was sick and so was Ruth. That was why she didn't come. They were back in the old house, and Mrs. Perkins was well-nigh sick herself with all the worry. Papa kept his eyes on Grace while I talked, and Mama came in with dry stockings. Silence filled the room momentarily as Papa looked at Mama, at me, out the window, then back to me. At last he spoke.

"Amelia, can you pack a basket with anything we might need?" Mama nodded. "Edith, you help her. Mark, Alan, get a bundle of wood tied up and ready to go. There is no telling how much they have. Maria, get into the warmest clothes you have."

I waited to hear no more, but flew to my room. Returning some ten minutes later, I suddenly realized that poor Gracie knew nothing of what was going on. The young girl was curled up in the chair and trying to look brave, though her chin quivered, and the cough which shook her thin shoulders sounded terrible. My heart went out to her. What would it be like, Emma, to be sick in another home where they didn't speak your language? To be there pleading for help for your family and not know if they even understood you or would help?

"Papa," I asked as he appeared with his medical bag. "What about Grace?"

He had no time to answer as Mama called from the dining room. I only had time to call out in French that everything would be all right. There was a flurry of getting things ready. Mama kissed me before she wrapped my scarf around my neck and face and whispered,

"Be careful, dear."

I nodded. I had a small hamper strapped on my back, and covered with a waterproof covering. Papa had a larger hamper and a load of wood on his back, while he carried his medical bag and a lantern.

"We are going, Grace," I called out, my voice muffled by the folds of wool about it. Grace looked up, startled. With a cry, she sprang from the chair and staggered towards us.

"No, Grace," Papa said gently, "you can't go out again tonight. Wait until morning."

At that, Grace became almost hysterical, stammering something and crying, trying to break away from Mama's arms and follow us. If she hadn't been so exhausted, she might have managed to reach us. As it was, Mama soothed her and spoke comfortingly to her in French, all the while tenderly drawing her back to the chair. Papa told Mark that tomorrow, if it wasn't snowing and Grace was up to it, he could bring her home. Finally, Alan opened the door; Papa and I stepped out into the cold, white world.

It wasn't snowing as hard as it had been earlier, but the wind off the sea was frigid. It seemed to go right through me. With our backs to the wind, we trudged off up the hill toward the path among the pine trees. Once we reached the shelter of the trees, the biting wind wasn't so keenly felt. Papa led, and I followed in his tracks as best I could, wondering how Grace had ever managed to come so far. Some drifts were higher than my knee! I kept a tight hold of

Papa's coat. At last we paused to rest, and Papa asked if I was all right. I nodded. My lungs were burning as I gasped in the cold air. The wind didn't seem as strong as we again pressed forward. Before much longer we could see the small light of a candle in a window just ahead. Then we could see the house. It appeared that someone had tried to clear the snow somewhat off the porch. We stomped our feet, and Papa knocked. The door opened almost instantly, and a little figure appeared, only to shrink behind the door at sight of Papa.

Only a short time was needed to set our burdens down and get out of our snowy wraps. The room we were in was large and dimly lit. One log burned in the fireplace, hardly enough to heat the area right in front of it. The furnishings were old and very sparse for so large a room. On one side was a table with a few rickety chairs. A lone candle burned on the table. On the other side, near the fireplace, was an old sofa. Only the back was visible, the front being towards the fire. Two or three equally old chairs, one of which looked ready to fall down if one sat in it, stood near by. All of this I took in at a glance after removing my wraps. Then Mrs. Perkins was clinging to me, exclaiming in her broken English,

"Maria, you have come! You have come!"

"Yes," I replied in French. "I brought my Papa who is a physician." I turned to Papa but found that he was already bending over the sofa.

"Praise the Lord, a doctor has come. But, . . ." and her face grew even more pale in the dim light. "Grace . . ."

"Is safe at our house," I hastened to assure. "After a good night's rest, Mark will bring her home."

Mrs. Perkins drew a deep sigh of relief, and I turned to answer Papa's call.

Hurrying to the kitchen a few moments later to fetch water to heat, I found Ruth huddled next to the slightly warm stove. Upon seeing me, however, she sprang up, threw her arms about me and burst into such a torrent of tears that she began coughing. I tried to calm her, and soon the tears stopped, but the coughing, once started, continued. Filling the kettle, and drawing Ruth with me, I hurried back. In the doorway, Ruth stopped, still coughing, and shook her head.

"Come," I urged, "you can't stay in that cold room."

Still hanging back and coughing, Ruth came. Papa looked up at the sound of the cough but said nothing, only nodded toward the fire, which was now blazing brightly. When the kettle had boiled, I made some tea.

I will spare you the details, as it would take a while to write them, and they all seem combined somehow in my memory from here, until all were finally asleep. To tell it briefly, Tom had a broken leg, which Papa set. Papa examined both Ruth and Baby, gave them some medicine and put them to bed on cots near the fireplace. The other rooms were like ice. We finally persuaded Mrs. Perkins to lie down on the other cot, for she looked ready to drop. I am not sure if Papa really persuaded her, or if he simply ordered her to lie down.

It was about that time, I believe, when I became aware that the other three children, Anna, Joseph and Hannah, hadn't been around at all. After several moments of looking, I found them huddled together in a corner on the other side of the room, staring wide-eyed at everything. Quite a little coaxing was needed to draw them over to the light and fire. Clinging to me and to each other, they looked timidly at Papa. When he held out biscuits to them, their timidity vanished at once. Before long, they too were asleep before the fire, wrapped in blankets.

Papa brought more wood in. The snow had stopped, and I could see hundreds of bright, twinkling stars through the window. The moon cast its silvery beams on the newly fallen snow, causing it to sparkle and glisten like millions of tiny diamonds. I could have stood and gazed for hours, but there was work to do. Ruth and Tom had a restless night, the one from coughing, the other from pain. It was a long night. I didn't get much rest at all, but that didn't matter. I was working in a sick room with Papa. How often over the last few years had I longed for just such a time as this. I wouldn't trade it for several nights of sleep in my own warm bed.

Around midmorning, Mama, Grace and Mark appeared. Papa sent me home with Mark to get some rest, while he and Mama stayed. Tom is still ill, fever having set in, but Papa doesn't think him in danger any more. Ruth, Grace and Baby are much better. Why do I call little Maria a baby when she is three years old? When the snow melted enough, the entire Perkins family was moved down into Grandmother's house, which has stood vacant for nearly a year. Everyone in the village has taken an interest in them though they persist in calling them "Maria's family." Mrs. Perkins still isn't strong.

They are coming to the feast. Why, Ruth told me they haven't had a real Christmas since her father left for the war! They don't know what happened to him, for his letters ceased to come, and yet he was never listed in the papers that they could find. How could he just disappear like that?

This morning Mama, Edith and I made Figgy Pudding for Papa. He said he greatly missed it each Christmas. I hope Uncle Lawrence in getting to enjoy some this year as well. On the second day of Christmas we will certainly make more, for no doubt we will have many guests come asking for it. Alan and David assured us that they would be here for it. When Edith told them they would have to sing for it, Alan said,

"Ony song ye wuss for my bonnie lass, ony song."

Wedding plans are for spring when the flowers are in bloom everywhere. Sheena is not engaged, yet I feel sure she won't be left a spinster.

Edmund-- Mark and Alan, yes, even Papa agree with you that the female mind is not to be understood. Do take care of yourself. A cough is nothing to fool with. Is it any better? I pray it is.

Do tell Georgie that spelling is an important part of life. He may be a business man someday with important letters to write.

Speaking of letters, the school children here, at least the older ones, were given an assignment of writing a letter to someone that was not to be opened for five years. That is quite a thought, isn't it? Mark and James exchanged letters. Lydia Ruth wrote one to Mama. Ruth and I were talking about it one day. We decided to try it. I also wrote a letter to each of the Perkins children. I can't help but wonder where they will each be when they open them. Five years ago we were about to celebrate our first Christmas with Papa gone to war. Andrew hadn't been born yet. So much can happen in that amount of time.

Do you have any law books that Vincent can read? Do you recall when I tried reading them once, but couldn't understand a thing? Edward Campton is now living in Halifax where he is studying for the bar exam.

Malcolm and Mabel were married the first of November. It was a quiet, simple wedding in the Burns home. They didn't take any wedding trip. I think their house would be quiet if it were not for Henry. Since being in complete charge of him, Malcolm has grown less moody and silent. No one talks of the war with him, for he cannot bear it. Mabel said that there are still days where it all seems to come back to haunt him, but they are growing less frequent. Much prayer has gone up for him. Would you please pray for him, too?

Mark and Papa have just brought in the Christmas tree, and the cookies are ready to be hung. All are gathering. May our Heavenly Father bless you this coming year, dear cousin. Everyone sends a Merry Christmas to all of you and wishes you a happy New Year!

      Your loving cousin,
      Maria

"Oh," Ria breathed. "I'm so glad the Perkins family came back. Mom, do you remember anything else about them?"

Mrs. Mitchell looked thoughtful and finally shook her head. "I think they stayed there in Princeville for a while, for I remember meeting them when Edmund and I went up there for that visit, but I don't recall what happened to them."

Mrs. Smith pulled out a paper from her pocket, and handing it to Mrs. Mitchell, said quietly, her French accent very noticeable, "I wanted you to see this."

Lydia glanced over. "It's the letter from the mystery person."

Her mother only nodded.

Mrs. Mitchell glanced down and then looked up, puzzled. "This handwriting looks familiar," she observed before starting to read again. Suddenly she looked up with surprise and delight mingled in her face. "Grace!"

Mrs. Smith nodded. "Yes, I am Grace."

"Grace?" Ria stood up and moved to her mother's side to see.

"Yes, Grace. The same Grace that went for help when my brother was hurt and my mother and sisters were sick."

Ria and Lydia stared at each other in disbelief.

"But, Mom, why didn't you know before? I mean, how did you come to know now? And . . ." Lydia was utterly bewildered.

Mrs. Smith smiled. "I didn't know until today. This morning, I finally received a letter from your Aunt Ruth, explaining who had written that," she nodded her head towards the letter still in Mrs. Mitchell's hands. "I couldn't quite place her in my mind, but when Ruth mentioned Princeville, I recalled where," she spoke to Mrs. Mitchell, "your cousin was from. So I made up my mind to bring the letter and show you. I still wasn't sure it was the same Maria, but when you read of Grace going to get help for her family, it all came back." Mrs. Smith fell silent.

Almost in awe, Ria half whispered, "You remember doing that?"

"Yes," was the simple answer.

No one said anything for a few minutes. Ria was trying to realize that her friend Lydia was the daughter of someone talked about in the very letters they had just finished reading. She shook her head, and then unable to keep quiet any longer, she burst forth, "I just knew something was going to happen from reading these letters!"

That broke the tension, and everyone laughed and began to talk at once.

It was a few moments later that Ria noticed Corporal coming across the yard from his house. She wondered when he had left, for she hadn't noticed. "Corporal!" she called excitedly to him as she jumped off the porch and raced to meet him, "Did you hear? Did you know that Mrs. Smith is Grace? She really is! The same Grace that went to Maria's house to get help when her brother broke his leg!"

Ria was so busy chattering about it that she didn't notice the startled look that crossed the older man's face as he allowed himself to be pulled back onto the porch.

"Corporal!" it was Mrs. Mitchell this time. "Are you all right? Here, sit down, you look pale."

Corporal sank into the chair, his hand shaking. "I didn't know. I mean, I have looked, but they said-- oh what am I saying?" He shook his head, took a deep breath and looked around the porch. Every eye was fastened on him. He gave a low chuckle before beginning.

"After you finished that last letter, I could hardly believe it. I've searched everywhere, but had come to believe that they had all been killed in the explosion at Halifax."

"Who had?" Ria interrupted.

"My family. The last letter I had from them was that they were in Halifax and then nothing. When I came back from the war, not a trace of them could I find. I finally gave them up for dead," his voice broke.

The only sound to be heard for a moment as the listeners sat in breathless silence was the singing of a cardinal in a nearby tree and a neighbor's whistle.

"Ria, thank you for inviting me to come listen today. You have found my family, for I am Thomas Joseph Perkins."

For once in her life, Ria Mitchell was absolutely speechless.

"Pa . . . Papa!" Mrs. Smith gasped, her face turning white. "Oh, Papa! Is it really you?" She clung to him and cried.

"It was all so unbelievable," Ria told her dad and brothers that night at the supper table. "To think that all these years we have lived right next door to Lydia's grandfather and never even knew it!"

"I still don't understand it all," Chris complained. "How could he just disappear like that, and why didn't his family know what happened?"

Mrs. Mitchell attempted an explanation. "Corporal isn't sure exactly what happened, but apparently his letters were not reaching his family, and after the explosion at Halifax, he no longer received any from them. He was wounded and taken to Germany as a prisoner. After the armistice was signed, there were American troops stationed in Germany for a while. One of them, a Captain Thorn, found Corporal, and taking pity on him, took care of him himself instead of sending him back to the States. His mind was injured, and he couldn't remember who he was or where he came from. Captain Thorn kept him with him, and when he was ordered home, he brought Corporal back too. Gradually Corporal's mind returned, and he set about trying to locate his family. However, they had by that time moved to the U.S. and left no trace behind them. Unable to find them, Corporal lived near the captain until he found the house next door. He said it reminded him of his old home in Quebec.

"As for the Perkins family, they moved around a lot, and perhaps that explains why Corporal's letters didn't reach them. In 1919, they moved back to Princeville until Mrs. Perkins came down with tuberculosis. Uncle Frederick sent them down south to Florida to live, in hopes of helping her. She died only a few years later, and the children were split up. They managed to keep in touch over the years, but only the three oldest remember much of their life in Canada."

Ria sighed. "Just think, Mom, if you and your cousin hadn't written those letters, Corporal would never have found his family. We did find a mystery in those letters, Mom, and we found some forgotten heroes to write about." She gave a little skip of excitement. "Oh, I can't wait until tomorrow to give our report! We changed it just a little, Mom, did I mention that?"

Ria and Lydia sat beside each other. Ria was eagerly awaiting their turn to give their report. At last Miss Bryant called them to come up. Lydia handed in the written report and then Ria turned to face her audience. Near the back of the crowded auditorium sat her parents. Her mom's face wore an expectant look and her Dad's one of pride. In the row in front of them were Lydia's parents and her newly discovered grandfather. Though Ria couldn't see it, she knew Corporal's eyes were bright with a feeling that a long-neglected honor was about to be given.

Ria threw back her shoulders and the room hushed. Her cheeks glowed and her eyes sparkled. She didn't even look at her paper, but taking a deep breath, she began to speak. Her voice, tinged with energy, reached to the very corners of the room.

"In every war there are heroes. Some are praised and rewarded for their heroic deeds. Others are never mentioned in the papers. They get no medals. No parades are given in their honor, yet they are heroes every bit as much as the others. Most of these forgotten heroes are known to only a few persons, yet their memory is sacred. There is one special group of heroes that will always be remembered in the hearts and minds of the soldiers of The Great War. These heroes, yes, and heroines too, will never be rewarded with press and ceremony, yet without them the war would never have been won. These deserve our heartfelt thanks and our deepest honor, for they are the fathers and mothers, the wives, sweethearts and children who stayed at home and kept the home fires burning. Without their love, help, prayers and support, the soldiers couldn't have done what they did, for they were fighting for their families. You may think that the war was all about defeating a ruthless enemy who wanted to destroy the world, but it was more than that. It was a war to preserve the right to have and keep the freedoms we hold dear. There were many mothers who gave their "glorious laddies" for this, many of whom never returned. There were many wives who gave the men they loved the best to buy this freedom, and many didn't return. There were many daughters who, without a word of complaint, watched their fathers or brothers march off to war while they stayed at home to wait and pray. These are the true unsung heroes of the Great War.

I would like to tell you now about a few of these very special heroes who bravely kept the home fires burning."

The End

GLOSSARY

A': all
A'body: everyone
Aboot: about
Aff: off
Aften: often
Ain: own
Aince: once
Auld: old

Bairn: child
Baith: both
Bannock: flat oatmeal cake
Begude: began
Bide a wee: stay a little while
Birkie: lively young fellow
Blude: blood
Bonnie: pretty
Brae: hillside
Braid: broad
Braw: brave
Burn: stream

Caddie: messenger
Callant: young man
Canty: cheerful
Capering: dancing
Claes: clothes
Claymore: great sword

Countrie: country

Daft: silly
Deid: dead
Didnae: did not
Doesnae: does not
Donnae: do not
Dour: grimly determined

Een: eyes
Eneuch: enough
Ettle: attempt

Faither: father
Forjaskit: exhausted
Frae: from

Gab: talk
Gae: go
Gang: gone
Gangin': going
Gin: if
Gowden: golden
Gude: good
Guidwife: housewife

Hae: have
Hame: home
Hasnae: has not
Havers!: exclamation of

surprise
Hert: heart
Hoo: how
Hoo's a' wi' ye?: how are things with you?

I's warrant: I feel sure
Ilk: the same
Ilka: every
Isna: is not

Ken: know
Kent: knew

Lang: long
Laochain: hero
Leal: loyal
Let-a-be: let alone
Linn: waterfall
Littlins: children
Loch: lake

Mair: more
Maun: must, man
Mither: mother
Mony: many
Morn's morn: day after tomorrow
Muckle: much

Nae: no or not
Naething: nothing
Ne'er: never
Nicht: night
Noo: now

O': of
Och: expression of dismay
Ony: any
Oor: our
Or: before
Ower: over

Puir: poor, pitiful

Runnel: stream

Sae: so
Sair: sore
Sally Lunns: tea cakes
Shouther: shoulder
Sic: such
Sinsyne: since
So: here
Sporran: leather pouch
Suld: should
Syne: ago

Thae: those
Toon: town

Wad: would
Wark: work
Wee: little
Wha: who
Whaur: where
Whiles: at times
Whist: national exclamation
Wi': with
Wuss: wish

BIBLIOGRAPHY

American Heritage www.AmericanHeritage.com/"BlackJack.
Axelrod, Alan. The Complete Idiot's Guide to World War I.
Indianapolis, Indiana:
    Alpha Books, 2000.
Balaguier Publications. Images of the First World World
War. Great Britain:
    Balaguier Publications, 2003.
Burg. David F. and L. Edward Purcell. Almanac of World
War I. Lexington, Kentucky:
    The University Press of Kentucky, 1998.
The California State Military Museum
http://www.militarymuseum.org/USSSanDiego.html.
The Canadian Encyclopedia
http://www.thecanadianencyclopedia.com.
Carrie: An Electronic Library www.ku.edu/carrie.
Castor, Henry. America's First World War: General Pershing
and the Yanks. New York:
    Random House,1957.
Caulley Corner www.caulleycorner.com.
Cooks Recipes.com
http://www.cooksrecipes.com/dessert/figgy-pudding-with-custart-sauce.
Cyclone Day 1918 http://www.tornadochaser.com.
Daniel, Clifton, ed. America's Century. New York, New
York:
    Dorling Kindersley Publishing, Inc., 2000.
Daniel, Clifton, ed. Chronicle of the 20th Century. Liberty,

Missouri:
>JL International Publishing,

For King and Empire - Canada's Soldiers in the Great War www.kingandempire.com.

Freidel, Frank. Over There. New York:
> McGraw-Hill, Inc., 1990.

Garst, Shannon. Scotty Allan King of the Dog-Team Drivers. New York:
> Julian Messner, Inc. 1953.

Gordon, Lois & Alan Gordon. The Columbia Chronicles of American Life 1910-1992. New York: Columbia University Press, 1995.

Guttman, Jon. Spad XII/XIII Aces of World War 1. Great Britain:
> Osprey Publishing Limited, 2002.

Haythornthwaite, Philip J. The World War One Source Book. London:
> Arms and Armour Press, 1992.

Heritage of the Great War, The www.greatwar.nl.

Hills, Ken. Wars That Changed the World: World War I. Long Island, New York:
> Marshall Cavendish Corporation, 1988.

History Learning Site www.historylearningsite.co.uk.

JackieJ's Home Page http://www.geocities.com/jackiej53/cyclone5231918news.html.

Jasen, David A. ed. For Me And My Gal and Other Favorite Song Hits. New York:
> Dover Publications, Inc., 1994.

Jennings, Peter and Todd Brewster. The Century for Young People. New York:
> Random House, Inc., 1999.

Kansas Collection, The www.kancoll.org.

Lawson, Don. The United States in World War I. New York:
> Abelard-Schuman, 1963.

Liberty Memorial Museum, The www.libertymemorialmuseum.org.

Library and Archives Canada
http://www.collectionscanada.gc.ca.
Long, Long Trail, The www.1914-1918.net.
Lorne's Lighthouses www.lorneslights.com.
Marrin, Albert. <u>The Yanks Are Coming</u>. Sandwich, Massachusetts:
    Beautiful Feet Books, Inc. 1986.
Monnon, Mary Ann. <u>Miracles and Mysteries The Halifax Explosion</u>. Toronto, Ontario:
    Nimbus Publishing Limited, 1977.
Mysteries of Canada
http://www.mysteriesofcanada.com/Nova_Scotia/halifax.htm.
Olian, Joanne. <u>Everyday Fashions 1909-1920 As Pictured in Sears Catalogs</u>. New York:
    Dover Publications, Inc., 1995.
Parks Canada
http://www.pc.gc.ca/dci/src/3d_e.asp?what=more&sitename=hfxcit.
Pershing, John J. <u>My Experiences in the World War</u>. New York:
    Frederick A. Stokes Company, 1931.
Reeder, Colonel Red. <u>The Story of the First World War</u>. New York:
    Duell, Sloan and Pearce, 1962.
Regiments www.regiments.org.
Rickenbacker, Eddie V. Captain. <u>Fighting the Flying Circus</u>. New York:
    Doubleday & Company, Inc., 1965.
Rickenbacker, Edward V. <u>Rickenbacker: His Own Story</u>. New York:
    Fawcett Crest, 1969.
RMS Lucitania www.ocean-liners.com/ships/lusitania.asp.
Rothenberger, Von. <u>Images of America: Osborne County, Kansas</u>. Charleston, South Carolina: Arcadia Publishing, 1999.
Scottish Tartans Museum www.scottishtartans.org.

Scuttlebutt and Small Chow - A Salty Old Harbor of Marine Corps History www.scuttlebuttsmallchow.com.
Seibert, Peter Swift. How We Lived 1880-1940. Atglen, Pennsylvania:
   Schiffer Publishing Ltd., 2003.
Stolley, Richard B. Life: Our Century in Pictures For Young People. Boston:
   Little, Brown and Company, 2000.
Terhune, Albert Payson. Bruce. Charleston, South Carolina:
   BiblioBazaar, 2007.
This Day in History www.history.com/this-day-in-history.
Thompson, Rebecca, ed. "The Great War."
   Learning Through History Magazine issue: 6 Vol: 3 2005.
Treadwell, Terry C. & Alan C. Wood. Images Of Aviation: The Royal Flying Corps. Great
   Britain: Tempus Publishing Limited, 2000.
Warren, Andrea. Orphan Train Rider. Boston, Mass:
   Houghton Mifflin Company, 1996.
Wheeler, Richard "Little Bear". Sergeant York and the Great War. Bulverde, Texas:
   Mantle Ministries, 1998.
World War 1 The American Expeditionary Forces www.thedigitalbookshelf.us/ww1_units.htm.
World War 1 - Trenches on the Web www.worldwar1.com.
www.newpaperabstracts.com.
www.freepages.military.rootsweb.com.

ABOUT THE AUTHOR

Rebekah A. Morris is a homeschool graduate who has a love for writing. She is the author of dozens of short stories and poems. After six years of loving labor, her first book, <u>Home Fires of the Great War</u>, came out in March, 2011. In October of 2011 her second book, <u>The Unexpected Request</u>, a western novel for the whole family, was published. Currently, Rebekah is writing the sequel to <u>Home Fires</u> as well as working on several other short and novel length stories. Every Friday her blog <u>www.rsreadingroom.blogspot.com</u> is updated with her work. In addition to her own writing, Rebekah enjoys sharing her passion for writing with her students.

Proof

Made in the USA
Charleston, SC
20 February 2012